Sarah Needs Saving

Sarah Needs Saving

DCR Bond

Chapter One

After all this time, Sarah still wasn't "one of them". She was dressed – like everyone else – in a skirt, blouse, and sensible shoes. She wore little makeup or jewellery and smelt only subtly of a light floral scent. Sarah had adopted this unofficial uniform for over a decade, but it was only camouflage; it gave her access, not membership.

Sarah shivered and buttoned up her cardigan. The room was vast with a long mahogany dining table at its centre and smelt faintly musty like an unused basement. Surreptitiously, she looked upwards to the ceiling twenty feet above, at white sweeping swags of plasterwork framing intricately moulded cupids, exotic birds, and Tudor roses. The effect was heightened by the subtle contrast of a pale blue background – stunning. One day, thought Sarah, when Freddy inherits.

The seat at the head of the table creaked as the chairlady deposited her bulk then tapped a short, manicured fingernail on the agenda.

'Let's begin,' barked Sandra.

Sarah's heart beat a little faster; it did that each time any of these ladies spoke. She let everyone else sit down before taking the last chair. Sandra leaned forwards as if speaking to all twelve ladies round the table, but her eyes – which were dark and small and reminded Sarah of a Guinea pig – didn't travel as far as Sarah, sitting at the furthest end.

'Pity, but the new owners of the Grange are Mr and Mrs *Frightfully* Pleased with Themselves,' laughed the chairlady, 'She told me she'd like to join us.' Sandra pulled a face, 'We're not a golf club!' she chortled.

There was a burst of laughter.

Sarah forced herself to smile, despite feeling a rush of sympathy for the unnamed woman – without Mary, Sarah wouldn't be attending this meeting either. Oh, these committees with their baffling, preordained hierarchy, dictated by a complicated mix of the size of one's house and how many hundreds of years you can trace your ancestors back to residing in a large house in the county. Sarah understood her place in the pecking order.

Sandra's high pitched whining voice echoed round the room.

'Right, who's offering to take the minutes with our secretary on hols?'

'I'll do it,' volunteered Sarah.

'Splendid. Let's start.'

Half an hour later they were still on item one. Unlike Sarah, Sandra – or Mrs Delegator as she was nicknamed – wasn't in a hurry, broadcasting demands but allowing the ladies to meander like uncontrolled dogs stopping to sniff each lamppost. Sarah scribbled notes, mentally rearranging her diary. She beamed down the length of the table at Sandra, 'I can do Penelope's share of baking if her Aga's on the blink. Can I drop it round at yours; we've no room at mine.' She put down her pen, 'Of course, there's heaps of space at the Dower House, but I don't want to impose on Mary.'

The chairlady was examining her agenda when she issued her instructions, 'Bring it all to the Hall, tomorrow, eleven o'clock sharp works for me. We can run through your draft minutes at the same time.'

Sandra's eyes circled the seated ladies. 'Now collecting tins this Saturday – I've got Amanda down; we need one more volunteer.'

Sarah saw the Guinea-pig eyes swivel towards her, '. . . Sarah is that one for you?'

Squeezing her eyes shut – there goes my Saturday – Sarah mumbled, 'Yup, I can help.'

Two hours later, Sarah swung through the gates and down the tree-lined drive towards the only appointment she didn't want to scrub from today's schedule. She could only spare an hour; she wanted to stay longer, had planned to, and was on track to, until that meeting overran, and her to-do list grew. Cursing her bad luck to be busy when wretched Sandra wasn't, she slid open her car window and inhaled the sharp scent of freshly cut grass. Unlike her own, the lawn in front was immaculate: crisp straight alternating stripes, the verges neatly trimmed with a spade; Mike's been busy! But then he is another "doer"; we're both like children in a game of musical chairs when the music stops, she thought, dashing about in a flap searching for a spare chair. Rounding the final bend of the drive, she caught a glimpse of the statuesque Georgian house; would today be one of Mary's good days?

Parking under an old cedar tree, Sarah checked her appearance in the mirror – dabbing on a little powder and rearranging her hair – then picked up a pot of homemade jam from the passenger seat. She crunched her way over the gravel to the house. The curtains were open, and she spotted her hostess by the fireside, legs pressed together and angled to one side, a sewing box on the table beside her, focusing on the needlework in her lap. Mary was dressed in the same pink woolen Chanel suit she wore fifteen years ago, at their first Sunday lunch together. Back then, Sarah's own outfit hadn't been much competition for Chanel: skintight trousers with four-inch heels to prop up her modest five-foot four slim frame, and a jumper that probably cost less than Mary's tights, peppered with bobbles where the wool was matted. Fifteen years ago, Sarah stumbled from one mishap to the next. Champagne was served in the lounge. Error: it was the "drawing room". Her then boyfriend, Freddy, gently eased out the cork, which emitted a lame, soft hiss – as if surrendering – rather than the triumphant explosive crack she'd been expecting. She was disappointed with her half glass, knocking it straight back like a shot of vodka, earning her a startled look from the hostess. Freddy recharged her flute. A few glasses later she was explaining the benefits of a bikini wax before summer to his bemused mother.

On their way home, Sarah burst into tears. 'It was a disaster. She didn't like me.'

Freddy pulled over, stopped the car, and stroked her cheek. 'Darling, first meetings are always a nerve shredder.'

She sniffed, her shoulders heaving, and lifted a wrist to wipe her face before peeking across at Freddy.

He was grinning and started to laugh. 'You're just a little unusual for her.'

'Don't make fun of me! I don't hunt; I don't even know how to ride. I don't own a Labrador or a pair of green wellington boots. I am not from your world, and I am not what your mother wants. You must teach me how to fit in!'

'You don't need to change. I love you as you are. Anyway, she did like you.'

'Did she? And Mike?'

'Mike's views don't matter.'

Back then, Sarah was confused by Freddy's statement; it wasn't until she was introduced to Freddy's brother that she discovered why Mike's views didn't matter then, and still didn't.

At least today she wasn't wearing *bold red cherry* varnish or sporting talon-like long nails. My husband's family is from a different world, she reminded herself, like cashmere compared to my sackcloth. When Freddy recounted childhood stories, they resembled episodes from a period drama, whereas Sarah's ancestral home was a three-bedder in Basingstoke. Her parents never held dinner parties and they didn't have "problems with household staff".

Sarah rang the doorbell. Mary didn't stir.

It was Mike – a stocky man with that weather beaten skin tone that comes from outdoor hobbies – who let her into the entrance hall, with its stone floor smooth and shiny in patches, worn down by centuries of human traffic. The Dower House: Sarah had fallen in love the moment she clapped eyes on her – the perfect package of amazing reception rooms without the inconvenience of acres of bedrooms. Mike led her into the cold octagonal staircase hall that always had a faint honey scent of beeswax. Sarah pulled her jacket a little tighter and gazed upwards at the glazed cupola, daydreaming this was her home. She held out her gift.

'She hasn't forgotten I'm coming, has she?'

'I reminded her. Fab, strawberry and vanilla.' He raised his eyes from the jar. 'She's always asking for your jam.'

'I know she hates shop-bought.' Sarah lowered her voice. 'How is she?'

'Bit hit and miss. You go on in; I'll get the tea tray.'

She watched Mike's retreating back and the jar being tossed from hand to hand. His hair was grey but still as thick as when she first met him. She would always remember thinking when they were introduced, that his job as a lighting technician in a London theatre sounded so cool. She gave a short laugh, recalling her mother-in-law's stinging rebuke that day when Sarah mistook Mike for Freddy's stepfather.

'Only *I* have a relationship with Mike.'

That was still accurate!

Sarah leaned against the heavy sitting room door. It jerked open and she peered into the room. Her mother-in-law glanced up. Mary was a tall lady. It was probably her genes which gave Sarah's husband his height of six foot three. Freddy had also inherited his mother's lean features, but not her hair. His was dark and curly, Mary's honey blonde like Sarah's.

Mary didn't get up, but she did put aside her needlework, and proffer her cheek. 'Sweet of you to pop round, shall I ring for tea?'

Sarah bent over, grazing against the older woman, and smelling the familiar mixture of musk, rose and sandalwood.

'No need, Mike is on it,' she said, lowering herself into a slightly battered chintz-covered armchair. Despite it being a warm day there was a small blaze burning behind the brass spark guard, and feeling beads of perspiration round her neck, Sarah took off her jacket and draped it over the side of the chair.

Mike brought in a tray, groaning under the weight of refreshments. There was an impressive array of silver, china, cakes, and sandwiches that wouldn't have embarrassed an Edwardian chatelaine of the Dower House. Sarah hid a smile, watching the couple cast their eyes over the feast, checking for any absences. She caught a tiny nod from Mary. Did she just dismiss Mike, like a footman?

The ladies nibbled and drank tea. Sarah spoke of her family, but, despite flickers of interest in the eyes of the older woman, there was no indication she appreciated she was hearing about her son and only grandchild, named Mary after the matriarch. There was no natural banter, no questions probing for details or interruptions to seek clarifications; merely minute changes in facial expressions, as if an acquaintance was talking about strangers. It was tragic to see the diminution of this once grand, vital lady who used to command proceedings, and had never been content to participate as a bystander.

Sarah reached for a crustless cucumber sandwich – the filling still firm and sweet – watching the same tawny eyes as her husband's, stare vacantly out of the window. Physically, Mary camouflaged her age by taking care with her hair and makeup, and never allowing her posture to slacken. Sadly, her mind was less well preserved. Days like this, thankfully, were interspersed with happier occasions – where the majestic lady Sarah feared in the early stages of her romance was still evident, running life at the Dower House from her power base in the morning room. Could I have cared for her? Sarah wondered.

After the diagnosis three years ago, Sarah had watched from the sidelines, dismayed at the speed of decline and the inability of Mary's two sons to agree on what to do. Sarah questioned if her mother-in-law was safe living alone, whilst the brothers debated speaking to experts and the merits of seeking second opinions – both hoping the other would miraculously find a solution, neither acknowledging the scale of the crisis. The men were poking at the problem like two children exploring an intriguing insect with long sticks; examining it from different angles, convinced there must be a more attractive perspective to view the conundrum, they just needed to find the right viewpoint. The truth was, there is no cure for dementia, and it wasn't just Mary whose way of life was threatened.

At least I seriously considered offering to care for her, she thought, unlike my selfish in-laws who wouldn't alter their perfect life at their grand country house. Harry never visited and that was cruel. But then Harry was a harsh man; when Mike and Mary split up – just a couple of years after Sarah met them – Harry had as much sympathy as a traffic warden for a harassed shopper, even refusing to speak to the older man. Mary's consequent move west had been driven by the combined pull of the imminent birth of a grandchild, and the push of leaving Mike who had been caught offering to sell more than a theatre program to an off-duty policeman. He was let off with a caution – Class B drugs, and his first offence – but the horror of the drugs squad rifling through Mary's underwear drawer sealed Mike's fate, and divorce lawyers were instructed. The family abandoned Mike; he spent years winning back Mary's affection, finally penetrating the combined Fetherston barriers when he offered to care for her after her diagnosis. Together, the couple had bought the Dower House – although mostly financed by Mary's fortune.

Hearing a teacup rattle, Sarah looked up. Mary was sipping delicately, holding the cup and saucer with her slightly shaky fingertips; surely that tea is cold! Sarah stood and collected the dirty crockery, dusted crumbs onto a single plate, stacked everything neatly onto the tray and then said goodbye, pecking the cheek thrust her way, sensing the slight leathery texture beneath the makeup. Closing the door softly behind her, she went to find Mike; Mary was clearly deteriorating.

After searching the grounds for ten minutes, she thought she'd try the Walled Garden, Mike's sanctuary. She'd never been in before; he didn't encourage the family into his "man cave". She opened the door and poked her head in. Her eyes swept across the beds of flowering runner bean plants and sweetcorn, then around the walls, where fruit trees hugged the warmth of the sun. Where was he? She glanced at her watch. *I'll just check those two polytunnels then I must go.* She advanced on the first wondering why it was so enormous, the size of one of those articulated lorries she detested having to pass on a motorway, and why the plastic was black. The polytunnel doors were shut. She pushed one open, and a blast of heat hit her: it was like stepping off a flight to a winter-sun holiday. Her eyes swiveled from Mike, bending over with his back to her, to the rows of spiky plants growing snugly, row after row after row of them, then back to Mike.

The plants were identical and all unmistakably cannabis.

She was speechless.

Chapter Two

The next morning in the kitchen of the Long House – a medieval farmhouse with dark interconnecting cosy, not grand, rooms – Freddy sat staring out of the window, transfixed by a tub of lilies. Behind him, the Aga was purring like a giant shiny blue cat, the room was warm, and he could smell toast cooking and hear Sarah bustling about organizing breakfast. Her heels clattered on the stone floor, but something was wrong. Had he upset Sarah?

Last night, returning late from a departmental dinner, he'd found her sitting up in bed frowning. He'd attempted to entertain her, explaining some of the fascinating parallels between historical and current events he'd been debating with his fellow professors, but she wouldn't engage. She'd claimed a headache when he slid eagerly into bed and sidled towards her, caressing her warm, smooth shoulder, and then refused the offer of painkillers. All through the night Sarah had been restless, and Freddy suffered alongside her, periodically woken by the duvet scrapping uncomfortably over his chin bristles as Sarah tugged at it. When the alarm sounded, Freddy reached over for a cuddle, but her side of the bed was cold.

Freddy stretched across the breakfast bar. 'Is something wrong, darling?'

'Nothing,' Sarah said, pulling her hand away from his touch.

'What have I done, or failed to do? Tell me . . . please?' he asked, shooting her one of his engaging smiles that normally melted domestic incidents.

But she turned her back on him, muttering that it wasn't him and there was nothing he could do to help. Freddy watched Sarah dither her way between the kettle and the toaster, as if she didn't have the energy to master both appliances simultaneously. He tried to recall his diary – could he stay and root out the problem? He might have a meeting with the other professors, or was it an early tutorial, something enticing about the Quaker movement, it was on the tip of his tongue, Quakers, or was it the battle of . . .

'What time are we leaving for Suffolk this afternoon?'

He screwed up his face. 'No, darling. Marston Moor is in Yorkshire not Suffolk!'

'Wakey wakey . . . the weekend in Suffolk.'

He smelt coffee and looked down at the mug being swung like a present-day version of smelling salts beneath his nostrils. 'Suffolk,' his wife continued, slowly, pronouncing each word. 'This weekend, with your brother, in Suffolk.'

'Ah, yes,' he said, taking the cup from her. Suffolk, with Harry, his older brother, his protector who always stood up for his sibling, prevented him being teased at boarding school, bullied as a swot.

'I'll be home by four o'clock, darling,' he promised. 'So, we can set off then.'

He took a gulp of his sweet brew, examining Sarah and detected the faintest traces of a smirk. When she spoke, it was a in a softer tone.

'Think I'd better oversee directions, make sure we don't head up the M1. You, darling, are a bit like a giant puppy always getting yourself into pickles that require a grounded adult to rescue you from!'

This was Sarah – his anchor – who smoothed away twenty-first century challenges allowing him to spend most of his life immersed in the seventeenth, filling his days with tutorials, guest lectures and writing. Freddy adored her and still had an inkling despite her denial, that something was upsetting her.

The kettle whistled its readiness. Their eleven-year-old daughter drifted into the kitchen, still buttoning up her school shirt.

'I'm not hungry. Can I just have milkshake?' she moaned.

'Please may I have a milkshake,' Sarah replied. 'But the answer is no, little one. Too much sugar. I'm just making tea and toast. Now, don't forget to brush your hair.'

Listening to Sarah take control reassured Freddy; perhaps it really was nothing. He ran his fingers through his hair as a rack of toast was plonked on the breakfast counter, rapidly followed by a tub of butter, marmalade, and a pot of local honey. He eyed the contents of the toast rack; no two pieces were ever the same, each had its own unique characteristics if you considered them carefully enough. He made his selection, puzzling over when marmalade was first made at the Long House. Were the occupants rich enough to buy imported fruit in the sixteenth Century? He heard Sarah saying something about his dinner suit. 'Eh?' he said, chuckling at the sight of young Mary whose bottom was in the air as she dug – like a frenzied terrier after a subterranean animal – in the depths of her school bag.

'Have you packed your dance kit?' Sarah asked.

'Ooops!' said Mary, grinning and rushing out, clomping up the stairs.

'Hair while you're up there,' Sarah yelled after the departing girl. Her gaze switched to him. 'Are we cancelling Spain?'

'Spain, ah yes Spain,' he murmured.

Sarah moved Mary's discarded pencil case to the arts and crafts copper tray: the family "lost and found" department, home to life's necessities with a habit of going astray: car keys, phones. That tray minimised frantic family searches where the three of them dashed around in circles like a pack of dogs doing the zoomies, turning their neat, organised house into rooms that looked like a named storm had just blown through. Freddy quite enjoyed those games.

'Ahhh, Spain,' he repeated. 'Can I get back to you on that one?'

'No, it can't wait any longer. It gets too expensive. I'll cancel.'

His head drifted back towards the lily pot. Why was she so snappy? Was she under pressure from that ghastly Sandra woman; he'd walk out and refuse to help at all, if "Mrs. Delegator" treated him so shabbily, why did Sarah put up with her? He grunted and started to count the lilies, ruminating on when the Long House might have started to grow tubs of flowers: certainly not in the seventeenth century – you can't eat a lily. He nibbled on toast, his mind meandering through his latest research project, why did Cromwell give so much leeway to the counties? There was a clicking noise and his head snapped back towards the sound. Sarah's hand was by his ear.

'Sorry, darling, what did you say?'

She waggled her eyebrows at him; at least she still finds my eccentricities endearing, not annoying. Maybe she's just tired, a bit anxious about something trivial.

'Fascinating place with Oliver Cromwell?' she said.

'Actually, with his major generals,' he admitted, stretching his arms up over his head, then adding, 'What people fail to appreciate about—'

She cut him off. 'Not now, please!'

Mary dashed past, crowing that she'd found her dance costume. He pushed back his chair. 'Darling, I must go. Did you notice what I did with my car keys?'

'Copper tray.'

Freddy leaned over, kissing Sarah then walked past Mary, rustling her neatly brushed hair.

'Dad!' she grumbled.

'Bye, girls!'

Sarah watched Freddy hesitate in the doorway, then twist round shooting her a last enquiring glance, his fringe falling low on his forehead. His hair was too long: another item to chalk on the nag list; *once I work out what to do about Mike.* She slid a plate of buttered toast in front of Mary, then listening to her child munching, snatched down the to-do list – written on the back of a used white envelope – and ran an eye down the seemingly endless roll call of duties. With one eye on Mary, Sarah squashed onto the bottom '*bake for fundraiser*', in tiny letters, ensuring she met the secret goal of keeping obligations to a single side.

She slipped the list under a ribbon on the padded noticeboard by her double sink and glared at it; she couldn't focus on trivia with her ship steaming towards an iceberg. Bloody Mike and his drugs! Mike was the guilty one, but justice frequently harms innocent connected parties. Damn Mike, why is he growing cannabis and how could he be stopped without causing collateral damage?

Yesterday standing confronting Mike, in the stifling heat, her temptation had been to stalk straight back to the morning room, but when she recalled those blank eyes staring at her, pictured her mother-in-law fumbling like a stray dog trying to find its way home, almost dizzy attempting to pin down who Sarah was – she concluded telling Mary was pointless. Mike was shuffling uncomfortably in front of her with a pleading expression on his face; he reminded her of a naughty schoolboy caught smoking behind the bike sheds, hoping to avoid an hour's detention. Mike was not frightened; doesn't he know this is a crime?

'Don't shop me,' he said. 'You've always been in my corner, just keep this to yourself.'

'No way! This is wrong. I have a young daughter. I need your word this will stop. And either I, or preferably you, must tell the family what's been going on.'

'Don't, Sarah.'

As she turned away, she felt his palm rest on her shoulder. She shrugged away his hand, wheeling round to face him.

'Will you promise me you will stop?'

'No,' then he winked at her, saying, 'It's hardly heroin!'

'Mike! This is unseemly.'

He rolled his eyes at her. 'Oh, come on,' he lashed out. 'Don't ape that lot and pretend you're one of them. You aren't. You and I are the same, neither of us toffs. They look down on both of us. Don't kid yourself they think you're any better than me. I've heard that arrogant shit Harry sniggering with his wife and mother behind your back.'

Her insides curled up. Her brother-in-law never hid his disdain for Mike as unbefitting Mary. He'd scoffed at Sarah too, when they first met. But she'd changed – apparently not sufficiently enough for Harry, or so she was being told. Harry's opinion of Sarah was evident the very first time she met him, when despite her boyfriend eulogising for days before their visit about his brother with the amazingly successful online wine business – like a parent carefully planning a child's introduction to broccoli – Sarah had suspected Harry would be trouble.

Freddy warned her that his brother lived in a large country house in Suffolk, but she'd still gulped when they arrived. What was *she* doing *here*? The entrance hall was the size of the combined reception rooms of her childhood home. The grand Ashe Hall foyer was welcoming, a pair of tall vases filled with white hellebores and pink heather resting on a wooden chest; her host, though, was not. Standing in the dim light, peering across the black and white flagstones, she saw a paunchier version of her boyfriend, but that was where the similarity ended.

Harry was running his eyes over her body, his tongue running round his lips as if anticipating an ice-cold beer on a hot summer day. 'Well, hello there. What have we got here, little brother?'

Sarah shuffled and wriggled like a nervous toddler, clutching Freddy's hand. He pulled her in front, and she sank back against his chest, inhaling the comforting sharp citrus smell of him, feeling secure with his arms encasing her.

'This is Sarah.'

Grinning, Harry looked over her head at his brother – she'd learned to wear lower heels – chuckling appreciatively as if Freddy was presenting an award-winning piglet. Sarah dipped her reddening face, her insides churning – would she ever be accepted by this pompous bastard?

She'd long given up trying.

And yesterday Mike had claimed – despite all her efforts – Sarah was considered a family joke; not just by Harry, but by all her-in-laws. Was he being manipulative, trying to stop her telling anyone about his illegal crop? Mike might have been exaggerating, but Harry probably did think his sibling had married beneath him. Unlike some of the wines he recommended, Harry had not improved with age, and Sarah suspected he tolerated rather than enjoyed her company. She certainly didn't enjoy his. Sarah had never warmed to Harry, like she had to her mother-in-law. It wasn't hard for Sarah to envisage Harry's arrogant manner, belittling her. And where Harry led, that snooty wife Amy followed. But she couldn't believe Mary shared their opinions. Or did she? Did it matter, anyway, what they thought of her? She still needed to figure out a way of preventing anyone else being affected by exposing Mike – especially not Mary.

Back from the school run, Sarah changed into boots and collected the vegetable peelings from the utility room. Whatever was she going to do about Mike? She rounded the corner of the house and stopped, the first smile of the day twitching at her mouth. Six hens were hurtling towards her. They were comical creatures, leaning forward, unbalanced. She unbolted the gate and serenaded by clucks, slopped through the mud towards the grain store: a metal dustbin. Removing the brick securing the lid against gusts of wind, she scooped out the feed, feeling gentle pecks against her boots. Sarah fought her way to the front of the flock and released the grain into their trough.

'What do I do about Devon's latest drug baron?' she asked her favourite hen, which had dark grey, almost black feathers, speckled with a little white. The bird ignored her, its beak darting up and down.

She replayed the same options that had circled round her mind yesterday driving back from The Dower House, and again when she made dinner, and all through the frustrating evening that followed trying to identify a solution to a problem she wished she'd never unearthed. This was not just about Mike. For the last three years, Mike had done a first-rate job caring for Mary. Whenever Sarah called, her mother-in-law was cosseted in the morning room, waited on hand and foot, like a rich dowager aunt from the nineteenth century. A dementia sufferer needed routine. A change of the magnitude of Mike disappearing could cause a serious wobble, and Sarah didn't want to risk that.

She checked the hen house, collecting four warm eggs from the laying boxes, tucking them into a pocket, then watched the hens dart about poking heads into bushes, beaks into soil, searching for titbits indifferent to their keeper's worries. Adding to her concern was the knowledge of who would become the new care provider.

Sarah.

Suffolk would plead the impracticalities of distance, and what was the alternative? Harry would resist paying for residential care and there was no help to be had from the State.She'd done her homework and they only contribute if the patient has no money or is certified mad: too dangerous for someone to live with!

She dug out another measure of feed, sprinkling it the length of the feeding trough, asking herself if she was prepared to risk picking up responsibility for her mother-in-law. That would have been a tough assignment three years ago, but now – stepping onto the stage a novice, without the benefit of learning how to play the part as the patient gradually deteriorated – she didn't want to be the catalyst forcing herself into that role.

Sarah pushed a black and white bird away from the feeding trough with her foot. 'Don't be so greedy, let the others have some!' The bird squawked, dashing round approaching the food from a different angle, dipping its beak back down and filling its craw with grain.

Should she call the police? Last night she'd queried if she was *obliged* to call the police? She didn't know a criminal lawyer, and how could she pose that question of a friend? What pretext could there be for asking, 'So, hypothetically, if someone discovered a drugs operation, do they have to report it?' Anyway, she couldn't tell the police. Not yet. That wouldn't be fair on the family. It was only right they were consulted before the panda cars exploded up the genteel driveway of the Dower House. When she did tell the family, whoever she told, they would summon the police; this was not the first time Mike had dabbled with drugs.

'Maybe he always kept those links to the drug world,' mused Sarah. Who should she tell? Certainly not that perfect twit Harry and watch him crow about Mike's second downfall with his bird's-eye view from the sanctimonious moral high ground of never having been in receipt of so much as a parking ticket. Her last option was to tell Freddy; somewhere in that muddled head, he knows something's wrong. Poor darling Freddy probably thinks he's the cause. But if she told Freddy he would immediately call his brother: back to square one.

She closed the gate on the chicken pen, ramming the bolt firmly into place. If only Mike had kept the door to the Walled Garden locked! Why didn't he come back to the morning room, clear away the tea tray and show her out like he normally did? The best option, still the only option she could think of, was to convince Mike to stop. He had resisted yesterday, today she must be firm.

When the phone rang, Sarah was deadheading roses. She peeled off one of her elbow-length protective gloves, and hearing Mike's voice, shouted, 'Hang on a tick,' then dropped her mobile to pull off the other pink gardening glove. 'That's better,' she said, retrieving the phone.

'I thought,' Mike said, 'as I haven't had a call from that arrogant shit Harry, and not heard any sirens, maybe I owe you some money?'

'I told you I don't want your money. You can't buy your way out of this, Mike.'

'It would help you buy that Georgian gem we all know you covet.'

'I will find a legitimate way to pay for that, thanks.'

She picked up her secateurs and gloves and headed for the utility room.

'It's only weed,' he said, and Sarah heard the echo of her father's voice when as a teenager she'd trotted downstairs to investigate the peculiar, sweet smell curling up and under her bedroom door. 'Don't be so bloody middle class,' Mike continued, 'it's a mild recreational drug. People use it for all sorts of medicinal reasons.' Was that why her father had smoked dope? She couldn't recall him in any pain. 'All the toffs use it; nothing to be embarrassed about!'

'Social acceptability doesn't make it legal,' she said, struggling to open a drawer with her full hands. 'Mike, don't badger me.' She pushed the drawer shut with her bottom. 'I think it's best you stop. If you stop, I won't say anything. I will give you a week to shut things down, how does that sound?'

'I won't stop.'

'You *must* stop!'

'Don't tell me what to do.'

'Stop or I will be forced to tell someone, probably Freddy, who will call Harry, and you know what that will mean.'

Sarah could hear Mike's short puffy breaths.

'Final answer?' he said.

'Final warning. Just stop, Mike. I mean it.'

The line went dead; congratulating herself on a tricky job well done, she slipped the phone into her back pocket and went upstairs. There was a party to pack for!

Folding Freddy's dress shirt, she felt the phone vibrate, pulled it out and was transported back instantly over a decade. The message with two attachments was from Mike:

"You tell, I tell. You have until Monday to decide."

Chapter Three

That evening Sarah stepped into the fairy tale existence of her in-laws at the grand Ashe Hall; she normally loved dipping into their world, but tonight she was haunted by the contents of a ten-second video clip.

Standing at the foot of the stairs, her hands on her daughter's shoulders, she watched the brothers disappear up the main Ashe Hall staircase. Admiring the elaborate cast iron balustrades and sweeping mahogany handrail, she could almost picture her mother-in-law in full evening dress posing on the half-landing. Oh, for those previous Suffolk trips, when there had been two Marys in the back of the car, chirping their way up the A12! This time, Sarah was forced to rely on Freddy's battlefield tour of the Civil War in East Anglia to distract her from her phone; she couldn't stop fiddling with it.

An arrangement of roses and flowering marjoram stood on the table, billowing out of a jug, sending fragrant waves across the hall. Her sister-in-law picked up a few rose petals that had fallen from the blooms and pushed them into her apron pocket then turned and a smile – that didn't reach her eyes – was forced onto her scrawny face. Although on arrival the hostess had rushed out and engulfed Freddy in a bearhug, she had yet to great her female visitors. *Is she as frosty with paying guests?* When Sarah had discovered Harry's haughty wife ran a boutique B&B, she found it hilarious. Amy, in the hospitality trade? Amy, whose face was so thin and pinched beneath her mouse-coloured hair – usually scraped back like it was tonight into a practical ponytail – that Sarah wasn't sure there was room for a smile? Now, Sarah stood with her arms wrapped around her child, thinking there was no way Amy would continue running a B&B once the couple inherited sufficient of her mother-in-law's fortune to pay off their £500,000 mortgage.

She took Mary's hand and followed Amy down the corridor. Would it hurt you to be warmer to your only niece, even if you still can't manage to pretend you like me? Yes, I suspect Mike was right; behind my back you mock me. Despite my efforts, you still see that gawky girl from Basingstoke, the one with the hapless father, who ensnared your charming unworldly brother-in-law and tricked him into marriage. You'll never accept it was Freddy's wish too, nor how happy he is. Except that video Mike had sent would shatter her husband's happiness and Amy would delight in telling him she'd always feared Sarah was a mistake.

'Informal tonight, ladies – can't cope with a proper dinner before a big event,' said Amy, letting them into the kitchen.

'I'm hungry!' shouted Mary.

'Supper is ready,' said Amy. 'Harry has chosen a splendid burgundy for the adults.'

What about your niece? You never give a second's thought to what a child likes to drink. It will be water. The three ladies waited for the men in uncompanionable silence. Amy was slicing up a crusty baguette into thick chunks. Mary sank to the floor and played with the dog. She was flicking a yellow-and-blue-striped rope, making it dance, chuckling at the dog whose head was whirling from side to side; its front paws simultaneously fumbling to grasp the twirling toy.

Her sister-in-law was silent: her head down. She could never have a heart-to-heart with Amy about what Mike was doing at Dower House, far less what he was threatening to do to her. There would be no debate – Amy would dial 999 the second she heard the word "cannabis". Amy wouldn't think about the implications. If Mike was whisked away, her sister-in-law would assume Sarah could shoulder the caring burden – juggling the additional responsibility into her packed schedule – while she and Harry maintained their charmed life and tutted their way through the drama from the safe distance of Suffolk.

Life at Ashe Hall seemed to be a whirl of hunt balls, riotous dinners, drinks parties, and resembled life at Lampton, the ancestral Fetherston estate her mother-in-law used to reminisce about, given any opportunity. Sarah still recalled how at their infamous first meeting, Mary's eyes had started glowing when she spoke about Lampton. Mary was sitting imperiously at the top of her dining table recounting memories as Mike scuttled around like an overworked footman. Sarah was treated to tales of weekend house parties, of butlers and cooks, of governesses and upstairs maids. In a gap in the storytelling, deciding it was safer to listen than talk, Sarah waved her fork at the wall.

'Do these pictures come from Lampton?'

'Ah Lampton,' said Mary, as softly as if speaking of a lover. She shot Sarah a steely look. 'They are portraits, not pictures.'

'Who are they? Have I heard of any of them?' she asked, peering at the elaborate gilt frames.

'What a peculiar question – they are Fetherstons. Those are my brothers, Harry, and Tom. They were much older than me; we lost them in the D-day landings,' explained Mary. "And that, behind Mike, is Lady Mary, my several greats grandmother – wasn't she divine?'

Sarah glanced at Lady Mary, then back at her hostess. 'Are you named after her?'

'Yes. It's a family name. Continuity is important, don't you think?'

'Continuity be damned! There's going to be an almighty scrap over who gets what when you shuffle on!' Freddy chortled.

When the room fell silent, fearing the spotlight might fall on her, Sarah quickly asked. 'Are any of them painted by someone famous?'

Mary gave her the sort of look Sarah used to get from her physics teacher, on those rare occasions she attempted to answer a question.

'They hang here because they are family. Money isn't everything, young lady.'

She remembered thinking that was an easy thing for Mary to say, because she was wealthy. Would her mother-in-law understand why Sarah had done what was captured on that clip, or would she be horrified that in a tiny way she had enabled her daughter-in-law's fall from grace? And what on earth would the committee ladies say if they saw it!

Sarah heard laughter in the corridor; the kitchen door opened, and Harry headed for the bottles of red wine lined up on the kitchen counter. Amy stopped him in his tracks.

'Darling, fire in the dining room!'

'Phuff, in the morning. Let's have a snifter.'

'*Now,* please, Harry.'

'Come on, Harry, let's do it tonight,' said Freddy. 'Won't take long.' His eyes were on her. 'Sarah and I will keep you company.'

Inwardly Sarah groaned as she trooped into the dining room behind the men. She had been introduced to the Harry "sport" of character assassination on her first visit to Ashe Hall and wasn't surprised when her brother-in-law took out his temper at having to clean out the fireplace, by indulging in his favourite game. Mike was tonight's victim. Each scoopful of ash was accompanied with another dig from Harry at a man that – although she had little sympathy for him given his earlier threat – Sarah didn't recognise. After a monologue of spiky comments, Harry sat back on his haunches, twisting round, shifting so he could see her and his brother, asking, 'Why did my elegant, charming, accomplished mother ever settle for that man?'

A flush swept over her; how often in her absence had Sarah been the target of these barbs? She felt Freddy's hand fold over hers, squeezing it, while his brother's petulant voice whined on. 'To justify a meaningful relationship with Ma, one must be a gentleman, not a common little man.'

Freddy leaned back against the sideboard. 'If you remember, he was painted as a gentleman. She described him, just before we were all introduced, as "my new gentlemen friend". Ha, ridiculous notion that was, eh?'

'Did you know, Sarah, his name is actually *Darren,*' Harry added, tittering loudly.

There was a rustle as Harry scrunched up a sheet of newspaper and pitched it towards the grate. 'Which was too much for Ma, so she always uses his middle name.'

'Which is of course "Mike", not Michael,' said Freddy.

Both brothers chuckled. Sarah suppressed a gasp of outrage. Her first boyfriend had been called Darren. What was wrong with these grown men, sniggering at someone's name? What was wrong with this *family?* It wasn't just the men – who did Mary think she was, judging a name not good enough, then dismissing the middle one: trying to select a replacement, as if for a rescue dog with a name the children can't manage? Poor Mike: acquiescing to their snobby plan, buying acceptance into their lofty world.

Harry was balancing logs onto a lattice of kindling, creating a tower of wood. He announced to the fireplace: 'Evidently, her suitor would not agree to being renamed Michael to satisfy his girlfriend's social preferences.'

Well, thank goodness Mike had drawn the line at rechristening.

'It must be "Mike", not "Michael". No gentleman shortens his name like that!'

'Frederick can be shortened to Freddy,' offered the younger brother.

'And Harold becomes Harry. If you want to shorten Michael, it should be Mikey, not Mike,' concluded Harry, standing up and admiring his handiwork.

Freddy was elaborating on Mike's deficiencies: '. . . and he never went to uni, so no claim to acceptability through education.'

'And the pièce de resistance,' Harry snorted, 'this "house in the country", Ma reported, was actually on a modern estate near Basingstoke!'

Sarah let rip, her voice slightly shaky. 'That's enough! That's where I was brought up, Basingstoke, and you know it. I doubt you've ever been there, so don't judge. And she *did* marry him, despite all these deficiencies. Why can't you just accept her choice?'

Freddy stroked the back of her hand, his eyes on his brother. 'I think I have accepted it, haven't I? Finished in here, Harry?' he asked reaching out for the ash pail.

'Come on,' said Harry waving a hand in Sarah's direction as if swatting away a fly. 'Snifter time!'

Back in the kitchen, watching Harry sniffing, slurping, and spitting the wine – why couldn't he just pour straight into the glasses? – Sarah asked how many guests were coming to the drinks party tomorrow.

'It's an *At Home,* Sarah. Not a drinks party,' corrected Harry, placing a glass in front of her.

Why did he still revel in each inconsequential mistake she made? Did it matter if she called it a party or referred to the cloakroom as a "toilet" rather than a "loo"? She bet he and Amy still sniggered about the first time she'd tried dessert wine, when he'd triumphantly told Sarah, 'It's a Sauterne, comes from Bordeaux, like the claret I served earlier. Or you can call it a pudding wine if you prefer. It's a sweet wine that pairs with a pudding, not a sugary wine with a sweet.'

Harry had missed his vocation. He should have gone into teaching; he loved correcting her. She picked up the glass of burgundy.

'Let it float round your mouth, swirl it into your cheeks,' Harry commanded.

Sarah bit her tongue. He just can't help himself; she took a large slug, exaggeratedly swishing the wine from cheek to cheek – as if she was gargling mouth wash – before swallowing and beaming across at her host.

'Delicious, Harry. Soft and delicate and wonderfully complex!'

She'd learned the lines over the years of tutelage. The wine was amazing. She suspected it was also staggeringly expensive.

'We're expecting about eighty tomorrow night, at least that's what we're catering for,' said Amy, passing around plates of chicken casserole, sending wafts of a rich earthy smell round the table. Sarah's stomach growled. She had seated young Mary between herself and Freddy, a buttress against potential onslaught from Harry or his wife and leaned over to ask if she had washed her hands since playing with the dog.

She heard a soft scratching noise and spun round. Her phone was on her side plate.

'I think that's yours, darling, found it in the car,' said Freddy.

She stared aghast first at him, then down wide-eyed at her phone as if it had become radioactive. Sarah wiped a hand over her face, listening to Harry's arrogant voice. 'So. What news of Ma?'

'Your mother, well . . .' she began. *Can Freddy open my phone, would he check my messages?*

Harry asked a second time. 'Yes. How is she, all well?'

Sarah was chewing her lip, her eyes on her lap. Should she reach for her phone? Was her life about to explode in front of her child?

'How goes it all at the Dower House?' asked Harry a little louder, pouring himself more wine, his eyes trained on Sarah.

Why can't Harry drop it! Stop talking about that bloody house, reminding Sarah of Mike, and trapping her in a revolving door she had no idea how to escape. She lifted her eyes. Freddy was smiling. He couldn't have seen; he wouldn't be smiling if he had. She snatched up the phone and stowed it in her handbag, then bowed her head again. Why hadn't Harry grown up and accepted Mike was part of the family? He wouldn't have to ask Sarah how his mother was if he had. As the only regular visitor, Sarah was the only person equipped to answer questions about the matriarch, and sensing the family's collective eyes, Sarah gave in, answering tartly, 'Not great, Harry. You might want to visit and judge for yourself.'

Always close to the surface, Harry's smoldering temper gushed out.

'It's a bloody long drive,' he snapped, his chin juddering. 'I know you've both got all the time in the world, with you not working and Freddy off on hols for months over the summer, you can both swan about enjoying Ascot and Wimbledon. *We* don't get the summer off. I can't think when either of us enjoyed any of "the season", can you, Amy?'

There was a tight shake of the head from Amy, and her clipped nasal voice confirmed that she hadn't been to the Henley regatta since they'd moved to Suffolk.

'What do you think Mike would make of Henley?' chortled Harry. 'He thinks a cox is a type of apple.' Tittering at his own joke, he carried on, 'No, Amy and I can't be expected to traipse halfway across the country every month. Mike should bring her here!'

It was tempting to snap back at Harry, but fifteen years of suffering her brother-in-law's outbursts had enabled Sarah to develop a thicker skin. She was probably busier than Amy, and certainly Freddy spent more time in his study than his brother. As for Mike, well, he was jolly busy too. For starters there was his cannabis farm. Wow – wouldn't she love to roll that little grenade into this evening's discussion! Except Mike would then message that hideous clip to Freddy, and her own world would collapse alongside Mike's. Sarah chewed thoughtfully on a chunk of dry bread, refusing the bait Harry dangled. She passed the conversational baton elsewhere and Freddy came to the rescue.

'I think Mike is doing an admirable job with Ma. You should be more grateful.'

'Ahha, do I spy a convert in our midst? Has your wife from the elegant spa town of Basingstoke convinced you to support her fellow tribesman from Hampshire?'

Harry raised his wine glass in mock salute to Sarah.

'I hereby humbly beseech the forgiveness of the saintly Basingstoke duo if I have not been grovelling enough with my thanks for your work at the Dower House.' He drained his glass, and then refilled it, returning to his theme. 'Enlighten us, Sarah: do the Basingstoke natives have their own language and customs?'

Sarah heard Mary sniggering, and looked across, meeting Freddy's eyes. Freddy shot Mary a warning glare. *Was Harry's childishness explained by the couple's childlessness?*

'Very funny, brother,' said Freddy. 'Seriously, why not come to Devon? You could stay with us, and we could visit Ma together? Tell you what; we could have another go divvying up the portraits?'

'She should leave them all to me as the eldest son,' spat Harry, using a fingernail to poke at a piece of chicken lodged between his teeth.

'Nice try. She's told us she won't do that. So, which is your top pick? Still fighting for my dashing cavalier? You only covet him because I do.'

When Harry claimed his sibling didn't have anywhere appropriate to display the portraits, declaring they needed to hang in a grand dining room, Sarah assumed Freddy had disarmed the conversation, but Harry wasn't finished.

'And if I want to stay at Ma's, I bloody well will. It's her house, not his. He owns a fraction. So, do we as a family think we should start demanding Mike ferries Ma about a bit?' suggested Harry, knocking back his wine and stretching over for the bottle. 'Can't be good for her, holed up in the same four walls all day?'

Wrong again: those four walls are her comfort blanket, not her prison.

Sarah's eyebrows rose when she saw Amy remove the bottle from her husband's grasp, saying sharply, 'Drop it, Harry,' before topping up the other three wine glasses. 'Remember, you've eighty guests tomorrow, darling, you might want to avoid a hangover.'

Interesting, she'd never seen Amy rattled. Even for Harry there was a lot of wine flowing – and mostly into the host's glass.

'Anything I can do tomorrow?' asked Sarah, reaching for the dirty plates either side of her.

By the sink Amy muttered, 'I'm sorry. Even for Harry, he's taking his twin hobbies of drinking and bad-mouthing Mike to extremes tonight. You're just getting caught in the crossfire. He has his reasons.'

'I'm a seasoned veteran. I'll cope!'

Sarah collected her handbag from the floor by her chair and pulled Mary to her feet, leading her out of the kitchen and the potential danger zone of Harry's mood. She had her own problems; she wasn't interested in her brother-in-law's.

Closing the bedroom door behind her, Sarah shivered. It was June – were these old houses ever warm? Freddy threw back the bedclothes and patted the bed beside him.

'Hop in, soon have you warm.'

'Wow – what's going on with your brother?' exclaimed Sarah, clambering in. 'He was hitting the bottle a bit hard.'

'We all have our demons. Not sure what's chasing him . . . best leave Harry to sort it out himself.'

Sarah snuggled down, warming her cold feet against her Freddy's legs. She couldn't contemplate anything more intimate. Until lunchtime she'd been looking forward to this weekend. Having given Mike his ultimatum, she'd skipped up the stairs to pack – lightheartedly stroking her silk nightdress and promising herself she'd make up for the cold shouldering she'd given Freddy last night. Then Mike's message had stolen the upper hand, and tonight she couldn't relax, avoiding Freddy's attentions by focusing hers on their daughter.

When Mike's text arrived, with its stark message, Sarah had collapsed on the bed, dropping Freddy's dress shirt, her heart pounding, scrolling through the attachments. There were only two. Who? Why? And how the devil had Mike got his hands on them?

There was only one way to find out. She dialed Mike's number.

He reminded her Covent Garden was in the heart of theatreland. *Why did I choose Covent Garden?* She'd inwardly groaned; it wasn't her choice. It was her mother-in-law who recommended the restaurant, close to the theatre where – until she'd left Mike for Devon two years earlier – Mary helped alter costumes. And of course, Mike still worked there. In those first years after their daughter was born, Freddy had not been a classic supportive modern husband, shouldering his share of the chores. It was Sarah's life that was upended, Sarah trapped with the toddler, Sarah who didn't have a day to herself, and when Sarah moaned to Freddy's mother, about him accepting yet another invitation to a guest lecture necessitating an overnight stay, she'd leapt at her mother-in-law's suggestion she have the grandchild to stay so Sarah could get away to meet an old friend.

That day, Sarah had been wallowing self-indulgently like a hippo in mud. It was the first day in over a year she didn't have to spend every second with all five of her senses on a war footing readiness for potential threats to another human being. It was like her ship had slipped anchor for a world cruise. She remembered her phone buzzing with a message from Darren – her first boyfriend – saying he was running twenty minutes late and that's when she ordered a second glass of wine. Halfway through the third, she spotted him on the gallery. He hadn't changed, still wearing the confident cloak of youth and good looks. She jumped up, knocking over her chair.

'Darren, down here!' She waved her hands around above her head, giggling. He was standing directly above her. 'Darren, down here, you muppet!'

Apparently, Mike – taking a stroll between rehearsals – heard a female voice calling out to him and looked down over the banisters at a drunken Sarah shouting and waving, not at him, it turned out, but to another man evidently called Darren as well: an attractive young stranger.

'I thought it was odd like, you with a man in London, so I circled back and when I spotted you snogging him . . .'

'You didn't have to take a photo,' shouted Sarah down the phone.

'You didn't have to snog a stranger!'

'He wasn't a stranger.'

'Well, he certainly wasn't Freddy,' said Mike, giving a little laugh. 'I wasn't spying on you, I just thought I might use the snap to get your support with Mary, help broker a reconciliation. It was two years since she booted me out, and once that prick Harry left us alone, well things weren't too testy with the lawyers, and I thought after a bit of time, she'd have me back. But I didn't need your help, in the end.

I worked my own way back in.'

'But why did you follow me?'

'You were clearly up to no good. It was instinct to follow you.'

'And video us!'

The ten-second clip showed the pair in the foyer by the lift, pressed up against each other, her blouse open, her breasts on show with Darren's head bent over nuzzling them. Neither of them would have noticed a circus parade nearby, far less Mike and his phone.

It wasn't until Mary went to primary school that finally Sarah forgave herself for her moment of madness. She'd drunk too much wine on an empty stomach, Darren showered her with compliments and attention, and she'd succumbed to his charm offensive. She was sure her guilt was written all over her face but decided after agonizing for the whole train journey back to Devon, she couldn't confess. It was not just her infidelity; Freddy would question the whole basis of their marriage. Sarah was the rock he relied on; how could he ever trust her again? For a few days Darren pestered Sarah, tugging at her conscience. But that stopped when she blocked his number.

Now she had to choose. Mike was adamant he wasn't stopping. If Freddy saw that clip, would her marriage be over? What if Mike posted it publicly and Sandra and all the committee ladies saw it; she might get away with it if she'd been snogging a Duke, but not Darren! Which way to jump? Dare she stay silent? Tonight, lying rigid, wrapped in her husband's arms, wracked with guilt, she asked herself why she was so determined to turn Mike in. It was only dope; she'd been with her father often enough when he bought weed. Was the inclination to report Mike born out of her innate desire to be a paragon of virtue in the eyes of this family? Mike had never bothered to adapt, like she had. Was that because of a stubborn streak: maintaining an independence from the family, flaunting his lack of adherence to their upper crust ways?

Sarah pushed Freddy's limp arm away – he never has trouble sleeping – and rolled onto her back gazing at him, stroking a curl off his forehead. She adored her husband; Mike must feel the same love for his Mary, he wouldn't deliberately embarrass her. He'd never shirked his share of the dinner bill when Mary was present, there was none of the patting of pockets and bemused expressions she or

Freddy encountered if the matriarch was absent. Sarah was convinced Mike never admitted to himself he was from a different class, hadn't acknowledged he had "married up". Unlike Sarah, Mike had failed to change for the simple reason he never thought to try.

Sarah pushed herself back against the pillows. Should she accept Mike's proposal, stay quiet about the clandestine Walled Garden farm? Would that solve things, or would she just be delaying her fate? He'd always have that weapon. If she ever did something he disliked he could retaliate, ruin her life with a simple text. She wriggled back down the sheets, huffing. Time had lulled her into a false sense of security, but she was as doomed as an insect lured too close to a Venus flytrap.

For one night Sarah was going to forget her problems. For all their faults, her in-laws did throw fantastic parties. The Ashe Hall reception rooms were like a stage set for a P.G Woodhouse movie, with silver wine buckets, free-flowing champagne, and couples in evening dress dancing to the sounds of Cole Porter's *"Anything Goes"*. Although always a dazzling affair, this Ashe Hall party had a particular buzz, as if the guests had been starved of social interaction and simultaneously emerged, determined to celebrate in style. She felt arms encircling her and rested her head back against Freddy's chest, catching a whiff of lemon.

'Enjoying yourself?' he murmured into her hair.

She turned round to face him, pressing her arm tightly against her ribcage to trap her clutch bag. 'Enormously. On an evening like this, I can almost forgive your brother's taunts. Dance?'

'In a minute, darling. There's someone I want to catch up with. Stay right here, I won't be long,' he promised, unwinding his arms.

Sarah ran her tongue around her dry mouth. She needed water. She looked through the gaggle of elegant guests. Rats, her route to the kitchen was blocked by Harry holding court with two men she didn't know. Drawing closer, she saw a magnum of champagne between her brother-in-law's feet, and he was twirling an empty glass in one hand, lecturing his two friends. Sarah hesitated. The men appeared innocent, but she'd made that mistake before. She cast around for Freddy, but he'd melted into the crowd. Should she turn away?

Harry would dance on the grave of her marriage; revel in revealing her mistake to all his mates if it was ever exposed. One of Harry's companions wore a tight purple velvet waistcoat: the buttons straining to contain the weight of his stomach, the folds of his white dress shirt hanging loosely over his waistband. The third man was sweating profusely, damp patches staining the fabric under his armpits and the upper portion of his dress shirt.

Sarah saw three sets of eyes swing towards her, and then spotted the tell-tale small smirks and widening eyes, the shifting of their feet. The boys were out for fun, and Sarah was cast as the quarry. Her host was beckoning her. She couldn't avoid him, not without being obviously rude. Horrid Harry would be delighted to be rid of his sister-in-law, and Freddy would turn to his brother in the same way their mother did after discovering Mike's indiscretion. And Harry's advice would be identical: divorce the scoundrel; you shouldn't be married to the toad anyway.

Feeling an unpleasant tightening of her throat, she took the last few steps towards the three men.

'Here she is, the lovely lass from Basingstoke,' announced Harry, running his tongue over his lips. 'Come here and meet my chums.'

She froze, biting her lip, her stomach clenching.

'This is the delicious Sarah, married to my lucky brother.' He let out a braying laugh.

Harry reached out to claim her, his clammy hand gripping her wrist, forcing her to stop. Caught off-guard, trying to free herself, Sarah's bag fell from under her arm, the contents spilling across the floorboards in a jumble of makeup, tissues and hairbands, her phone in the centre of the mess, shining like a warning beacon. She ducked to scrabble on the floor, but Harry was faster, seizing the phone and holding it round to face her, close to her eyes so it unlocked.

'Ha ha, Barnaby, Randolph, let's have a gander. What have we in here, eh lads?' he chortled, re-gripping her arm.

She stiffened, holding out her free hand. 'I'll have that back, please.'

Sarah had never worked out how to deflect these ambushes without creating a scene. She felt like a fly imprisoned in their spider's web of arrogant social superiority. Why hadn't she deleted that message? Harry didn't have any scruples.

She tried to wrest herself free but the clamp of his slippery hand on her arm tightened. The sweaty man, Barnaby, took her other hand and bowed over it, dropping a slobbery kiss on her wrist. Randolph was smacking his lips. Harry transferred his grip to her waist, scrolling through her phone one-handedly, his eyes raking across the screen.

She raised her voice. 'Harry, this isn't funny. I am asking politely for my phone back.'

He chuckled; his eyes were glued to the screen. 'Just checking if you've got anything interesting on here.'

She could feel beads of sweat on her forehead, and under her arms. *Not this way, please let me have a chance to explain to Freddy first!*

'And what do you do with your lovely self all day in Devon?' asked the velvet-waistcoated Randolph, leering down at her.

'I manage to keep myself occupied,' replied Sarah, trying again to shake herself free from Harry's grip and lunging for her phone.

He danced away from her, holding the prize high in the air. 'Oh, touchy touchy. Remember I'm family; nothing should be secret within a family. What're you trying to hide, sister?'

She should be used to this lot by now: why did they paw her? Harry didn't do it to any of the other wives, so why did he always pick on her when he'd had too much to drink? Even if Freddy did forgive her, his brother never would, and no doubt Harry would encourage his pack of arrogant friends like Randolph and Barnaby to assume Sarah might be game for a "quickie".

'May I have my phone back please, Harry!'

'I don't detect a Basingstoke accent, do you?' asked Barnaby, cocking his ear and grinning at each of the other men.

Why did she always become tongue-tied, lose her confidence, when Harry or his monstrous friends toyed with her? Why, after so many years of enduring these attacks, could she never think of anything to spit back?

'I know what you do all day. Elocution lessons,' suggested Randolph, chortling at his own jibe.

'Ha. No, Sarah does nothing. Absolutely naff all. She's just a bored little housewife padding out her day playing on committees. Just a pretty little parasite living off my brother, aren't you?'

Parasite! How dare he!

Harry freed her and passed back the phone, then retrieved the magnum at his feet, and sloshed champagne into glasses extended by Randolph and Barnaby in slightly wavering hands.

'Top up for you?' he offered, shaking the bottle, his piggy eyes ogling her.

She held her head high. 'No thanks. Parasites don't drink champagne, Harry. I'll settle for a glass of water.'

She stalked off, discretely consigning Mike's message to the bin. *Phew, that's done!* It didn't solve all her problems. Mike had the original and goodness knew how many copies, but maybe there was a way of disarming Mike's weapon after all.

Chapter Four

On Monday, driving towards the Dower House, Sarah was surprised to notice the back gate open. The back drive opened onto a corner of a busy road, so the gate was usually kept locked. It was safe for her to enter that way, but precarious to exit, necessitating turning right onto a main road on a blind corner. She bumped her way down the track, dodging the worst of the ruts in the un-tarmacked road and parked by the potting sheds. Mike was waiting, a hoe in his hand – the man was permanently busy – and a frown creasing his weather-beaten face. He led the way, swinging open the door to his sanctuary and releasing a powerful scent of cherry blossom.

The irony was not lost on Sarah. Here they were in the peaceful setting of an English Walled Garden, symbol of the Victorian upper classes, with its neatly planted rows of vegetables and espaliered fruit trees, and it was she and Mike – the two "outsiders" in the Fetherston family – who were about to discuss a crime.

Mike and Sarah stood side-by-side, their backs to the South-facing wall, spring sunshine warming their faces. Mike was leaning forward, his arms propped on the hoe, its blade anchored into the grass. Both stared out on the tranquillity of the garden, and at the black polytunnels straddling an elegant cream-coloured Victorian greenhouse: two smudges staining the beauty.

Sarah cleared her throat. 'I wish for all the world I never stepped foot in this beautiful garden.'

'I know.' He rocked on the hoe.

'Why? Why are you doing this?'

'Don't tell Mary, but it helps with her anxiety. I bake some into the afternoon cakes.'

Sarah gasped, rounding on Mike and shouting, 'I eat those!'

'Not when there's visitors, you prat!'

She took a deep breath, exhaling slowly; so that was why he was growing dope – for Mary. That changed things. Why hadn't he said?

Despite her illness, Mary still dictated so much of our lives.

'OK, I won't have anything to do with all this, but I am prepared to stay quiet about what's going on for the sake of Mary, *provided* I can be sure all copies of that video are destroyed. How many copies are there?'

'Thought you'd come to your senses,' Mike said quietly, shifting his hands on his prop. 'There's only two. You've got one and the other is on my phone.'

'You *are* blackmailing me. How can I trust you?'

He wrinkled his face. A few moments elapsed. She lapped up the warmth of the sun, trying to spot the bee she could hear buzzing in the nearby herb bed. Eventually, Mike spoke. 'Logic? It's not exactly hard-core porn, and you're not a celebrity, so it's not worth anything except to you.' He looked over pointedly at her chest. 'Lovely pair of tits, though.'

She closed her eyes – how many times had Mike given himself a thrill watching that ten-second clip?

She held out her hand. 'Phone.'

'Not so fast. I want to make sure *you* don't change your mind either. We'll be in this together. You don't have to get fully involved, but you'll be paid for your silence.'

'I thought you said you were doing this for Mary.'

'Not all of it.' He chortled, pointing at the poly tunnels. 'She can't use that much!'

'So it's a business, is it? I don't like the sound of that. What do you do with the rest of the stuff, who buys it?'

'Nick does all that. He liaises with the buyers, I just grow it and pick it, he does all the packaging and deliveries, and he has a little team that helps him. You can meet Nick if you like.'

'No. I don't want to meet Nick,' she shook her head, 'and I told you. I don't want your dirty money.'

'It's not a suggestion. You don't have to *keep* the money. Just receive it. That's the deal.'

What choice did she have, and did it matter? She could donate the money to charity. 'OK. But I'm doing this for Mary.'

'And yourself!'

'No, not for me. For Freddy and my daughter.'

'As you like,' he said, passing her his phone. 'It's quite a sophisticated operation, with lighting and proper ventilation, all temperature controlled.'

Sarah cut in, 'Too much information. As I said, I am not going into business with you – I'm just not going to shop you. There's a big difference between the two.'

He rested the hoe against the back wall.

Sarah's curiosity got the better of her. 'How the devil do you keep this a secret from Mary? Doesn't she ask about the size of the electricity bills? And why the polytunnels are black?'

He laughed.

'No, she's no interest in gardening, only ever been interested in plants once I've got them inside, into that flower room, or any fruit and veg she can eat. And let's face it; she's not really up to worrying about utility bills anymore.'

She handed back his phone after deleting the clips.

'How is she today?'

He beamed across at her. 'We've had a visitor for the weekend, and it's been a tonic for her. Some friend of a friend who hosted a big party on Saturday night. The freeloader didn't want to pay for a hotel when he could sponge off us. Let's go in and get you ladies a cup of char, Mary's been her old self all weekend.' He retrieved the hoe and walked towards the door, asking over his shoulder, 'How do you want to be paid?'

Mike could have been offering to settle a fee for cinema tickets, not pay over drug money! Sarah had her own private bank account where she kept the money her parents – who both died young – had left her. Freddy never checked the joint account, but even so she wanted this money separate, cordoned off from the rest of her life. Anyway, she wouldn't be keeping it long.

'I've a personal account.'

He chuckled, shutting the door behind them. 'We're not setting up a standing order for a gas bill!'

'Well, I certainly don't want a brown paper bag of cash,' she shot back.

Mike introduced her to an alternative payments system, telling her to download the Metamask app.

'I get paid that way. It's just safer, no one can trace payments without knowing your private key,' he explained. 'Let me know when you've installed the app and chosen the currency.'

Rounding the corner of the house, Sarah spotted her mother-in-law, framed by one of the morning room windows. Mary waved and lifted her arm in response: how marvelous to call on one of the good days. There was a taxi parked by the cedar tree, its engine idling. A tall slim man was getting in; he was vaguely familiar, but Sarah couldn't place him, was he married to one of her committee ladies? The man stopped, his legs straddling the open door, spoke to the driver, and then trotted over saying, 'Glad I didn't miss you, thank you so much for your hospitality, Mike, you're an amazing cook!' He winked, 'Take great care of her, won't you!'

Mike walked the stranger towards the waiting taxi without introducing him to Sarah. Was he keen to get shot of him?

'Don't want to miss your train, do you? Go on in, luv,' he called to Sarah. 'I'll get the tea tray.'

Sarah was filling Mary in on Suffolk news when Mike appeared in the drawing room. Spotting a fruitcake, Sarah sat upright, shooting an enquiring look at Mike. There was a swift shake of Mike's head.

Mary gushed on. 'Over eighty guests and just a few helpers from the village. My my, Amy is brave, isn't she?' The tea tray was lowered into position. Mary pointed a perfectly manicured finger at the pot. 'Is that Indian or China?'

'Indian, but I can fetch a pot of Lapsang, if you prefer?'

Mary inclined her head to one side like a bird. 'Oh, would you be a darling?'

The door closed behind Mike.

'I gather you've been hosting this weekend?'

'Yes. Mike was grumpy about it, but he must learn that living in this house brings responsibilities. The man was a charming guest.'

Sarah sat upright, smiling. 'He's on telly, isn't he? I thought I recognised him.'

Mary wrinkled her nose. 'Is he?'

'Yes. I've got it now, he's on that antiques program.'

Mike reappeared with a second silver teapot. Mary sat back in her chair, batting her eyes at him. 'Ah, there you are, delightful, I am parched.' She turned to Sarah saying, 'Everyone thinks they're a celebrity today. Now, which will you have, Indian? I've something important to tell you.'

'Either.'

Mary poured as she spoke. 'It's about Thomas.'

Mike got up, his eyes flashing a warning at Sarah. 'Oh no, here we go. She's exhausted herself, luv. Away with the fairies again.' He knelt before Mary and said softly, 'Sarah's not interested in your dead brother.'

Mary was glaring at Mike. She raised her voice, 'Sarah, I must tell you about Thomas!'

Mike crossed to Sarah, took the untouched cup of tea from her hands. 'Best if you go, luv, I'll get her upstairs for a little lie down.'

Mary stood up, 'Sarah, wait, don't go yet.'

Mike rolled his eyes, 'She needs a rest. I won't get her to move until you're gone.'

Sarah rose, whispering to Mike, 'You are so good with her.'

He clicked his tongue. 'It is hard work sometimes.'

'Why not tell me another time?' Sarah said crossing to her mother-in-law's chair and pecking Mary's cheek.

She drove home with mixed emotions. Spending time with Mary on one of her good days was an unexpected treat that only served to reinforce Sarah's decision; her mother-in-law deserved to be protected. The time spent in the Walled Garden negotiating with Mike was less pleasant, but she did feel a slight thrill from dabbling with danger, tinged with a feeling she might just have taken a decision she would regret.

By the time she arrived back at the Long House it was midday, but she took a shower. Why did she have the same grubby feeling she'd had when her mother gave her that tiny tight smile the morning after Sarah's first teenage fumble with her boyfriend Darren? Massaging grapefruit-scented granules into her limbs, she scrubbed her body clean then wrapped herself in a dressing gown, poured herself a glass of water and took it into the sitting room where she downloaded the Metamask app.

A week elapsed and Sarah began to hope Mike had forgotten about paying her – then this whole drama would be gone. He summoned her, threatening to bring over cash if she didn't finalise the payment details. She arrived to find him in the Victorian Greenhouse, where he was snipping side shoots from his cucumber plants.

'Must concentrate the energy into the fruits,' he explained, lifting each leaf to check for hidden growth and dispatching another small tendril. 'Got those account details for me?'

She passed over her Metamask address on a slip of paper. He scrunched it up, pushing it into a pocket. 'Do you have your Metamask seed phrase written down?' she asked.

'Blimey, yes. Lose that and you lose your wallet, luv. I am far too old to remember a random nine-word phrase, and there's no help desk to call if I do!' He turned round. 'Right, that's done. Currency?'

'Bitcoin,' she said with a smug expression.

'Okey doke. I get paid in Bitcoin, too.'

Sarah could have asked Mike to pay her in pounds. It was, after all, a wallet, and funds could be paid in whatever currency she wanted – pounds, Euros, or any of the cryptocurrencies, but some people considered Bitcoin a racy investment and it would provide a smokescreen if anyone asked where she'd earned the chunky sums she was about to start donating. She was excited by the idea of speculating; her father had been a keen gambler.

Sarah had enjoyed a close relationship with her father who juggled childcare while ostensibly "working from home". Sadly, his weakness for daytime television – especially afternoon racing with a sneaky spliff – had stymied any entrepreneurial aspirations. The family did celebrate the occasional windfall, but his relationship with the bookies was never symbiotic. Would her father have dabbled with cryptocurrencies?

Mike clambered onto a stepladder. Sarah held the steps steady, listening to Mike's grunts and groans as he struggled to secure the cucumber plant to a bamboo pole angled upwards to the greenhouse roof struts. She was enjoying the heat of the sun streaming through the Victorian glass panes; the gardens were as lovely as the house!

'You adore this place as much as she does, don't you, Mike?'

He grunted. 'Gardener's paradise, but I chose this place for her, she insisted on moving to a proper house. Wanted all her knick-knacks around her, to get all that stuff we had in Wiltshire out of storage!'

Sarah closed her eyes against the sun, remembering helping her mother-in-law pack up to move to the Dower House. She had expected to be the only helper and was gobsmacked when Harry and Amy offered to help too. What a frustrating morning that had been! Mary refusing to part with anything: clutching at decade-old, half-finished crosswords like ancient family heirlooms. Sarah had solved the problem, starting to refer to the boxes they were stuffing with items all three helpers knew should be jettisoned, as "for consideration", knowing the older woman would soon forget those things.

Mike had turned up just as the family took a break and disappeared with Harry, leaving the three ladies in the drawing room drinking tea. He reappeared, with the purchase agreement for the Dower House – Sarah's perfect Georgian gem. Sarah nearly cried when Mike held the document flat on the table next to Mary with the palm of his hand, passing Mary a pen.

'I've signed already, luv, and Harry's witnessed me. Pop your squiggle next to mine then I'll drop it with the lawyers.'

If only Sarah had offered to care for her mother-in-law it would have been her and Freddy signing that document, and no one would be growing cannabis in this walled garden.

The summer was punctuated by a succession of disturbing calls from the Dower House. Initially, Sarah fielded them – cheerfully chatting to Mike or Mary before relinquishing the phone – but, as the months wore on, she became reluctant to speak to either of them. Mary seemed to have become fixated with her dead brother Tom, starting each conversation insisting that she speak to Sarah about him.

'Don't let me forget. I must tell you about Thomas.'

But she never did. Something always distracted the older woman, and Sarah would listen patiently as the conversation rambled around like a driver circling a car park searching for an empty space. Freddy, too, reported an obsession with his uncle, who had died decades before he was born.

'I don't recall her saying they were particularly close. She was so much younger than either of her brothers; they were both killed while she was a child.'

'Maybe the Dower House reminds her of Lampton?' suggested Sarah.

'Yes, but why Thomas all the time? What about her older brother?'

Sarah shrugged. As an only child she didn't understand the interaction of siblings.

A few of the summer calls from the Dower House were harrowing. During one, she overheard Mary complaining to Freddy that Mike was trying to steal her money. Sarah listened to Freddy painstakingly explain that the workings of the power of attorney precluded Mike from doing anything without Freddy's consent. Thankfully these tense occasions were interspersed with more cheerful conversations – wherein mother and son would happily recount their day-to-day lives – but by mid-August, all the calls from the Dower House were challenging. Mary couldn't follow the thread of conversations anymore, unable to recollect what had already been said. Sometimes just a few minutes were all it took for her to forget what her son had told her. He reported having to repeat the same story: each time backtracking to an earlier point, saying it was like pushing in vain against an incoming tide, slowly but surely being forced to retreat further each time.

That summer there were pleasing personal episodes. Sarah chose her first charity – a drug rehabilitation centre in Exeter. The Bitcoin balance built up fast and she started drip-feeding her trading profits into her personal account. Whenever she spotted an opportunity to pay a bill in cryptocurrency, she did, siphoning off money from the joint account to repay herself, then swiftly donating that money. Silence was proving to be very lucrative. After her second donation, she received a personal invitation from the chairman of the centre to join them for a musical recital in aid of their charity; she was keen to attend her first fundraiser as a guest, not one of the aproned helpers.

It wasn't just Sarah's capital that was boosted; maybe it was from dabbling with danger, but Freddy didn't question the unexplained increase in Sarah's libido, frequently driving home for early afternoon trysts like an Iberian businessman visiting his mistress during siesta.

On the day she received her third payment, in September, Mike called Sarah. He was on the verge of tears.

'She bit me.'

'She did *what?*'

'She bit my hand when I was trying to get her to take her pills.'

'No!'

'Oh luv, it's not my hand I'm upset about. They've sectioned her. She's gone into a clinic to be assessed. I can't even visit her yet.'

Mary sectioned!

Her mother-in-law was released to a residential home which Mike chose after diligently inspecting every option within a fifty-mile radius of the Dower House.

Freddy withdrew from family life, barricading himself in his study. Day after day Sarah's heart nearly melted, seeing Freddy silently skulking back from meals to his hallowed den. One evening Sarah tried to talk to him, using a cup of cocoa as an excuse to enter his lair.

'I just feel so useless,' he said. 'Is it really my mother anymore, or has sufficient of her mind been destroyed that the essence of what I love and have loved all my life is no longer there?'

Sarah took a tentative sip from her own mug, but the chocolate burnt the edge of her tongue. 'You need to come to terms with this disease,' she counselled. 'For all his faults, Mike has done that.'

Sarah had too.

From the comfort of the chintz armchair, over the summer she'd watched Mary lose her desperate struggle to control her mind. Sarah had looked on in admiration at the ramrod-straight posture, elegant clothing, and genteel mannerisms of her mother-in-law; but those were merely physical manifestations of the character she once admired, and that summer Sarah witnessed Mary's character being subsumed by the disease. Then, one day in late August, the mantel slipped; Mary entertained her daughter-in-law wearing bedroom slippers.

Two weeks after Mike's call, with a heavy heart Sarah drove to the clinic to visit her recently sectioned mother-in-law. It was the last time she saw Mary. Despite staying for over three hours, Mary didn't recognise her visitor. Sarah couldn't admire or love the changeling, other than as a symbol of who she once was. The easy path would have been to follow the well-worn charade of duty visits that were pleasing to neither visitor nor visited. To avoid disturbing memories of the woman she loved with the husk of what remained, after floods of tears, Sarah vowed not to visit her mother-in-law again.

She still grieved for her loss. If only Freddy could accept that the mother, he knew was no longer with them. There won't be any more good days, she told him. And now Sarah drank her cocoa, listening to Freddy pour out his torment.

'Every time I'm with her, I want to cast her in aspic, preserve the small pieces of her that are still there, before they too disappear. This last visit she didn't have a clue who I was. She was quite ambivalent, accepting my presence as you might a stranger you're forced to sit opposite for an hour on a train journey. How much worse will she get?'

She stood up, reaching for Freddy's empty mug. 'I'm so so sorry, darling. Don't try and endure this alone, lean on me.'

Mike telephoned often, reporting on Mary's day. Even with her confined to a residential home his life still revolved around her – cooking nutritious meals he took in for her, forcing her to eat or to take exercise. Mourning the loss of a lady she loved, Sarah asked herself why Mike was prolonging a life Mary would shun if she could. Was it guilt for allowing her to be sectioned? Or was it selfishness – not wanting to allow Mary the dignity of departing and leaving him alone?

Mike's care of Mary didn't interfere with his farming. Autumn turned to winter, then spring, and the payments bounced in then rapidly out of her wallet. She selected another two charities to donate to. Who would have guessed cannabis was such a money-spinning crop? Sarah congratulated herself on her decision; her secret was safe. There was no harm being done, she wasn't advocating using drugs, or involved in distribution, she was just siphoning off part of the profits for worthy causes.

It was a fine spring day and Sarah was driving towards a meeting in Exeter. She was giving a lift to a tall lanky lady with black hair held off her face by an Alice band. Lady Penelope, who rarely used her title, sat on many of the same committees as Sarah, and like her, was a "doer" not a "delegator". Her family had lived in the same, now crumbling, manor house for over six hundred years. Penelope was married to William, an older recently retired colonel, who devoted his days to chairing often obscure local organizations grateful both for his time and the elevated stature his baronetcy bestowed on them. William's spare time was split between running the estate with the same attention to detail he had meted out on the parade ground, and helping his wife raise their demanding brood of three sons.

Drawing up at a set of traffic lights, Sarah turned towards her friend.

'Do you mind me asking a personal question?'

'Fire away.'

'Do you have your own income? Is that where you make your donations from?'

'No. But then I've never really worked. Mama sent me to finishing school, and not long afterwards I met William at a regimental ball.'

The lights turned green. Sarah pulled away; accelerating to pass a bus, then drew in front of it. She trod on the clutch to change up to third, mistimed, and the gearbox let out a few protesting screeches.

'I had my own crash course finishing school'. She stabbed on the clutch, wrenching the gearstick into place. 'From my mother-in-law when she moved down here.'

'Was Mary a tough teacher?'

Sarah didn't answer for a few moments, thinking Mary didn't teach me, she instructed me precisely what to do.

'I was told to give up my job. What was it she said, ah yes,' Sarah imitated her mother-in-law's voice, *"beneath you, darling."* And I was told *"a governess would be more appropriate but without suitable assistance perform that role yourself."*

The ladies tittered together but Sarah had not enjoyed being taught how to behave like a Fetherston, how to change her life to become a genteel lady who devoted spare time to charity committees.

'I used to be a little scared of Mary,' she admitted, flicking a look in her side mirror then turning left. 'I dreaded having her to stay. Back then I had no idea how to host the woman. No one told me.'

'Not even Freddy?'

'No, bless him.' She wagged her head. 'But it wasn't his fault. I wasn't hosting a seventeenth century reenactment, so he didn't really notice the minutiae like his mother did. It's my sister-in-law I blame, she could have tipped me the wink before I had Mary to stay, rather than gleefully reel off all my mistakes in front of her odious husband after she'd heard about them from Mary.'

Penelope put her hand lightly on Sarah's arm. 'You've got a bit of a cross to bear with that pair in Suffolk. You can't have got it *that* wrong, surely?'

Sarah could laugh about it now, but initially she had struggled in her strange new "Fetherston world" - spiked with booby traps primed to catch the novice; her first hosting of the matriarch was a social disaster.

'I didn't put any flowers in the guest bedroom or provide champagne, which I should have known was her favourite tipple. The fact I was pregnant was of course irrelevant, but I didn't know any better.'

'Ah!'

'Back then I don't think I'd have thought of flowers in mid-summer, let alone January.'

Her sister-in-law had explained in a tone that implied she was revealing how to boil an egg that Sarah didn't need to buy flowers. It was worse than that! The hostess was expected to create an artful display of whatever was on offer in her own garden, even in winter!

'My third slip-up was not putting toiletries in the guest bathroom. I thought Amy was pulling my leg when she accused me of that! I wasn't running a B&B like her. Guests brought their own soap and shower gel, didn't they?'

Nope. Amy told her a hostess was expected to leave a generous selection of bath oils, soaps, even colognes! Fortunately, unlike her habit of pilfering the toiletries from hotel rooms, the Mary's of this world only use what they require, leaving the bottles for the next guest.

'But you did learn.'

'The hard way!' Sarah said, battling again with the slippery clutch.

'William says to stroke the clutch.'

'William doesn't have this slippery monster to deal with,' said Sarah smiling across at the other woman. 'Do you know I think I'm going to buy an automatic car next time! I don't like to ask for one, not earning myself. Do you ever wonder what you've missed out on, I mean not having your own career, earning your own money, and deciding what to do with it?'

'You can't miss what you've never known!'

'But you can be curious about what it would be like, surely?' pressed Sarah, glancing at Penelope.

The other woman inclined her head, adding with a hint of warning, 'Or you can avoid the torture – accept that you don't know, never will – and enjoy what you do have.'

Sarah squeezed the brake pedal to allow a gaggle of chattering schoolgirls, who hadn't considered traffic before launching themselves across the road. The girls were all smoking.

'Outrageous, just yards from school!' exclaimed Sarah, taking a hand off the steering wheel and waving at the campus. The girls strutted along the pavement, taking it in turns to blow smoke circles at each other, giggling as they demonstrated their skills. 'Shouldn't we do something, pull over, have a word?'

'You can't be the moral policeman for every child. I've enough trouble keeping my own brood on the straight and narrow. William caught young Angus smoking cannabis last week, said he could smell what he was doing down the corridor. He's only fifteen!'

Keeping her tone neutral, Sarah asked how the family was coping.

'He's gated all week. No parties, no outings unless accompanied by William or me. He's flatly refused to tell us where he bought it, which enrages William.'

Sarah chewed at her lip, telling herself teenagers sourced drugs from school.

'I'm so sorry! Where do you think he's getting it from?'

'He won't say. Claims we shouldn't try and force him to "reveal his source." Penelope snorted, 'He's not a journalist; he's a silly boy.'

Penelope hadn't finished. 'We need to stamp it out before he starts popping pills or sniffing cocaine.'

Sarah waited for a car to pull out in front of her, and then placated her friend. 'Come on, he's just a teenager experimenting. It's only dope, my father used to smoke it!'

'Sadly, we're not talking about the innocent wacky baccy your father smoked. It's powerful stuff now.'

Penelope's warning sent Sarah's heart racing. Had she got herself tangled up in something more serious than Mike led her to believe? And if she had, what was her route out?

Chapter Five

Some days Sarah wished Freddy was more involved in their daughter's life, and today was shaping up to be one of them. She stood at the foot of the stairs, tapping her car keys on her leg, bristling like a greyhound keen to be released from the traps. Freddy was not going to be any help, having set off for university earlier while she was coaxing Mary out of bed for the second time. Mary wasn't a difficult child; she'd just slipped into her twelfth-year sloth-like. Some mornings, Sarah found herself chivying the child through the succession of necessities like a pilot performing preflight checks. Was Mary up; had she showered, dressed; had she eaten; got her homework? Until finally, lift off – the school run could commence.

The day had started badly. Having woken the child, Sarah was distracted by Freddy wanting to explain the latest chapter of his book. He wanted an opinion, not just an audience, and years of marriage had given her a thorough grounding in her husband's chosen period of history, so she was a decent foil. But right now? Really? Couldn't it wait until tonight? She was a much better historian with a large glass of wine in hand.

By the time he relinquished her attention, an unsupervised Mary had drifted off to sleep again. Gritting her teeth, Sarah tossed the girl out of bed. She would have loved to climb back into her own after managing only a few hours herself. She urged Mary into the shower and thumped her way back down the stairs: it was going to be one of those days where it was toast in the back of the car. Freddy met her at the foot of the staircase. He leant over to kiss her goodbye and she pressed up against him. He opened his eyes, murmuring, 'No time, darling, and you've the school run, but I'll come home early,' he suggested, winking at her and grinning as he opened the door and let in a chilly blast of spring air.

'Coat, Freddy?'

He chuckled, reaching back, snatching one randomly off a peg.

Sarah glared back upwards, willing Mary to appear. Five minutes later the child stood on the landing at last, yawning, and rubbing her eyes with the back of her hand. Sarah closed her eyes and groaned; Mary was plodding down, step by step, as if unsure of her footing. Sarah shepherded her charge outside, passing her the toast in a paper napkin, and the pair finally set off.

Briefly.

At the end of the lane Sarah did a U-turn, and the car returned to collect Mary's ballet dress and shoes.

Sarah gunned the engine, watching Mary; she was strolling back down the path toward the house, key in hand, with the lack of urgency of an aged Labrador on its evening walk. They were going to be late. Ten minutes later the languid child reemerged, now clutching the precious bag and Sarah set off, bowling along the narrow Devon lanes faster than she normally would and arriving with a full two minutes to spare. She applied the brake, flicking a look in the rear-view mirror at Mary, sprawled on the back seat; her school tie askew; her jacket sleeves pushed up to the elbows. Mary looked like one of the scarecrows Mike had set up to ward off birds from his prize cabbages.

'Thanks, Mum. You haven't forgotten I have a dance class, have you? I just need dropping. Caroline says her mum will give me a lift home.'

Was Sarah the only parent who wanted to reply tartly to these helpful prompts with the statement that it is technically impossible to forget something you've not been made aware of? *Rats.*

Eight hours later, Sarah returned to the school gates after a frenetic day: a charity coffee morning, then rushing home to change for tennis, followed by a slip-shod rushed job on the hoovering. Lunch was an apple eaten in the car on the way to tennis. Now, with Mary buckled in, Sarah set off, following the satnav to ensure she didn't have to recall the way to the tiny hamlet. She pulled up at the instructor's house and Mary grabbed her bag from the back seat and shot off to the fun.

'Catch you later little one, have the best of times!' Sarah hollered.

Putting the car back into first gear, she drove off. How long has that been red? She realised she was driving on fumes. Where was the nearest petrol station? She didn't trust the satnav: it was several years old and couldn't be relied on to direct her to a garage not already converted to houses. Did she know anyone who lived locally? She ran through her small list of north Devonian contacts, the engine idling its way through the precious reserves of petrol. Sarah gave a loud tut – she was minutes from the Dower House. Perfect. Mike was bound to have a jerry can of petrol, with all those gardening machines.

She drove towards salvation: caressing the accelerator, urging the car to limp along, expecting to hear a spluttering noise warning of imminent stoppage. The back gate was temptingly propped open but approaching from the opposite direction than the Long House, she needed to turn right. She stopped, indicating, then spying a gap, swept in, taking her foot off the accelerator, allowing the car to coast down the track and come to a halt beside the potting sheds. There was a small green car already parked at an angle on the grass verge. She switched off the engine before it could die and climbed out of the car, stretching her arms above her head, feeling the tightness in her shoulders dissolve.

Where was Mike? *Please not visiting Mary.* She tried the Walled Garden, opening the door wide and peering round, listening for signs of activity. She called out but there was no response, so she trekked to the house and rang the doorbell. She stood on the doorstep, jiggling her keys, stamping her feet to keep warm; April could be such a cold month. She didn't have a plan B. She pushed the bell again and let out a quiet hurrah – footsteps, then the rasping sound of the bolt sliding back. The door opened.

'Hiya, come in, we're in the kitchen.'

'Thank goodness you're in!'

She followed him into the octagonal staircase hall – it was over nine months since she'd been here: she'd missed this house – then down the corridor and through a green baize door, letting it swing behind her. She was in the kitchen, a room she wasn't familiar with; her mother-in-law never regarded a kitchen as the hub of family life. It was old-fashioned, with small red quarry tiles on the floor – and pine, yards of pine. There were pine units, set around the Aga; a large pine dresser stood opposite her, and a long pine table was positioned in the centre precisely where Sarah would choose to locate a kitchen island if this was her room. An unshaven middle-aged man was sitting at the table, staring directly at her with unsmiling, hard eyes.

'Nick, this is Sarah. She's one of the daughters-in-law,' said Mike as the baize door finished swinging and shut behind them. Crossing the room to the sink, he added, 'This is the nice one, not the snooty one. I'll make us a fresh brew.'

Nick's gaze settled on her chest, a little smirk now on his face (*Mike hadn't, had he?*). He was dressed for the outdoors, with stout boots and thick socks pulled up over the bottom of a pair of slightly crumpled trousers. His hair was hidden beneath a blue woollen hat; gloves and a scarf sat discarded in front of him, next to a Tupperware box with its lid askew, offering a glimpse of something soft, brown, and tempting inside.

Sarah sat opposite Nick, moving the Tupperware box a little further along the table so she could place her bag in front of her. So, this was Nick: the one who dealt with the grubby side of the business. She peeked into the plastic box. Her stomach growled – chocolate brownies – she helped herself.

Sarah heard the kettle being filled and Mike opening and shutting cupboards, chattering about vegetables. She bit into the cake, chewing slowly, and letting the chocolate ooze in her mouth. Mike asked, 'How thirsty is everyone: a pot, or mugs?'

'Mug please, Mike. I must get back to do some baking.'

She took another bite of the brownie, refusing to catch the eye of the man opposite her who was grinning and stroking his bristly chin. She dipped her gaze to the table, sweeping the crumbs she'd dropped into a pile.

'Enjoyed that, did you?' asked Nick.

Mike spun round; his eyes were wide and staring her way. 'Oh Nick, you haven't!'

Sarah glanced from one man to the other. Nick had tipped back his chair, so it rested on the back legs and – controlling it by adjusting his feet – was rocking backwards and forwards, chuckling. Mike stood with a mug in each hand and an expression Sarah had last seen when she walked in on him tending his cannabis plants.

'They're delicious, Mike, wonderful soft texture,' said Sarah. 'Sorry, I shouldn't have eaten one without asking, I've just hardly eaten all day. Are they a present?'

Mike huffed. He glared at the younger man as he shouted, 'You let that happen, Nick! Not funny.'

Nick chortled. 'Don't blame me, Mike, I didn't make them.'

Mike switched his attention to Sarah. 'They've got resin in them.'

She arched an eye at him. 'Sorry?'

A long "ummm" escaped from Mike. 'The brownies, I added some resin.'

The cakes were meant for her mother-in-law!

'Don't eat any more, or you may start to feel a bit odd.'

'Oh heck, Mike. I only popped over cos I ran out of petrol. I was hoping you might have a jerry can, I wasn't planning on getting stoned! I need to get home to sort supper, and I've got two cakes to bake before tomorrow!'

Mike placed a mug in front of her, then Nick, and turned to fetch his own. 'That might be challenging. I could bake a couple of cakes,' he offered. 'Could Freddy make dinner?'

Sarah put her head in her hands. She didn't have time for this!

Mike disappeared into what Sarah assumed was the pantry, reappearing with a tray of ingredients. He pulled a set of scales out of a drawer and busied himself with weighing flour and sugar, then cracking eggs. Allowing her tea to cool, Sarah told the men about her petrol drama. She directed her tales at the stranger, but Mike didn't, he was ignoring the younger man, excluding him from the conversation, speaking with his eyes focused on her as if it was just the two of them in the room. She gave up and drank her tea, watching Mike beat eggs and grate chocolate, listening to his little triumphs at the nursing home. Mike was being overcautious: she'd eaten the brownie twenty minutes ago. She shook her head; she was fine, she was really hungry, but fine: maybe she chose a piece without much resin in it. She reached over towards the box.

Nick burst out laughing, slapping his hands on his legs.

'Got the munchies, have you, darlin'!'

Mike dropped the spatula and ran over, pushing Sarah's hand away. 'No. I'll make toast. Nick, put the lid back on that lot and get them out of the way.'

Sarah ate the toast, enjoying every morsel, licking her fingers to catch the last buttery crumbs. 'Mike, this is simply the most amazing toast. Gourmet toast – you superstar . . . the champion toast maker!'

Mike was glaring at Nick. Why does he dislike him so much?

'Now, gentlemen if you'll excuse me for five minutes.' She rose, swaying slightly. Why am I feeling every muscle involved in standing up?

'I think you'd better rest,' said Mike. 'I'll call Freddy and tell him you're not feeling too clever, that you'll be home late. I'm sure even he can manage to heat up a tin of baked beans for supper, just this once.'

Mike took Sarah's arm and steered her out of the kitchen and up the back staircase.

'Wow, aren't these stairs simply *amazing!* Just think how many servants have used these steps, slaves to their upstairs master's every whim,' said Sarah, leaning heavily on the banister, and gaping at the hallway below. 'What must life have been like for them? We love these old houses but always envisage life as it was lived upstairs, we never think of those who were downstairs.'

She stopped halfway up and sagged against the wall. Mike gripped her under the arm, hefting her up the last few steps.

'Very profound,' he said. 'This way, let's get you to a comfy bed.'

He opened a door and led her into a bedroom. Its walls were covered with faded wallpaper: a soft green trellis with pale pink roses climbing against it. It was fascinating, especially the section immediately in front of her.

'Sarah!'

Oh, the soft green trellis. The pink, pink roses!

'SARAH!'

Pink roses . . .

She felt his hands on her shoulders.

'Sarah, come on, luv.'

She was still staring at the wallpaper. 'It's the jungle bedroom, a jungle of roses!'

Sarah was giggling, but Mike was frowning.

'Spoilsport!'

'In!' directed Mike, pointing at the bed. 'I'll check on you in a couple of hours. Give me the keys so I can sort your car out.'

Sarah fished out her keys, then kicked off her shoes and clambered in fully clothed, pulling up the old-fashioned sheets and blankets. Exhausted from lack of sleep and a busy day, she was soon asleep.

Mike woke her handing over a glass of water. She tossed it back like a dose of medicine. The light was fading outside, and she could no longer make out individual plants in the border – it was like a homogenous landmass at the end of a green sea of lawn. She glanced at her watch; eight o'clock. She'd been asleep for hours.

Mike was dangling her car keys from his fingers.

'I called Freddy, he said not to worry, young Mary is already home and will be fed. I've baked two cakes, and I've put them both in a box on the back seat of your car, which now has petrol. I put twenty quid's worth in, and I reckon a fiver for the ingredients.'

'Thanks.' She handed him the empty glass and bent over to pull on her shoes, then dug out her purse.

They walked into the kitchen and Nick stood up. Why did this scruffy man have to witness me being silly, and what's he still doing here – waiting for another laugh?

'Sorry about that,' she said.

Nick shrugged.

'Hardly the first time I've seen one of you lot stoned – all la-di-da in front of us ordinary folk, but out of sight you're just as bad as anyone else. Surprised it's your first time, though. Why the heck you involved if you don't use?'

Nick insisted on showing her round the little enterprise. Sarah was a reluctant participant in his guided tour; she was uncomfortable being drawn further into a murky world she never wanted to enter. Although her Metamask wallet enabled her to make generous donations, mentally, Sarah had severed the connection between the cash and its seedy source. Mike traipsed round silently behind them; his hands stuffed into his jacket pockets. The younger man switched on the lights in each of the potting sheds in turn. Inside the first was an old wooden table – a sheet of plastic nailed over it – covered with fresh leaves. Against one wall was a solid metal shelf unit, stacked with boxes full of small bags of cannabis. Nick bounced into the last shed with the same enthusiasm Freddy evidenced if asked a question about Oliver Cromwell.

'This is the lucrative stuff,' explained Nick, running his fingers over the crop as tenderly as Sarah brushed her hands through her child's hair.

'It's what the punters want. You get far more of a hit from the bud.'

Was that what Penelope meant when she claimed cannabis was more powerful now? Had her friend been referring to the bud?

Mike closed the door of the last shed. It's only weed, Sarah told herself, just a few dropouts like your father smoking dope to pass time or alleviate the pain of arthritis or anxiety like your mother-in-law.

'I'll be off then,' announced Nick, opening the boot of the little green car. Mike popped a box in, and Nick slammed it shut.

'Welcome to the team. Try not to eat all the profits,' he said to Sarah as he slid into his seat. 'Bye for now.' The window was wound down in jerky stages. 'Back in ten minutes,' he added, winking at Mike. 'Never like to carry too much, just in case.'

He pulled away down the back drive, crunching his way over debris, the headlights picking out a tangle of small branches blown onto the side of the track by a recent spring storm. Sarah tracked the taillights until they disappeared. She opened the door of her own car and sat down sideways, her feet still planted on the drive.

'You don't like your business partner much, do you?' she said.

Mike gave a snort. 'He's not my business partner.'

She arched her eyes.

'He's my jailor.'

Mike leaned his backside on the bonnet of her car, crossing his arms. He looked over at her.

'Why do you think I'm operating on such an enormous scale?'

'I hadn't thought about it.'

'I started years ago, just a couple of plants to earn a bit of extra cash to buy Mary some of the little extravagances she takes for granted. I fell in love with that lady when I saw her dressed up for one of the opening nights at the theatre, couldn't believe my luck when she allowed me to buy her a drink, then wondered how I could ever afford her when she asked for champagne! She was one hell of an expensive date on a lighting technician's salary.'

'Well, it's hardly a couple of plants anymore!'

He rubbed one of his hands down his face, as if trying to erase the memory.

'When I followed her down here to Devon, I stepped up scale. Someone put me in touch with Nick and he sold everything I gave him, kept egging me on to grow more. So, I did. It's quite easy to hide in the countryside. I wasn't working anymore; I had the time. And I wanted the money to buy, well, to buy things for Mary, to buy back her affection – she doesn't know how much those baubles cost me.' He paused before explaining that when the couple bought the Dower House, he was determined to stop. 'Cut back to just a few plants for her anxiety. But Nick wouldn't let me. He saw how perfect the setup was, insisted I expand: grow two polytunnels, not just one. He started stashing the stuff in the potting sheds. Threatened to tell Mary if I didn't co-operate.'

'So that's why you couldn't stop when I asked you to. Nick wouldn't let you.'

'Yup!'

Sarah had a mental picture of her mother-in-law in her prime, the horror she'd spat down the phone from Wiltshire after she discovered Mike mixed up with drugs.

'But surely Nick's threat is hollow, now she's in a home.'

'You've only just met him. He was on his best behaviour. Take it from me; he's not a man to cross.'

If that was his best behaviour, Sarah didn't like the sound of Nick. She swung her feet into the car and started the engine.

'Freddy will be getting worried. Thanks for the petrol and for baking those cakes.'

She bumped down the back drive. Later she'd ask herself why she did that. Was it because Nick had shot off that way, or because they had spent the past half hour discussing the little enterprise and this was the route used to ferry drugs out of the Dower House? At the road, Sarah paused, checking her tricky exit, her indicating light flashing to turn right. She leaned forward over the steering wheel, craning to see round the corner. Maybe she should reverse and go out the front gate. She glanced down at the dashboard. Eight-thirty! She leaned forward over the steering wheel as far as she could, her nose touching the windscreen, checked the road again and eased the car out.

A motorcycle careered round the corner.

Sarah screamed and braked as the bike tipped over, ejecting the rider – like a slingshot – in its attempt to avoid Sarah's car. There was a jarring clang as the bike hit the tarmac followed by a drawn-out screech as the metal slithered across onto the other side of the road, coming to rest against the grassy bank. Then silence, except for the soft purr of her engine. Sarah's hands cupped her face; she was mesmerised by the leather clad body spread-eagled on the ground. She heard an ear-splitting scream of brakes, dragged her eyes off the leather to see a second car; it cannoned into the helpless biker, pushing the body forwards. She stared at the crumpled form, her hands now clenching the steering wheel, her foot still hard on the brake pedal.

The biker was motionless. *Man, woman, or child?*

Sarah reversed back into the driveway. In her mirror, she saw Mike running down the track. She pulled up the handbrake and got out, shaking.

What have I done?

'What's happened?' asked Mike, breathing heavily.

'A bike, it came out of nowhere. Mike, I don't know if he's OK, he's not moving.'

Together, the pair ran back towards the road. There was a horrid stench of burning rubber, and Sarah pinched her nose with her fingers. The headlights of the other car illuminated the scene, with the driver kneeling beside the injured biker.

'Is there anything we can do to help?' called out Mike.

The driver raised his head. It was Nick.

'He's either unconscious, or I'm afraid he's dead. He's not talking.'

Sarah shuddered. It was a man, but that didn't make much difference. Why had she been so stupid?

'One of us needs to phone for an ambulance,' she said, chewing her lip.

'And the police,' added Nick, standing up and jogging across to join them.

'Shit, that's not what we need, the cops on the edge of our little enterprise,' mumbled Mike.

'It was an accident, Mike. The police will see that, and that's all they'll be interested in,' pointed out Sarah, staring directly at Nick who had taken out his phone.

'Yes, but I don't want them to *see* anything else! Nip back to the house and get a blanket off one of them beds, keep him warm until help arrives.'

She heard the words, but her brain felt fuzzy. She stayed rooted to the spot, unable to get her legs to move.

'Nick, is there anything in your car that shouldn't be there?'

'All clean, Guv'nor.'

Mike was staring at Sarah. 'Blanket?'

'Yes, yes, I'm off.'

She was running down the drive, she heard Mike yelling after her, 'Then go back and stay in the kitchen. I'll deal with this. I don't want the cops round you. You will still have traces of cannabis in your system.'

Sarah stumbled down the drive, trying to block out the image of the crumpled biker. What have I done?

Chapter Six

'Mike called,' whispered Freddy, 'Ma… died this morning.'

Sarah stared aghast at her husband. Dead? How did Mike know the motorcyclist was dead, and why tell Freddy? She hadn't told Freddy much; just that she'd witnessed an accident and had to give a statement to the police.

'He's *dead*?' She didn't even know the victim's name, just that it had been a young man.

Freddy gave her a quizzical look. 'He? I said Ma. She died earlier this morning,'

She felt a rush of love for Freddy. 'Darling, I am so sorry. You must be devastated.' Sarah wiped her slightly sticky hands on her apron and hugged him, feeling his body slump against hers – as if transferring some of his grief – she pulled him tight, inhaling the lemon smell of him. Poor Freddy. She led him over to a breakfast stool and with her hands on his shoulders, asked if his brother knew – Mike would never call Harry.

'Yes,' he said, softly. 'He's gone into organisational overdrive, talking about the funeral, notices in newspapers, allocating me my share of distant relatives to call.'

Freddy pulled across the tray of cooling jam, and she watched him rearrange the hot jars, handling each one quickly as he arranged them in groups according to shape – tall and skinny, short, and angular, or dumpier.

'Oh, and Ma's Will – and evicting Mike from the Dower House.'

The jars now segregated by shape, he reached across the counter, dipping a finger into the abandoned ladle, scraping off some of the congealed jam and popping it into his mouth. Sarah pushed his hand away.

'That's pure sugar, Freddy.' She scolded, stalking to the other side of the kitchen. 'How compassionate of your brother. Mike has served his purpose.' She opened a cupboard and pulled out the biscuit jar. 'Yes, I can see Harry turfing a grieving man out of his home at the first opportunity to get his hands on the money.'

She shook out a few chocolate chip cookies, telling herself to concentrate on Freddy's pain, but she remembered eating the brownie, the crash, the crumpled body, and the start of a drama she feared was out of her control.

Last night, Mike had come back to the Dower House. 'Sorry, luv, but they want a statement.'

She'd shuddered, why couldn't she have run out of petrol, and never made it to the Dower House? That poor injured man. But he was wearing proper biker's leathers and a helmet; he'd be OK, surely?

'How is he? Did he wake up? What did the paramedics say?'

'No one's saying much, but they blue-lighted him off so he's alive.'

'Thank God. How do we find out how he's getting on?'

'Come on, luv, let's not keep the coppers waiting, eh?' He was holding out a hand as if she was a child that needed guidance. 'They may be able to tell you more. They're not happy you moved your car.'

'But I was blocking the road.'

'The cops are doing that, anyway; they've cordoned off the area, it's got more chalk on it than a teacher gets through in a whole term. Come on, they're waiting.'

Sarah walked slowly behind Mike, following the beam of his torch as it bobbed along the pathway. Heading up the back drive she started to cringe but forced herself to keep taking steps closer to the unquantifiable danger: it was as if, unable to swim, she was being ordered to jump into the sea with no lifejacket, and no idea what to expect from the churning waves.

Nick stood by her car. Her eyes drilled him.

'You saw, I just poked my bonnet out,' she said, her breath coming in short rapid puffs. 'If he hadn't been speeding, I would have had ample time to get out of his way.'

Nick shrugged.

'Didn't notice much, that's what I told the cops – too shocked by what was happening on the road to look anywhere else.' Then he winked at her, added 'partner' in a patronizing voice, and sauntered off to his own car.

Sergeant Grindley and PC Matthews introduced themselves. They were polite, but not friendly. The junior officer interviewed her; she addressed all her answers to his left shoulder, she couldn't take her eyes off the camera strapped to that side of his utility vest.

Above the sound of his crackling radio, she heard words she never thought would be directed at her!

'You do not have to say anything, but it may harm your defence—'

Sarah was breathalysed and her statement taken down. The officers couldn't tell her much more than Mike; the victim was a young man, and he was alive, they wouldn't tell her his name, but they did tell her which hospital he'd been taken to. She could have guessed that herself, it wasn't far away.

First thing this morning, on the pretext of feeding the chickens, she'd tucked her mobile phone into her apron and jogged out to call the hospital but learned nothing other than the victim was with his relatives. At least that meant he was still alive. Surely, he would recover, unlike her mother-in-law. She must channel her energy into helping Freddy now. Sarah dipped her hand back into the jar, and then took a large bite, allowing the soothing taste of chocolate to fill her mouth. Freddy was reminiscing about his mother; she tried to listen to what he was saying rather than let the words wash over her.

'I offered to talk to the lawyers about the Will.'

Her ears pricked up; fifteen years of untangling muddles had taught Sarah it was better to wrench administrative tasks away early from Freddy. He would make a complete dog's dinner out of sorting out his mother's affairs and if she dealt with it, that might help divert her mind from the accident. If only she knew the victim's name, she might be able to learn more about his injuries.

'Let me sort things out. I know it was ages ago, but I went through it all after my father died. There could be hours of talking to lawyers. You won't want to get bogged down with that.'

Later that morning, Sarah spoke to the family's solicitors, who told her she needed to locate the Will. They confirmed they had the original power of attorney but claimed no knowledge of a Will and were adamant they didn't have one stored in their vault. Yes, of course they would check, but they did keep meticulous records.

She called Harry.

'There's definitely a Will, Ma told me there was,' Harry informed Sarah testily, implying she was at fault for not uncovering the important document.

'Well, it's not with the Devon lawyers. What's she done with it? Do you think she kept it at the Dower House?'

'Could have.'

She gritted her teeth, spat a goodbye, and dialed the hospital. Fortuitously a junior nurse answered. Claiming to be an old friend, Sarah learned that the man was in a coma.

Yikes! Concentrate on the Will.

She paced the Long House, a basket of freshly ironed laundry in her arms giving off the restful scent of lavender. Where was the Will? There were so many places to hide a small document. Could it be in Mary's sewing box? She dropped two school shirts into Mary's drawer, gently closing it on them; could it be hidden amongst her mother-in-law's jewellery? What about in one of her travelling cases? But thoughts of travel catapulted her back to the injured biker, so she sped past to another possible location. Was the Will behind a picture? She folded Freddy's underpants, pushing them in next to the balled-up socks, then glanced at her watch; she must get cracking, nearly pick-up time. Was Mary's obsession, the constant refrain of, 'Thomas, I simply must tell you about Thomas,' a clue? Had she taped the document to the back of Uncle Tom's portrait? She hung up Freddy's shirts, and then trotted downstairs to collect her handbag, irritated to notice the collection of mugs strategically hidden behind it. Why couldn't Freddy manage those extra steps to the sink, or, joy of joys, rinse them and pop them in the dishwasher himself?

Starting the car, she sat with the engine idling for a few minutes, thinking about the motorcyclist's family. Her phone was ringing, clicking into the car's hands-free system. *No caller ID* flashed up. She pushed 'accept' with her thumb.

'Sarah Fetherston speaking.'

'Mrs. Fetherston, it's Sergeant Grindley.'

'How is he?'

'There's no news.'

'Can't you tell me anything?'

The police officer spoke crisply. He wasn't rude but nor was his the slightly supportive voice adopted on the night of the accident.

'There's no news, he's in intensive care with his family by his bedside. I'm calling because we need to ask you a few more questions.'

'I've given you a statement.'

The voice was firm. 'Mrs Fetherston, I said we need to question you again.'

Sarah stared across the expanse of scuffed red leather. Two hundred years of use had left a spiders-web of scratch marks etched into the top of her husband's desk, but he refused to have it restored, claiming they were a calming historical reminder of the many previous owners. Sarah fixed a determined look on her face, dragging Freddy back to the twenty-first century, like a medium summoning their favourite spirit. She maintained her gaze until he gave in, stopped typing, and sat back in his chair.

'I just got off the phone to Harry. He now says he recalls your mother saying she sent the Will off to one of those custodian companies for safekeeping. We need to find out which one. I can't call them all! Any ideas?'

Freddy was stroking his chin. Sarah could sense the alluring seventeenth century receding a little further to be replaced by the less enticing present.

'Ah, yes,' he said. 'I do recall that being mentioned.'

'And?'

'Actually . . .' He screwed up his face, confessing, 'I think she may have given me an envelope, and told me to pass it on to you.'

'When?'

He gave Sarah one of his enchanting smiles. 'Four years ago, shortly after she moved. I just have no idea what I've done with it,' he admitted, pulling a face in apology.

Sarah groaned. 'Oh Freddy. Mind, what did the silly woman think she was doing giving something so important to you in the first place!'

She rested both hands on the edge of his desk and leaned over. 'Right, out – off to the university. You are never going to remember what you did with that envelope, and I can't search for it with you underfoot.'

Freddy scuttled out.

'On the off-chance if you do remember what you did with it,' she called after him, 'feel free to phone me.'

That wasn't going to happen this side of Christmas. Not that Sarah minded running Operation Will Hunt; it was a useful distraction and would stop her calling the hospital so frequently that she was in danger of being reported for stalking.

She claimed Freddy's chair, staring at the chaos around her. To Sarah, her husband's study reminded her of a scene from a spy movie in which the hero has rifled through the room searching for top secret papers before being rumbled and forced to scarper out of a window. Freddy didn't have a filing system; his papers were left wherever there was a free space, or, failing that, wherever they fell. What would Freddy have done with that envelope four years ago? Preoccupied he may be, but he wasn't a stupid man; he would have known how important it was. He'd have put it somewhere sensible, or somewhere he thought sensible at the time.

For the first hour, Sarah picked through each of the desk drawers. Then she tackled the bookcase: clutching each book by the spine and giving it a good shake. She opened dust jackets to check behind the flaps; several scraps of paper covered with handwritten notes fluttered to the floor, but no promising-looking envelopes.

She called Penelope.

'Where would you search in William's study for an important document?'

There was a pause. Sarah took the phone with her into the kitchen and ran herself a glass of water.

'Not sure I would start in the study,' Penelope replied. 'In fact, I think I'd try his gun safe.'

Sarah swallowed a few mouthfuls, and then carried the glass back with her to the study. 'Unhelpful. Freddy doesn't shoot.'

Penelope chuckled. 'I can't help that. What are you searching for?'

'An envelope his mother gave him, with details of where she sent her Will.'

'Ahh! Not sure I'm going to be able to help. How's things? We haven't spoken since you told me about the accident. Are you OK?'

'He's in a coma!'

'I've never witnessed anything like that, it must be difficult. But you must try not to dwell on it. It's no help to the victim; he's in the best possible hands!'

Sarah toyed with her glass. The man shouldn't need to be in the best possible hands. 'I can't stop worrying. What if he's paralysed or has lost his memory, I'd never be able to forgive myself.'

'Sarah, you didn't do anything wrong. He was going too fast; it was an accident. You've got a lot on your plate with Mary's funeral to arrange, and now it sounds like you've got to track down a missing Will. Try and forget about the man. Anyway, if you want more drama, you can help me.'

'Oh no. What's happened?'

Sarah heard an exasperated cough, then Penelope said, 'Angus has been caught smoking again. Cannabis. We can't work out how he got hold of it. He's gated. William and his pack of spaniels have the house locked down like we're under siege. The dogs bark if a stranger comes within sniffing distance of the house, and Angus hasn't been out the front door except to come to that Open Garden event with me, so how the devil has he got his mitts on the stuff?'

Oh my God, I know his source. Mike was on that invite list!

'Maybe he just hid the last batch somewhere you haven't thought of?' suggested Sarah, knowing how unlikely this sounded, visualizing William rolling up a rug and kneeling to check under the floorboards.

'That's an idea – must dash, William's calling! Try not to worry.'

Sarah finished the call; was she inadvertently supplying Angus his dope? She didn't want to be sucked deeper into the drugs business, but maybe she should speak to Mike. Not now, she'd find the right time.

Focus on the Will!

She let her eyes wander across the stacks of papers haphazardly dotted around the room. She would have to get in for a good spring clean. Freddy protected his study like an old dog with a smelly basket, preventing potential invaders seeking to alter an environment he had carefully nurtured and wished to preserve. On spring-clean days, he hovered like a protective parent when a child's stabilisers come off their bike for the first time, clucking his teeth and swooping in to reclaim precious papers Sarah lifted from the floor, returning them – once she'd finished vacuuming – to precisely the same spot.

Her eyes roved around, pausing at a pair of Regency knife boxes sitting as bookends on the table under the window. Elegant wedges of wood long since shorn of their intended contents, they were a gift from Mary to Freddy on the birth of their daughter. She darted to the table, lifted a lid, and peered inside.

An envelope!

Sarah plucked it out. It was bulky and quite heavy. She tore at the top – in the same frenzied way she scolded Mary for opening new packets of cereal – spilling the contents onto the floor and pitching her thoughts back to the motorcyclist spreadeagled on the tarmac. For a few moments she stared sightlessly downwards, gauging how the relatives might react if she turned up at the hospital; she wouldn't welcome a stranger if it was Mary lying in intensive care with tubes strapped round her little body and machines beeping either side of the bed.

Sarah blinked and looked properly at the floor. A garish plastic card lay beside a thickish wad of papers – were these the custodian's contact details? Had she found the Will? She scooped it up, her heart beating a little faster.

She unfolded the document, her hands shaking and was about to read what it contained when her conscience kicked in and she folded it back up. Was she being greedy, wondering what Mary had left her family? Should she just let Freddy know she'd found it? Her curiosity got the better of her; she'd have a peek and get the gist.

In the comfort of Freddy's chair, she unfolded the pages and skimmed, stopping at interesting words. Mary's sons were asked to be the executors – not surprising. After a few small gifts to relatives and charities, she got to the meat. A sum of £10,000 was bequeathed to Mike – wow he's going to be thrilled with that after the hefty divorce settlement he was paid! Spotting the word "jewellery", she sped on only to discover she and Amy were left to divide the collection between them – so much for continuity. Would her sister-in-law leave her half of the hoard to her niece?

"And to my granddaughter Mary . . ."

What was her daughter getting? The house?

"I bequeath the portrait she and I both admire of her namesake Lady Mary Fetherston. Continuity is important."

Was that it? To the only grandchild! Mike was singled out for a decent sum, and the granddaughter left a pretty family picture!

Unless . . . had Mary done the right thing with the rest of her fortune? She held her breath and read on, spitting out a strangled 'WHY?!' when she saw that the balance of the estate was left equally to the two sons. Equally? What did the Suffolk Fetherstons need money for? Mary hadn't even allocated the family paintings between her sons, instead adding an extra battle between their two wives over jewellery.

Stapled to the Will was an additional sheet of paper – a list of Mary's principal assets. Sarah bit back her irritation, curious to discover how much was involved. She had never asked Freddy what his mother was worth. There was no point. He never showed any interest in his inheritance and would not have discussed the topic; to Freddy it was unseemly to speculate about money. Sarah's eyes scanned the list. There was Mary's seventy-five per cent share of the Dower House, listed at its purchase price of £1,500,000. There were various investments in unit trusts and stocks and shares worth an additional £750,000. And those were the values four years ago! Nursing home fees had not depleted the estate. The local council was obliged to pay those once Mary was sectioned and deemed too dangerous to return to live with Mike.

Sarah reread the Will, slowly. Had she missed something? She had not. There was no separate provision for Mary: no special gifts of jewellery, and no dreamed-for bequest of the Dower House. Half of the fortune was destined to enrich her odious in-laws. Sarah slammed the document onto the desk. Had she learned nothing about this family? Why had she ever allowed herself to think Mary would do what normal people would? Freddy always told her the money would be split equally, saying that was the best she could hope for. If the Lampton estate was still in the family, he was adamant the whole lot would have been left to his brother!

'Even though he owns Ashe Hall?'

'Yes!'

'Why?'

'That's the way things are done.'

She picked the plastic card up off the floor; it was the contact details for a Will custodian company, but she had the Will. She dropped it on the desk scolding herself for dreaming about moving house, she was lucky to be living where she was.

Gathering up the papers and her empty glass, it occurred to her that it wouldn't be too expensive for Freddy to buy out Mike's portion of the Dower House, and when she explained what she wanted to do, her in-laws might agree to let Freddy keep the house. Provided Amy and Harry repaid their mortgage, what more did they need? She walked to the kitchen, allowing a smile to creep onto her face. Sarah photocopied the papers and scanned them, sending a copy to Harry, then chose a bright yellow file from her stationary drawer. *'Mary Fetherston Will'* , she wrote on the spine. She popped the originals in an envelope together with the custodian's card to drop off with the lawyers. She would ask for a quote; Harry wouldn't want anyone appointed without agreeing fees first.

Her fingers were on her phone texting Freddy when it rang.

No caller ID.

She answered and immediately asked. 'Any news?'

'No. Mrs. Fetherston,' said the officer. 'That's not why I called. I must make that appointment to reinterview you.'

Chapter Seven

Rhododendrons were Sarah's favourite shrub, the brief flowering season – that burst of yellow, red, or purple, lasting just a few weeks – a shortcoming worth overlooking. She circled the rhododendron stand, ignoring those in flower or bud, scanning the spent plants. Penelope had told her about the Cornish Early Red, which, when planted in a south facing position, flowers in February, a month when there is little else but snowdrops and hellebores. She was leaning over scrutinizing a label when a shadow fell across her vision, and she straightened.

'Can't be doing with them rhodies, don't pull their weight,' said Nick.

He was standing beside her in the same pair of crumpled trousers he'd been wearing when they met three days ago. Sarah spun round in a circle, her eyes flickering over each customer. How could she possibly explain how she knew this man? She smoothed down her skirt.

'What does pull its weight then, Nick? Flowers you can sell in small plastic bags?'

He coughed. 'I've come to buy a present for me wife. Any ideas?'

At least he didn't want to talk about the accident, or their shared horticultural interests. Sarah didn't need her conscience prodded; what she needed was to know the man was out of his coma, but no one at the hospital would give her an update.

'Bit of an open-ended question. Depends on what she wants to do with it. Is she into flower arranging? Does she keep potted plants?'

'She's more of a gardener than a florist.'

'A woman after my own heart! I can't stand flower arranging. Waste of my time. My mother-in-law insisted I try. She thought a room wasn't complete without flowers, warned me all the other ladies would think I couldn't be bothered if there aren't any.'

Sarah recalled how initially she'd assumed it was a joke – women don't judge one another on their ability to produce an arresting display of flowers – before realising her mother-in-law probably did!

'My arrangements don't bear much resemblance to a selection of flowers assembled with artistic thought. They look more like they've been abandoned together in water.'

Nick rubbed a hand over his chin – still stubbly – then said he wanted something special. 'Posh like, it's our anniversary.'

'Ahh, well, what about a rose?'

She hefted her handbag back up her shoulder and moved quickly in her flat-heeled pumps towards one of the attendants who was spraying a fine mist over the roses. 'This one's pretty,' she suggested, fingering the leaves of a pink-flowered *Boscobel*. 'Mmmm,' she said, smelling myrrh with a hint of almond. 'Lovely bouquet, too.'

Nick snorted.

'Bouquet,' he said, pronouncing it *bookay*, elongating both syllables. 'Why don't you just say smell?'

'OK.' She made a loud tutting noise. 'Well, this rose has a lovely smell.'

'How much?'

She pulled out the plastic marker, passing it over. He examined it and then handed it back, whistling. 'Nah, didn't want to spend that much. What's cheaper?'

She pushed the label back into the pot.

'What do you do for a living?'

'I've a delivery van, drive long distances. It doesn't pay much, but absence makes the heart grow fonder. I'm not under the missus' feet.'

That sounded like a useful job for his little sideline; crisscrossing the country legitimately, no doubt delivering a few extra packages along the way.

Nick was rocking on his heels, his hands thrust deep into his trouser pockets, pushing the pants downwards as if he was trying to take them off without unfastening them. She led him towards the lavender plants – surely even Nick would stretch to a few of those – imagining Freddy pushing across a paltry six-inch potted lavender on their wedding anniversary. It was soon, though she couldn't muster the same enthusiasm she had last year – she'd become totally disinterested in sex since the accident, allowing Freddy to attribute the change in appetite to his mother's death.

'So, what's your line?' asked Nick.

She picked up a six-pack of French lavender – each tiny plant confined to a two-inch square of compost, the purple fronds towering above the leaves – then a single, larger specimen in a more generous-sized pot: comparing each, viewing them as presents.

'Charity work, fundraising.'

'Unpaid?' he asked, incredulously, as if she'd suggested she was an astronaut.

She stood a little straighter. 'Yes, it's voluntary.'

'So, you're a kept woman?'

Sarah bristled. At least Nick hadn't called her a parasite, like Harry had. 'It's the way we choose to run our family. I deal with domesticity; my husband has a career.'

'And what does he do?'

'What a lot of questions. He's a history professor. Now what about one of these lavenders? Personally, I would prefer the single large one to the six-pack.'

He took the pot from her outstretched hand and peeked at the price. 'Ta, that's more like it, we don't all have a professor's salary to spend.'

He let his arm drop, resting the pot against his leg.

'So, you never worked then?'

'Actually, I did work,' she said, feeling herself bristtle. 'I used to work in Exeter full-time.'

Why was she defending her way of life to this man?

'Why did you stop?'

Sarah considered the six-pack of lavender plants still in her hand, confined to their tiny cubicles. She hadn't given up a career, she'd been temping in the human resources department of a firm of accountants, but she'd been content, with no plans to stop working. Not until she met Freddy. *I stopped because my mother-in-law told me to.* Pathetic though that sounded, the compliance didn't convey the magnitude of her action. She'd surrendered her independence, shunned her friends. Her ex-flat mate Kate tried to keep in touch and was still connected on Facebook – but when had they last spoken, let alone met? Kate was still in Exeter, working for the same firm of estate agents. They used to have such fun, searching the Exeter nightlife for soulmates, but Sarah doubted her old Exeter friends would recognise her now. She didn't go to girls' lunches in pubs anymore; this week she would be joining one at Langton Manor – Penelope's home – and she doubted a bottle of wine would be drunk between six or eight of them.

'Oh, it seemed the right thing to do at the time. Stay home and take care of the baby.'

Nick shrugged. 'Hey, if that's what makes you happy,' he said, turning on his heel and walking away, towards the till, the lavender plant bouncing against his trouser leg.

Sarah returned to the rhododendrons. Was she happy? Maybe not right now, but once that man was out of hospital, and her mother-in-law's affairs wrapped up, all her problems would evaporate. Even if her family didn't move to the Dower House, it would be sold, and the little enterprise would stop.

Spotting *"Cornish Early Red"* on a white sticker, she picked up the plant without checking the price. With all her problems about to be resolved, she should help solve a friend's troubles. She would go and ask Mike about Angus.

Someone was shouting. Sarah swung open the door to see Nick and Mike facing each other, Mike with his back to the double doors of one of the polytunnels his arms outstretched.

'No more, Nick. Not until you've paid me for last month.'

'Get real, Grandad, you get paid when I get paid,' said Nick, reaching out towards the older man. Mike dodged him, still protecting the entrance – like a mother hen sheltering her chick.

'You can't keep taking stuff on credit.'

Slowly, quietly, Sarah closed the door. Not quietly enough. Nick spun around and yelled, 'What the bloody hell do you want?'

'I wanted a word with Mike.'

'What about?'

'It's private. I can come back. I've got some baking to do.'

Nick was looking from one to the other of them, his arms folded across his chest. 'Shit, it's like being in business with a couple of toddlers. You two have no frigging idea.' He imitated her voice, 'I've got some baking to do. You don't have to deal with the men I do, one of these days my missus will be identifying me body on a trolley. You with your fancy houses and your fancy ways, leaving all the real work to me, and then Mike moaning if I'm a few days late paying. Move!' he demanded, now standing chest to chest with the older man.

Nick shoved Mike out the way, as if clearing a path past overgrown brambles. The older man stumbled.

'Don't!' shouted Sarah, reaching out a supportive arm.

Nick didn't wait for the outcome of Mike's struggle with gravity; he took a running jump, kicking open the flimsy double doors, which crashed inwards. Sarah yelped as if she'd been scalded as Nick stormed into the polytunnel.

By the open doors, Mike was on all fours, pleading. 'Nick, stop.' He sat back on his haunches. 'You don't know what to pick. You could damage the plants.'

Nick's voice boomed out at them. 'You can either come in here and help or leave me to it. Your choice, Mike. And you can clear off, Sarah. Take your whining posh voice somewhere I can't hear it – before I change the shape of your face.'

Mike glanced up at Sarah, scrambled upright and disappeared into the polytunnel, leaving her staring at the black plastic. Nick was a nasty piece of work!

Fifteen minutes later, from the safety of her car, Sarah saw Nick close the boot of his car and once he was in the driver's seat, she slipped out of her own and trotted back to the polytunnels. The doors were closed. She nudged one open and stepped inside, feeling the heat smothering her.

'You OK, Mike?' she asked.

He was on his knees, sweat running down his face, a box by his side, reaching into the spiky plants. He sat back on his heels and swiped a hand across his brow. 'Thanks for asking, luv. He didn't hurt me.'

'He didn't care if he did, though, did he?'

'Don't worry about me. Nick's not going to mess with his best supplier. He's under pressure; some of the deliveries are late.'

Hearing the jarring whining noise of someone struggling to start a car, she quipped, 'Sounds like they could be getting later.'

'Oi, Sarah, I need you,' hollered Nick.

She pulled a face at Mike, who stood up, shrugging, and lifting his t-shirt, used the end to mop at his face and neck. 'What did you want to chat about, luv?'

'Sarah!' The voice was getting closer, Nick was at the mouth of the polytunnel. 'You deaf or something?' His eyes were cold, dark little menacing dots, and she began to breathe a little faster under the unblinking gaze. 'I *said* I *need* you.'

'What for?'

'Me car won't start, and there's deliveries to make.'

She swept her eyes over to Mike. 'Well, ask your partner.'

'This 'aint a request.' His hand gripped her arm, fingers digging into her flesh. 'Mike's picking, so you can be the chauffeur.'

The shopping list was on the kitchen counter near the sturdy bags. Close by, was a foldable cool bag – it was May and forecast to be hot – that Sarah had unearthed from the depths of a cupboard in the utility room, turfing out picnic blankets and plastic cutlery last used for family beach outings the previous summer. This would all be very handy if she'd still been at the Long House, rather than at a supermarket ten miles east in Exeter, wrestling to release a trolley from the vice-like grip of its friends. Two forgotten items and now the uncooperative trolley – *am I in the clear, does that count as my three unlucky episodes?* She released the trolley and set off round the aisles, tossing in items that appealed rather than those that matched her carefully laid-out weekly meal plan. If that was her run of bad luck over, she could stop fretting about Sergeant Grindley, his sidekick, and her interrogation later that morning – at the Long House.

'Unless it would be more convenient for you to drop by the station, Mrs. Fetherston?' Grindley had offered.

'No, at home would be better for me, please.'

She was not going to volunteer to assist the police with their enquiries at the station!

She examined the contents of her trolley, crammed full of sinful foods: cheeses and chocolates and packets of crisps – even a large, white, crusty baguette had crept in unnoticed. *This must be my subconscious secretly comfort- eating*. She removed some of the excess calories and headed for the breakfast cereals, before making a quick detour down the poultry aisle, adding a plump chicken. She had no idea what the weather forecast was for the weekend, but she could roast it, or they could barbeque it if the fine weather held, and then steered towards the checkout.

She chewed her lip and tried not to glare at the elderly man in front of her grappling with his shopping bags with quivering hands. She folded her arms and checked the time. The man had his bags open, was feeding in his purchases one by one. With just a few items left, he went into reverse, removing a few vegetables, picking up a can of beans and inserting it snugly in a corner so the bag went rigid, then surveying the remaining goods. He picked up a single banana, found it a home, then selected a second. Sarah watched a further two bananas being packed, closed her eyes, clenched her teeth, and kept her hands pinned to her sides.

She arrived home to the unattractive sight of a panda car squatting in the corner of the parking area, like a predatory animal waiting for dinner to amble past. The police were five minutes early. Maybe this was a deliberate ploy to catch her off guard. Rats, no time to gather thoughts. She parked and popped the boot open, then tooted the horn, the noise startling her. 'They are early, you are not late. Get a grip,' she muttered under her breath.

The police got out of their vehicle as she got out of hers. She glanced at a puddle by the front door fast-evaporating in the spring heat, feeling powerless: like part of the food chain caught unawares at a waterhole.

'Let me help you with those bags, Mrs. Fetherston, and before you ask, no news, the lad's still in a coma,' offered Sergeant Grindley, reaching into her boot, and picking up two of the flimsy plastic carriers she had been forced to purchase. He had large hands. Do the police deliberately recruit people with large hands, does that help when fastening handcuffs round criminals' wrists? Sarah led the way inside and into the kitchen where she heaved her shopping onto the counter, on top of the missing list – and turned to the officers.

'Take a seat. Please make yourselves comfortable.'

They pulled out chairs, scraping them nosily on the flagstones.

'Tea, coffee, glass of water?' she offered, crossing to the sink to wash her hands.

The officers replied in unison. 'No thank you, Mrs. Fetherston.'

PC Matthews pulled a notebook out of his shirt pocket. Sarah could feel Sergeant Grindley's eyes on her as she darted round the room like a pigeon startled into flight, noisily opening, and shutting cupboard doors, bobbing in and out of the utility room trying to play the role of the calm housewife caught up in a mishap.

'Why don't you sit down, Mrs. Fetherston? This really shouldn't take long.'

'I'll just unpack. I forgot my cool bag and I've some frozen items.' She waved in the direction of the groceries. 'How can I help, though? I'm a girl, so I can multi-task. Fire away.'

She peered at the sergeant over the tops of her carrier bags – a token barrier between her and the law. She couldn't look the men in the eye. It was so damn difficult dealing with this alone. The only other person who had witnessed the accident was Nick, and she didn't want to talk to him.

'Now then,' Sergeant Grindley began. 'On the night in question, you told us you dropped by to visit Darren Smith. You say you stayed for a cup of coffee and a chat about his wife, your mother-in-law, who's in a nearby retirement home.'

'Yes. That's correct. At least she was then. Sadly, she has since died,' she replied, opening the freezer to find room for a bag of peas. She manhandled a joint of lamb out of the way. That's what we are having for lunch on Sunday; I didn't need that chicken after all, she thought.

'Was there anyone else present when you were at the Dower House?'

'Someone else?' she asked, closing the freezer door. Should she mention Nick?

'Yes, was there anyone else at the Dower House?' repeated the senior officer.

Did it matter if they knew Nick was there? He was involved already, had been driving the car that collided with the victim, given a statement. 'Umm, well yes, there was someone, but I didn't know him,' she said, hiding a tiny smirk behind a family-sized bag of spinach she tossed into the salad drawer.

'Was his name Nick Henderson by any chance?' suggested Sergeant Grindley.

She wheeled around from the fridge.

'Now you mention it, I think his name was Nick. I don't think Mike told me his surname.'

'So, there were four of you in the kitchen. This man Mike was present too?' asked PC Matthews, shifting in his chair, making it squeak.

'Sorry,' said Sarah, pulling boxes of cereal out of the bags. 'Mike is Darren. We just don't know him as Darren. The family all call him Mike, it's a long story.'

'It's this Nick we're interested in. He's a shady character, part of the Devon drugs world. We want to establish what he was doing at the Dower House that evening,' revealed PC Matthews.

Sarah gulped.

She saw the senior officer shoot his junior a warning look.

'It's surprising how crime investigations can pan out, Mrs. Fetherston,' explained the sergeant. 'You think you're investigating a traffic accident and sometimes you end up uncovering something far more sinister.'

Was she expected to reply? Sarah crumpled up the now empty bags, pushing them into the cool bag then stood by the Aga despite the uncomfortable heat – her heart thumping. The policemen were staring at her. Could they see her terror? They were trained to notice these things. How would a normal respectable woman, married to an eminent university professor, with a young daughter, be expected to react to news about the shady Nick Henderson? She tried out her voice.

'Involved in drugs, you say. That sounds worrying.'

They were still watching her, like a pair of tabby cats waiting to pounce on a mouse. This interview was not going well.

She dropped her head as the next question was fired at her by the sergeant.

'So, Darren introduced you to Nick Henderson. Did he indicate why Nick was there?'

She shook her head.

'Did you notice anything suspicious, or hear any discussion about anything unusual?' queried the senior officer.

'Like what?'

'Unexplained packages? Do you recall if Henderson had any bags with him?'

The police were on to something; someone must have tipped them off. Did they know Nick's visit was connected to drugs? Oh shit. It was tricky enough dealing with the trauma of the accident; what if they discovered what was going on in the Walled Garden? And her involvement in the little enterprise was not confined to keeping quiet. Not anymore. Instead of stopping Mike supplying Angus with cannabis, that visit to the Dower House had ended with Nick loading boxes onto the back seat of her car and Sarah ferrying him around Devon, praying no one would spot her with an unshaven man in her passenger seat. Despite Nick urging her to go faster, she'd stuck like a learner driver to the speed limit, even when she caused a tailback of traffic on the Barnstaple new bridge. She wasn't going to risk being pulled over for speeding! Worse, when she dropped him back at the Dower House, telling him tartly the expedition was not going to be repeated, his reply was a short snort.

The heat of the Aga reminded her of the polytunnels, and she stepped away, looking at the officers blankly, 'I don't recall anything odd.'

'One further question for you, please, Mrs. Fetherston,' said Grindley. 'In your statement you say you inched out of the driveway, just a few feet, and didn't see the bike coming. And that the motorcyclist sped round the corner, braked, and fell off? You are sure you weren't further out in the road, forcing the motorcyclist to take evasive action?'

Where had that idea come from? Had Nick said she was responsible for the crash? No, that couldn't be right. Nick made his statement *before* her. If he had suggested it was her fault, they would have asked her that question on the night of the accident.

'No. I only poked my nose out.'

'OK. I think that's all for now,' said Sergeant Grindley.

She waited for PC Matthews to finish scribbling and pocket his pad and pen then showed them out, staying in the porch as the pair walked across her driveway. Did they believe her?

Chapter Eight

Sarah stood by her mixing bowl, tapping her fingers on her leg. She was listening to a lawyer who had fifteen years' experience, why couldn't he send her a quote; it was a simple enough matter.

'What I've got in front of me appears straightforward, I agree, especially as there's already a list of the deceased's principal assets. But this is not the original Will, it's just a copy. I need the original. Do you per chance have that document?'

Sarah pushed her cake mix aside.

'A *copy*?'

There was a short silence on the line, which the lawyer filled with further bad news.

'I called the number of the custody company you gave me. They don't have the original either. Apparently, she withdrew it over two years ago. I've asked them for a copy of the correspondence affecting that withdrawal and they have undertaken to furnish me with the same.'

Why would Mary withdraw her Will?

'I'd like to see that letter too, please.'

'Of course. Now, this list of known assets, it's quite a considerable estate. Do you think this list is accurate? I am not referring to the valuation of the assets; my question pertains to the assets themselves – do you think their composition has changed substantially since this helpful list was drawn up four years ago?'

Ten miles to the west, Sarah chewed her lip. Having triumphantly scored a thick blue line through 'find the Will', she would have to add it back.

'There was a power of attorney. My husband's consent was needed for any changes to the investments. He would have talked to me before making any.'

'That's useful to know. Now, moving on, another question for you. The Dower House forms the bulk of the estate. She hasn't provided for Mike to continue to live there for the duration of his life: a life tenancy, we legally refer to that provision. Is that going to surprise him?'

She gasped. Mike may be in his mid-sixties, but he was fit and healthy and might have a good thirty years to go. This was the first time she'd heard the phrase 'life tenancy'. Four years ago, had anyone been aware of that danger? It wasn't mentioned at the 'family council of war' convened by Harry to chew over 'Ma's alarming plan', as Freddy dubbed the crisis. The couples were gathered round speakerphones either side of the country. The younger brother was firmly against the scheme of Mary and Mike buying the Dower House together. Surprisingly Harry, was remarkably sanguine, and supportive – concerned only that his mother's money was protected.

'It's a good plan. He'll take care of her.'

'Why does it have to involve Mike?' Freddy moaned.

'Are you offering, Freddy? Because I can't do it from here.'

Sensing Freddy's gaze fall on her, Sarah chipped in, 'I've spent the day with them, they've found the most gorgeous house to move to and I think she wants Mike back in her life.'

'Why?' the brothers said simultaneously.

Harry ran on. 'If the price of him caring for her, is they buy a house together, that's fine, provided we protect the money. He was already given a generous settlement when they divorced. I'll explain the facts to Ma.'

'Why don't they rent a bigger house? I accept her cottage is too small for them both to live there, but why buy?' Freddy asked.

'You can't rent something like the Dower House. Things will work out fine, Freddy. Ma wants a retreat into memories of Lampton surrounded by family furniture and pictures; to reminisce while she still can. I'll speak to her and make sure she gets the legals straight.'

Harry did speak to Mary and reported everything was taken care of. In all their discussions, the family never contemplated a life tenancy provision for Mike. That was a lucky escape, and it sounded like Sarah had found the right lawyer – this Percy Wilson was on top of his game.

'Mike won't be expecting anything from the Will,' she said. 'He was given a generous settlement when they divorced a decade ago.'

She dipped a finger in the chocolate cake mix and popped it in her mouth, then trotted to the sink to wash her hand.

'Hmm, let's hope so. I've been told that a few times before. Mrs. Fetherston, could you have a hunt around for the original Will? Did your mother-in-law have a favourite hiding place, or a safe? Maybe a secret compartment in her desk?'

Percy was running through what Sarah suspected was the lawyer's 'helpful list of hiding places for Wills'. He rambled on suggesting Mary might have passed it to a trusted friend, or her bank manager.

Sarah finished the call, thinking Percy needed to update his list; where would Mary have found a bank manager, they were on the endangered species list. She pulled the mixing bowl back over and picked up her spatula. Her mother-in-law had fully understood her diagnosis and put her affairs in order while she still could. What possible reason could she have had for altering that plan?

The next morning, Sarah glanced up from her screen and giggled at the sight of Mary slouched in the kitchen doorway, aping her mother's usual morning expressions. Her child was exaggeratedly glancing at her wrist, tutting.

'Aren't you ready yet, Mum? We don't want to be late.'

'Two minutes, little one,' she muttered, clicking open the attachment Percy had forwarded; her lawyer did seem to start work early. In front of her was the letter Mary had written to the Will custodian.

Dear Sir / Madam
I would like you to return my Will, which you have for safekeeping, to the above address.
Yours sincerely

And it was signed.

Mary Florence Fetherston

Why had her mother-in-law done that?

Sarah printed off a copy, pulled out the yellow file.

'Right, let's go,' she announced, snatching a coat, then jerking the front door closed behind her and struggling into the jacket.

Driving back home from school, she called Mike – he might know where the crucial document was. He appeared unsurprised by her questions and claimed to know all about the recalling of the Will. It had started to rain again: large drops falling and slapping against her windscreen. She stabbed at the volume button.

'She asked me to take her into town to the Citizens Advice Bureau to make a new one,' he explained, to the background drumming of rain. 'They told her they couldn't help. They weren't comfortable; they felt the dementia was too advanced. It was on the way home she told me she was going to ask for her old one back. When it arrived, she tore it up in front of me. Ripped it to shreds and threw it in the bin. I am happy to tell your lawyer that's what happened; that she destroyed it, if it helps?'

'Er, thanks, Mike. Get back to you on that one.'

The windscreen wipers were working diligently to clear a half moon of window for Sarah to peer through briefly. *What next?* Ask an expert? She called out 'Percy Wilson' to the handsfree system.

The lawyer picked up on the first ring.

'Hmmm,' was Percy's response when she'd relayed what she'd discovered. 'So, it is alleged that the original Will, which you have given me a copy of, was destroyed, implying she died without a valid Will. That is, legally she died intestate?'

The rain had eased off; Sarah could talk rather than shout. 'Yes, and if it helps, I can get Mike to confirm that,' she said, steering round a large pool of water at the road's edge. 'So, we might as well call the hunt off.'

'That depends,' said Percy.

'Surely if we have a copy, that's enough, isn't it?' Sarah challenged. 'We know what my mother-in-law intended. After all, we've only got Mike's word that she destroyed it. She may not have – she could've squirrelled it away in any number of nooks and crannies, that Dower House is huge. What matters is we know what she wanted done, so don't we just proceed on that basis? We pay out the small bequests, and then it goes equally to my husband and his brother, job done?'

There was a soft chuckle.

'I didn't have you down as a client who would become an overnight specialist in the field of probate law, Mrs. Fetherston. Hold on while I just check my file note of our first teleconference.' There was a short silence, and then she heard the phone being picked up.

'Me again,' announced the lawyer. 'This Mike you say witnessed the alleged destruction: he is presumably the former husband bequeathed £10,000? Checking my notes from our initial teleconference, your mother-in-law divorced him a decade ago?'

A tractor chugged past on the other side of the road, sending a cascade of filthy water over her windscreen. Sarah cursed under her breath, turning up the speed of the wipers to maximum, and raising her voice.

'Not actually divorced, no. Technically, they legally separated.'

There was another silence. Sarah leaned forward, straining to catch the response above the whirring of the wipers. She heard an intake of breath.

'Separated, you say, not actually divorced. Now that does complicate matters somewhat. Legal separation does not actually terminate the marriage in the same way as a divorce does.'

'So?'

'So, Mrs. Fetherston, Mike was still her husband when your mother-in-law died. He is her next of kin and entitled to her entire estate in the event she died intestate.'

The entire estate? No, that's absolutely not what Mary wanted, continuity is important, her fortune must not go to Mike.

The rain was driving down hard, crashing against her windscreen as if in sympathy with her mood. Was Mike behind this? Had he really seen Mary destroy her Will or was he lying? He might want revenge against Harry, but why do this to Freddy? The family had to find the original Will. What if it didn't exist, what if Mike was right and it had been destroyed? She turned into the driveway of the Long House, stopped by the front porch, and made a dash for cover. Misjudging the puddle, she felt the water seeping in through her trainers, soaking her feet. She slipped off her shoes and socks leaving them by the door, and ran upstairs barefoot, wet socks in one hand, damp feet slapping on the uncarpeted stairs.

She should warn Harry. Was she up to the inevitable explosion? Outside the bathroom door, she fired off a quick message. The soggy socks dripped their way across the bathroom floor. She stopped with the lid of the laundry basket in one hand, the socks in the other.

'Oh Freddy!' she exclaimed, hurling the damp socks into the basket.

She walked over to the bath. It was full. Sarah plunged her hand into the icy water, feeling around for the long-ago detached plug. If Freddy changed his mind from a thought-provoking soak to a quick shower, why couldn't that decision be accompanied by thrusting his own arm in while the water was still warm? She listened to the gurgling sound, feeling her spirits sink with the water. What would happen if they couldn't find the original? Would Mike do the decent thing and follow the instructions in the copy of the Will, or would he stay at the Dower House, wrecking her plans to move house and trapping her in his drugs world?

Later that evening, the family was spread out in the sitting room, enjoying tea and crumpets. Freddy was gazing at the fire burning in the inglenook fireplace imagining a cavalier leaning against the mantelpiece, with soft leather boots folded over at the knees, a hat in his hands, a long white feather dangling towards the floorboards. His phone rang. It was his brother.

'I got Sarah's message, and I don't think Ma destroyed her Will.'

Freddy felt the fingers of his left hand being unwound and the cup and saucer lifted. He winked his thanks to Sarah and moved the phone a little further away. Why was Harry shouting? Out of the corner of his eye, he saw Mary's hand dart out to claim the last unguarded crumpet.

'Nor do I. Sarah and I are hot-footing to the Dower House tomorrow to find the bloody thing. It's got to be there somewhere.'

Sarah was holding a warning finger at him: her eyes indicating Mary, sitting squirrel-like in the seat in the inglenook fireplace, hunched over, and munching her prize. Freddy would miss that seat if they moved; the Georgians built to impress, not for practicality.

'I'm coming too,' shouted Harry. 'I'm not letting that toad have my inheritance!'

He folded away his phone and took a refilled cup of tea from Sarah.

'Do you think Mike appreciates the significance of the Will being destroyed?' she asked.

'Let's just be diplomatic and say I think we need to find the original, and quickly.'

The following morning, Freddy rang the doorbell at the Dower House, and then took a step back from the front porch. Why did Sarah covet this place? Was it the symmetry she admired or was it the lure of the power the house projected? Was Sarah's desire driven by a lack of connection with the history of the Long House? Where he saw charm in the channels on the dining room floor – knowing it was the original milking parlour, and how practical they made it to clean the room by throwing pails of water – she saw trip hazards for ladies' high heels. Sarah complained about dark rooms while Freddy respected the astute planning required to maximise natural light whilst minimizing exposure to the draconian window tax. Would agreeing to move house restore Sarah's happiness? Was she worried that because the inheritance was his, he'd dictate how it was spent? Maybe that's why she had a perennial headache lately and kept moving her body away from him in bed.

Freddy heard footsteps approaching.

'Mind your temper, Harry,' he hissed. 'We need his cooperation. No one's going to issue a search warrant for the blasted thing. As far as he's concerned, we are here to finalise the order of service for Ma's funeral and have a rustle through her papers. That's all.'

Mike showed the Fetherstons into the morning room. Freddy hadn't stepped foot in the space for over ten months, yet it was as if his mother still lived there. He felt an almost physical stab of misery: the pair of chintz armchairs bookending the fireplace, her sewing box on a side table and the butler's tray table he had known all his life close by, as if waiting for tea and cakes. *I wish she was in this room with us. What I wouldn't give for one more day with her!*

He sat in the chair opposite his mother's empty one. Harry skirted round the chair, perching on the fender, and Sarah sat beside him. Mike pulled out a little stool. It was as if the empty chair was keeping an eye on the four of them as the order of service was finalised. Mike offered round homemade biscuits, and Freddy spotted Sarah staring at the chocolate brownies then selecting a piece of shortbread – why, she loves brownies – shaking excess sugar off the biscuit back onto the plate. He picked up a brownie thinking she might be on a diet; that could be what was making her miserable.

Taking advantage of the atmosphere, Freddy asked if Mike minded them having a quick rummage through his mother's boxes and drawers. He helped himself to another brownie. Sarah scowled at him. He arched an eyebrow, was he being greedy?

'Personal papers, photos, that's what we're after,' added Harry, 'We don't expect you to know what's sentimental to the family.'

Mike was polite. 'Help yourselves. Sarah can let me know when you're done.'

The Fetherstons sat where they were, eyes glued to the door as Mike left. It clicked shut and as if a starting gun had gone off, the three jumped up to recommence Operation Will Hunt, charging out of the room like they were off to hide for a game of sardines. Freddy started in the dining room. For a few minutes he gazed at all the pictures remembering meals with his mother and wondering which portraits would end up at the Long House. What would Harry fight for? Freddy still wanted the cavalier but had developed a fondness for Uncle Tom; he pulled that portrait a few inches away from the wall and ran his hand up, slowly, methodically sweeping across the wooden back feeling for anything that might have been taped there – either the document itself, or a clue to where his mother had hidden it. He stood on tip toes to reach the top. Nothing.

An hour later – each having searched through pre-allocated rooms – there was still no sign of the crucial document.

'Let's just try her flower room,' suggested Harry.

'I'll pop out and say goodbye to Mike.' Sarah offered. 'Meet you both back at the car.'

The brothers poked around the musty-smelling flower room, pulling out drawers filled with florists' tape, scissors, and balls of string. Taking in his brother's scowling face, Freddy asked, 'What do you think?'

'I think we're in trouble. It's not here because I reckon that thief has destroyed it.'

Sarah trudged out to the gardens, picking her way down the pathway to avoid the wet lawns. She stopped briefly by the potting sheds, gazing down the back drive, and offered a little prayer for the motorcyclist, asking for him to regain consciousness and to have suffered no lasting injuries. She ran the last fifty yards and let herself into the Walled Garden.

Mike was leaning over one of the raised beds, sprinkling slug pellets, bright blue granules raining down on neat rows of pale green spring cabbages with pointy heads. He was in shirt sleeves. She shut the door, and he turned around.

'All this rain doesn't half bring the slimy army out on munch parade. On your own?' Mike quizzed, screwing the cap back on the slug pellets.

She chewed her lip, 'Just came to say we're off.'

'Have the police been again?' he asked, walking towards the greenhouse. She followed him inside wanting to retort, 'None of your business.' Instead, she told him they had dropped by and asked a few more questions but had no news about the victim.

'Have they interviewed Nick again?' she asked.

'Ask him yourself,' suggested Mike, angling the packet of pellets at Nick, crouched on the floor, stuffing packets of drugs into a large canvas bag. Mike grunted. 'Nick, you shouldn't be in here. Polytunnels or potting sheds, but I don't want dope in my greenhouse.'

'Too hot in them tunnels today. I'll only be a few minutes.' He grinned up at Sarah. 'No calls, no visits, not interested in me and my life at all.'

'Why are they interested in you then, it was Nick's car that hit the man?' Mike asked Sarah, dropping the slug pellets on a shelf next to packets of ant powder and sprays for troublesome insects.

She perched on an iron Victorian table, feeling the sharp edge dig into her bottom. 'They're not interested in me; it was a routine follow-up in case I recalled something I didn't mention on the night,' said Sarah, pushing aside a tub of fish blood and bone and shifting to a more comfortable position.

'Cops don't waste their time, girl,' said Nick. 'They didn't call to check out your fancy kitchen. Don't assume you're in the clear.'

Sarah huffed. 'If I need advice, I'll call a lawyer, not you.'

He laughed as he buttoned up the canvas bag. 'You've never been interviewed before, 'ave you? Bit of a shock, was it, hearing that caution read out? Not something you want to blab about at the next tea party!' He grinned up at her, and adopted a high-pitched nasal voice, 'Oh it was simply ghastly, darlings, I can't tell you how many 'h's the policeman dropped.'

A door banged against a wall and Sarah spun round. It was Freddy and Harry! She could hear their cut-glass accents ring out contrasting with those of the men in the greenhouse, who were discussing when to harvest more buds.

Sarah pushed herself off the table, crying out. 'We need to get rid of those two!'

Nick grinned, but the mirth didn't soften his eyes. 'So, hubby doesn't know, eh? Not going to introduce me to the professor?'

'Stay here, out of sight,' snapped Mike.

Sarah darted out of the greenhouse, Mike followed shouting, 'Shut that door! Only takes a second for a rabbit to get in, destroy me crops before I could catch the blighter!'

'There you are, darling,' said Freddy. 'We wondered where you'd got to. Shall we go?'

There was a note of sarcasm in Mike's voice as he asked, 'Find what you were searching for?'

Sarah looked at Freddy, who looked at Harry, but neither brother spoke. Mike snerred, 'You've been after the Will, haven't you, you clots!' Mike switched his gaze to Sarah. 'It's like I said to you on the phone, luv. She destroyed it, died without a Will, so the whole lot comes to me.' He started to laugh, speaking to Harry's pouting face. 'Of course, if there are one or two small sentimental items you would like as little keepsakes, I won't stand in your way.'

Chapter Nine

Sarah said a tart goodbye and pushed the phone into her back pocket. The man was supposed to be an expert; why couldn't he identify the problem? She was standing by the kettle, and from behind her she heard Freddy ask, 'Who was that darling?'

She gave the kettle a hopeful shake. The weightlessness confirmed it shared her thirst.

'That, darling,' she spat, 'was the second set of builders. Not good news. Like the first they have absolutely no idea why water is seeping in and down the sides of the wall of the fireplace in your study.' She ran water into the kettle, popped it on the Aga and stood with her back to the warmth. 'Just like the first crew, their suggestion is spending several thousand pounds of our money building a scaffold so they can get onto the roof and have a jolly good snoop around. Again, absolutely no guarantee that if we do spend the money they will diagnose the problem – far less come up with a cost-effective way of fixing it.'

'Hmmmm,' said Freddy.

'Yes. Hmmmm indeed,' Sarah replied, flushing hot water round the teapot then spooning in fresh leaves. 'I don't think there's any point me getting a third opinion, unless you particularly like the distraction of men poking around in your study?'

She pulled out a stool and plonked herself down.

'Freddy, that's just the latest in a rather long blacklist this house has accumulated. Isn't it time we moved? Isn't this yet another sign we've been here long enough?'

Freddy took the chair next to hers, reached for her arm, patting it gently, running his other hand through his curls.

'Sarah, if it was as easy as that I would agree, but I know what you want and I'm sorry, I can't give it to you. Certainly not without my inheritance. You married the wrong brother – I'm the steadfast salaried one, not the racy entrepreneur.'

The kettle sang triumphantly. She pulled him towards her, kissing him firmly. 'No, I did not marry the wrong brother. I wouldn't put up with that irascible, opinionated Harry – no idea why Amy does. It's just I do despair of this house sometimes.'

'You don't despair of this house. You fear not achieving the status of living in a manor house.'

'That's a little unfair,' she said, getting up and pouring boiling water into the teapot. 'Mary has hardly any natural light in her bedroom,' Sarah said, 'She will ruin her eyesight. All the windows are the size of postage stamps, and I know you're thrilled that they retain their original glass, but that distorts the light as well.'

Stirring the tea, she saw Freddy reach into the cupboard where the mugs were kept and pull them all out, one by one, lining them up on the counter. Sarah watched the mug inspection parade unfold. It doesn't matter, don't snap, the tea needs time to brew.

'I hear what you say, darling,' he said. 'I just don't think it is possible. I would love to have the capital to buy the house of your dreams!'

She poured the strong tea into the champions of the mug parade.

'How apt. Yes, house of my dreams. This has and always will be the house of your dreams!'

The doorbell rang. Sarah peered out of the kitchen window. It was the police; she must get rid of Freddy.

'I'll deal with this. Why don't you take your coffee back to your study, I'll rustle up some biscuits.'

He picked up his mug, winked at her and left. Sarah dashed to the front door, and showed the officers into the kitchen, offering tea or coffee. Neither accepted. Did they ever accept, or were they precluded from doing so, just in case someone slipped a banned substance into their cup, like cannabis resin?

'It's bad news, I'm afraid, Mrs. Fetherston,' said the senior officer.

Bad news? She felt her body tense up; how bad, was he paralysed? She stared blankly at the officers.

'Sadly, the young motorcyclist died earlier this morning.'

She sagged backwards, felt for the Aga rail behind her, grabbing it.

'Oh, my goodness!'

She stared down at her cooling cup of tea, seeing instead the leather-clad body of the motorcyclist tossed like a pile of autumn leaves, by Nick's car. Should she have tried to visit after all, paid her respects?

No one spoke as the seconds ticked past. It was as if the three of them were observing a minute's silence for the victim. She wanted to ask his age, if he'd been married, were there any children, but it was nothing to do with her, the police would just think she was being voyeuristic. How must his family be feeling after keeping vigil for the last week?

Sergeant Grindley told her she was to be interviewed again – formally. They would call to arrange a time. Sarah closed the door behind them, choking back the tears welling up inside her. She fought for a few moments before starting to cry, unable to stop the drops spilling down her cheeks. She wiped her face with the back of her hand, then fished around in her pockets for a tissue and blew her nose. *Dead, is this my fault?*

She stood in the hallway, with the comforting sound of the grandfather clock ticking in the study. Freddy was in there, she imagined herself running in and burying her head in his chest and howling. But she couldn't do that. She gave a final long sniff, screwing up her eyes to stop the tears. It wasn't right feeling sorry for herself – someone was dead. She should never have eaten that brownie; she should never have used the back drive; she should never have got herself involved in the whole wretched cannabis farming business.

She blew her nose and sniffed loudly, why did the police want to reinterview her? Of course, the incident was more serious: the victim was dead, but they had her statement. The clock chimed slowly, eleven long beats. She should tell Freddy what really happened that night, but then Freddy would want to know why she hadn't told him the full story to start with; and even if she did reveal the truth about the accident, even then she wouldn't be telling him the whole story, not about eating the resin, not about the cannabis, and not about why she was involved with drugs.

The next morning, the alarm summoned her out of a fretful slumber; a sleep-deprived Sarah dragged herself into the shower and let jets of cold water pummel her sagging body. She pictured the motorcyclist lying stiff and cold, and tried to dispel that thought by turning up the temperature and inhaling the smell of lavender as she rubbed shower gel into her skin. She must focus on the Will hunt. She could not let Mary down: her mother-in-law never wanted her fortune going to Mike.

Sarah sat down on the bed and dressed quickly; she prodded Freddy's sleeping form, rustling the dark curls which emerged above the duvet, then set off to Mary's room once she saw Freddy heading for the bathroom.

Rousing Mary took longer, but ten minutes later Sarah was guiding a sleepy child into the still steamy room, silently cursing her mother-in-law. It was so unlike Mary to be slapdash about something important like a Will. *I bet she didn't destroy it!* Sarah folded towels, replacing them on the heated rail, which Freddy failed to appreciate was where they needed to be for them to dry, not hanging from the hooks on the back of the bathroom door under his later-discarded dressing gown, or over the side of the wet shower screen.

Mary, a hazy figure behind the shower screen, shrouded in a fog of mist, was singing. It was a Cole Porter song; Sarah had heard those lyrics so often at parties in Suffolk where her in-laws liked to play music from the twenties and thirties.

'Birds do it, bees do it . . .'

That Ashe Hall *"At Home"* four years ago – when her mother-in-law vacillated between being the socially adept asset she always had been, to a stranger devoid of basic interpersonal skills – that was when the brothers accepted their mother needed to visit a doctor. That was the first time her mother-in-law put a proverbial foot wrong: getting herself locked in a cloakroom she must have used a hundred times before – and on release, when offered a restorative glass of champagne, insisting she never touched the stuff, claiming she was a whiskey drinker.

'Even educated fleas do it, let's do it, let's fall in love . . .'

That was it! It had been hovering at the back of her mind. She threw the last towel at the heated rail, rushed downstairs into the kitchen, and reached for the yellow folder, pulling out the typewritten letter to the Will custodian. It was brief and to the point. It was also grammatically incorrect.

Dear Sir / Madam
I would like you to return my Will, which you have for
safekeeping, to the above address.
Yours sincerely

When it should, of course, have concluded with *'Yours faithfully'*.

Sarah shook her head. Maybe the Mary currently soaping herself in the shower would make that mistake, but not my mother-in-law! Had Mary written that letter? Or had someone else done it for her? Could that be the innocent explanation for the schoolchild error: that all Mary did was sign, failing to check the contents thoroughly before she did?

Her eyes dropped to the signature, and she peered critically first at *"Florence"* then the surname. Sarah was very familiar with the way Mary formed the letter F – with a distinct curl under the stem and two wavy lines across the top – she had seen that flourishing F on numerous occasions. These F's weren't quite right. Who would forge Mary's signature? There was only one person who stood to gain. The swindling little shit.

Freddy stood in the kitchen doorway; Sarah had her back to him, but she looked a little more herself this morning. The table was laid for three, he could smell toast and proper coffee, and she was bustling about with a letter in her hand and her usual in charge manner. Good! She kept denying it, but Freddy was sure something was wrong. Sarah was perpetually morose; if something was bothering her, why wouldn't she talk about it? She was uninterested in his research, or him, even their daughter was a bit overlooked: last night Mary had knocked on his study door and pulled up a chair to discuss her geography homework. Sarah was fixated on overcoming the problems with his mother's Will or the latest invitations to fund raising events for the charities she'd started supporting. Strange how Sarah's role was not dissimilar to that of seventeenth century ladies, who would spend their days tending to the poor and needy.

'Are you visiting sick parishioners today, darling?'

She turned round and started to giggle. That's more like it; she used to giggle all the time! 'We have social services for that now, Freddy. My, you're colourful. Are you lecturing today? You may wish to change if you are!'

'Eh?' He looked down at his scarlet shirt, then his purple trousers. They were both clean, pressed, what was her point? He'd wear his lime green corduroy jacket for the lecture, but not in the house!

'Look at this,' Sarah commanded, thrusting a letter at him.

He took the page and read it, keeping half an eye on Sarah who was pouring coffee into mugs.

'Don't you see? There's no way your mother wrote that letter,' she declared when he'd finished, pointing to the grammatical error with a teaspoon.

Freddy handed the letter back in exchange for a cup of coffee. Odd that his mother had made such a trite error, but at least Sarah was animated about something.

'And the signature – is that really hers?'

Freddy looked again at the looping letters, at the elongated F's; Sarah had a point, they weren't quite right.

'So, who do you think did write the letter?' he asked, sitting down at the breakfast bar.

Sarah raised her voice, spitting, 'Who do you think? Who is the only person who stands to gain if your mother's Will is destroyed?'

'I know this saga is a shock, but like the rest of us, my mother could make grammatical errors. We can't start accusing Mike of forging Ma's signature to withdraw her Will then destroying it. I'm not his biggest fan, but he's not a criminal,' he said.

'Freddy, you can't see evil when it stares you in the face, can you?' snapped Sarah.

'*Evil?* There must be an innocent explanation.'

She slammed a rack of toast in front of him, and Freddy knocked out a slice with his knife, spraying a scattering of crumbs around the toast rack. He pulled the top off a jar of marmalade.

'The question I can't answer is how the devil did he know there even was a Will?' Sarah demanded, snatching the marmalade jar off him. 'Let alone that she'd sent it away to a custodian and which one.'

Animated and angry. Freddy bit into his toast, watching Sarah use a teaspoon to scoop out several dots of butter from the marmalade, smearing them onto a side plate. He gazed down at his knife; was he responsible for the blobs of butter?

'He knew, all right. Harry told him,' explained Freddy, pouring milk over a bowl of cereal Sarah pushed in front of him. He would eat and run. 'It was at one of those peculiar dinner parties – you know, where we all dressed up in evening clothes and Mike darted about acting like the butler, serving us all and answering the bell if Ma decided she required something from the kitchen.' He spooned in some cereal, alternating with a bite of toast. 'Mike was complaining that Ma was becoming a tad aggressive, saying it was lucky we had put the power of attorney in place, claiming it was too late for a Will. Harry took great pleasure in correcting him.'

'That brother of yours should learn to keep his mouth shut!'

Freddy looked at the pool of milk at the bottom of the cereal bowl. He put the dirty bowl on his toast plate using the surplus sticky puddle of marmalade as an anchor.

'Just because he knew where the document was doesn't mean Mike did anything, darling,' he said, gathering up the cutlery and collecting everything on the table, freeing Sarah from the chore, placing it neatly in the leftover milk, then pushing the pile to one side. 'Motive and opportunity don't automatically lead to a crime.'

'Must you do that?' she snipped, snatching up the pile of dirty dishes, and turning to the sink. 'Most of that cutlery was clean, it was for Mary to use.'

'Fascinating how cutlery has evolved, isn't it? From the humble spoon to the fork and then knives. We all use knives now, but it was your Georgians who made them utilitarian.'

Sarah was staring out of the window – wasn't she interested, not even in the Georgians? 'Where are the two-pronged forks?' he asked. 'I haven't used one recently. And pewter plates, we never dine off them anymore.'

Sarah shot past him. What have I done wrong now?

He heard her call out from the utility room, 'Just taking last night's vegetables out to the chicks.'

Taking a last slurp of coffee, he collected his car keys and went to fetch his briefcase. Sarah was behaving most oddly.

Sarah rushed out of the house banging the utility room door behind her. Thank goodness it was her who had glanced out of the window and spotted the flicker of movement. She stalked over to where Nick was strolling round as if he'd been asked to pop over and mow the lawn, grabbed his arm, and marched him to the chicken pen, which couldn't be seen from the kitchen.

'How did you find out where I live? Did Mike tell you?'

'I don't need Darren to tell me where Professor Fetherston lives!'

'What are you doing here?'

Nick smirked at her, and then said slyly, 'Nice set up you've got here, Mrs. Fetherston. Big old stack must be worth a few quid. Going to invite me round for tea and croquet on the lawn?' He chuckled, 'Pretty handy for Exeter, mind.'

She unlatched the gate to her chickens and to avoid getting mud on her shoes, stretched out to scatter the vegetable peelings, shaking out the bag to dislodge the last stubborn few clinging to the inside.

'Don't get any ideas,' she said.

'I was just thinking maybe we could stash some gear here, much closer to the market?'

Sarah shouted back, 'In a word, NO.' She closed and latched the pen stuffing the empty bag in a pocket.

Nick was smiling at her, but there was malice not mirth in his expression. She bit back her anger, not wanting to fan the flames of his.

'That's a bit hasty, isn't it, Mrs. Fetherston? You've no idea what I have in mind yet.'

'Go, and don't come back. Leave me and my family alone!'

He winked at her. 'Maybe, but me mum always told me not to look a gift horse in the mouth.'

He lunged at her seizing her arm. She cried out as pain shot through her shoulder; he was twisting her arm up behind her back. He pulled her closer; she could smell the rank stench of an unwashed body.

'Ouch, get your hands off me.'

He was holding her arm so hard she was sure she'd have a bruise. She tried to wriggle free, but his grip tightened as he pushed her limb up towards her neck. His mouth was by her ear, she felt warm moist breath as he hissed, 'I come and go where I like, when I like. I'll be here when you're back from the school run, and whatever plans you've got, change them. You and I are going for a little drive again. You're in this up to your dainty little neck, so stop trying to boss me around.'

Sarah drove home from school slowly, stopping to let cars out of side roads, allowing buses to pull out in front of her and pedestrians to cross. Nick was bluffing, he wouldn't be waiting for her, and he wouldn't want an unenthusiastic amateur involved in his business.

She pulled into her driveway. Nick was perched on the edge of her log pile, a phone glued to his ear, a cardboard box at his feet. He stalked towards her car, yanked open the passenger door and placed the box as gently as if it contained eggs in the footwell.

'Took your time.'

He got in, bringing the stench of stale sweat with him. Sarah chewed her lip averting her eyes as he buckled up; he wasn't a big man, but his presence filled the car. She heard the click as the belt slotted into the buckle and slowly spun the car round.

'Drive towards Exeter.'

She did as she was told, but her hands were trembling, and her foot kept slipping on the clutch. There was a loud screech as she battled to change gear.

'If you want to draw attention to yourself, you're doing a fine job of it,' muttered Nick.

On the outskirts of Exeter, she was directed to a housing estate. She inched her way along a road lined with small houses, cramped together as if in mutual support against the bleak surroundings. She gawped at cracked windows, some with cardboard for curtains, untended front gardens littered with bulging bin bags. They passed a spruce lawn edged with borders planted with the same care and attention Mike lavished on the gardens at the Dower House – a little beacon of hope in a desert of despair.

'Over there,' Nick ordered.

Sarah parked. In front of her was an old sofa with a dog lounging on the soiled cushions. The dog bared its teeth. She tensed; she wasn't expected to leave the car, was she? There was a deep throated growl, then savage barking and spittle was flying from the animal's jaws. Sarah shuddered; Nick chuckled and got out. The front door opened and a short skinny man with his hands shoved in his trouser pockets and a hood drawn over his head shuffled down the path, yelling at the dog as he shambled towards the road. On the pavement, Nick spoke to him, slapping him on the back. The other man was grinning, except now he was closer Sarah could see he was only a child, no more than fourteen, little tufts of stubble dotted on his chin.

Nick got back in the car, shoving a wad of cash into the box at his feet.

'Left at the end of the road.'

The car didn't move.

'What you staring at me like that for?'

She put the car in gear. 'He's a child.' She spat.

'He's a lucky lad, he's got money.'

'I am not helping you criminalise children.'

'We both know what you did that night, Sarah,' he said. 'If you don't want the police to know, you can help with deliveries. Unlike me and me van, or me little green car no one questions a lady toff driving round dropping packets off in dark alleys.'

The car stalled.

'Just my bleedin' luck. How long you been driving? Get a move on we've four more drops to make and then I've got the day job to do.'

With shaky fingers Sarah turned the key. She was taken to parts of a city she thought she knew well that she didn't know existed: to boarded-up pubs and deserted playgrounds she wouldn't want to walk through, far less allow a child to play in. She took Nick to a nightclub, then an industrial estate and another young lad – he should be at school! Were these children intermediaries, running drugs further down the chain? There was nothing she could do. The drugs would be delivered with or without her assistance. She just needed to ensure she scrupulously obeyed the Highway Code.

Chapter Ten

In the flesh, Percy Wilson bore a remarkable resemblance to how Sarah had envisaged him: late thirties, of medium height, wearing a well-cut dark suit and wire-rimmed glasses. He was either blessed with fortunate genes or followed a strict diet and exercise regime. Was there an equally well-maintained Mrs. Wilson and maybe a fleet of mini-Percy's? As he bustled into reception, a legal notebook tucked under his arm, there was an air of calm confidence radiating off him.

Sarah and Harry rose when Percy invited them to follow him. He led the way into a boardroom, laying his notebook on the table. Sarah sighed; somewhere there was a lawyer dealing with the dead motorcyclist's affairs.

Percy was opening his notebook, smoothing down the pages.

'This is a slightly complicated situation. For the purpose of this meeting, I think we should assume the original Will no longer exists. Our goal must switch from finding that document to obtaining grant of probate on the copy we already have.' There was a pause. Percy was peering over the top of his glasses at Sarah. 'Probate is the term for acknowledging that a Will is legal. Once probate has been granted, we can gather and subsequently distribute the assets in accordance with the copy Will.'

Leaning back in his chair, Percy raised his right index finger.

'Let's explore the first possible line to pursue. Do you think Mike would agree to the copy of the Will being treated as if it was in fact the original?' he enquired, his eyebrows lifted as he looked first her way, then at Harry. 'If so, it would be quite straightforward – I would apply for grant of probate on the copy Will.'

Harry exploded. 'Not a chance! In fact, we think he's behind this whole charade and that he's been plotting to steal my inheritance for years.' Harry hissed the words, and then apologised. 'It's been a long drive down from Suffolk. I just wanted to be here in person, to make sure this is sorted out.'

Harry explained the family's suspicion that Mike had forged the letter recalling the Will and then intercepted the post and destroyed the document.

'He plans to take the lot, that's pretty obvious now.'

Why couldn't Harry learn to control his temper? Sarah assessed the lawyer's reaction to her brother-in-law's explosion. Percy was nonplussed; this wouldn't be the first family feud their lawyer had encountered.

'We think, initially the scoundrel was unaware there was a Will,' Harry continued. 'Thought he didn't need to do anything, and that she'd die and the whole fortune would fall into his lap. But then I stupidly told him, and where it was, too. Bit of a coincidence, isn't it? The letter recalling the Will being written a week after I told him all about it?'

Percy was drumming his fingers on the edge of the boardroom table, as if playing the piano. 'Hmmm, I agree it doesn't sound like that route is viable. I would encourage you not to distress yourself about what Mike might or might not have done with the original Will for now, Mr. Fetherston. I will explain why shortly. So, let's consider an alternative solution to our little conundrum. I know you won't like this, but we must accept facts. Mike is legally the next of kin. They were not divorced, and there did appear to be reconciliation as they purchased a house together subsequent to their separation. If she dies intestate, he is her sole legal heir. You could contest it, but ostensibly Mike would be entitled to the entire estate. For the family to inherit, it is imperative there is a valid Will bequeathing the estate to her sons.'

It was all bad news today. A tearful Penelope had telephoned while Sarah was crashing through the gears, trying to get to Percy's office on time after another impromptu delivery run with Nick. Despite Angus's allowance being stopped, somehow, he was still getting hold of dope. William had found it in their son's room on one of his snap inspections. Where was the money coming from? Sarah didn't offer her own theory – was Nick using the fifteen-year-old child as a runner?

Percy was still speaking.

'Secondly, it would appear she did not intend to die intestate. There is a Will, dated four years ago, of which we have a copy. Now let us assume that the original version of that copy Will no longer exists. It has either been destroyed or lost.' He was peering over his glasses again, but this time his eyes were trained on Harry. 'In your mother's case, I don't think it would really matter which, but Mike has told us he witnessed its destruction and so let us proceed on that basis. Thirdly, there is no suggestion she drew up a new Will subsequent to the one you have a copy of. Mike does say that she planned to do this, but he admits this never happened.'

'We've only his word on that,' Harry butted in, 'but I agree. Mike has never suggested there is a new Will.'

Percy took off his glasses, gripping them by a single arm and punching the air with them as if to emphasize the importance of his next point.

'Mr. Fetherston, I know you don't think your mother would have visited a Citizens Advice Bureau of her own volition and would have approached a qualified lawyer to amend her Will. Whilst I applaud the sentiment of supporting the legal community, these CAB centres are staffed with perfectly competent professionals; it is not a bunch of amateur do-gooders relying on the internet for their knowledge.'

Interesting. So, Percy believed Mike's CAB story. What if Mike drove her there, having sown the idea she should write a new Will?

'Whoever the deceased saw that day judged she lacked the mental awareness to draw up a new Will; judged that, sadly, the disease had progressed too far. Now that's a bold assessment to make, especially on, we are told, a first encounter. The advisor did not know her. He or she could not have detected there had been a significant deterioration from their previous meeting. So, it must have been a very easy conclusion to reach.'

What was Percy's point? Was the date Mary tried to write another Will significant? The lawyer was speaking again so she gave him her full attention.

'It is another of those legal phrases we always have in Wills.' Percy assumed a mock judicial voice, *'I, John Smith, being of sound mind.'* Then he reverted to his usual voice. 'The legal test, technically, is does someone possess sufficient testamentary capacity to sign their Will? Is someone in sufficient control of their mental faculties to understand fully what they are directing to happen with their estate when they die? Indeed, are they even able to comprehend the extent of their estate? Whoever she saw that day assessed that Mary Fetherston lacked the testamentary capacity to draw up a new Will.'

His glasses were off again, and he was squinting myopically at Sarah, sprinting for the punch line.

'If she lacked the testamentary capacity to draw up a Will, ergo the law says she lacked the testamentary capacity to destroy one,' he declared, stabbing the air again with his spectacles.

Sarah blew out a long 'Yes,' and turned to grin at Harry. Who would have thought it; she'd been rescued by the law.

From one of her dramas.

The ringing phone was leaning against a carton of flour. Earlier, Sarah had clumsily snatched a handful out of the box to sprinkle onto her pastry board, dropping some along the way, leaving a dusting of flour like a white cap, perched on top of the phone.

No caller ID.

What did they want now? She had given them a statement; they'd checked she hadn't forgotten anything; there was nothing more she could do. With this internal dialogue she'd managed to distance herself from what the police had told her three days ago: that they wanted to re-interview her.

Peeling her eyes away from the phone, she wound the pastry round her rolling pin, eased the load over to the baking tray and slowly unwound it over the pie tin, moulding the pastry to fit snugly against the sides. The phone bleeped. *Maybe it would be better to just come clean.*

Sarah busied herself tidying up: methodically brushing the unused flour into her palm; rinsing then stashing the dirty utensils in the dishwasher. It was no good; she had to know what they wanted. Wiping her floury hands on her apron, she retrieved a voicemail that erased all thoughts of pastry-making from her mind.

'Mrs. Fetherston, it's Sergeant Grindley. There has been a further development concerning the road traffic collision you were involved in. I would like to invite you to attend the police station for a voluntary interview. Please could you call to arrange this?'

And he left his phone number – twice. Your choice madam, come to the station voluntarily, or we will fetch you.'

That same afternoon, Sarah walked into the police station. The foyer was cramped, but then, this was hardly the place for a queue. There were three metal seats along one wall, bolted to the ground. A disheveled young woman in a baggy tracksuit sat in the middle seat, hunched over staring at her phone. She could have been there for hours, and had a dejected, almost lost look about her, as if she had given up expecting anything positive to happen in her life. Sarah pushed the bell, flicking her eyes over the other woman; she didn't want to spend a moment longer than she had to, Sarah didn't belong here.

Sarah moved to one side when she realised that standing in the middle of the counter was causing the automatic doors to reopen and whilst that didn't disturb her, the woman in the tracksuit was throwing Sarah dark looks each time the door slid open allowing in a gust of wind, and she didn't seem the sort of person who took kindly to being inconvenienced.

A smartly dressed woman appeared behind the reception desk, and Sarah told her – as if reporting her arrival for a cut and blow-dry – that she had an appointment with Sergeant Grindley. She didn't say but managed to convey with an elaborate display of switching off her phone and placing it in her designer handbag, that she was doing the sergeant a favour and did not expect to be kept long. She was shown into a room the size of a large pantry, with no natural light and entirely blank walls. Sarah took a seat on one of the two leatherette sofas and distracted herself by planning the rest of her day. She had arranged for Freddy to collect Mary from school as she had no idea how long she would be, supper was ready, but she still had to bake for a village hall fundraiser.

Grindley didn't keep her long. She was collected, led through to the body of the station, and down a flight of stairs to the interview suite where he showed her into another small windowless room where Matthews was waiting. Neither officer was smiling as they squeezed in after her and sat down, inviting Sarah to sit opposite them. Grindley turned on a recording machine and explained, 'For the record,' who was present in the room, adding, 'Mrs. Fetherston has agreed to a voluntary interview.'

She was told she was free to leave at any time, and that she was not under arrest. Sarah was offered the services of the duty solicitor or the ability to summon one of her own; she declined, fighting to keep her heart rate under control. Why would they think she needed either of those? For the second time in her life, Sarah was cautioned. Earlier, when she telephoned to make the appointment, Grindley had warned her that the interview would be recorded but he didn't tell her what the mysterious further development mentioned in his phone message was. Now he did.

'Mrs. Fetherston, the victim was wearing a camera on his helmet. His mother told us he always wore one. We couldn't find it at first, the accident dislodged it, but we kept searching and have now retrieved the file from the night in question and it appears to contradict your statement.'

Sarah's eyes flickered. She pictured rows of police officers with long sticks poking through the hedges and under clumps of grass like rescue workers searching for the black box flight recorder after a plane crash. She hadn't considered a dashcam on the biker's helmet! Her breathing started to accelerate; how clear was the film and what did it show?

'Can you explain to me the events leading up to the incident?'

'I already have.'

'I am going to play you the dash cam file and ask you some questions about what it shows. Before I do that, would you like to reconsider if you want the services of the duty solicitor?'

Oh shit.

'No thank you.'

'We are now showing Mrs. Fetherston exhibit ten, the dashcam file of the incident. Right, Matthews, let's go.'

Sarah saw her car hiccupping out of the back drive. She chewed her lip; Matthews paused the machine; his boss fired the questions.

'Is that you driving the motor vehicle, Mrs. Fetherston?'

There was no point denying she was the driver.

'Was there any mechanical problem with your motor vehicle that evening?'

What was the point of that question?

'No.'

The film restarted and she saw her car stationary in the middle of the road, the motorbike approaching, then veering round her car, then she saw Nick's oncoming vehicle.

Then the film stopped. The younger officer fiddled with the machine, addressing Sarah, 'The digital file has not been corrupted; it will be admissible in court.' The sergeant asked a barrage of questions, each one probing further into the murky truth of that awful night. How much trouble was she in? Should she just confess to her part in the death, give the family closure even though it wasn't entirely her fault? She'd had no idea her judgement was impaired by drugs she'd never intended to eat. But what would happen to her – and to Freddy and Mary – if she confessed, and what possible good could come from it? Sarah answered each question the only safe way she could.

'Why didn't you tell us you were obstructing the road?'

'No comment.'

'Were you under the influence of an illegal substance?'

'No comment.'

'Would you like to revise the statement you have given us about the events of that night?'

'No comment.'

Matthews joined the fun. 'Do you have anything more to say? Mrs. Fetherston, this is your opportunity to set out your defence.'

Neither of her interviewers was playing the role of 'good cop' as they pummeled her with questions. They would be familiar with, but they wouldn't like liars. She had not only lied but very nearly got away with killing someone through her thoughtless, careless actions. She didn't want to be uncooperative, but she couldn't risk incriminating herself. She had no idea how serious this was.

Grindley was speaking, his voice authoritative. 'I am giving you a special warning that this is your opportunity to tell your side of the story.'

Sarah didn't say a word, she didn't trust herself. What was a special warning?

'Mrs. Fetherston, we are going to report you for consideration of process.'

Sarah peered at the officer, screwing up her face. 'What on earth does that mean?'

The officers exchanged a glance, and then the sergeant locked his eyes on her. 'This is very serious, Mrs. Fetherston. You would be well advised to seek legal advice without delay.'

Sarah was escorted back to the foyer. The woman in the tracksuit was still sitting in the same seat and gave a slow nod as Sarah ran out with her head bowed, tears streaming down her face. She sat slumped in her car, sobbing. The front of her blouse was damp and still, drops fell from her chin like a leaking tap. She had no idea how dangerous this was – and there was no one to confide in. How could she tell Freddy what had happened today, when she'd yet to admit she hadn't just witnessed, but been involved in the accident? She hadn't even told him it happened by the back gate. She'd been so stupid. She deserved to be in trouble; but for her carelessness, someone might still be alive.

Chapter Eleven

Although positioned halfway down the vast dining room table, Sarah could still hear every word as Harry droned on about defeating his arch enemy and preventing a thief making off with the family fortune. The man on her left – who, until his attention was captured by their host, had been amusing her with tales of his beekeeping hobby – was now tuned in to Harry. Sarah wanted to be entertained: her mind deflected onto anything other than that ghastly interview, seeing her own stupidity displayed on that screen.

She gazed across at Freddy, resplendent in black tie. She preferred these dinners to be black tie affairs; not only did she enjoy dressing up, but it also prevented Harry from wearing his trademark – and in her opinion slightly ridiculous – bright red tartan suit. After fifteen years the joke was wearing thin. What will Freddy do when he finds out, she thought, and how could she explain why she hadn't been honest, either with him or with the police? At least Sarah now had another lawyer; maybe that lady could produce a rabbit out of her legal hat, just like her colleague Percy had done.

Freddy had commandeered his own audience at the other end of the table, and with the use of the condiments set – parts of which she suspected were doubling as Cromwell's model army, parts cast in the role of the doomed cavaliers – was narrating a story. The salt cellar was marched forward a few inches. The mustard pot rapidly followed. One of the women asked a question. Freddy ran his hands through his hair, teasing those lovely curls. He answered the woman's question, manoeuvring the salt cellar backwards and forwards. *Was she going to lose him?*

Sarah took a large gulp of wine, identifying the flavours to blot out Harry's whining voice. Horrid man. Plums, maybe liquorice.

'I will not let that common little man get away with this. You need to be bold to win and I will win.'

She took another sip, allowed her eyes to drift to the head of the table, mentally poking out her tongue at her host as she added vanilla to her list.

'I've chosen an excellent lawyer in this Percy Wilson,' declared Harry, draining his wine, and picking up the claret jug. 'Justice will be done!'

Sarah didn't like Mike any more than Harry, but Percy was confident the family would win, so Mike wouldn't be stealing anything. And how dare Harry claim credit for sourcing Percy!

Sarah peered closely at her host; his face was unattractively flushed. Was he slurring his words? If anyone had an excuse to get roaring drunk tonight it was her, not her brother-in-law, whose ugly booming voice was still dispensing legal advice to its attentive audience. He was drinking in the praise for standing up for his rights against the "upstart Mike". It sounded like Harry had been rereading his boyhood comic adventure books – he'd be referring to Mike as a cad and a bounder next. *I struggle to find any aspect of his character to respect or even like.* Both brothers were rooted in the past, but while Freddy semi-dwelled in the seventeenth century, at least he didn't expect the outside world to join him there. Whereas Harry acted out the life of a privileged Edwardian aristocrat and imposed his arrogance on everyone around him.

'I've spent my life defending this family's interests against Mike's persistent money-grabbing. I shouldn't be surprised by his latest antics. It's just so dull having to fight these people off all the time.'

'Sounds like this Mike has picked a battle with the wrong man,' said the beekeeper, returning his attention to Sarah.

Sarah didn't share this opinion of their host. She didn't want to embarrass Freddy, nor jeopardise future trips to Ashe Hall; Mary liked these Suffolk sojourns, sitting in the kitchen helping her aunt bake without being chastised for licking spoons and wiping fingers round gooey bowls. Sarah viewed visits to her in-laws as quasi-dress rehearsals; she would replicate these dinner parties in her own Ashe Hall someday, which would be decorated with Freddy's share of the family paintings. Earlier, she'd overheard Harry boasting about the value of the silver laid out along the dining table and pointing out *which* of their mother's paintings he intended to hang on *which* wall. Freddy had been non-committal; there was no point fighting yet. Let Percy work his magic before dividing the spoils.

In the morning, Amy asked Freddy to go for a walk, just the two of them. A low front had blown across East Anglia overnight, bringing a cold dampness. The pair shrugged themselves into jackets and boots stacked in neat rows in the back hallway, as if lined up for inspection. Amy opened the door and called out to the black Labrador, Claret, who was sitting rigid, her snout inches from the fresh air, her tail sweeping wide strokes across the floor.

They set off across the lawn, leaving a trail of footprints in the damp grass. The long border down one side of the lawn was ragged; gladioli leaned drunkenly against drooping hydrangeas dragged down by the weight of the overnight dump of rain. Claret cantered over, wandering in amongst the bushes and shrubs, her tail alternating between languid wags and bolt upright.

'I'm sorry Harry isn't being more grateful to Sarah for her help on the Will front. He is, really. We both are. You know what he's like, tends to play up his own importance when there's an audience!'

Freddy coughed. 'There's no need to apologise. I know my own brother!'

'Not as well as you think,' Amy turned to Freddy. 'The reason I singled you out for a walk is I've something to confide. Harry hasn't told you because . . . he doesn't know how to.' She paused, scuffing at the wet grass with the toe of her boot. 'The embarrassing fact is we need Mary's money quite desperately.'

Freddy coughed; he didn't know it was supposed to be a secret. 'It's OK, Amy. Harry told me all about your loan to buy Ashe Hall. He explained it's an interest-only mortgage and unlike ours you haven't paid off any of the debt yet.'

Amy gave a little moan. 'That loan was planned for. The wine scam was not. This gorgeous house,' she turned and waved her arms at his brother's home, 'is going on the market. We can't afford to live here.'

'What?!'

Amy brushed water off a wooden bench and sat down, inviting Freddy to do the same. He lowered himself slowly, trying to sit on his jacket, but felt the damp creeping through his trousers.

'Harry is a bit slapdash. He is either too trusting of people or else too embarrassed to ask the right questions. He's lost everything.'

'Everything?'

'Just about. He remortgaged this house. He took out a business loan which he personally guaranteed.'

Freddy stayed quiet. His brother was to lose Ashe Hall! Where would he hang the family portraits? Harry was destined to live in a grand house; he'd shrivel in anything modest like the Long House. He peeked at Amy. She had always been welcoming to him, but that hospitality was never extended to Sarah or Mary, allowing the two families to develop a bond. The transformation from relation to relationship had never occurred. Their bond was like a fully functioning lamp, bulb intact, plugged into the socket, but the electricity had never been turned on. Freddy didn't believe Amy and he were friends, and so he couldn't pry.

After a few moments, Amy broke the silence.

'Don't try and discuss this with Harry.'

'But where has the money gone?'

Amy looked down at her feet then back up at Freddy.

'How much do you know about buying wine en primeur?'

'Nothing. I don't visit shops unless they specialise in the seventeenth century. I think Sarah buys most of our wine from the supermarket.'

'Keep it that way, it's safer.' She paused, then said, 'This is so difficult to say kindly.'

'Just tell me.'

'Your brother has been a bit foolish. He invested hundreds of thousands of pounds into the en primeur wine market. You pay for wine up front, and pay for it to be stored in what's called a bonded warehouse, so you don't have to pay any tax: import duty, VAT. You gamble on the wine increasing in value. Sell when it does.'

'I never knew people bought wine without drinking it.'

'Oh yes! There's even a dedicated trading exchange. A buyer knows the wine's been stored in a temperature-controlled warehouse and can either keep it there as an investment or pay the taxes and have it delivered for drinking.'

Freddy stared sideways at Amy. This tale didn't make sense. 'Harry knows everything about wine. Has the market slumped?'

Amy shook her head, and stood up, smiling. 'The value of his investments rose spectacularly. He really does know what he's doing.'

'So, what's the problem? Have we been drinking the investment wines?'

Freddy saw Amy stare across at the crumpled border, then run her hands down her face. She spoke softly. 'When Harry tried to sell,' she stuttered, 'he discovered . . . he discovered there was no wine. His partner had stolen it.'

Freddy gaped at his sister-in-law; his eyes were wide. 'But he still has to repay all the debt?'

Amy called out to the dog which was patrolling the border.

'Yes, we are still saddled with all the debt. Your brother created his own Ponzi scheme. As the value of the wine went up, he borrowed against it to buy more which the horrid man stole too.'

'No wonder Harry keeps referring to Mike as a thief.'

'He didn't catch his business partner, but he is determined to catch Mike.'

Freddy couldn't take his eyes off the dejected face of his sister-in-law, her hand resting on the silky head of the trusting dog. Amy's life was in turmoil, through no fault of hers, yet outwardly there was little sign of distress. She had told her story unemotionally, sought no sympathy from him.

'Has he spoken to the police? Can't he get the money back?'

Amy swallowed. 'It's long gone. Our money has been financing this crook's lifestyle for over a decade. We are stony broke.'

It was Freddy's turn to swallow. He had to speak to Sarah about skewing the inheritance Harry's way; they didn't need the money like his brother did.

On Monday morning, Sarah stumbled downstairs after another sleepless night. She switched on the kettle, trying to focus her mind as she did most days, onto the Will drama. Untangling the messy web Mike had woven was complicated, but it was a welcome diversion from her other legal saga.

At their first meeting, Lesley Bridges, Sarah's criminal lawyer – who was a little taller and a little slimmer than her client and dressed in a dark blue suit – listened to her client without interruption. Sarah recounted the police interview, then her version of the events of the fateful night, watching Lesley scribbling furiously into a legal notebook as if finishing an exam question against the clock. Sarah stammered a little, recounting eating the resin-loaded brownie. The lawyer stopped writing and raised her eyes from her legal notebook, running a hand through her neat black bobbed hair.

'Cannabis resin in the brownie?'

'Yes,' mumbled Sarah.

'Was there any suggestion you would be charged with driving under the influence of an illegal substance?' Lesley asked in a flat, non-judgmental voice.

'No.'

'Are the police aware that you had consumed cannabis resin a few hours before the accident?'

'No.'

The lawyer probed. 'But you were under the influence of cannabis at the time?'

'Not intentionally.'

Lesley put down the pen. Sarah felt the lawyer's eyes settle on her.

'But you were aware of what you had ingested, and you still chose to drive, Mrs. Fetherston.'

Sarah shrank from the penetrating gaze that followed this statement, and then sat up, saying, 'That's a little harsh. I didn't mean to eat it, and I've never eaten cannabis resin before, so how could I judge how long it would take for the effects to wear off? I felt fine.'

Her lawyer inhaled, letting out a long sigh. 'I'm sorry, Mrs Fetherston, but that won't wash as a defence. It's the same as a drunken person claiming they didn't ask for their wine glass to be topped up. When you get behind the wheel of a car, it's your responsibility to ensure your judgement isn't impaired.'

'I'm not trying to duck responsibility, just explaining how it happened.'

She was treated to a long stare.

'Right, easy stuff first. The fact you haven't been arrested is not something you should take any comfort from. It's a technicality. You were there on a voluntary basis so they couldn't arrest you. It will be up to the Crown Prosecution Service to decide if you are charged with an offence.'

Sarah ran her tongue over her lips. 'Do you think that will happen? Should I just confess and take the punishment, what would that be?'

'Yes, I do think they will charge you. It sounds like they have a very good case to charge you with *Death by Dangerous Driving*. You should expect a summons in the post in the next few months.'

Sarah closed her eyes; Freddy mustn't open that letter.

'Ever been in trouble with the police before?'

Sarah shook her head.

'Any current points on your licence?'

'No.'

'How long have you had a licence, and have you ever had any points?'

'About twenty years, and no.'

Sarah could hear the faint scratching noise of the biro as Lesley made notes.

'All good answers, Mrs. Fetherston,' said Lesley. She put down the pen and favoured her with the same look Sarah had given Mary earlier when her daughter confessed to forgetting to do any of her summer household chores.

'Frankly, this is a very serious offence. Assuming you are charged, the trial will take place at the Crown Court, and I should warn you, it may result in a custodial sentence. It's not—'

'What!' Sarah exclaimed, her hand flying up to cover her mouth. 'Good God. I never thought it could be that bad,' she exclaimed through her fingers. She felt her chest heaving above her racing heart. How could she confess if they were going to send her to jail? No matter what Lesley said, she didn't feel totally responsible. Why hadn't Mike or Nick stopped her driving home that night? They dealt in the wretched drugs; they must have known she wasn't fit to drive? If she was jailed, she would lose Freddy; he would divorce her and take Mary; she would lose her whole life; no one would stand by her.

'As I was trying to say, it's not helpful that you lied in your first statement.'

'I don't mind being punished, but I didn't do this intentionally. I was the butt of someone else's joke. Please, I just want to avoid going to jail.'

'Step by step. I will ask for the dashcam file, check it's not corrupted, review it, and then we can meet again to plan out your defence – consider some character witnesses, come up with a credible explanation for your existing statement. Meanwhile, Mrs. Fetherston, be a model citizen. Don't put a foot wrong. Nothing. Don't even think about doing thirty-one in a thirty zone.'

Vivid images of white wigged judges in scarlet robes flooded her mind. She had a mental picture of Sandra in the witness box. No chance. Who could she ask to be a character witness? The list would shrink like woollens on a boil wash if the business of the drugs came out – genteel ladies don't mix with drug dealers.

Why weren't laundry accidents and domestic tussles her only problems? That's how it should be, as it always used to be before she'd got mixed up in the drug world. Now, standing in the kitchen Sarah watched the kettle come to the boil. She heard giggling and turned round to see Freddy and Mary walking into the kitchen together.

'We're both starving, Mum, what's for breakfast?'

Sarah groaned. She loved them both so much; *please don't separate me from them.*

After dropping Mary off early at school, Sarah drove straight to Exeter and her meeting with Percy. If Nick was loitering waiting for her return from the school run, he would be disappointed. It was so much more pleasant listening to Percy than Lesley. In his presence, Sarah was still the respected client soon to inherit a fortune thanks to his canny advice. The meeting was short. Harry dialed in from Suffolk and reported the results of his research into the value of his mother's estate.

'Mr Fetherston, the combined total is significantly above the inheritance tax threshold.'

Just now, that's the only quality problem I have!

'While we are talking about values, Mr. Fetherston,' Percy continued, 'is there anything amongst your mother's personal effects of individual significant value – any important family heirlooms? Fabergé jewellery? Chippendale furniture?'

'Can't be. There was a sale of the contents of the family estate in the sixties. The only stuff not put up for auction were sentimental things like family portraits. There were a few lots that didn't sell, but Ma never suggested they were valuable.'

Percy laid out a plan to get the court to grant probate.

'Mike seems to believe destruction of the Will entitles him to her estate. He is wrong, but let's not enlighten him. I suggest a letter from me, explaining this firm has been instructed to act by you and your brother as the executors of what is believed to be your mother's last Will. I propose to state that we have established the Will was returned and ask him to confirm he witnessed its destruction.' He switched his eyes from the phone to Sarah, as if seeking permission.

'Sounds like a good idea,' she said.

Percy had one more item on his agenda.

'We need the deceased's medical records subsequent to the dementia diagnosis. Mrs Fetherston, is that one for you?' His eyes were searching her face for an answer. 'What we want, is something from her general practice doctor, an expert whom the court can rely on, that backs up our allegation that at the time the Will was destroyed, she was no longer legally able to do so. Armed with this evidence, I would apply to the court for probate, and get us to the starting line.'

Sarah shrugged acceptance. What was one more item on her blasted list, at least he wasn't asking her to do anything illegal, unlike Nick who appeared to be in tune with her school run routine, each morning waiting by the little shed the family used to store their seasoned logs, then forcing her out on a delivery, threatening to change his statement if she refused. The irony was the police now knew what happened that night, but if she wriggled off Nick's hook that way, he might threaten to tell Freddy, and that was worse than chauffeuring him around Devon.

Chapter Twelve

Sarah was munching her way through a lunch of fresh poached eggs on toast – the yolks thick and a rich orange yellow, the sourdough crunchy – and reading Percy's latest email. There were three attachments: a draft letter applying for probate, a copy of a letter from Mike, confirming destruction of the Will, and a copy of a doctor's attendance notes, five days before the date the Will was destroyed, recording that his patient appeared confused about her address. Of greater concern to him – and useful for the Fetherstons – the doctor recorded Mary had no recollection she didn't have a car anymore, nor that she couldn't drive anyway, as, on medical advice, her licence had been revoked four months earlier.

Sarah dipped a forkful of toast into a yolk, declaring game, set and match to Mary. For Sarah, this feud was not between her and Mike but between her mother-in-law and Mike. Sarah was fighting Mary's corner, ensuring her last wishes were carried out; it was Mary's money, it should be distributed as Mary wanted.

She coughed, choking on a mouthful of food, dropping her knife and fork. There was a face pressed up against the window in front of her. The stranger leered in, then sniggered and walked away.

'What?' she exclaimed. This time it wasn't just Nick, there were two more mangy-looking men standing by her rose bushes. She pushed herself up and stalked into the utility room, past a basket of shirts now stiff as if starched, long past their optimum ironing point; she must get a grip of her life!

Once outside, she shouted, 'Nick, this has to stop or else I will call the police.'

'Don't bother. Trespass ain't a crime, darlin''

Nick's companions were huge, muscly arms sticking out from faded un-ironed t-shirts ending in enormous hands that hung loosely but managed to convey menace as if they were not used to lying idle. She kept her distance.

'Wanted to introduce you to some mates of mine.'

She exhaled slowly. 'I have asked nicely. Please just leave me alone.'

Nick held his hands up, as if surrendering, 'Hey, we don't need to disturb you, but you don't mind if we have a poke around, find somewhere discrete like to stash some gear.'

'There isn't anywhere. My husband and daughter would find anything you store here, so as I said before it's a no.'

'We'll be the judge of that, ta,' said one of the companions, running his eyes over her approvingly. 'You don't know what we're after, but I can show you how you can help me inside if you like, bored little housewife like you, fancy a bit of rough?' He grinned at her and rubbed his oversized hands down the legs of his trousers.

She took a step back as he moved towards her. Nick did nothing to stop him. The man was standing so close she could smell beer on his breath.

He lunged at her, snatching her wrist. She jumped back, catching her leg on one of the terracotta flowerpots and fell over. A jolt of pain shot through the side of her face. She could smell lavender. The man leaned over, she smelt beer again and his fingers clamped around her side, squashing her against the ground. The rancid smell of beer intensified, and she twisted her face away, wincing as it hit the pot for a second time.

Nick's voice rang out, 'Leave it mate. Enough. She's hurt herself.' He spoke slowly as if to a child, 'Now Mrs Fetherston is going to go back inside and leave us to finish off out here.' He paused, and then yelled, 'Aren't you?'

Sarah scrambled up and ran into the utility room, banging the door shut behind her. She tried to turn the key, but it jammed. She glanced up, through the glazed top of the door, straight into the face of the man who'd trapped her on the terrace. She jiggled with the key. 'Come on, come on, please just turn!' With slippery hands she wiggled the key, and then shouted 'Yes!' as she felt it slide into action. Sarah shot the security bolt and ran into the kitchen, slamming that door behind her too, and then groggily climbed the stairs to the bathroom, a palm pressed against her throbbing cheek. She pulled her hand away, taking in first her shaking fingers sticky with blood, and then staring at her face in the bathroom mirror; it didn't look much like the one she was used to seeing reflected back.

Sarah trooped back down to the kitchen but couldn't finish her eggs. She tried to concentrate on Percy's email, but her eyes kept being drawn away from the page out towards the three men casing her garden. If only she could speak to Freddy. She gently pressed against the plaster, releasing her fingers as the pain jolted through her cheek. What was Freddy going to say about her face? And what excuse could she give the ladies – when was the next meeting? This was ridiculous, that man was going to attack her and now she was concocting cover stories, sitting impotently watching a gang of drug dealers decide if her garden would become a staging post for the Exeter cannabis market.

She reread Percy's advice for the third time. Sarah lifted her eyes from the screen and muttered, 'thank goodness.' Three backs were walking away from the house. She got up, went to the corner window, and blew out a long breath. All three men were getting into Nick's car.

Sarah returned to her cold lunch, pushed the plate aside and read Percy's email for the fifth time. He was advising they copy the application for probate to Mike, to demonstrate to the courts that the only person likely to object was fully in the picture. Good advice! Would Mike consult a lawyer and see the Fetherstons in court? Or would he recognise he was beaten, and back off? Sarah wiped down the kitchen table, clearing away crumbs, and then paced the garden to check the three men really had gone. Would they return?

A few days later Sarah coasted down the drive of the Dower House. She could hear a high-pitched engine, and as she rounded the bend she spotted Mike by the border, pruning back a rambling rose with a pair of loppers. There was a small mobile wood-chipper at his side, and he was feeding culled branches into the jaws of the machine.

The family had cut their way through mountains of tortuous legal barbed wire, strand by strand, to free Mary's fortune. They were nearly there, and their success would force Mike out of this amazing house. She didn't like the man, resented what he'd done to her, but it didn't seem right to bear a grudge when Mike had spent years of his life ensuring her mother-in-law enjoyed the last few years of hers.

This wasn't just his home; it was a way of life, and he was going to have to leave it all behind. Why didn't he just ask for one last growing season? Even Harry might have agreed to delay putting the house on the market until the summer.

She switched off the car engine, the high-pitched noise stopped, and in the rear-view mirror she saw Mike put down the loppers and peel off his thick protective gardening gloves.

'Hiya. Long time no see,' he said, opening the door for her. His eyes widened.

'Sarah, whatever have you done to your face?'

'Oh silly me, tripped and fell on a flowerpot.'

'Ouch, bet that's sore!'

Sarah wanted to be inside, but Mike was keen to show her his harvest.

'I've peaches and nectarines. There're raspberries and blueberries.' He pointed to the south-facing wall. 'And there's going to be a bumper crop of plums and damsons. How's everyone at the Long House?'

Tense – that was the atmosphere at home. Sarah was constantly on the lookout for Nick or one of his goons, demanding she hide a carload of cannabis, or ferry them around, or worse that one of them would pick up where Nick had stopped that gross man who tried to attack her. And she couldn't speak to Freddy about any of it. Poor Freddy, he'd looked like he'd been hit with a medieval poleaxe when he saw her cheek swollen to double its normal size. She played down the injury, telling him the truth that she'd tripped over a flowerpot. She didn't tell him what caused her to trip, or that it was too painful to chew, claiming she wasn't eating because she wasn't hungry.

At nighttime she lay, heart racing, replaying in her mind those two short video clips. The one Mike messaged her then the one from the motorcyclist's helmet, each with the power to destroy her life. By protecting herself from the first, she'd allowed the second. Then, sleep became elusive; hours of tossing and turning fighting with the duvet, looking daggers at a slumbering Freddy, wanting to scream, 'Why can't I sleep!'

Now watching Mike reach up behind a net curtain and pluck a peach, she was honest. 'I'm having trouble sleeping. Ever happen to you?'

He handed her the peach, and she brushed the warm downy skin then bit into the pale, creamy flesh. She was planning to ask him to get Nick to back off, how could she broach the subject?

'Nah. Out like a light, me.'

A dribble of peach juice escaped down Sarah's chin; she wiped away the stickiness with her fingers. The door to the Walled Garden opened. Sarah swiveled round to see Nick saunter in, wearing the same crumpled trousers. Did he own another pair?

'Hiya, all. Thought I could hear voices. I'm off to Bristol, thought I'd stock up before I go.'

Sarah fixed her eyes on the greenhouse. At least he wasn't suggesting she chauffeured him.

'You've got your own key to the potting sheds,' muttered Mike.

'We're getting a bit low on supplies. When you picking again?'

Mike grunted and walked towards the polytunnels, leaving Sarah alone with Nick.

'I presume you're going to stop pestering me now you've poked around and seen there's nowhere to store any of your stuff?' asked Sarah, politely.

He grinned, bouncing on the balls of his sneaker-clad feet. 'Lovely shiner you've got there,' he said, angling his head at hers. 'Yeah, you've no bloody outbuildings, have you? Odd for an old house.'

'I did tell you,' she said crisply, taking a step further away, repelled by the sharp whiff of stale sweat. This man needed a shower, but at least she could stop worrying about becoming a storage depot and that hideous man who threatened her wouldn't be calling again.

Mike poked his head out of the black plastic and called over. 'I'll do some picking later today.'

'You staying to help with the harvest?' jested Nick. 'Or too busy with the charity stuff to do an honest day's work?'

'It's hardly honest, is it, Nick? And it's none of your business what I do.'

'Touchy madam, ain't ya?'

'Mike, it's jolly hot,' she said. 'Might I have a glass of water?'

Thankfully Mike took his cue. 'I can do better than that. Come in for a glass of homemade lemonade.'

Lemonade was served in the morning room, where Sarah wanted to be, not in the kitchen, reminding her of the cannabis resin. He loaded a green plastic tray covered in a pattern of bright yellow sunflowers with a jug, glasses, and a plate of puffy macaroons, and carried it through the octagonal hall into the morning room, setting the refreshments down on the butler's tray. The flashy plastic was incongruous, jarring with the beeswax-polished surface. Sarah stood by the window, assessing the garden, and listening to the clink of ice, as behind her Mike poured drinks.

How often had her mother-in-law stood admiring this same view? Mike handed her a glass, and she took a sip. It was sweet, lemony, and slightly creamy, with no bitter aftertaste: nothing like the cans Mary drank.

Sarah sat in the chintz armchair, recalling her last visit nearly a year ago. The same pictures hung on the wall; the chinoiserie papier mâché spill vases sat either end of the mantelpiece; Mary's sewing box waited like an obedient spaniel next to her chair. Everything looked the same, but it wasn't. Opposite her should be Mary: perched, ankles crossed, sitting erect; not Mike: slumped, legs splayed out.

'Mike, I wanted to ask you to do something for me, help me out.'

Sarah jumped, bashing her lip on the side of her glass. Someone was hammering on the window behind her. She turned round to see Nick's face smudged against the glass.

Mike got up. 'Wait here. I'll deal with him, luv.'

The door to the morning room opened a fraction, and Nick leaned round.

'Engines packed up again.'

She glared at him.

'So, when you've finished your drink, I need a lift.'

'I don't have time.'

'Well, make time.'

'I'll drive you, Nick,' offered Mike.

Nick shook his head. 'I like the way Sarah drives.'

Two hours later, sitting in the driver's seat, on the edge of an industrial estate in Bideford, Sarah accepted she was becoming horribly familiar with Nick's route round Devon. His patch stretched from

Taunton, just inside the Somerset border, across to the North Devon coast and back down to Exeter. The drop-offs were usually quick. She hovered like a getaway driver as he met his customer, before hurtling off, quickly moving up through the gears. She tried not to watch the handovers – she didn't want to see or be seen – but glancing down an alleyway in Taunton she saw Nick's contact and did a double take; *surely that isn't?*

At least the Bideford stop was the end of the line. Nick was running back over the road and Sarah braced herself for the smell, winding down her window. He got in saying, 'Last stop now. I'll give directions. Left at the roundabout.'

'I thought that was the last stop,' she grumbled, opening her window a little further then putting the car in gear.

She sat in silence, following Nick's directions. Ten minutes later she saw the gates of Mary's school; a stream of cars she would normally be part of was indicating to turn in. Sarah held her breath, releasing it only once safely past the entrance.

'Next left, then pull up over there by that line of recycling bins.'

Her heart was pounding as Nick got out of the car and jogged down the back entrance to her daughter's school.

Chapter Thirteen

The authorities were not as impressed with the doctor's attendance note as Sarah was. 'As I see it,' explained Percy, 'they are taking the easy line. We have given them proof the deceased lacked testamentary capacity at the pertinent point. They have decided they don't want to be responsible for assessing that proof.'

Sarah was listening to the lawyer from the comfort of her deckchair, with one eye on Mary and two friends who were retracing a complicated dance routine on the lawn, counting out their steps to the beat of the music. It was quite exhausting just watching the twists and jumps. One of the girls was a little slower, tripped up, and then all three collapsed against each other, panting, and laughing in a jumble of arms and legs.

Percy was still speaking, 'I think that, rather than assess the evidence, they want to be told by an expert your mother-in-law lacked capacity. I am sorry, but I think you are going to have to commission an independent expert to write a report on the deceased's mental faculties at the date she withdrew her Will.'

Sarah's eyes swept across her lawn, taking in the sectioned-off vegetable plot and the children's play zone long since shorn of the chunks of brightly coloured plastic that had once decorated the grass; a surviving swing hung limply from the branches of an oak tree, the ropes frayed after a decade of rain – Mary hadn't sat in it for years. Although more demanding of Sarah's time, back then, Sarah had felt more in control mothering a small child than as the parent of a teenager. The girls had switched to lying down: listening to the music with their backs on the grass, propping themselves up on their elbows, their faces turned up to the August sunshine.

Percy rumbled on. 'Having reviewed the medical records myself, I do believe an expert will conclude that, on the balance of probabilities – which is the threshold in a civil case – your mother-in-law lacked the requisite testamentary capacity.'

Back to the future, another roadblock to navigate her way around.

Percy rang off, but as soon as he did, Sarah's phone sounded again,

'Penelope!' she said.

There was a tiny gulp, then a sob.

'Penelope?'

Her friend fought to control her emotions, and then spluttered out, 'It's Angus.'

Sarah listened to a few soft moans, imagining her friend's eyes screwed up and a hand fiddling with her Alice band.

'What's happened?'

'He's been beaten up. He came home for the weekend; we only let him out for a walk and he . . .' There was more gulping as Penelope told how they were sure he'd been attacked, but he claimed he'd not been looking, tripped up and hit a lamppost. 'I know he's lying; William says he's clearly been hit and not just by fists. What's he mixed up in? Why won't he talk to me?'

It was Sarah's turn to gulp. She'd been right, that delivery out near Taunton, it was Angus she'd seen. Nick and his goons were using her friend's son as a drug mule, and it appeared that Angus had done something to upset them. She must talk to Mike and beg him to get Nick to find someone else. The boy had only just turned sixteen. What could she say to Penelope?

'Do you think perhaps Angus just upset a rough crowd round here, and was punched for being a toff?'

Her friend tutted. 'I can't think how, unless that's where he's been getting the drugs from. I'm scared to let him out of my sight. If only he'd talk to me. I keep telling him I won't be angry, but he knows his father will be, he's just clammed up.'

'Perhaps he would talk to me, as outside the family?'

There was a short silence. 'It's an idea, isn't it? Let me ask him. Thanks, Sarah.'

As she hung up the phone, she heard a car's tyres scrunching on the gravel drive and heaved herself out of the deckchair. Inside, she paused to quickly rifle in the utility room drawers for a tube of sun lotion, keeping an ear cocked for the doorbell. Locating the sunblock – thankfully still in date – and wondering why she hadn't been summoned, she went through to the front door and opened it, but there was no one outside.

She closed the door, and spotted an envelope on the doormat, with her name misspelt, written in slightly crooked childlike capital letters. She used a fingernail to slit the top and pulled out a torn scrap of paper.

I KNOW ABOUT THE TRIAL. BUY A GARDEN SHED WITH A PADLOCK.

A medical expert was appointed, and a few weeks later the report was ready, tempting Sarah when she downloaded her emails on returning from a meeting in Exeter. There was also an email from her other lawyer; the subject, *'update on process'*. Sarah didn't open that one. She checked there was sufficient paper in the printer and unpacked the groceries to the whirr of the machine as the pages of the medical report chugged out; all forty of them.

She stowed the food neatly in the fridge. Why was she being so careful? It wouldn't take long before chaos reigned. The four-pack of yoghurts would be ripped apart by the Long House tooth fairy: no one ever admitted to a fridge crime. No doubt the surrounding cardboard would be abandoned for someone else – aka Sarah, the only one who cared – to clear away. The rigid containers for grapes and berries would gradually empty, save for those last bruised, unappealing fruits left, squashed, with the remaining plastic, for her to deal with, too. No one else appeared to mind the fridge contents being dispersed as if a tornado had whipped through.

Armed with a mug of coffee and a biscuit, Sarah settled at the breakfast bar with the report in front of her. Someone needed to understand the evidence, and she didn't trust Harry; he would skim-read. The initial pages were devoted to the author's impressive credentials in the field of treating dementia patients. Percy had explained that this would provide reassurance that a qualified expert was advising that probate was granted. There was also a secondary purpose; those credentials should convince Mike he would be wasting his money questioning the report.

The expert had spent decades treating patients like Mary. Would that be a rewarding career? Wouldn't it be frustrating, knowing that all you could do was delay the inevitable, that you could never offer any real hope? Wouldn't it be soul-destroying to witness the gradual transformation – as Sarah had with her mother-in-law – as the cruel disease robbed its victims of their dignity, being the expert but powerless to intervene?

She got up and retrieved the biscuit barrel, then pushed the jar to the back of the cupboard, out of sight. She nibbled as she read on. Once past the author's CV, Sarah started to relive Mary's decline, and there was no sugarcoating. Was it necessary to read the entire document, could she skip to the conclusion? She jumped off the stool and walked to the bank of cupboards, reaching in and easing the cookie jar back out of its hiding place and refilling her coffee cup whilst she was up.

Sarah took another slug of coffee and progressed into the deterioration of Mary's mind, a stark medical description of what was happening to her mother-in-law's brain as Mary lived out her last years at the Dower House, enjoying those family dinners and the little girly talks in the morning room. Sarah was prying into the gritty detail of a distressing slide downhill. Having to read the report did nothing to assuage her guilt. She was intruding. Mary had always involved herself in the health and wellbeing of her sons and that of both of her daughters-in-law – even when they were all middle-aged – but this was a one-way street: discussing her own ailments had been out of the question.

Mary's life in those weeks leading up to the withdrawal of her Will, were recorded in regular trips to the doctor's surgery. Alongside records of mundane visits for minor medical issues was documented the gradual eroding of Mary's faculties. Each attendance note assessed how the disease had progressed. All those anxiety attacks, in those last months before she was sectioned – had the relationship between the two occupants of the Dower House altered? Were Freddy's fears correct – had his mother been controlled by Mike?

Sarah's mug lay abandoned. She poured the cold coffee into the sink, adding water to wash the congealed mess down the plughole with brisk strokes. Looking up, she gazed at the new garden shed, delivered earlier in the week, and poked her tongue out at it. How long would it be before Nick asked for a key to the padlock? Freddy hadn't questioned the need for a padlock, didn't question Sarah's sudden desire for a shed, either just told her to order one.

'Get the size you want, the one that will make you happy.'

Did he long to add "again" at the end of that sentence?

Maybe this report was the tonic she needed, to put her back onto a path that would solve her problems and restore her happiness. Their expert concluded that, on the balance of probabilities, Mary lacked the testamentary capacity to destroy her Will. This was the final chapter in the Will saga, Mike would be forced to accept the copy Will as legal, but the war with Mike had become a constant reminder for Sarah of a diminished Mary. She wanted to recall the lady in her prime, not the person she became. She closed the report and filed it in her yellow folder.

Sarah clicked on Lesley's email. Her criminal lawyer reported she was waiting for copies of a few technical reports but suggested a meeting. Lesley expected her client to be charged and she was encouraging her to come clean with her family, pointing out how much harder it would be to explain if they were unaware of the trial, and she was found guilty. Sarah had no intention of following this last piece of legal advice.

Sarah glanced up at the kitchen clock: time to collect Mary. She grabbed her keys and was selecting a jacket when her eyes spotted an envelope on the doormat. She grimaced, slowly opening the flap.

THERE'S A BAG IN YOUR GLOVE BOX. THE GROUNDSMAN STEVE WILL MEET YOU AT THE BACK GATE 3.30. DON'T BE LATE

Harry had been badgering his brother about collecting their mother's furniture, claiming Mike would steal and sell the more valuable pieces. He didn't offer to do anything; just moaned. He was pushing the unwelcome problem round his plate, like a toddler discovering a strange vegetable hidden under the pasta, hoping it would miraculously disappear with enough poking. Finally, exasperated, Sarah called Mike, smiling when he suggested the boys collect Mary's bits and pieces and get rid of the clutter. If he accepted the family was entitled to the furniture, he wouldn't be contesting the experts report. Mary's wishes would be honoured.

Escorting them into the drawing room, Mike offered to make tea.

'We're in a hurry,' spat Harry.

Freddy shot him a look.

'But thank you for offering,' added Harry in a neutral tone.

'I'll leave you to it then,' said Mike. 'You know your way around.'

'We do,' Harry replied, turning his back on the older man, and removing a landscape from the wall.

Mike looked at Sarah, who shot her eyes heavenwards, allowing herself a faint smile. She followed Mike out, muttering to him, 'Wouldn't have hurt him to wait for you to leave the room before he starts to denude the house!'

Sarah wandered through the reception rooms alone, mentally arranging her own furniture and envisaging it where Mary's stood, ear marking a few items she wanted to keep. The brothers marched past her in the octagonal hallway, a rug slung between them. Harry was either being alarmingly thorough or vindictive; time to save the curtains, she thought.

She was sitting in the drawing room – its walls now forlornly marked with dark rectangular patches of wallpaper where pictures had recently hung, protecting the paper from the bleaching sun – when Mike walked in.

'Got a moment, luv?' he asked, closing the double doors behind him.

'Harry's being spiteful today. Sorry.'

Mike flicked his hands up, as if shaking a duster. 'That's our Harry, a spoilt brat who's never grown up. Needs a good punch in the gob from life, that one!'

An image of Ashe Hall popped into her mind; Mike would roar with laughter if he knew Harry had to sell his pride and joy.

'Nick says the cops have been to see him again.' He pulled a quizzical face. 'They want him to review his statement, says there's going to be a trial, he's not sure what to do. Thing is, they haven't arrested him. Do you think he should speak to a lawyer?'

That explains how Nick knew about the trial – lucky him, he's not the accused. It was Sarah who'd been summoned to appear at the magistrates' court to answer the charge of causing Death by Dangerous Driving. Sarah chewed her lip for a few moments. 'It's not good to change your statement, he shouldn't do that.'

'But why have they suggested he might want to? That's what neither of us understand – what do they think he got wrong?'

Freddy was calling her from the hall, asking for a hand. *Damn.* 'I can't talk. Let me finish up here, and then I'll come and find you in the Walled Garden. I've something I'd like to talk to you about.'

She tracked Freddy's voice down. The men were in the dining room either side of a partially dismantled table: the middle leaves stacked against the wall. The brothers had already taken down the family portraits and were attempting to divide them. There were two piles either side of the fireplace. Most, including the cavalier, were still waiting to discover where their next home would be.

'Last room now. Help required, please, darling,' announced Freddy.

Harry dumped one of the brass fasteners that anchored the wooden leaves into place onto the marble mantelpiece. Sarah picked them all up winding bubble wrap around to create a parcel, then taped it securely to a table leg. This was her table; pieces were not going astray.

Harry's phone rang, and he left the room to take the call.

'While he's gone, darling, can we talk about Ma's pictures?'

She went to stand beside Freddy. He linked his fingers through hers; his thumb stroking her palm, as together their eyes ran over his ancestors.

Here we go, did she really want to witness this?

He gave a short laugh. 'This has been a family joke for decades. Any of them you particularly want?' he asked, squeezing her hand.

'They're your family, darling, I shouldn't be involved. But I have become rather attached to Uncle Tom. Make sure you fight for the ones you want, like him,' she said, pointing at the cavalier. 'Don't allow them all to end up with Harry.' She bit her tongue to stop herself adding 'After all, he won't have a proper dining room to hang them on.' She reached up and kissed him. 'I'll go and find Mike so we can say goodbye.'

She swung open the door to the Walled Garden, and peered round.

'Mike,' she called out, softly.

'Over here, luv. Just spraying for weeds, while there's no wind.'

He wound the protective plastic gloves down to his wrist, and then wriggled them off, inside out. 'You lot done?'

'Pretty much, just the family portraits. I want to ask you something. Could you have a word with Nick, I think he may be using a teenager called Angus?'

'For what?'

'As a runner for distribution.'

'Not really my side of the business, luv.'

'I know, but the boy's only just sixteen,' she pleaded. 'Can't you ask Nick to find someone else?'

'Know him, do you this lad?'

'He's the son of a friend of mine.'

'Ahh. I can speak to Nick. But I can't promise anything.'

'Thanks.'

Taking their leave of Mike was awkward. Sarah stood aside while the brothers shuffled uncomfortably – like schoolboys forced to apologise to a neighbour for playing with their ball too loudly. The Will dispute hung unmentioned between them. The removal works now complete, there was no furniture to hide their distrust behind. How did you say goodbye to a person who used to be part of your family – someone you'd shared Christmas lunch and other celebratory meals with – whom you were unlikely to ever meet again, unless it was in the law courts? Eventually the brothers' manners got the better of their evident dislike of Mike. Shaking hands formally and murmuring 'thank you' and 'see you soon', the brothers backed out of the room, as if concerned Mike might attack them from behind if they didn't keep an eye on him.

'That's probably the last time we'll visit this house, Freddy,' Harry said as they steered their hoard towards the Long House.

'It was the right decision to buy it. She was happy there, Harry,' Freddy replied.

'So was Mike. He won't be happy once we evict him, which shouldn't take too long,' promised Harry. 'Wonder if he'll stay in Devon.'

Sarah didn't join the discussion about Mike's dilemmas; she had her own. If Mike knew about the trial, should she tell Freddy? That was lawyer Lesley's advice, who had no good news, and plenty of bad. Lesley had reviewed the dashcam file, and in her opinion, it was compelling evidence. It hadn't been corrupted and it was very clear. She was still waiting for a copy of the victim's blood samples, but that was not unusual, they'd turn up.

From the driving seat, Harry was crowing about the family beating Mike.

'He's going to get such a shock when old Percy tells him to clear out. How long shall we allow him to pack up his horrid little flat-pack furniture?' chortled Harry, turning into the driveway of the Long House.

'Don't be cruel. We never understood why, but Ma chose him,' said Freddy. 'Anyway, no point having a dog and barking ourselves, let's rely on our lawyer – Percy will tell us what's reasonable.'

Sarah opened the van door and jumped down onto her driveway. Yes, Freddy was right, she should rely on her own expert, Lesley, and stop worrying about the trial. This was only a first stage, to transfer the case to the Crown Court. There was plenty of time for a miracle.

Chapter Fourteen

Freddy slammed the tailgate shut, banged the side of the van, and waved at the wing mirror. His brother waved back, and the van pulled away. Freddy cast his eyes over his share of the family portraits propped against the closed garage doors. He crouched down and stroked the side of the cavalier's face, tracing his finger over the moustache of his ancestor. He heard the front door open and glanced up. Sarah was standing wiping her hands on her apron.

'Has he gone already? He didn't even say goodbye! I was going to make him a sandwich for the journey.'she said.

'He got a bit tetchy divvying up Ma's stuff. In fact, he was downright greedy; we didn't part on the best of terms.'

She was walking towards him, and he stood up, put an arm around her waist. She pulled away.

'You got him then!' Sarah said, smiling at the cavalier.

'I got them for you too.' He said pointing to his great uncles. 'Sarah, what's wrong? Please tell me what's bothering you, it can't just be Ma's Will, that's what's on my conscience, it shouldn't be on yours.'

A gnawing sense of failure had been tugging at Freddy's conscience for weeks. He'd become disturbed by memories of those anguished calls in the months running up to his mother being sectioned and was starting to question his reaction to his mother's pleas for help. That summer, was his mother more in control of her mind than the family assumed? Had she been fighting to keep her fortune? Had Mary known Mike had recalled her Will, and suffered the humiliation of Mike destroying it, powerless to write another? If Freddy had been more suspicious about what was really going on at the Dower House – been more supportive of his mother, and questioned what Mike was doing instead of automatically siding with him – could he have prevented his mother enduring the dreadful experience of being sectioned and sent to that clinic?

He took both of Sarah's hands in his, waited until she rasied her eyes to his, then said. 'I know you fought tenaciously but you've done your best, what will be will be – don't let it trouble you.'

She gazed up at him, 'Shall we get your family inside, and up on the walls?'

'Sure, there's nothing troubling you? You would tell me wouldn't you, Sarah? You know you can tell me anything, darling.'

She closed her eyes and whispered. 'I'm fine, just got a lot on.'

He leaned down and kissed her. Her lips lingered on his, and when he drew away and opened his own eyes, hers were still shut as if replaying the memory of the intimacy.

Sarah looked up at him and said, 'I am determined to win this Will battle for your mother.'

'Mike has not covered himself in glory over this saga, has he?' said Freddy, picking up a picture and hugging it to his chest. 'He's not given much thought to the family.'

He carried his ancestor inside and propped the picture against the wall then walked back out and picked up Uncle Tom. Sarah was carrying a smaller portrait, saying, 'I think Mike may be a bit colder and more calculating than we've previously given him credit for.'

'I hope you're wrong, darling.'

If Mike had conducted the same research into dementia as Freddy had, Mike would know the significance of a patient being sectioned. The Council picked up the cost of the residential home. Had Mike – thinking he was to inherit his mother's fortune and wanting to preserve it – connived in dispatching his mother to the ignominy of the clinic like an eighteenth-century husband disposing of an unwanted spouse?

A week later, Sarah was sitting on grass still damp with morning dew. In front of her, dark green hedge clippings lay amongst the flowers and shrubs waiting to be raked up and wheeled to the composting pile. She peeled off her gardening gloves to release her hot sticky hands and reached into her jacket pocket for her phone. Shielding her eyes against the sun, she saw there was an email from Percy. She opened the message, read it, then dropped the phone in her lap and leant back, her eyes closed. She let the sun fall on her face: feeling its warmth, seeing the red hue behind her eyelids, and recalling her mother-in-law helping her plan the outside space. Not just this border but a rejuvenation of the whole plot, transforming a lawn surrounded by low-maintenance, forgiving shrubs – azaleas, rhododendrons, and a lilac tree – into a family garden.

Mary had drawn up a proper plan, with Latin names for the plants, allocating space for the main flower border, another for raised vegetable beds, a space for children to play, and an area for adult summer drinks with a view of the flowers from May to September. Now they would be leaving all this behind; at last, probate had been granted, and the family could afford to move house.

Sarah stood up swiping at the seat of her trousers to check for moisture, then collected her sheers and gloves and went inside, leaving the laurel clippings where they lay. She surfed the internet, with a calculator by her side, printing out pictures of possible alternatives to the Dower House and trying to gauge what the Long House was worth. It was a weird sensation; this time her search wasn't daydreaming. Her family could afford these houses! Finally, the last piece in the jigsaw; no more bowing and scraping, she could sit at ease at those meetings. Less exciting for her in-laws – their slice of the money would only buy them breathing space with their creditors – but Harry had been the architect of his own downfall.

In the evening, Sarah heard the front door slam shut, then Freddy calling out, 'Darlings! I'm home.'

She opened the kitchen door and popped her head out. 'Supper ready in ten minutes. We're having a pasta bake. Fancy a glass of wine? I've put out the last bottle of that special claret your brother recommended?'

'Lovely, and yes, please. Are we celebrating something?'

She left the door open, conscious of the pungent smell of fried onions permeating the house.

'Darling,' she called. 'Hold the front page, probate has been granted on your mother's Will.'

She heard footsteps, felt his lips on her neck, and the tension eased out of her body.

'Well done,' he said. 'That was a bruising battle!'

She turned round, slotted herself into his arms for a proper kiss.

'Later,' he promised, releasing her.

She closed the kitchen door he'd left open and watched him cross to the pine table. A flower arrangement stood on top: a polished silver rose bowl with late yellow roses billowing over the sides. The silver candlesticks – equally shining – a gift from his mother, sat on either side of the flowers. Linen napkins were folded next to the two-pronged forks, and pewter plates beside them. Freddy picked up the wine glasses, carrying them over to the cupboard used to store glassware. He put them down, and pulled out several others, took a step back and examined the collection. Sarah shook her head – she should have saved time and put all the wine glasses on the table.

There was a clattering noise as Mary danced into the kitchen and slumped in a chair. Her shoulders were close to parallel with the table, her arms dangling down either side.

'Forgotten how to sit properly, little one? Or did someone shoot you while my back was turned?' enquired Sarah, tossing a green salad.

The teenager altered her position, slightly. It was a token adjustment. Sarah pulled out the baking tray. One night off discipline wouldn't hurt. Tonight, the persistent tightness in her chest had dissipated. The Will battle was over; she had handed over a key to the shed to Nick but given him the wrong one – his would unlock her oil tank. It was a small gesture, he would soon find out, but it still gave her a warm glow. There was the trial hanging over her, but she wouldn't think about that tonight.

Freddy was still examining glasses, holding each one up to the light, twirling the stems.

'I'm ready to serve here,' she announced, tapping the side of the dish with a spoon.

'Won't be a moment, darling. You two start if you're hungry.'

Over dinner Mary talked of school life. The teenager's jolly, lilting voice was the perfect entertainment for a celebratory meal and the parents chuckled at her silly jokes. The adults lingered over the wine, chewing over the implications of the inheritance long after Mary had departed to enjoy a virtual world in her bedroom.

'What happens next?' Freddy asked.

'In a nutshell, Percy gathers the money together and pays it out to you and Harry.'

'How long does that take?'

'Shouldn't take more than a few weeks. He has the relevant information. The tricky asset is the Dower House, which is the bulk of the estate.'

The wine had loosened her mind, they were so lucky to inherit all that money. The family could move to a Georgian gem; their first move – how exciting! Sod the trial. She couldn't do anything to alter the outcome, and if only she could stay out of jail, she'd readily accept her punishment. Lesley had called to tell her the victim's blood tests had turned up. Not to be dwelled on tonight.

'The plan is to sell the Dower House,' said Sarah, running her finger round the edge of her wineglass, making a humming noise.

'Mike won't like that, being turfed out of his garden.'

'He doesn't have the money to buy us out, even if he wanted to, so he will have to move.'

Lucrative though his farming enterprise was, she couldn't believe Mike had enough capital to stay, and even if he had amassed over a million pounds –the amount he would need to buy Mary's seventy-five per cent share – no English lawyer would accept payment in a cryptocurrency without proof it had been earned legally.

'Your brother has no sympathy. He says Mike's been squatting while we unraveled the mess he created.'

Sarah had told Harry not to be so spiteful; the family had won. But her brother-in-law had scoffed at her.

'Not likely! Let's send the rascal a bill for rent. I refuse to feel sorry for him. He'll have plenty of money to buy somewhere more appropriate; he doesn't belong in a house of that stature, anyway.'

Maybe Mike didn't, but she and Freddy certainly did!

'Once we've had the Dower House valued, can we suggest to Harry we move there, instead of selling? I think we'll find the Long House has appreciated very nicely.'

She watched Freddy, swirling the wine appreciatively around in his glass, sniffing at the delicate aroma, then sipping gently, rolling the wine around his mouth as Harry had taught him to.

'Let's think about it, darling. Let Percy write to Mike.' He chuckled and then added, 'I don't think Mike has ever been taught how to behave in a gentlemanlike manner when you lose, so stand back, there's going to be an explosion from the Dower House.'

Sarah dressed carefully, wanting to create the right impression without appearing to have made the effort. A suit was too much, trousers might be considered too casual. She tried on a tartan skirt and stood in front of the mirror, holding up three different blouses. It's not the blouses, the skirt is wrong! She stepped out of it, discarding the skirt on the pile of crumpled, rejected clothes on the bed. A bed she had yet to make, just as the remains of breakfast still covered the kitchen counter downstairs.

She leaned into the cupboard, pressing the clothes to one side. Hangers screeched as she dragged them across the rail. At the back of the wardrobe, she found a navy-blue skirt in a dry-cleaning plastic wrapper: the paper tag still attached to the waistband with a safety pin. She had been fond of the skirt in her working life, and pulled it on, recalling a riotous night with her flat mate Kate. A quick post-work drink had turned into a late night out, the pair dancing round their handbags still dressed in formal office clothes. What would Freddy have thought if he'd spotted Sarah that night! She sucked in her tummy, but still couldn't do the zip up. Less of those biscuits, girl! The skirt joined the pile on the bed, and she started rummaging again. She stopped and pulled out a dark green, almost black skirt, then chose an olive silk blouse and a pair of sensible low-heeled shoes – she certainly didn't want to appear sexy.

Trial date. Sarah still hadn't talked to her family; she was allowing a flame to burn down the length of fuse wire towards the stack of dynamite, relying on a last-minute miracle reprieve to prevent the explosion of her life. Today would not be the climax to her ordeal, but she would be standing in a dock accused of killing someone. Lesley would be there to support her; her lawyer had tried to reassure her client that today was a formality, that she wouldn't have to answer any challenging questions: the magistrates would just be transferring the case to the Crown Court. And Sarah would be required to enter a plea.

She didn't want to take Lesley's advice to plead guilty and there was no one else to discuss it with. Every flashback – to the crash, the interview, and the dashcam images – had to be endured alone. There was no one to talk through her 'what ifs' with. What if she had been sensible and not run out of petrol? Or if Nick had prevented her eating the resin, or if she'd never wanted to try the brownies because she'd had a proper lunch not a snack? Why hadn't one of the men warned her not to drive, or, if only she had driven out of the front gate – as she should have done, as she had always done before she got messed up with drugs.

Freddy found her one morning, crying as she stared down at a batch of chocolate brownies baked for a fundraising event at the village hall that were cooling on a rack on the kitchen table.

'They smell delicious, darling. What's brought this on?' he asked, gently folding her into his arms.

She couldn't say. She would never be able to explain why the sight of a chocolate brownie would forever be distressing.

Should she plead guilty? Not today. She could change her plea at the real trial. Sarah cleared up the debris on the bed, re-hanging discarded skirts and blouses, and then made it, smoothing down the sheet and plumping the pillows. Next, she tided the kitchen – polishing the counter diligently. If only she could stay, and spring clean the whole house.

She sat in the car, keys in her lap, closed her eyes for a few moments, taking deep breaths before she set off in slow motion, teasing the seatbelt into place, and slowly turning the key. As she drove, her mind clutched onto Lesley's last piece of news – was it good or bad? At the magistrates' court, her lawyer was going to start a discussion with her opposite number – the prosecuting counsel – about possible leniency in exchange for a guilty plea. Could Lesley persuade them not to press for jail?

Thirty minutes later, Sarah walked up the steps into the court building. It was silent, modern, rather bleak, and desperately dark. Lesley was waiting, dressed in an inky grey suit that matched Sarah's mood. The lawyer took her into a little room.

'How are you feeling?' she asked.

Sarah sat down and tried to return her lawyer's smile. 'Bad question. Try another.'

'There's been a last-minute development that might help your case.'

Sarah felt her heart start to flutter and chewed her lip.

'The prosecution has asked to have a word. You remember I told you earlier this week the results of the deceased's blood tests finally showed up.'

'The poor man still died, regardless of what was in him that night.'

'Don't give up hope,' said Lesley, patting her client's arm as she stood up. 'I'm going to find opposing counsel.'

Sarah followed her lawyer outside and sat on a chair in the corridor. She licked her finger and scrubbed at a mark on her sleeve. That wasn't there when I put this on! She scrolled down her emails, then read a few news articles but her eyes kept being drawn towards Lesley, pacing up and down, her head bowed, talking to a thin, sandy-haired man whom Sarah presumed was the lawyer for the prosecution. Lesley was gesticulating; her counterpart had his hands clasped behind his back as if using them to force himself into an upright position. Sarah dropped her eyes back to her phone, and checked the weather forecast, then lifted her gaze again; the lawyers continued to walk up and down, as if measuring the length of the building with their footsteps. Neither turned her way. Sarah opened a few WhatsApp messages; the pair was still talking.

Now Lesley was shaking her counterpart's hand. Sarah's breathing accelerated; her lawyer was walking towards her. She stood up, running clammy palms down her skirt.

'Well?'

'Well, the deceased had been drinking on the night of the collision. Rather a lot, he was twice the legal limit. What's more, he had previously lost his license for driving under the influence of alcohol.'

Sarah screwed up her face. 'He still died.'

'Yes, but he is partially to blame. He shouldn't have been driving, his judgment was impaired. It makes the case against you that bit less secure, calls into question whether it's in the public interest to pursue the prosecution.'

'So we were both at fault.'

'Yes. And' Lesley face was beaming at her, 'they are prepared to lower the charge to driving without due care and attention, provided you plead guilty.'

'Will I still go to jail?'

The answer came swiftly.

'No. Three points and a fine, maybe £200?'

A fine and a few points. 'I still killed him even if he was drunk. It was my car he had to dodge.' She looked at Lesley, and then said, 'But I didn't know I wasn't safe to drive.'

'And you going to jail won't help the man.'

At least by pleading guilty she would enable his family to move on, and she had her own family to consider. With this ordeal over and the Dower House changing hands – even if not into hers – no one would have a hold over her anymore.

'Thank you, Lesley, please tell them I will plead guilty.'

She drove home, singing to the radio; she wasn't sure she deserved her reprieve, but her family certainly did. Sarah pulled into the driveway of the Long House, vowing never to complain about being bored with charity committee meetings again and scowled. There was a green car parked by her log store. Well, this is going to be a short conversation!

Sarah locked her car and strode to the front door without making eye contact with Nick or his goon, who was holding a box out to her as if he was collecting for a food bank.

'Not so fast!' Nick grunted, running to catch up, 'Give me the right key to the padlock.'

She let herself in and was closing the door behind her, but it wouldn't shut. She looked down and saw a sneaker-clad foot jamming her door ajar. She gave a hard shove, flipped round so her back was against the door and leant her full weight against it.

'It's over. Case dropped. So, you can both piss off.'

She felt the pressure against her body. The door was reopening; inch by inch, her body was being jerked further into the hallway.

'I said I need the key to the shed. The right key.'

'NO!'

She peeked down through her legs, now there was a foot-wide gap and Nick's leg was inside her house.

'Leave, or I will call the police!'

His head was inside, angled towards her, smirking, 'I gather from Mike you'd like to discuss a youngster called Angus.'

She stepped away from the door and both men stumbled into her entrance lobby.

Nick was grinning. 'Thought that might be the password. Mine's white two sugars. H, what do you fancy?'

Sarah saw the man ogling her, and her stomach clenched.

Nick snorted and added, 'To *drink*, H, what do you want to *drink*?'

Sarah opened the kitchen door; she could smell the pair of them following her in. Why don't they shower before they visit me? She filled the kettle saying, above the noise, 'He's sixteen, Nick. I don't know how you got your claws into him but please find someone else.'

She flicked the kettle on and turned round to see the men exchanging an exaggerated look.

'Can't think of anyone as trustworthy to replace him, can you, H? No one suspects a toff boy in his school uniform.'

Sarah made two cups of coffee, plonking them on the table in front of the men. She could hear her phone ringing and took it into the corridor, closing the door behind her. It was Penelope and she was in bits. Angus had come home with a broken wrist. This time the boy had used the excuse of mistiming crossing the road and tripping on the kerb. He was lying; Angus was right-handed. His knee jerk reaction would hardly have been to use his left hand.

'What am I going to do? He insists it was another accident.'

'Can't the school do anything?'

Penelope grunted. 'It's not happening at school. Do you think I should go to the police?'

'Ooooh,' Sarah said, sucking in her breath. 'How can the police help when the victim insists these are all accidents?'

Her friend raised her voice, 'I've got to find some way of stopping whoever is doing this!'

Sarah let out a deep sigh. 'Let me see if I can think of something. I've got someone here. Can I call you back for a proper chat in a few minutes?'

Sarah tossed the phone onto the hall table and ran her hands down her face. Poor Angus, he was still a child, three years older than Mary. How would she have felt if this was happening to her daughter? There was a burst of laughter from her kitchen. She glared at the door, her eyes pinched into slits, as if she had the power to hurt the men by beaming her venom, laser-like, through the wood.

As she let herself back into the kitchen, Nick took a noisy slurp of coffee and winked at her. Hideous man: he was using a child and abusing him too. She made herself a mug of coffee, pulled out the biscuit jar, and sat down opposite the men.

'I'll do it,' she said. 'Stop using Angus, and I'll do the deliveries to Taunton.'

Chapter Fifteen

Two days after the trial, and the day after her first solo delivery round the slightly down at heel town of Taunton, Percy called, insisting Sarah attend a meeting in his office. Harry was going to be there too – in person.

'He needs to drive all the way from Suffolk?' she queried, trapping the phone between her cheek and shoulder, leaving her hands free to finish the breakfast washing up.

'Yes, Mrs. Fetherston. I rather think he does.'

She dried her hands, retrieved the phone, and pressed for more information.

'Why, what's this about? Is something wrong?' she demanded.

'I can't be sure. There's been a most unexpected and unwelcome development – only Harry can determine how serious this is.'

'That sounds ominous! What sort of unwelcome development?'

Percy wouldn't be drawn, ending the call abruptly but not rudely, 'Please excuse me, Mrs. Fetherston. I must call your brother-in-law.'

She ran warm water over the last of the plates, rinsing off the suds then pulled the plug, watching the water level subside, leaving a grubby tidemark round the basin. She swooshed water towards the plughole, trying to dispel the gurgling noise. This had to involve Mike – had he found another Will? Or maybe commissioned his own expert's report? Could he mount a challenge now probate was granted? How exasperating the man was; maybe he did deserve to be evicted and charged rent.

The following afternoon, Harry met Sarah in Percy's reception area. He looked exhausted, as if the journey south had taken twelve rather than six hours. Sarah raised a limp hand in greeting. He shuffled over and slid into the chair beside her, for once a welcome sight.

'Did he tell you what this is about?' she hissed. 'I couldn't sleep.

Freddy told me to stop worrying, what will be will be, but I reckon your brother would have preferred a night in the spare bedroom. I was wriggling more than one of my hens in a dust bath.'

'No, Percy wouldn't tell me,' admitted Harry, clenching and unclenching his hands as if preparing for a fight. He blew out a long breath, 'I've been worrying away at what Percy did say, trying to puzzle it out.'

'Why are we whispering?'

A few moments passed then Sarah nudged Harry, lifting her voice to a natural tone. 'What did Percy actually say?'

'He just said I would be the one who'd be able to clear things up,' replied Harry, wringing his hands together.

Their lawyer's bespectacled face appeared in the doorway. There was no attempt at small talk; silently, the Fetherstons filed into the familiar boardroom and sat opposite their lawyer, butterflies fluttering in Sarah's stomach in the way they did whenever she spotted a police car driving behind hers. Sarah wasn't thirsty but she unscrewed a bottle of water and poured herself a glass. She held up the bottle towards Harry, and then kept her eyes on both the rising water level in Harry's glass and Percy who was walking slowly round the desk towards his clients. He laid a legal document in front of Harry.

'Mr. Fetherston. This is a copy of the purchase agreement for the Dower House.'

Sarah took a sip of water, keeping her eyes on Harry; he looked up at the lawyer, then back down at the document, propped open by one of the complimentary pads of paper left on the table for clients.

'Could you please carefully consider those witness signatures and tell me if they are indeed yours and your wife's?'

Harry glanced down, then swiftly back up.

'Yes. Those are our signatures.'

'There's no problem with either of them?' pressed the lawyer.

Of course there wasn't. Sarah had been there when that document was signed. What was Percy driving at?

Harry shook his head. 'Nope.'

'No. I didn't think there would be,' said Percy, pursing his lips.

The lawyer's hand snaked between her and Harry. He retrieved the contract, returned to his seat, and for a few moments he sat silently rubbing a page between his thumb and fingers, as if assessing the texture. Sarah drank water she didn't really want and tuned in to the sounds of traffic outside the office window. When was Percy going to reveal why they were here? Why was it important to check her in-laws' signatures – was something wrong or not?

Percy was looking her way.

'The problem is not with any of the signatures,' he said.

Sarah stared at the furrowed brow of a man she had grown to trust. With a sharp intake of breath, Percy switched his gaze to Harry.

'Mr. Fetherston, when you and your wife signed this contract four years ago, you were both doing precisely what you had been asked to do – to witness the signatures of the two purchasers. What you were not invited to do, and so what I presume you didn't do, was check the contents of the document your mother and Mike were signing.'

Sarah heard a faint voice beside her, barely more than a breath.

'He lied to me.'

Percy turned a few pages of the contract pressed down firmly to ensure it stayed open and pushed it back towards the Fetherstons. Sarah couldn't take her eyes off the document. It sat between her and Harry, an unexploded grenade, waiting to be claimed. Sarah pulled the contract over the last few inches. There was a pink post-it note on the open page, the sort she used herself to leave messages for Freddy, sticking them to the side of his desk where they couldn't be ignored: *'Remember to collect dry cleaning when you're in Exeter'*, or *'Lunch is in the oven, I am out all day.'* This note had an arrow pointing towards a section where purchasers choose one of two boxes to indicate if they are buying as tenants in common or joint tenants. There was a mark in the second box, joint tenants.

'I am so very sorry, Mr. Fetherston, but yes, it would appear he tricked both you and your wife. I suspect he tricked your mother too. If she'd intended to buy the Dower House as a joint tenant, knowing her prognosis meant she was effectively leaving that money to Mike, she would not have included her seventy-five per cent share on the list of assets she attached to the Will a few months later.'

You could have heard a baby sighing. Sarah and Harry were

staring at the mark, as if willpower alone could shift its positioning across into the other box – the one everyone had assumed was marked that day, the one Harry had instructed his mother to choose to protect her fortune, then failed to check it had been!

'This of course, has enormous ramifications for you, Mr. Fetherston, and for your husband, too, Mrs. Fetherston.'

She was speechless. Mike had stolen the bulk of Freddy's inheritance!

She heard Percy clearing his throat.

'You are aware of the legal consequences of purchasing as joint tenants; the survivor inherits the other person's share of that asset. Legally, the Dower House does not form part of your mother's estate. It became Mike's on her death.'

The three sat like passengers on their first lift share journey, forced to sit in close proximity with strangers, each wishing they were alone. Percy appeared to be concentrating on the view out of the window; she guessed he was avoiding locking eyes with either of his clients. Harry – whom she assumed was in shock – couldn't take his eyes off the contract. Sarah didn't know where to look, certainly not at Harry. Mike had stolen the Dower House – the cunning, thieving shit. How could Harry have been so stupid? He should have checked not just accepted Mike's word. It was his responsibility. What a prize idiot. The trouble was, this time his sloppiness didn't just affect him, it would cost Freddy most of his inheritance too.

After a few minutes, the spell was broken by Percy. 'You don't have to tell me now, but . . .' He paused, and Sarah looked across the table to where a legal pad was doubling as a stress ball, being squashed and stroked as Percy continued, 'I must ask you to consider if either you – or Mrs. Fetherston, if your husband – wants to challenge this document?'

Sarah recalled that day at the cottage four years ago, the two men disappearing off to the dining room with mugs of coffee to deal with the paperwork, like Victorian gentlemen after dinner, dismissing the ladies so they could be left in peace to pass the port and discuss business.

She had to know; she would always wonder otherwise.

'Harry. Just what did happen in the dining room at Mary's cottage four years ago?'

Harry closed his eyes, drew in a long breath then released it. 'He was charming.'

'Most con artists are,' said Sarah, tartly.

Harry didn't look at her, training his eyes on the contract as if selecting something that couldn't criticise him. He said he'd been reassured that Mike was adapting to the role of caring for his mother and remembered wondering if he had misjudged the man.

'Mike told me he'd just been with the lawyer who was acting on their purchase. He asked if Amy and I could witness their signatures, to save Ma from having to go into town. He told me that new surroundings unnerved her. Ironic, really, that I was thinking so well of the chap seconds before he robbed me.' He coughed out a short laugh, 'As we were out of earshot of Ma, just being friendly, I told Mike about our de-cluttering plan.' He lifted his eyes towards Sarah. 'Do you remember, we filled up those boxes with stuff we thought she should get rid of, referring to them as "for consideration"?'

That had been Sarah's idea; was he about to blame her?

'That's what sealed our fate. He told me there was a charity shop on his way home that would be grateful for new stock and offered to take our "for consideration" boxes with him. So, instead of going back into the drawing room and keeping an eye out for Ma, I went upstairs to get those wretched boxes.'

'So, it was just us girls when your mother signed and Amy witnessed. We kind of assumed you'd taken care of business. But you hadn't done that, had you, Harry?' Sarah snapped.

She searched for a sign her brother-in-law accepted what he'd done. There was no nod, no shake of his head, but neither did he try and defend himself. He took a gulp of water and stumbled on.

'Mike told me it was a standard contract. Said he had done a full structural survey, which hadn't unearthed anything and that the house was well maintained.'

Sarah felt a tingle of excitement at the news about the structural survey, then remembered her family wouldn't have anywhere near enough money to buy the Dower House, and it wasn't for sale anyway. She bit back her anger; maybe this was payback for not going to jail.

'I was so cautious, so mindful that most of Ma's capital was being used to buy that blasted house. I asked him how the purchase was structured. He told me what I wanted to hear, said they were buying as tenants in common, that her stumping up seventy-five per cent was accounted for. And I signed.'

As she listened, Sarah recalled Freddy revealing how his brother had been swindled by a business partner, how Amy had let slip that sometimes Harry could be too trusting or too embarrassed to ask the right questions. That day four years ago, Harry had spectacularly failed to ask the right questions; to probe for any details at all – he'd just accepted what was presented at face value. Why hadn't he checked through the document, made sure he was being told the truth?

'Don't blame the packing boxes, Harry. Mary should never have been allowed to sign that document without you checking it first,' said Sarah, swilling back her water and standing up. 'There's no point wasting any more of your valuable time, Percy. Thank you for alerting us to the problem.'

Percy was gathering up his notepad and spectacle case, suggesting the family discuss matters amongst themselves and let him know if they wanted to take legal action against Mike. Together, the three walked in a stiff silence to the reception area, where Sarah stood to one side, watching Percy dancing about, ensuring Harry had his coat and didn't forget his umbrella. Harry thanked the lawyer, shook his hand, and turned towards her.

'I don't know what to say. I can't speak to Freddy yet,' Harry mumbled, then added, almost as an afterthought, 'sorry,' and left.

Was he apologising for not being able to speak to Freddy, or for having lost the family fortune?

Percy and Sarah stood at the office door, watching a hollowed-out Harry shuffle back to his car; his shoulders slumped, head bowed. Sarah tried but failed to muster any sympathy; Harry would be destitute without his inheritance, but in scuppering his own future, he had scuttled her dreams too.

'Can I buy you a glass of wine, Mrs. Fetherston?'

She had dinner to cook, and endless letters to stuff for a charity tennis tournament.

'It's Sarah. And thank you Percy, yes please, a large one!'

Sarah took a seat in reception. She saw Percy trot up the stairs, still clutching the poisonous document. She picked up a copy of Country Life, gazing sightlessly at the cover picture, unable to dispel the mantra: 'This is not what Mary wanted,' and dismissing half-hearted plans to deal with Mike. She would take Percy's advice; it was probably about to be dispensed for free and with a courtesy glass of wine. Then she would work out how to deal with the villain.

Chapter Sixteen

Sarah stared out at the late October afternoon; shoppers were scurrying past in the fading light, bags in gloved hands, warm jackets zipped up, buttressing them against the cold. What a mess Harry has created and now he's ducked responsibility. The selfish man has skulked off with his tail between his legs, casting himself in the role of chief victim, ignoring the impact of his stupidity on anyone else. You reap what you sow, she thought, you knew what the family was like, how careless they were with their fortune. She must shoulder her share of the blame. She shouldn't have left Harry in charge that day any more than she would have trusted Freddy to oversee the paperwork.

Percy reappeared by her chair, Sarah buttoned her coat, and they stepped out to join the throng. The lawyer escorted her towards a boutique hotel: a tall Regency building in attractive, sandy-coloured Bath stone.

'This is our office local, hope you like it,' he said, opening the door for her and ushering his client inside.

It was only five o'clock and the brightly lit bar was empty save for a man standing behind the counter wearing black trousers, a white long-sleeved shirt, and a slightly lopsided bow tie, who was polishing glasses in readiness for the post-work rush.

Sarah chose a round table in a window bay, unbuttoning her coat and shrugging it off. She could see Percy examining the menu, consulting the barman. All the pent-up excitement – the anticipation of fulfilling her plans – had evaporated in that short, shocking meeting.

Percy returned with a tray; two glasses of white wine and several small porcelain bowls filled with the sort of food Sarah was always telling Mary not to eat – crisps, dry roasted peanuts, and pretzels. Tonight, Sarah didn't have the willpower to resist.

'This is an interesting Muscadet,' said Percy. 'Such an underrated wine. See what you think.'

'Anything!' Smiling up at him, she took a glass, setting it down. 'So, go on, out with it – what happened? How did you discover what he did?'

Percy was removing his suit jacket, bending round to arrange it on the back of his chair. He shot a look at her, as if gauging how much of the ugly truth he should reveal.

'I wrote to Mike. I was very polite, made the usual noises about condolences for his loss, and then I told him that probate had been granted, and, under the terms of his late wife's Will, it was necessary to sell the Dower House. I asked him to call me at his convenience to discuss progressing the sale.'

Sarah tried the wine: welcoming the fresh, clean taste with the slight hint of sweetness, as it slid across her tongue. It was indeed good, although she would have settled for her cooking sherry if that was all that had been on offer.

'I was stunned when his reply came by return of post. It was quite terse.' Percy was drumming his fingers on the table, a faint rumbling noise. 'No, it wasn't terse, that's not the right word. Frankly the letter was downright rude. He said he was the sole owner of the house and had no intention of selling it. He might as well have signed with "bugger off".'

Percy took a swig of his wine then returned to his tale. Sarah helped herself to a handful of crisps, feeding them in individually to avoid crunching too loudly.

'I was so disturbed by his allegation, that the house was his, that I personally checked on the Land Registry website, to ensure the man hadn't just invented the claim. The only hope was that the witness signatures were forgeries. That was why I insisted Harry came down from Suffolk – but I never put favourable odds on that happy outcome. I am sorry you were ambushed, that I didn't alert you to my suspicions; it didn't feel right when there was the faintest possibility of this turning out to be a hoax.'

She voiced her fears. 'I don't think either of the brothers will challenge Mike.'

He pulled his face into a grimace.

'I know. I suspect Mike knows that too. I did run it past one of my litigation partners, but the odds aren't stacked in your favour.' He picked up his wine again, took a small sip, then put it back precisely in the centre of the mat. 'It would be Harry's word against Mike's. He could deny there had been any conversation that day in the cottage, insist it had been Mary's intention he inherit the house from the get-go, as a thank you for caring for her. If the conversation had indeed occurred, why didn't Harry check the contract supported the alleged words?'

Good question, she thought. Why hadn't Harry done just that?

'It's fraud, isn't it?'

'Between you and me,' he looked up at her, his eyes steady behind the glasses, 'yes, I think this was a deliberate act by Mike. I don't doubt Harry's account of the matter, not for one second.'

Percy had said it; her business partner was a crook. She'd always known he was dishonest – had suspected, like Harry, that his actions surrounding the disappearance of the Will were underhand. The most encouraging outcome Percy could envisage was if the lawyer who acted for Mary on the house purchase could be shown to have been negligent. Had they even met her? Were they aware of her dementia diagnosis? If not, why not? And if so, what additional steps had they taken to protect her? Percy speculated that maybe – as the lawyer had been acting for Mike on the sale of his house as well as the purchase of the Dower House – the solicitor just followed Mike's instructions and failed to involve Mary. If they could prove negligence, the sons would have a claim against their mother's legal firm. The contents of her Will and the list of her assets, both helpfully dated shortly after the house purchase, should be sufficient to show Mary never intended to leave her share of the Dower House to Mike. It was clear she believed she had a seventy-five per cent interest in the house to leave to her children by listing that as her principal asset.

It was hopeless. A big hurdle would be getting hold of the legal files for the house purchase. They had first-hand experience of how difficult that would be as they already bore the battle scars from retrieving Mary's medical records which had taken weeks of chasing. The records had only been handed over after Percy wrote a letter confirming they would not be used in a medical negligence claim. The insurmountable challenge was even getting to that obstacle. She would do it, but this wasn't Sarah's battle. A decision to sue the lawyers was for Freddy or his brother: they were the beneficiaries who had lost out, not her. All she'd been left was half the jewellery, and that was unaffected.

Neither of Mary's sons would consider it appropriate for a gentleman to take legal action against their mother's lawyer. In ensuring their mother's copy of the Will was adhered to, like Sarah, Mary's sons had been pushing to distribute the estate as their mother wanted. To unravel this fraud was a fundamentally different proposition. The brothers would be seeking compensation. Sarah would have done that if she could, the brothers would not. The way the men would view this was – even if they won – it would be the lawyers who ended up paying the price for Mike's duplicity, not them. Mike would still be living at the Dower House. Despite his predicament, Harry wouldn't be desperate enough. Harry always played the perfect gentleman – the role model for his younger brother – so he wouldn't suggest they prosecute, and Freddy would never challenge a decision made by his sibling.

The bar was starting to fill up: the end of another working day, office workers discarding wrinkled suit jackets, rolling up their sleeves, taking off security passes and attracting the barman's attention. The background noise of laughter and the buzz of conversations was a contrast to Sarah's own spirits.

Percy lightened her mood.

'When that ghastly silence fell in the boardroom, I was so thankful Harry didn't ask that classic question, so frequently asked of us lawyers by flummoxed clients: "What would you do if you were in my situation?"'

'What would you have said if he had?'

'There is only one answer. That a lawyer wouldn't allow himself or herself to get into the pickle their client evidently has somehow managed to achieve.'

Sarah accepted a second glass of wine, thinking back to her first meeting with Lesley, and pleased she hadn't asked that question herself! Lesley had performed a miracle. No more worrying about a life-changing confession to Freddy, no trial by jury, no criminal record – she could never have imagined feeling this low again by the end of the week.

Percy was threading his way back through the crowd of office workers, the plastic tray balanced in front of him. She talked as he unloaded the drinks.

'It's a fascinating field of law,' she said. 'You must get so many interesting cases.'

He passed Sarah her wine, then removed their dirty glasses, and replaced the empty bowls with fresh ones. Sarah tucked in. Supper might be late.

'When I started, the field of probate had a reputation for offering a junior lawyer a slightly dull, but safe career. Unlike conveyance, which was my alternative choice, probate isn't dependent on a cyclical market. I do often ask myself when and why my field of law became so contentious! It never used to be.' He lifted his glass for a short sip. 'But now my department is no longer viewed by the firm's annual crop of trainee lawyers as a steppingstone to a more exciting placement elsewhere.'

She saw Percy's fingers reaching over to fumble in the empty crisp dish.

'Sorry,' she said, 'must be nerves!'

'No matter,' he said, smiling and shaking his head. 'What was I saying, yes, we have monthly meetings to discuss our caseloads, and do you know, I notice a few of my fellow partners anticipate updates on some of my trickier cases with the same eagerness my wife does for a new episode of a period drama. Only the criminal lawyers surpass my enticing anecdotes.'

Sarah imagined a crisply suited Lesley dishing out the latest on her own juicy cases. Did the lawyers name their clients in those meetings? Was Percy aware of what Sarah had been through? She'd better review the partners list, check no one was connected to any of her charities.

'When I brought the copy Will to you,' she said, 'I honestly thought we'd just be plodding through a dull process that would result in a chunky bank transfer. I don't mean that rudely, implying your work is dull. It's just it was all so simple after my father died.'

She glanced at the remaining snacks. Percy caught her eye and nudged one of the fuller bowls towards her.

'Maybe it's because the growth in housing wealth has increased the proportion of estates, where life-changing amounts of money are at stake to be squabbled over by warring offspring. Has the fact those children are now so often deprived of housing wealth themselves exacerbated that? Or is it the increased rate of second and sometimes third marriages, each bringing another layer of previously unrelated people into the mix? In my experience, these complex family structures often turn out to be frighteningly fragile once the matriarch or patriarch is no longer there to act as the glue. Fifteen years ago, I did not envisage I would, like those in the matrimonial department, hear so much vitriol being poured down the phone by people about those, who at some stage in their lives, they professed to love.'

She ran her finger round a dish, forcing out the last few nuts.

'And where is the Fetherston case on your list of war stories?' Percy arched his eyebrows.

'I thought I had encountered some dubious behaviour before, but with Mike it isn't just his self-serving act of cheating the children out of their mother's portion of the Dower House that bewilders me. No, this was a devious plot. That man researched the law and his quarry, the two sons, meticulously. Was his motive really money or was it more complex?' His eyes were penetrating, she felt as if she was being challenged. 'Maybe an element of revenge for some earlier slight whilst he had been married to their mother?' He picked up his glass, asking, 'What do you think?'

Sarah took a large swallow of wine. Percy would never understand the politics that had underscored the Fetherston family over the last twenty years – the rivalry, the snobbery, the judging and being judged, the striving to be accepted.

'And another thing,' he continued. 'Just why did Mike choose to add insult to injury by putting everyone through the charade of the destruction of the Will? Wasn't the house enough? Do you think Mike believed that by destroying the Will it would automatically follow his wife died intestate, and all the money would come his way? Did Mike suspect the fortune was significantly larger than it was, that the home was not the major asset, and he wanted the lot, not just the house?'

Sarah listened to the lawyer theorizing about Mike's motives. Percy was both entertaining, and his subtle advice had enabled the sketch of a plan to form in her mind. However much she deserved her dreams to be shattered, her family - probably not the intended victim - didn't, and her mother-in-law didn't deserve to have her fortune stolen.

'What usually drives a person to commit a fraud like this?' she asked.

'Well, I've encountered fraud in my caseload before and have my own theory.'

'Go on,' encouraged Sarah.

Percy allowed a burst of laughter from the bar area to subside before speaking.

'Maybe there was a subtler reason behind Mike's actions. When an inexperienced person is thrust into the role of care provider – having total control over another adult in the same way a parent has over a toddler – gradually, sometimes, I think the line between caring for and controlling becomes blurred. The care provider discovers their charge is entirely beholden to them; that they can decide every aspect of that other person's life. All the choices – from the minutiae of when to get up and what to wear, to what to eat for breakfast – are down to the care provider. I think that power affects some people: they start to extend their remit to other aspects of their patient's life, such as what to do with their money.'

Sarah let Percy's words sink in. Having read the expert's report, she feared that towards the end of that summer, before Mary was sectioned, Mike had started to control her mother-in-law rather than care for her.

'So, the nurse becomes the jailor?'

'I suppose so. To date I've witnessed this control syndrome manifesting itself in breaches of a power of attorney, where the care provider uses their charge's bank account as if it was their own personal piggy bank. In some instances, clients find tens of thousands of pounds have been siphoned off the estate illegally. Maybe Mike started to think of Mary's money as his own? Not content with taking her share of the house, he believed he was entitled to all her money?'

Sarah's lawyer finished his wine with a delicate sip. This man had fought tenaciously for her and been outwitted at the last hurdle by her business partner. Mike had not been pilfering petty cash from Mary's bank account. He had stolen not just the money but Sarah's dreams, too. He was as rotten to the core as Nick. How had she managed to get tangled up with a common thief? She couldn't allow him to win.

When Sarah told him about her meeting with Percy, Freddy dropped his briefcase. He picked it up, slowly, setting it on the kitchen table. How was his brother going to repay all that debt? Sarah was spitting out the story, darting about the kitchen, pushing trays into the aga, setting vegetables to boil. He offered to help, asked what he could do, but she told him she was running late and there wasn't time for that.

'I need to lay for supper,' she said, snatching his briefcase off the table and tossing it back to him.

Freddy clutched it to his chest like a hot water bottle.

'Then I've got laundry to do, and Mary's lunchbox to make up.'

Her back was towards him, he heard a jug being filled with water and he seized a gap in the torrent of words, 'So, what you're saying is the Dower House is Mike's, not part of Ma's estate?'

Sarah turned round, waving the jug of water as if she was about to throw it over him, 'Unless one of you challenges Mike.'

He pressed the leather of his case with alternating fingers, as if playing an accordion. 'Challenge Mike?'

'Yes,' she said, tartly. 'As the beneficiaries who have been defrauded, you could contest what he's done.'

'*Defrauded.* That's a strong word.'

Her face was screwed up, why was she angry? Disappointed, he'd understand as there could be no house move now – but angry?

Sarah stalked to the cutlery drawer, wrenching it open and rattling the contents as she spat, 'Freddy, Mike has stolen your inheritance!'

Wowzah, where was this going!

He put his briefcase back down on the table. 'Come on darling, that's a bit unfair! We don't know for sure Mike is to blame.'

She was staring at him, her eyes wide. 'How can you be so naïve?'

She marched to the table, picked up his case, tossed it back at him again, and slammed the cutlery into place, piece by piece.

'Sarah, this has upset you, I can see that, but—'

Mary interrupted their discussion, ambling in rubbing her tummy. 'I'm hungry, when's supper?'

'Your mother is on it, little one,' said Freddy. He locked his eyes on Sarah. 'How long, darling?'

He was thrown a dirty look. Sarah crossed to the Aga and stabbed at the pots of vegetables, wielding a knife with as much venom as Macduff slaying Macbeth. 'It's ready,' she said, dropping the knife and snatching up a saucepan. 'You can both sit down, and I'll serve.'

Freddy tried to jolly his girls through the meal, but no one wanted to discuss his theory on how Charles I might have persuaded the Rump Parliament to allow him to continue as their monarch. He watched Sarah push her vegetables to the side of the plate and looked down at his own portion of fish pie congealed into an unappealing gloopy mess. Mary had eaten the pastry, and picked at the fish, and was asking to get down, claiming she wanted to rehearse a dance routine. Maybe it was best if she left, and then the adults would be able to pick over the wreckage of Sarah's dreams alone.

'Off you go,' he said.

'Thanks, Dad.' She finished her glass of water and got up, leaving her unfinished plate of food.

Freddy leaned over, patting Sarah's arm, and she looked up at him, her face screwed up in apology.

'I shouldn't have snapped,' she said, 'let my frustration show. I never expected either of you to challenge Mike.'

'I know it's a blow, darling, but this won't affect us like it will Harry. Whatever is he going to do?'

She dropped her gaze. 'I don't think Harry is close to working out a plan. He's not in a good way.'

'How will he pay off his debt without his inheritance?'

Sarah rose, picking up Mary's plate and Freddy leaned back to allow her to collect his too. 'Just what can he do,' he said. 'Poor Harry, what a disaster.'

The phone disturbed their morbid postmortem. 'Penelope,' Sarah mouthed at him, and he waved for her to take the call. Penelope might calm Sarah down; he was content to listen to half of the conversation.

'Nothing I didn't want interrupted,' Sarah said. 'Take me out of myself, please, divert me. 'Cos believe you me, not even you can sort our mess out.'

Poor Sarah, she'd set her heart on moving house. He noticed a smile at the corners of her mouth and felt an answering twitch at the corners of his own.

'What a good idea,' she said. 'A new school, a new start and still close enough to weekly board.' There was a short silence, and then Sarah said, 'Now, I wanted to bend your ear about this charity dog show next spring. Tad concerned about the timing . . . last time we organised anything for April it was raining, and we can't have an indoor dog show, we've nowhere for the show ring. Question is, has Sandra already got the bit between her teeth?'

How did women keep track of conversations? They bounced from one topic to another like children on a trampoline. Freddy didn't like this new thread. Sandra's name had not been hissed at him so much in the last few months, not since Sarah started donating to the rehabilitation centre, where Sandra was the treasurer. But despite all her efforts, Sandra still seemed to regard Sarah as beneath her – almost as if Sandra were a school prefect and Sarah a mere first-former: there to be bossed around, told what to do, how to do it and when to do it. Sarah needed to stand up to the woman!

He listened to Sarah saying goodnight to her friend. A few minutes later, his own phone rang. Harry. Watching Sarah scraping the remains of the fish pie into the food caddy, Freddy listened to his brother, yet to reach Suffolk, berating himself and questioning why he hadn't been more careful, why had he naively accepted that Mike was telling him the truth?

'Freddy, why did I allow that cunning fox into the chicken house? I knew he was untrustworthy. That's why Ma was determined to leave him when she discovered she was living with a drug dealer.'

Sarah topped up his wine glass but refilled her own with water.

'But no,' Harry continued, 'when Mike suggested they buy a house together, instead of hearing alarm bells as you did, I thought what an elegant, convenient solution it was for me. And I sold you into the idea. I know you had misgivings, but your older brother knew better. I persuaded you to go along with what were always Mike's plans, not ours.'

Sarah was working around Freddy, preparing the kitchen for breakfast. He stroked the stem of his wine glass; his brother's voice rolled on, uninterrupted.

'I wouldn't blame you if you said, "I told you so". I looked at the fox leering at me, and then I opened the chicken coop and ushered him in. Why am I now surprised by the devastation?'

Harry grudgingly admitted Mike had been clever: calculating Harry wouldn't ask to look at the contract. Mike had assumed Harry's gentlemanly demeanour would prevent him checking. And Mike was right. The document everyone signed that day probably didn't have either of the boxes marked. That was done subsequently, Freddy guessed. That way, if Mike's gamble hadn't paid off – if someone *had* checked – he wouldn't have been exposed, just forced to mark the correct box and no doubt blame the lawyers.

'But why,' demanded Harry of himself, 'did I miss a second opportunity to stop things by leaving the room to collect blasted boxes, giving that oik a clear run to get Ma to sign? I should have been there to protect Ma, to damn well make sure she checked the contract before signing away her fortune. Leopards and spots.'

'You were being told what you wanted to hear. It's understandable you believed him,' Freddy soothed.

'But I have cheated you out of most of your inheritance.'

'No, you haven't, Mike has. Please, Harry, don't feel guilty on my account. I am moved by historical events. I've never been materialistic; I'm perfectly content to live out my days at the Long House.'

He saw Sarah freeze, covering her reaction by rearranging the breakfast cutlery. Freddy kept his eyes on Sarah as he continued, 'I know Sarah is disappointed, but she'll get over it. She may have set her heart on a Georgian gem, but I don't think she bears you any ill will.' Sarah moved out of Freddy's vision, as he added, 'It's your life that is affected by this. You need to think about Amy, not us.'

He heard a crashing sound and looked round; Sarah was holding a smashed cereal bowl. He wrapped his hand round his phone.

'Sarah, is everything all right?'

'Why aren't either of you fighting back?! Where is Harry's backbone? Why is he being so limp?' Sarah spat, stalking out of the room.

Freddy said goodnight to his brother, drained his wine and poked his head round the utility room door. Sarah was throwing laundry into the washing machine with more force than the average baseball pitcher.

'Coffee, darling?'

She closed her eyes, slammed shut the machine door, then shouted.

'Why aren't either of you angry? I just want to hear a flicker of resistance from one of you. There is no suggestion of attack, of taking Mike on. Is this what the gentlemanly code of conduct requires?' she snapped, sarcastically. 'That, if you are outsmarted by a cad, you must walk away with your head held high, and ensure the bounder doesn't know you care?'

'Steady on, darling. It's only money!'

'No, you need to hear this. Is this the way your great uncle Harry– now resting peacefully on our sitting room wall – would have reacted if someone had defrauded him out of the Lampton Estate?'

'Sarah, what on earth's wrong?'

'Why aren't you fighting back!'

'Fighting back against Harry?'

'No, I get that apportioning blame is a tempting distraction – but it won't solve anything.'

He stared at Sarah. She rolled her eyes at him.

'It isn't a gentlemanly code of conduct protecting Mike, and you aren't the reason Mike will go unchallenged. If the money had been left entirely to you, I think you may have challenged this. But because the money was left jointly, sibling reverence directs this is your brother's decision, and the bully in Harry conceals his underlying cowardice. Harry has lost his battle with Mike and won't risk another encounter, too scared he might be outwitted a second time. If anyone is going to take on Mike, it will have to be me.'

He took a step backwards as she stabbed at the control panel of the washing machine, then stalked past, giving him a withering look, and spitting out, 'I will not allow your mother's intentions or my dreams to be shattered without a fight.'

Chapter Seventeen

Reaching the top of the drive of Langton Manor, Sarah cursed. A last-minute summons by Nick had necessitated a dash from the school run via the Dower House and up the M5. She counted the cars already parked and grabbed her hastily purchased gift: a box of chocolates from the Taunton Deane service station. It was a poor replacement for the jars of homemade crab apple jelly which – when she'd stabbed on the brakes – had rolled off the passenger seat smashing against each other leaving a mess in the footwell and all over her copy of the agenda.

Sarah yanked off the gardening Jersey she'd begged from Mike to cover her sober silk blouse – an incongruous garment in her drop off point, a shuttered night club – tossing it onto the back seat. She picked up the sticky agenda. If Angus was settled at a new school, once she'd checked it was sufficiently far away, Nick was going be told to clear off.

Sarah let herself in through the front door, with its glazed top half and lion's head door knocker. The door needed redecoration. In areas, curls of paint hung like strips from a peeled orange. Penelope had left the door unlocked, allowing the ladies into the hallway with its floor of alternating black and cream stones: each one set at an angle to the front door, presenting guests with a diamond lozenge chequerboard. There was a fire, glowing – the long logs balanced on black fire dogs, creating a medieval atmosphere with flames licking up the sides of the cavernous chimneypiece – but it failed to raise the temperature in the hallway beyond the few feet immediately in front of the blaze. Sarah jogged through the impressive entrance hall: down the less impressive, windowless corridors floored with ancient uneven flagstones to the service wing and rushed into the warmth of the kitchen. A dozen ladies were ranged round the long kitchen table. Penelope straightened her Alice band and beamed at her, saying, 'Here she is, girls. You look a bit frazzled, Sarah. Don't worry, we haven't started yet.'

Sarah mumbled her apologies and held up the box of chocolates. Sandra was sitting at the middle of the long table, patting an empty chair on one side of hers.

'Saved you a seat.'

Sarah tossed the chocolates onto the dresser. Sandra save Sarah a seat, and beside her, why? She darted round and sat down.

'Item one,' barked Sandra, 'is it a dog show? Are we all agreed on this plan?'

Penelope pointed out potential pitfalls, but no one had any alternative suggestions and Sandra saw off the ambush, claiming the house owner hosting the event had come up with the idea herself.

'Item two, allocation of key responsibilities,' boomed the chair lady.

Sarah heard a ping from her handbag. The room fell silent.

Sandra huffed, 'Is that yours?' she asked, focusing her piggy black eyes on Sarah's handbag.

'Terrifically sorry, Sandra, but I think so.'

Sandra rapped her pen on her agenda. 'Well check if it's important. Penelope, maybe we could get a cup of tea during this interruption.'

Her face scarlet, Sarah fished out her phone.

You only gave them one box. Stupid tart.

There was a box of cannabis in the boot of her car! She gasped and dropped the phone in her lap.

'Is it life threatening?' asked Sandra.

'No, no it can wait.'

'Now can we get on, ladies? Item two. I want to propose that Sarah acts as the sponsor of the dog show.'

Sarah coughed, gulping down a mouthful of hot tea. *Sponsor!* She had never been asked to sponsor an event, ostensibly still second in command beneath Sandra, but given the chairlady's skill at delegation, effectively running the show. Why now? Had they heard about Freddy's inheritance, did they think they were talking to the next chatelaine of the Dower House? Or was it someone senior at the drug rehabilitation centre, wanting to massage the ego of a key supporter?'Her eyes roved round the table. Penelope gave a quick clap; the other ladies were all smiling.

'All those in favour?' asked Sandra, raising her hand but keeping her eyes on her agenda. Including the chairlady's there were twelve arms in the air.

'Now item three, raffle. Who's volunteering?'

'Rachel?' suggested Sarah.

A wisp of a lady with prematurely grey hair raised her hand, saying, 'Happy to help.'

Rachel was famed amongst the ladies for guarding the entrances to fundraising events like a vixen at the mouth of the den shielding her cubs. Her looks were deceiving. She wielded her twin weapons of raffle ticket books and cash tin as efficiently as any fly fisherman, casting her chosen decoy at unsuspecting fish.

By the time they reached "Any other business", Sarah was drawing neat circles around the blobs of crab apple jelly on her agenda.

A second WhatsApp message announced its arrival on Sarah's phone, and she lowered her eyes to her lap, peaking at the message.

They've changed their mind, they want buds. Drop the box off at the school.

I will not do that! She typed back, stabbing out the message.

Cut the crap. I can't do it and you've got the dope. Steve will meet you at 3.30.

Sarah had not seen Mary this upset since one of the chickens died. Unfortunately for the child, the demise of the bird had coincided with a morning Mary offered to feed the chicks alone. Mary had stumbled into the kitchen, tears streaming down her face, her mouth puckered with the combined effort of crying whilst simultaneously whining out the reason for her distress. Today, Sarah was yet to discover why her teenage daughter was sobbing in the back of the car on the way home from school. Sarah had been a little later than usual; the groundsman had kept her waiting, and she'd taken a circuitous route back to the main entrance not wanting any questions about why she wasn't coming from the direction of the Long House. But being collected late couldn't be the explanation for Mary's distress.

'Mary, I can't help if you won't tell me what's wrong.'

She glanced in the rear-view mirror again; a red face with swollen eyes peeped back.

'S'nothing.'

'Well, that's not true. Please little one, your father is at home; I would like to know what's upset you before he sees you like this. Has someone at school been nasty? Have you fallen behind with one of your projects?'

The sniveling sound continued.

'Did you miss out on a part in the school play? Has one of the boys been mean?' Sarah asked, taking another look in the mirror.

The crying subsided into sniffing; a sleeve was wiped across the puffy face.

Sarah tried again. 'Has something happened to one of your friends?'

There was a long sniff from the back seat, and the faintest nod, but still no indication of what had happened, to whom, and why it was so distressing.

When they reached home, Sarah pulled to a stop and a snuffling Mary divulged another snippet. 'Caroline has to leave school and I'm going to miss her so much,' she mumbled, unbuckling her seat belt, and dragging herself out of the car, clutching her school rucksack as a makeshift comfort blanket.

Was this a money problem, Sarah wondered. Could the girl's parents no longer afford the fees?

'Just because she's not going to be at the same school,' she said, following Mary inside, 'doesn't mean you won't be able to see each other. You'll just have to make a bit more of an effort, plan things. We can ask her over whenever you like. I'll even drive over and collect her. Cheer up.'

Why should a friend moving schools cause such histrionics? Opening the emailed letter from the headmistress a few minutes later revealed that Caroline's exit had not been voluntary, and whilst Mr. and Mrs. Fetherston should be reassured their daughter had done nothing wrong, the headmistress wanted to meet with the parents as a matter of urgency to explain the circumstances surrounding Caroline's departure.

Mrs. Williams was a large lady, in her early fifties. It wasn't the first time Sarah had met her, but this was the first meeting in the headmistress's office. Today, Mrs. Williams' bulk was encased in a sage-green tweed skirt and plum-coloured jumper, matched with practical flat shoes and what Sarah's mother had referred to as 'American tan' coloured tights. The office was like its inhabitant: large and purposeful. The walls were covered with framed certificates evidencing the many talents and qualifications of Mrs. Williams, as well as landscape photos of school year groups; there were no unnecessary pictures, no flowers or potted plants or framed photos of family to distract from the day's academic responsibilities.

Sarah perched on the edge of the sofa. Beside her, Freddy reclined with his long legs stretched out in front of him. It was all right for him, he'd sailed through school with top marks and no blemishes; he'd only ever been inside a headteacher's study to be congratulated. She copied Freddy, shuffling backwards on the cushion and trying to drag her eyes away from the window. Steve's head is not going to pop up demanding a delivery, she told herself.

Opposite the parents, Mrs. Williams was sitting in an upright armchair that looked uncomfortable. The stiff back was not softened by a supportive cushion, and the seat was a little too low: forcing the occupant to reach up and grip the chair arms rather than resting her elbows on them. Maybe the chair kept Mrs. Williams alert in tense meetings with parents, who were forced to lounge on the squashy sofa at a slight disadvantage to the teacher. The headmistress straightened her skirt, smoothing it down over her knees, and then gripped the arms of the chair with her hands. It was an authoritative voice, but mildly comforting, reminding Sarah of her mother's soothing nurse's voice: 'Mr. and Mrs. Fetherston, I wanted to meet in person because I want to reassure you that we are on top of this. The school has a zero-tolerance approach to drugs.'

Sarah's eyes widened – was Steve's name about to be mentioned? Beside her, Freddy stiffened.

'Drugs, Mrs. Williams? That's the first I've heard of that word.' Freddy was running a hand up and down his trouser leg as if smoothing away wrinkles. Sarah hadn't seen him do that for ages.

'Yes, sadly, drugs, Mr. Fetherston. A girl in Mary's class has been caught in possession of drugs. She has been expelled and a thorough investigation is being conducted.'

'What sort of drugs?' asked Freddy.

Sarah sucked in her breath while Freddy rushed on, demanding to know who was conducting the investigation, how widespread the problem was and if the police were informed. So those are the sorts of questions an innocent mother asks if she learns about a drug dealer close to home.

Sarah listened to the headmistress battle to regain the upper hand.

'It's not as simple as that, Mr. Fetherston. Nowadays theses pills are frequently not technically illegal. They refer to them as, "legal highs".'

Sarah dug her hands into the squidgy cushion to push herself upright. At least Caroline hadn't been caught with cannabis. But she must stop this talk about drugs; the girl had hardly been caught pushing heroin on the lacrosse fields. It was the groundsman who should be sacked; a victim had been penalised instead of the perpetrator.

'What's this got to do with Mary?' she asked. 'And if the pills aren't illegal, why has Caroline been expelled?'

The headmistress rounded on her. 'Mrs. Fetherston. As the Americans say, "If it walks like a duck and it quacks, it's probably a duck". In her favour, when challenged, Caroline admitted what the pills were. Recreational drugs are strictly prohibited. Her parents have accepted our decision with no pushback.'

The headmistress folded her hands neatly in her lap, as if clasping a flower posy. Sarah was forced to suppress a giggle: deprived of the supporting armrests, Mrs. Williams was sinking down into the chair, her elbows now six inches below the chair arms.

Freddy asked in a firm tone Sarah didn't often hear him use. 'Is there a suggestion Mary is taking, or has in the past taken, any of these pills? Is that why you want to talk to us?'

What on earth would he say if he knew what his wife was doing?

'No, Mr. Fetherston,' gushed Mrs. Williams. 'As I said in my letter, your daughter has done nothing wrong. I merely wanted to ensure you are fully informed. Caroline and Mary were friends, and I suspect your daughter may not be as fulsome with the facts as I have been. Caroline may try to keep in touch, and I would strongly advise you against allowing that,' purred Mrs. Williams.

Freddy stopped fiddling with his trouser leg. He leaned back on the sofa. Sarah felt his fingers on her hand, opened it, and let his warm hand wrap around hers.

'Frankly, it's the slippery slope syndrome,' the headmistress continued. 'As you can imagine, this is a much-vexed topic at our conferences. A pupil starts experimenting with recreational drugs and then when that's not giving them a sufficient hit, they move up a notch. Before you know it, cannabis is replaced with cocaine.'

Where had that come from?

'So, are you recommending we ban Mary from meeting Caroline?' asked Sarah.

'That's what I am advising the parents of *all* Caroline's former chums to do. Thankfully, we think the drugs were uncovered before any real harm. My strong advice would be to ban your daughter from future contact, both physical and electronic. I know the former is easier to enforce than the latter.'

Freddy was now lounging back against the sofa, her hand gripped in his, giving it a comforting squeeze.

'I agree, Mrs. Williams,' he said. 'It sounds like we were lucky. It can be a problem for us at the University. We have children sometimes from very sheltered backgrounds suddenly given so much freedom. For most, the worst they suffer is a bad hangover from too much cheap Devon scrumpy. But sometimes they get mixed up with a seedier side of Exeter.'

Freddy rose, signaling the end of the meeting. 'I appreciate your honesty and your advice.'

The plum-coloured jumper was rising, too, and Sarah hefted herself forwards, accepting Freddy's offered hand.

As Mrs. Williams opened her office door, she spoke again. 'It's been a pleasure to see you both, even if the circumstances are not to my liking. I felt sure you would be understanding of the predicament these legal highs cause for those of us in positions of authority, being such a modern couple – there's only one other child whose parents pay our fees in bitcoin!'

Sarah hid her sharp intake of breath behind a spluttered cough. Freddy had his eyes on her; she imagined it was the same look he gave to an uncommunicative student in one of his tutorials.

'Yes, bitcoin,' he murmured.

'Sarah?'

She made a fuss of collecting her handbag from the side of the sofa. 'Got to move with the times,' she murmured. 'Balance my husband's passion for history.' She said, smiling at Freddy, who was holding the door open for her. Then she ran for cover via a shower of questions asking for technical advice about how to block Caroline electronically.

On her way home, Sarah mulled over the meeting. Freddy and the headmistress were united; Mary had been lucky but needed protecting from her former friend. Both the academics believed if Caroline hadn't been caught it was only a matter of time before peer pressure pushed a teenage Mary to experiment with those tablets, potentially precipitating a slide into ever stronger drugs. United in their understanding of the challenges posed by legal highs, and their relief that timely discovery of Caroline's habit had protected Mary and her classmates, neither of the academics had considered Sarah's opinion. She was the mother, whose naïve and sheltered existence protected her from the ugly realities of the harsh drug world. Or so the pair assumed. She had every intention of separating Mary from Caroline, but she would have preferred to see a little more sympathy for the child's plight, like a referral to the drug rehabilitation centre Sarah had been donating to.

The mention of cryptocurrencies had caught Sarah off guard. Given the number of overseas students, she'd not expected to be noteworthy for paying fees in bitcoin. Freddy was absentminded, but at some future point he would remember, and want to know why his conventional wife was behaving in such an unconventional way.

Chapter Eighteen

Behind the thick cream-coloured curtains, rain was lashing against the bedroom windows. Sarah lay listening to Freddy snore, ignoring the plip plop sound of the water, dripping onto the windowsill just a few feet to the left of her head – sneaking between the cracks in the woodwork created by a combination of time and the seasonal expansion and contraction of the wood. She was not going to spend the rest of her life in this house worrying about ancient leaking woodwork, weighed down under Nick and Mike's spell as they ran their little enterprise.

The alarm rang. Freddy rolled over, trapping her under his arm, snuggling into her back. She gently shook him off and sat up, reaching down for her slippers.

'Big day today, Freddy. Got to get going.'

Freddy snuffled. His dark curls disappeared under the covers as he hunkered down. To Freddy this morning was no different to any other, but this was the day Sarah was going to do something to wrestle back control of her life.

By mid-morning the rain had cleared, and Sarah took this as a good omen. She drove through the winding narrow lanes with their high Devon bank beech hedges lining either side: now brown and frayed at the edges where the leaves, buffeted by autumnal storms, had started to shed. She'd come prepared for the chilly day, with a coat, scarf, and hat. She was expecting the meeting to take place outside and had pushed a pair of wellingtons – thick socks crammed into one of them – into the boot, ready to cope with the aftermath of the morning rain. She splashed her way through the puddles, steering towards her morning mission. Driving past the back entrance and the sharp bend the motorcyclist had shot round, she felt her heart flutter. Would that night ever leave her alone? Could that man have avoided the collision if he wasn't drunk, or had his death been her fault?

She parked beneath the branches of the old cedar tree, pulled on her boots, and shored herself up against the cold with a hat and gloves, then wound a scarf round her neck, pulling it tight. In the Walled Garden she found Mike crouched down, sowing seeds into a trench a few inches deep. A line of string was stretched taut between two sticks along the side of the channel, ensuring the seeds were sown in a straight line. Did he use a tape measure to be sure each seed was planted equidistant?

She shut the door behind her, and he looked her way.

'Morning, luv. Planting some overwintering broad beans. Bit of a soggy job, but I've been putting it off for days. Wasn't that a dump of rain we had last night!'

Why did Mike persist in pretending they had a cordial relationship? And now, of all times?

'I brought back your jumper,' she said, holding out the garment she'd borrowed to cover her blouse on her last trip to Taunton. 'But I didn't really come to discuss gardening tips or the weather.'

Mike stood up, raining a few seeds back into the packet before folding the top over, holding the packet closed with his thumb.

'Right then, what's this all about?'

'I had a most unpleasant session at the lawyer's office last week. You'll be pleased to hear Harry was there too, and it was probably one of the most excruciatingly embarrassing moments of his life.'

Mike scuffed at the earth of the vegetable bed with his shoe, a smile puckering the corners of his mouth. 'Couldn't happen to a more deserving chap,' he quipped, not bothering to hide his broadening smile.

'But that's just it, isn't it, Mike? What about those of us who don't deserve it? What about Freddy? What about me? What about Mary? And I mean both my daughter and your former wife!'

The seed packet was being crushed in Mike's right hand; his left was playing with his lip.

'I am not going to let this happen! You are not stealing my inheritance.'

Breathing hard, she stood in front of the family adversary, hands on her hips, like a chasing terrier hoping a field mouse wouldn't scarper down its hole in the nick of time. Would he defend his actions?

Minutes of silence passed.

Mike pushed the seed packet into his pocket and inclined his head to one side. 'What's done is done. The Dower House is mine; I have no plans to part with it, and certainly not to benefit that arrogant twit, Harry. Anyway, what's all this talk about "my inheritance"? She never left you the house! You've got half her jewellery. Mary has her picture; and Freddy has a wodge of cash.'

'So, you don't deny what you've done. And that's all you have to say, is it, Mike? No apology, no explanation? You think it's fair the granddaughter is just left with a pretty picture!' Her voice had risen to a screech. 'You've nicked the best part of a million quid – half of which is rightfully mine – and why? To live in a big house you don't use. You spend your life growing illegal drugs, unnecessarily now – what are you going to do with the money from that?' She took a few deep breaths. 'Why? Why did you do it? Why do you want to live here all by yourself?'

Mike shot back at her. 'Why are *you* so desperate to live here?'

Sarah did a double take. 'What do you mean?'

'What's so wrong with your house? Have you reverted to your true class, obsessed with,' he adopted a mocking tone, '*hob-nobbing* with the gentry?'

'Don't start bringing class into this, Mike,' Sarah spat back. 'The people who came to visit Mary won't have anything to do with you, not now she's gone. They tolerated you for her sake; they never accepted you into their world. There won't be any more invitations to Open Gardens or Musical Evenings.'

'And they accept you, do they?'

'Yes. Unlike you, I don't make them feel uncomfortable.'

'Well, I'll just have to enjoy my own company then.'

'And you can live with your conscience, knowing you've stolen so much money?' She tried her second line of attack. 'You know I don't like Harry any more than you do, but what about me? What has Freddy ever done to you? What about just sorting my family out? Sod Harry, I'm not here to plead his case!'

Mike threw his head back and laughed throatily at her.

'Now we're at the bottom of the pit, where you belong. It's always really been about the money for you, hasn't it?'

'Don't patronise me. I am fighting for what's rightfully mine: mine and my daughter's – certainly not yours. You're a liar and a thief.'

Mike jumped out of the confines of the raised bed, shaking off the excess soil from his shoes. 'I suggest you learn to fight battles you can win, cos this isn't one. Learn to live with it. You don't know how lucky you really are, luv.'

'OK. Final question. How much will you enjoy the Dower House if you're parked in a cell? It's your choice. Either I tell the police about the little enterprise, or you give Freddy what's rightly his. This house should belong to him, not his brother and certainly not you. Mary should have left it to us because we have the grandchild, it should never have been left equally.'

'Another piece of free advice. People in glass houses shouldn't throw stones. If you tell, I do. How would you explain all that money to the cops? We'll go down together: then what happens to your life? All I have to do is open my Metamask wallet, show them the address I've transferred money to. Don't expect your husband to stand by you: that lot run a mile from the first whiff of a crime – don't I know it.'

She glared at his smug face. How had she ever agreed to be part of his blasted venture? She should have turned him in when she first discovered what he was doing.

'There's not much in there,' she said. 'Despite you thinking I'm driven by money, I've given it all away.'

'What you've done with the dosh is irrelevant. You still took it and that's illegal. I'm not sorry for what's happened. It took me years to worm my way back into Mary's affection after the cops caught me all those years ago.' Mike was wagging a finger at her. 'All stuff and nonsense; we should have been left to sort it out as a couple. It was only a caution. But oh no, that cocky little bastard of hers, Harry, persuaded her otherwise and used it as an excuse to separate us.'

'It was Mary's decision. Don't blame her sons.'

He shook his head at her. 'I'm just warning you, them sons will do the same to you. The family would disown you if they knew. Oh, and if you are suggesting we have a chat with the coppers, then I might also mention your new career as a delivery driver.'

She took a step back.

'That's unfair. I am protecting a child, and anyway he's moved schools so now Nick can't reach him you can tell your chum to make his own bloody deliveries.'

'Tell him yourself. Nothing to do with me!'

They stood in silence, Sarah breathing heavily. *How do I calm things down?* Hearing a loud squawk, she looked up; a large cock pheasant that had been sitting on the top of the south wall gazing at the warring humans was fluttering down to the ground. It scuttled over towards one of the still-laden vegetable beds behind Mike, lowered its neck and pecked at the crop, its vivid green neck darting up and down.

'Mike, you've got a hungry vegetarian enjoying your winter cabbages,' said Sarah, pointing at the bird.

Mike turned round and ran towards the pheasant, waving his arms around to shoo it away, then pulling over a protective net and bending to secure the ends into hooks fastened round the edge of the bed. He spoke over his shoulder as he worked, 'You've said your piece, now go.'

'But will you think about what I've said?'

He grunted. 'All right, I will think on it. But don't raise your hopes.'

On her return, via the supermarket, Sarah dropped the grocery bags on the kitchen floor. There was a little note from Freddy propped against an army of dirty mugs grouped together on the kitchen table beside four used plates and a scattering of breadcrumbs.

'Popped back for an impromptu lunch with colleagues. We finished the bread.'

There was even a PS seeking absolution on the grounds he knew today was weekly shop day. Thank you, Freddy, where did you think I was when you were creating as much mess as a party of teenagers? She scooped up the mess, seeing Mike's smug face as she dusted away the crumbs and polished the marble worktop with extra vigour. Had she penetrated Mike's defences? Surely the man had a conscience, and if he wasn't living at the Dower House, he could stop growing drugs for Nick.

Collecting Mary from school, she watched her slide in and hurl her dance kit onto the back seat. Sarah started to chatter, but each attempt was rebuffed with grunts and monosyllabic answers. Mary was engrossed in a more absorbing dialogue with friends: the telltale *ping*s from her phone announcing the arrival of another riveting comment to be pounced on.

'I'm just going to pull over and get a loaf, sweetheart. We've run out and they sell that wholemeal you like here.'

Mary raised her head from the screen.

'I'll go, you always do the shopping,' she offered, unbuckling her seatbelt as she spoke.

Sarah's eyes widened in surprise. Teenagers are so fickle. One minute you can't penetrate their world, the next they cast themselves as Florence Nightingale and can't be more helpful. Mary skipped across the forecourt and through the automatic doors.

Would Mike change his mind? She was on her own again, she couldn't talk to Freddy; maybe she could talk to Penelope? She didn't have to explain the stick she prodded Mike with. There was a *ping* on the seat beside her. Intrigued at her competition, she leaned over. 'Oh no!' she cried, reading the incoming WhatsApp message:

'You don't need to tell them it's at mine. Say the party is at Clare's house, and you've arranged a lift.'

The picture of the author confirmed it was from the pill-toting, banned Caroline, masquerading under a new profile.

Freddy walked into the kitchen, his mind spinning with the mistakes Oliver Cromwell made that led to the downfall of the protectorate. In his view, the final nail in the coffin was the ludicrous idea – as Cromwell grew sicker – of a hereditary Protector: the roundheads fought the civil war to end a hereditary monarchy, that dog was never going to hunt! Freddy dropped his jacket and briefcase in the middle of the kitchen table, sending the cutlery slithering across the surface, scattering to the four sides of the table.

Mary looked up from her phone. 'Hi, Dad!'

'Hello, darling,' said Sarah.

Could they have survived the death of Oliver Cromwell, if they'd opted for a more democratic way of selecting a new leader or was the

Protectorate always doomed once the lynch pin was removed?

He heard a raised voice. 'Darling!'

'Eh?' He kissed Sarah and she whispered in his ear, 'Could we have a chat after dinner, please? Nothing urgent.'

"Nothing urgent" in Freddy's experience roughly translated into "Suspend any plans you may have for the evening. Not in front of our child, but the very second we have privacy."

'So,' he said, closing the kitchen door behind Mary after dinner, 'what's up?'

She was rinsing plates and speaking with her back to him. 'In a word. Caroline.'

Freddy wrinkled his nose. Why did Sarah want to talk privately about history? He'd have happily discussed the Caroline period with her over dinner.

Sarah turned round and was staring at him. 'Caroline,' she said loudly as if trying to attract his attention. 'Mary's friend?'

He tutted. She didn't want to talk about the reign of Charles the first after all – the Caroline period, after the Latin for "Charles". 'That's the girl we've barred Mary from seeing?' he said slowly.

'Yes.'

Freddy sat down and reached for his wine glass, allowing Sarah to fill him in on the contents of the WhatsApp message. She wiped her hands then joined him at the table.

'There are two problems here, aren't there?' he suggested. 'She shouldn't have been in contact but, more dangerously, even if she hadn't pursued Caroline's ghastly suggestion of fibbing, Mary was prepared to discuss the idea of going to a party at this Caroline's house.'

'A party where those legal highs, or something even stronger, could have appeared,' added Sarah.

'She's bound to test the boundaries, darling, she's a teenager,' observed Freddy, topping up their wine glasses.

Sarah was glaring at him, her hands clenched. 'Are you condoning this?'

'No, of course I'm not.'

'Then what do you mean?'

'I'm saying we shouldn't be surprised we haven't kicked the

problem into touch at our first attempt. I, like Mrs. Williams, have a zero-tolerance policy towards drugs.'

Was it his imagination or did Sarah just blush? He peered at her, but her face was hidden behind her wine glass.

'We have to be able to trust her,' Sarah said.

'I agree.'

'She promised she wouldn't get in touch with that girl. I thought she was being so mature, that she understood what we were telling her about drugs and accepted her friendship with Caroline was over. Now I don't know if she took in anything we said at all.'

He ran his hands through his hair. Discipline was mostly Sarah's department, but this was serious.

'Do you think she has any idea we know?'

Sarah shook her head. 'No. I left the phone where it was and didn't say anything when she got back into the car.'

'Hmmm, tricky one. By the way, why *are* we paying Mary's fees in bitcoin? Have the trustees forgotten their fiduciary duties? That's hardly a gilt-edged investment.'

Sarah put her glass down.

'No. It's me, not them. They still pay into the joint account, and we make up the shortfall. I've been dabbling a bit with my parents' legacy. I was intrigued by bitcoin, and frankly I've done quite well with it. I must have paid out of my personal account instead of the joint one.'

Freddy gazed at Sarah for a few moments. She had told him all about the antics of her father, had she inherited a gambling streak?

'Done quite well?'

'I've been donating my profits to charity. That's why we've got ourselves onto the invite list for those fund-raising events.'

'Just as long as you don't expect me to go. It's your money. I don't like to interfere, but if you want to branch out into alternative asset classes, why not talk to Harry about wine? It's a lot safer than cryptocurrencies.'

'In the meantime, what are we going to do about Mary? Do we have another heart-to-heart? Do we gate her?'

Freddy finished his wine. 'We can do better than that. If she won't be told, she shall have to be shown.' He pushed the glass away. 'I will arrange a trip for her to meet one of my mature students. Heroin delayed his university studies by over a decade and by all accounts nearly killed him as he went in and out of rehab. She can hear a real story about the harm drugs do.'

Why had the colour just drained from Sarah's face?

Chapter Nineteen

Sarah crept down Penelope's drive in first gear: avoiding the worst of the potholes by weaving her way from one side to the other, like a skier between slalom poles. William – content to tackle the treacherous craters in his ancient Land Rover – wouldn't allocate money to road repairs, despite the storms washing away a little more of the tarmac each year. It seemed to Sarah that there was now more crater than there was driveway.

It was a week since her confrontation with Mike, and Sarah and Penelope were taking Mary to the RHS gardens at Rosemoor. Freddy had cried off the family outing to prepare for a guest lecture at St Andrews University, a fixture that now stalked Sarah's days like an upcoming FA Cup Final did in other households. A few days ago, he'd bounced into the kitchen like a little puppy, waving the invitation like a winning lottery ticket.

'Such an amazing opportunity, it's a real honour. I shall have to stay overnight, but you don't mind that, do you darling? I'm trying to decide what the theme should be. It needs to be thought-provoking.'

She didn't get a chance to offer an opinion before he wandered off, clutching the invitation to his chest like a love letter. Sarah was thrilled for him. She admired Freddy; he was besotted with history, he was genuinely gifted, had a rare talent to explore his subject matter from a new perspective, not just regurgitate hackneyed theories.

Sarah wasn't surprised Freddy had chosen Oliver Cromwell over RHS Rosemore, and bemoaned her fate to Penelope, who suggested she take his place. William was taking their teenage sons on a clay pigeon shoot, and Penelope preferred a girly outing to her husband shouting "pull" all morning and having to gauge which shots were "clean kills" of their clay targets – to be congratulated – as opposed to mere "wings".

'So, what news on the frightful fraud front?' asked Penelope.

Sarah glanced in the mirror and saw Mary's head bobbing up and down, her earbuds inserted. She turned towards her friend whose hands were flat against the seat bracing herself as the car lurched from one side to the other of the drive.

'To quote Frances King: "No answer came the stern reply!" said Sarah.

They reached the bottom of the drive and Sarah indicated to turn right. Penelope's head was trained to the left.

'All clear my way.'

Sarah looked anyway – since the accident she always checked three times before pulling out – and pressed a little harder on the accelerator to celebrate reaching the main road without damaging the car.

'Not necessarily a bad sign,' said Penelope. 'He hasn't said no. I don't understand why Mike stole the house. He's always struck me as kind. Was it revenge against Harry, or old-fashioned greed?'

'Fingers crossed it was the former – that way I'm in with a chance!'

'Yes, what possible reason has he got to be greedy? What could he want that a lack of money precludes?'

'Reason doesn't always drive the greedy. Do you think I should call him?'

Her friend pulled a face. 'No. What more can you say? He knows he shouldn't have done it, the scoundrel, only he can decide to make amends. You've no stick to prod him with.'

'True,' said Sarah.

Well, no stick her friend would ever know about, recalling a stick being wielded by someone else two nights ago, when she was alone. Freddy was giving a guest lecture in London; Mary was on a sleepover. She'd made herself a cheese omelet for supper then lit the fire in the sitting room and curled up on the sofa, her legs tucked underneath her. Sarah was enjoying a sneaky second glass of wine, half reading a book to the background crackle and hum of the burning logs and dreaming about living at the Dower House. She glanced at the picture of Lady Mary – now dominating one wall of the sitting room – whose dusky blonde eighteenth-century hair was stacked fashionably high, with startlingly white ostrich feathers attached to the top of the pile, hair curling down the creamy pale neck in cloudy waves; was this portrait destined to rehang at the Dower House – would Mike say yes? She'd begun to contemplate a complete makeover of the kitchen, stripping out the acres of orange pine, replacing it with modern units, the question was – what colour? Would dove grey be too cold, would sage green be better? Suddenly, she sat bolt upright.

'What was that?'

She dropped her book. Was that a bang? Had it come from the kitchen? Her eyes were wide, heart fluttering, she could almost physically feel her ear muscles straining; had she been mistaken?

There was a crashing noise. There *was* something going on in her kitchen.

Something or *someone*?

Surely, no one could be in there. If Freddy was away, she always locked the back door and checked the window catches before making supper. She sat up straight, breathing rapidly, her heart racing. What should she do? Her hand was rigid round the stem of the wineglass. She put it down, running through her options; they were limited. She was alone and her phone was on the copper tray.

Sarah stood up, dashed to the fireplace, and picked up the poker, standing with her back to the blaze, her eyes flickering around the room hunting for somewhere to hide.

The door was flung open, crashing against the wall; Sarah jumped backwards feeling the heat burning on the back of her legs. Nick took a couple of paces into the room and laid his hands on the sofa, leaning over it, his dark eyes staring straight at her, a little sneer playing at the corner of his lips.

'Evening, Mrs. Fetherston. Didn't startle you, did I?'

He laughed, but it sounded more like a cackle.

She held the poker tightly in her hands, upright like a samurai warrior. The metal was warm and felt solid. She tried breathing through her mouth, exhaling in breathy puffs.

'How did you get in?' she asked, trying to control her breathing.

He walked around the sofa towards her. She took another small step backwards, but it was too hot to move further away from him.

'I'm a man of many hidden talents.'

'Stay where you are, no closer.' Her voice was shaking. 'What do you want?'

Silently, he walked past her. Sarah tracked Nick's steps, moving her body in an arc, shifting her stance as he sauntered across the carpet as if it was his own and sat down in Freddy's armchair. Grinning up at her, he slowly folded his arms.

'You can put that poker down. I didn't come to hurt you, just to warn you. Mike told me you want to move in. Stop messing with my business or you *will* regret it. It's not just me you'll have to answer to; I'm quite nice compared to some of them. But then you've met one or two already, haven't you?'

She shivered, despite the heat. 'Does Mike know you're here?'

'No. But I don't need Darren's permission. No, what I need from *Mike* as you call him, is for him to keep growing stock.'

She lowered the poker; her wrists were starting to ache, but kept a firm grip and said softly, 'I'm not messing with your business. I just want what's rightfully mine.'

'Well, your wants clash with mine.'

'What do you mean?'

'We can't carry on the operation if you're living at the Dower House with your kid, and nosy husband!'

'The house isn't rightfully Mike's.'

'You stupid bitch.' He mocked her voice, 'the house isn't rightfully Mike's.' Then he continued, 'I don't give a damn if its rightfully his or not, and you shouldn't either. It works for me if he lives there, and it doesn't work for me if you do. End of.'

He got up, shaking his head. 'Sort out your priorities, Sarah,' he said and stalked to the door, where he paused. 'I'll see myself out, shall I? Would you like me to shut the door?'

Sarah didn't answer.

The door closed, and she counted to twenty to give him time to leave, then – carrying the poker – ran into the kitchen to retrieve her phone. She could feel a cold draft blowing from the utility room. She pushed the phone into her bra, and still gripping the poker, ran into the utility room which was bitterly cold. The door was wide open.

Shivering, she closed, relocked, and bolted the door, then shot up the stairs and locked herself into the master bedroom, pushing a chair up against the door.

She undressed and slid into bed, lying stiffly, wide awake, heart pounding. Why wasn't Freddy beside her? What would have happened if Freddy had been there? But there was never a chance Freddy would have been there; whatever he claimed, Nick had not come to warn her, but to frighten her, to demonstrate his power, choosing a night when she was alone. Sarah shuddered, imagining Nick outside casing the Long House, checking Freddy wasn't just running late. She pulled the duvet up to her neck; would Nick still have broken in if her child was at home?

Now, accelerating along the main road to Rosemoor, Sarah questioned Nick's motives for frightening her that night; it had to be connected to drugs. She cleared her mind of the scary memory, flicking a look in the mirror at her child, then asked Penelope, forcing a casual note into her voice, 'How's Angus?'

'Much better, and I am so relieved. He must have been getting the drugs from another boy at school. Since he's moved to Wiltshire, he's his old self. I can't even smell cigarette smoke on his clothes anymore!'

Brilliant. Wiltshire was beyond Nick's reach, someone else's "patch", and now Sarah was certain Angus had escaped Nick's clutches, she could hand in her notice. The odious man could deliver himself.

A couple of days later, Mike called, asking her to pop over for a chat. Sarah turned the car round; she'd come back and buy chicken food another time, there was still half a bag left.

Mike sat her down at the kitchen table. It had become remarkably untidy. There were piles of unopened post mixed up with unattended bills – bright red warnings poking out of torn envelopes, and seed catalogues: the mixture jumbled up as if lumped together in a recycling bin. He put a brown teapot on the table, pushing a multicoloured tea cosy which was dark brown, with jagged orange and yellow lines on its body, over the top. Where had he hidden that while Mary was living here?

Mike sat opposite her. 'Sorry about the pot,' he said. 'Your lot took all the silver; I don't have anything smarter.'

He brushed aside some papers, creating a space, and plonked down a carton of milk, a bag of sugar and two mugs.

'Does the same job,' she said, thinking back to the tea trays Mike had carried into the morning room, the silver all polished and sparkling. Mary would have hated to know they were meeting in the kitchen, sitting like two housemaids drinking tea from mugs with a brown teacosy-shrouded pot.

She was trying not to question why she had been summoned. If the answer was no, he'd have told her over the phone, wouldn't he? Mike picked up the teapot, gave it a shake, and then poured into both mugs. He pulled over the milk carton, dropping his nose and sniffing then added milk to one of the mugs and pushed the other in her direction, followed by the milk carton. Mike fussed over his own drink, stirring in sugar, blowing on it, and taking a noisy slurp.

She gritted her teeth, kept her eyes trained on her tea.

'Right, luv,' he said. 'I've got a proposal.'

Her head shot up as quickly as it would have if he'd shouted "FIRE".

'A house swap,' he said.

'You want the Long House?'

'No.' He gave her a sharp look. 'I swap this place for a farmhouse with a bit of land.' He handed her a brochure – two pieces of paper, stapled together, with small photos of the property on offer. 'This one.'

She scanned the pages. It was a small but pretty farmhouse; red-bricked- like Freddy's childhood home in Wiltshire and located – if the selling agents were to be believed – in the middle of nowhere. The asking price was less than the value of the Long House.

'It's a smallholding, forty-five acres. Too small to farm properly, but it'll do me nicely.' He stared into his mug as if waiting for the brew to give him inspiration and then admitted, 'You're right, it's never been the same for me since she moved into that home. I don't care if the toffs don't visit anymore, and it's not so much that this house is too big for one person. It's more that there's very little point without her here too.'

The Dower House had never been his dream, he explained. It

had been a prop; the last bauble dangled to persuade his wife – who fantasised about her Lampton childhood – to take him back. What Sarah wanted to know was why, if he never really wanted to live here, did Mike commit the fraud? Was it a simple case of revenge? 'Why . . .' she asked, picking up her mug and blowing on her own brew.

'Can't stand that Harry. He never visited her like you and Freddy did, Harry didn't love her like I did.'

She was right, his motive was revenge.

'You adored Mary, didn't you?'

'Oh yes, I worshipped that lady. You saw that.'

On one of her many visits, Mike delivered a tray with toasted tea cakes oozing with butter, followed by a basket of logs, later returning when summoned by the bell to clear away the cups and saucers, staking them as carefully as a trained parlour maid. Sarah had asked Mike if he minded being at Mary's beck and call, as she imperiously pushed bells and issued instructions, specifying what time she wished tea to be served, how many guests were expected to join and if she 'required' China or Indian tea leaves that day.

His reply was a simple no.

'Really?' she asked.

'Really. I don't begrudge her ringing that bell whenever she wants. Keeps me fit! She was born in an era when her class meant she was entitled to privilege. She's not a snob; she's just a lady from a bygone age. Until that disease took hold, she behaved like a proper lady every day of her life.'

Now Mike was stirring sugar into his second cup of tea. Sarah let him talk, learning he'd reached his decision batch-cooking pumpkin soup, questioning when he would ever eat it all, now there was no one to cook for, no visitors and no one to visit.

'I watched them onions sizzle in the pan, chopping up this year's bumper pumpkin harvest, and I was reliving those family dinners, all the anticipation I used to share with my Mary. For weeks we'd have such fun planning the menus. I spent days in this kitchen, loved every minute of it.'

Sarah saw his eyes circling the pine kitchen units.

'Oh, I loved preparing special treats to delight that lady with.' He said adding another spoonful of sugar to his tea. 'And all that effort was always rewarded. When I served those dinners, her eyes sparkled up at me. Mind, I resented cooking for that arrogant Harry. Not Freddy,' he held up his teaspoon and wagged it at her, 'I've nothing against your Freddy, just don't understand the man – what's so scary about the twenty-first century that prevents him wanting to live here with the rest of us?' He dropped the teaspoon onto the kitchen table, held his hands around the mug of tea as if to warm them. 'I miss those days.'

'We all miss Mary.'

'What's my life become, I asked myself. It's shrunk to the garden, really, and Nick's spoilt that for me.'

Sarah listened to Mike spilling out his heart. Mike talked about the garden cycle: sowing the seeds, potting on the seedlings, nurturing the crops, picking them, and composting down the inedible parts of the plants to fertilise the soil in preparation for the following year, and dealing with the harvest, making soup out of surplus vegetables. She couldn't begrudge her time, not after what he was doing for her family. They would have the house and Freddy's share of the money! Harry would cry foul, but she didn't care; it was how Mary should have divided the fortune in the first place, to ensure continuity.

Mike pointed to the brochure.

'I thought I might farm those forty-five acres, start growing organic fruit and veg, set up a little stall, travel around to farmers' markets. Give me a new sort of life.'

He confessed that without Mary to shape his day around, the garden and those polytunnels dominated his days.

'How I miss that woman. No bells summoning fruit cakes and scones, or homemade lemonade. No special requests for Welsh rarebit if she was feeling a little peckish of an evening. No one to fuss around and no one to force me to use the house as it was designed to be used.'

Sarah's eyes dropped to her mug, then across to the carton of milk and the tea-cosy clad teapot. She shouldn't judge. Mike had lived in this house the way his wife dictated, why should he continue to do so now she was gone? Was Sarah really going to prepare a tray of silver for herself, carry it through to the morning room and drink her tea out of a bone china cup and saucer?

Mike picked up the brochure, flicked through the scanty details.

'I know it's small, but it's all I need. I don't really go anywhere but this kitchen and my little bedroom now.'

She arched her eyes at him. 'Your little bedroom?'

'I moved out of the main one, when she was taken to that clinic. I just couldn't bear the nights alone in that master bedroom, lying awake recalling her sleeping beside me.' He looked up at Sarah. 'I think I knew I'd already spent my last night beside her.'

Sarah didn't comment. Had Mike's conscience been troubling him, did he deliberately let his wife be sectioned to avoid paying care home fees?

'So I moved. I chose a much smaller one.'

Had that been a form of penance?

'Just a shower, no bath. Mary never approved of taking showers.' He sat back and took a swallow of tea. 'She used to say,' he gave a little laugh, 'they were far too Continental, she wanted to soak in scented water, with candles for company.'

Sarah said, 'Yes, I learnt the hard way about her habit of using expensive bath oils!'

'I still can't bring myself to clear away them bottles of oil and her scented candles. Last night, I found myself drifting into our old bathroom and lifting a half-used bottle, pulling out the stopper and just sniffing the memory of her.'

They sat for a few minutes, drinking tea, lost in their recollections of a woman they'd both loved. Sarah sensed Mike was finished; she picked up the brochure, looking from it to Mike.

'So, if we buy Tiddleworth Farm for you, in return you make over the Dower House to me and Freddy. Is that the deal, Mike?' she asked, imagining herself walking from the pantry to the Aga, preparing evening meals for Freddy and Mary, her own kitchen table stood where she now sat, Mary's pencil case and headbands discarded in this room, the copper tray resting on the pine dresser.

'Yes, that's about the size of it. One small favour, though: would you mind if I had the picture of Lady Mary? I just want a keepsake to remember my own Mary by. I'd rather have it than the £10,000 she left me. I've no use for money. Do you think young Mary would agree to a swap?'

Sarah thought through the question.

'I don't think Mary is particularly attached to anything but her phone, and frankly, Freddy's favourite picture is the dashing cavalier. Let me speak to the lawyers. I think you can vary a Will, if all the beneficiaries agree. Harry may not like it, only because you are making the request, but I suspect Freddy and I may end up giving him some money – every dog has his price.'

'There's also the little enterprise to consider.'

She sucked in her breath. Surely, he wasn't going to suggest she took over the cannabis farm!

'I've told Nick I'm stopping in a year. That will give him enough time to find an alternative supplier. I have a fancy for a legitimate crop in them tunnels instead, some early salad leaves, rocket maybe. Just need to change the black plastic and that's not too dear.'

'I imagine he didn't like being given notice.'

Yesterday Sarah had also given Nick his marching orders, messaging *"find a new driver"*, then deleting him from her contacts list and blocking his number.

She shuddered, 'He's a nasty piece of work.'

Mike shrugged. 'Softest part of him's probably his teeth. That's why I've agreed to carry on for a year.'

If she wasn't expected to keep the polytunnels, what was Mike asking her to do? She wasn't prepared to start delivering again, even to secure the Dower House.

'I can move the plants and the polytunnels across to the farm. But the thing is I can't run the whole lot from there.' He lifted his eyes from his mug of tea, locking them onto hers. 'Not straight away.'

Whatever he said next, it was part of the deal.

'It's going to take longer to set up storage. I have to put in a track and convert a barn. I want to do it anyway, for me veg business. But we'll need to keep using the potting sheds here, for about three months after the swap.'

He rushed on; reassuring her he and Nick would only come during school hours. Three months didn't sound too bad. She had waited over a decade for her Georgian gem, and this deal would ensure Mary's wishes were – mostly – realised. Surely, Sarah could manage a few months after all she'd been through. Mike leaned over and poured more tea into both mugs, adding milk to his.

'Deal?'

'Back drive only!'

'OK.'

Sarah picked up the milk carton. Searching for a spoon amongst the mess on the table, she stretched out to reach the one Mike had used, and then stirred, thinking through everything that had been said.

'Deal. Provided you stop paying me. I don't want any more money.'

'Fine.'

At last! No one would have a hold over her anymore!

The couple didn't often row, but there was an almighty show down just before Freddy left for St Andrews. Sarah was looking forward to the trip as much as he was, but for different reasons. She had lived through each iteration of the debate about possible themes for the lecture, discussing the merits of each until he'd settled on: *'The significance of the Quaker movement on the demise of the Protectorate'*. For the last five days, Freddy had regularly trotted into the kitchen or tracked her down in the utility room, reciting paragraphs, explaining the significance of the argument, his eyes dancing and seeking praise like a cat dropping the spoils of a nighttime hunting expedition at its owner's feet.

She'd planned her ambush as thoughtfully as any mercenary soldier, timing it to coincide with Mary being at school and selecting the territory for the skirmish – his study, where the swashbuckling figure of the Cavalier watched over his descendant who was focused on his packing. Papers and charts were strewn across the floor; books were propped open on the desk; Freddy's bag was on his chair and was getting ever fatter as he pushed in journals and files and folders of notes.

Was this necessary when he'd written a speech?

She fired the first shot. 'I've got something to discuss.'

'Now?!'

'I've been discussing something with Mike.'

He grunted, straining to squash a book into the bag. 'You shouldn't have gone to visit that man on your own. He can't be trusted. He might have harmed you!'

'He never harmed your mother,' she retorted.

As she began to reveal the details of her conversations with Mike, Freddy stopped packing and his head shot forwards. 'What did you think you were doing, discussing my mother's estate?' Cramming yet more papers into his briefcase, he snapped, 'I know you think I'm a bit of a bumbling twit, but I wish you had discussed this with me before you went accusing him of meddling with Ma's money. That is not your business! Now where did I put that article, I wanted to show Professor Harding? Have you seen it? I'm sure I brought it into the kitchen for you to read last night?'

Sarah stalked into the kitchen, retrieving the missing pages from where they lay propped against the toaster, and returning to the study, tossed them at Freddy.

'Could you sit down?' she pleaded. 'And stop vacillating between centuries. What I'm telling you is not bad news. This is good news.'

He stopped, holding a sheaf of papers in one hand.

'Really?'

'Yes. Mike has agreed to help. He knows he shouldn't have done what he did, and he wants to put that right by giving us the Dower House.'

With his hand on his briefcase he exclaimed, '*Give* us the Dower House?'

'Yes.'

'*Us?*' repeated Freddy. 'The money was left to me and my brother jointly – what about Harry?'

'No, it's just for us,' reiterated Sarah. 'In exchange, we buy him a small farmhouse. I've spoken to a couple of local agents. We can easily afford to buy what Mike wants once we've sold the Long House.'

Freddy put the briefcase on the floor and sat down, cocking his head to one side. 'You and Mike have agreed a house swap? What about Harry? What about his share of the money?'

'He's not part of the deal.'

Freddy started shouting. 'Do you expect me to condone this scheme, and deprive Harry of his share of our inheritance? You cannot ask that of me, Sarah. He's my older brother; he's protected me all my life. I simply will not do that.'

'Freddy, this is his *entire* fault. He shouldn't have been so stupid. He doesn't deserve your adulation, and you don't owe him any favours,' she hissed back.

'It was a mistake any gentleman might have made.'

Sarah threw her hands up, shaking her head.

'Now I've heard it all. You two are so fixated on being gentlemen. There are aspects of your mother you should never have copied; some things simply have no relevance today. Her approach to money was one of them. She never understood money because she never had to make any herself.'

Freddy leaned back in his chair. He was gazing at her, wearing a puzzled expression.

'When did you become so fixated on money?' he said. 'Your life is charmed; why can't you just be happy with what we have? You have a wonderful daughter, we love each other, we have plenty of money and a really special home. All three of us are in rude health.'

'This would never have happened if the family took more care when she bought the house.'

'Are you blaming Ma for not checking the contract?'

'No, of course I don't blame Mary. I blame your brother. He should have stayed in the drawing room that day and forced Mike to talk to us *all* about the contract. Your brother should have smelt a rat when Mike insisted they talk in private – who did they need privacy from? It should have been obvious he was up to no good. Harry deserves to lose his share of the fortune. We don't.'

Sarah ran out of the room, stopped in the corridor, and stamped her feet like a child. Why was Freddy resisting? She felt a light grip on her arms and relaxed into his embrace, but he drew away. She turned to face him.

Softly he said, 'Just for a minute, think about what is happening to Harry and Amy. How can you be so selfish?'

'He's done it to himself,' she snapped.

Freddy spun round and with his back to her said slowly, 'You were there too. You could have suggested Ma review the document before signing it.'

'That's a bit cheap for you, Freddy. You know I've never bought a house. I wouldn't know which sort of purchase method to choose.'

There was a short silence. Freddy took her hand, pulling her gently back into his study where he cleared a chair for her and then sat down behind his desk.

'What about Harry and Amy?' he said. 'They were relying on this money. They are about to become homeless. Don't you care?'

'Of course, I *care*, but I'm not prepared to share their pain.'

Freddy opened his hands as if preaching. 'And what about me? What if I care enough about them to want to share their pain?'

Sarah got up and walked to the edge of the desk, put her hands on the leather top and leaned over. 'Freddy, I am sorry your brother has got financial problems, but he caused them, and he is also responsible for losing his inheritance. I haven't negotiated this deal to sort out Harry's mess. For once I am taking care of team Sarah, because I have always been taking care of someone else. I spend my life doing things for other people. You, your mother when she was alive, our daughter, or a charity. For once in my life, I'm putting my wishes, my hopes, and dreams, centre stage.'

His hazel eyes looked wounded; she turned hers away. Sarah wasn't going to refuse Mike's offer because Freddy didn't think it was fair to his brother!

'So, your mind is made up,' he said.

'Yes, it is.'

She told him she had already arranged for estate agents to value the Long House and get it on to the market. Then she stormed out of the study, throwing a final pithy message as she clattered up the stairs: 'I have never insisted on anything in our marriage before. Now I am!'

Chapter Twenty

Sandra was in full stride, barking out requirements. Sarah held the phone with her left hand, jotting notes with her right. Momentarily she allowed her eyes to drift across to the sky-blue cardboard box sitting on what had been her mother-in-law's desk. It was eighteen inches long, a foot wide and six inches deep. There was a ribbed cream ribbon wound round it like an old-fashioned parcel, with an elaborate bow tied on the top. Just finish this call, she told herself. Remember your responsibilities; the contents are your reward.

'I am sorry it sounds like a lot to load on you, on top of all you've done already. Everyone's offered to do a little bit more. But we all know what a super cook you are, and you've so much more storage space now.'

Yes, she had much more room. Sarah glanced at the list, and then put her pen down, stroking the side of the blue box as if it was a slumbering cat.

'Don't worry about me, Sandra, I shall make the time. It's so unlucky for two of our crew to be struck down by flu. You can't bake if you're stuck in bed, can you?'

She had become more confident in managing people's demands since the move and brought the call to a close – 'Now if that's all?' – before laying her phone down next to the baking list and undoing the cream ribbon. As she pulled the lid off, the tissue paper within rustled in protest. She brushed it aside to reveal the contents – two piles of invitations.

Mrs. Frederick Fetherston
At Home

And in the right-hand bottom corner

RSVP
The Dower House

She snipped the ribbon that held the cards together and lifted one out. A stiff white card, edged with a gold trim so slim it was barely visible – stunning. She kissed the card and skipped down the corridor through the green baize door into the kitchen, where she propped it on the pine dresser next to her favourite mug, just above the copper tray, where Freddy would be able to see it.

The family had been living at the Dower House for over two months. The move was made more awkward by Freddy refusing to involve himself, as if somehow by ignoring the mounting evidence of the imminent sale of the Long House he could prevent its loss. Single-handedly, Sarah showed enthusiastic house-hunters round their home, explaining the embarrassing presence of her sulking husband – holed up in his study like a grumpy teenager – with a casual, 'Sorry, he has a pressing deadline on his book.'

All the arrangements for the sale of the Long House to the young couple moving to their first house in the country from Bristol were dealt with by Sarah: price negotiations; the legal papers; haggling over the curtains and carpets and light fittings. She found and appointed a removals firm, dealt with the packing boxes, tied things up with the utility companies, and quarterbacked the purchase of Mike's new home as well as the transfer documents for the Dower House. She hardly had a moment to herself for months, but she had the widest smile as she coasted down the drive on the day of completion: her daughter by her side. Mary was chattering, bouncing from topic to topic like a little puppy exploring a box of toys pulling each plaything out and bobbing straight back for another; the chickens cowered in a large cardboard box on the back seat, no doubt speculating on their fate.

Freddy drove over alone, the car crammed with the contents of his study. Even Sarah was prevented from helping with his packing. She did prepare several boxes – taping them securely at the bottom and stenciling FREDDY STUDY on the top flaps in black felt-tip pen, leaving them just inside his hallowed space. Later that evening, tidying the coats and hats away from the hallway, she heard his study door click open. A box emerged, followed by an arm. The box was placed in the corridor, and then the arm withdrew. She watched the procedure repeated multiple times, and then the door shut with a soft crack. Sarah stalked down the corridor and gently kicked the pile of cardboard. Empty.

The following evening Freddy returned from Exeter with his own slightly smaller boxes.

'Why?' she demanded, as he walked past her without a greeting.

'These have cut-out handles.'

'So?' she said.

'More suitable for my papers.'

Was it a last act of defiance; an impotent demonstration that Freddy still controlled a portion of family life, albeit one that no one else intruded on anyway?

The winter day of the move, snowdrops formed a white carpet of welcome, their penny-sized flowers rustling in the winter breeze; the larger, more colourful heads of the hellebores cheerfully greeting their new mistress. Sarah was the new chatelaine of the Dower House! Freddy would come round; time would heal the small rift formed since she forged ahead without his support.

Freddy had tried to talk her round. Returning triumphant from St Andrews – where his lecture was hailed as "thought provoking" and "casting a new light on a forgotten force in history"– he'd asked her to change course. Pushing his hand through his curly hair in that gesture she still loved, he pleaded with her. 'I don't like this plan, darling, and you know I can't support it. This is simply not the way our family behaves. Please think of Harry and Amy. It isn't like you to be selfish.'

He folded her in his arms. She cuddled in feeling secure as he gently pulled her towards him, nuzzling his face in her hair.

'That doesn't mean it's not right for us. For our family,' she murmured into his shirt front, inhaling the familiar sharp citrusy scent.

He leaned back, his tawny eyes looking down on her.

'But if we sold the Dower House,' he said, 'rather than lived there, would Mike care? And he couldn't do anything about it if he did, not once it's ours. We could share the money with Harry, exactly as Ma wanted.'

She gazed up at him.

'She shouldn't have left it equally, Freddy. She always said continuity was important, she should have left the house to us; we've got Mary.'

He drew away a little, but still holding her in his arms. She peeked up at Freddy feeling cossetted as – stroking a strand of hair off her face – his fingers lightly brushed her cheek.

'No. You are wrong, darling. If she was going to leave the house to only one of us, it would always have been to Harry as the oldest son. It would never have been left to me. I feel we've colluded with Mike, that we've diddled Harry out of his inheritance, behaved just as badly as Mike.'

She squirmed in his embrace.

'I'm sorry, but my mind is made up. Harry has always scoffed at me. Why should we help him? Can you honestly say if the positions were reversed Harry would help me?' She gave him a hard look. 'We must think about us for once. Please come with me on this one, Freddy – I'd so much prefer us to be a team.'

'Sarah, this is about you, not us. It's not about our family, or our team. You want to live at the Dower House. You always have.'

Never having moved house before, Sarah was unprepared. It was the little things that kept tripping her up: locating the kettle on move day; forgetting to turn the Aga up to cooking temperature – unhelpfully Mike had turned it off; arranging for a plumber to connect the washing machine – she'd never heard of a jubilee clip and if she asked Freddy, who'd shut himself into his new study, he might not even laugh at her, he might just scowl. As she chivvied her family into new routines, she pointed to all the fun they were going to have. Their very own Walled Garden! Summer evenings, when she and Mary could set off with a wooden trug to pick their own fruit, selecting berries for jams and puddings, popping a few in their mouths as they harvested; winter Sunday lunches when Mary could choose which home-grown vegetables she wanted to eat. They would grow leeks and dark leafy spinach, purple and white sprouting broccoli, and a mixture of colourful squashes and cabbages. Mike had left some of his winter crop. He'd offered to come and dig in the green manure growing in the raised beds, pointing out it would be an easy job for spring and that he could fit it in alongside a trip to the potting sheds. Sarah refused, claiming she wanted the exercise – a little free gardening labour was a poor exchange for risking three months storage extending to four. Sarah had reneged slightly on the deal, restricting her former partners to a single potting shed. She told Freddy she'd agreed to let Mike store some of his gardening tools for a few months.

Only a month until I'm free of that pair! She cracked an egg and used the shell to separate the white, sliding the bright-yellow yolk into the cake mixture. Her hens were comfortable in their new fox-proof enclosure beside the Walled Garden and were just as pleased with their new accommodation as she was with hers. Heaven for a chicken, with windfall fruit and brussel sprout stalks regularly tossed in for them to scrap over. She had arranged for contractors to dig down two foot, fencing beneath the surface to prevent burrowing foxes, and staked out a generous plot, large enough for them to be able to dart about and clean or cool themselves in dust baths in summer. The hens settled quickly but it took weeks for the family to adjust to their new routines. Freddy moaned about the length of the commute, but even he mellowed when Mary announced it was "fab".

'I mean it's good to be living where Grandmamma lived, isn't it?'

On the family's first weekend they wrapped up against the winter chill to tour the gardens. Freddy had no plans to help outside, but Mary did, suggesting they invest in a polytunnel to replace the two that had stood in the Walled Garden either side of the Victorian green house; strips of bare earth standing out from the surrounding grass. Sarah rebuffed that idea.

'Let's see how we get on with just the greenhouse and the raised beds,' she replied, standing together with the two people she loved. This was her responsibility now and Mike had never grown vegetables in either of those missing tunnels.

Their new home was close to Mary's specialist dance teacher, and she could cycle there. Instead of the occasional group lesson, she now had individual tuition twice a week after school. She was also enrolled in a local amateur dramatics group that met each Thursday evening in Bideford, too far to cycle to, but Sarah had not expected to relinquish all chauffeuring responsibilities. There was another trip

Mary often took; the Dower House was closer to Langton Manor, and when he was home from boarding school, Mary frequently cycled over to meet Angus, also keen on drama. Penelope claimed she could date her son's sudden fascination for the arts, to his meeting Mary at a family Sunday lunch party at the Manor.

Sarah's in-laws had also moved house. The gorgeous Ashe Hall was sold; their debts cleared. There was no money left over. Freddy floated the idea of giving his brother £100,000.

'I think that's a good idea. Tell him I will speak to the lawyers and ask them to vary the terms of the Will, so he gets an additional slug of the cash when it's distributed. Harry might find it easier to accept if it's done that way.'

She was rewarded with Freddy's first smile since the agent was appointed to sell the Long House.

With a sizeable mortgage, guaranteed by Amy's father, the money enabled her in-laws to purchase a small flint cottage close to Ashe Hall on the Norfolk Broads. He still ran his wine business: sitting rather pompously behind his grandfather's antique partner's desk in the garage, dispensing advice about wines he could no longer afford to drink himself. Sarah suspected the more valuable of her mother-in-law's possessions that found their way to Suffolk would serve as a piggybank; that her brother-in-law would sell them piece by piece to top up his income.

Harry recast himself and Amy in the role of "impoverished victims of a fraud" to be indulged by rich county friends and the scarlet tartan suit still enjoyed plenty of airings to smart dinner parties. Life would never be the same for them. They were muddling through. Sarah told Amy that Mike had gifted them the Dower House, claiming he suffered a pang of conscience about young Mary. Her sister-in-law was speechless for a few moments, then ended the call with a strangled, 'You bitch!'

Harry called Freddy, demanding to know why his brother was allowing his "scheming vixen of a wife" to swindle him out of his inheritance. Which presented Sarah with her current dilemma – should she invite her in-laws to her *At Home*? Would her brother-in-law consider an invitation rubbing salt in his wounds? Would he consider it a snub if he wasn't invited? Harry had no right to be offended; Sarah deserved to be living at the Dower House. For all Harry's airs and graces, and Freddy's genteel mannerisms, they had both forgotten what allowed them to lead their privileged lives. All these lofty families could trace their lineage back to an ancestor who was rewarded for doing something outstanding – being indispensable to a King or Queen; instrumental in winning a battle; innovating in the Industrial Revolution. Somewhere in all those histories was an overachiever recognised for their accomplishment. The descendants, including Harry and Freddy, reaped the rewards earned by their predecessors. Occasionally the spirit that spurred the original success resurfaced in the lineage, though that hadn't happened with either of the Fetherston boys. Harry had all the determination to succeed, but for all his bluster he lacked the attention to detail; Freddy possessed all the attention to detail but was indifferent to the trappings of wealth. It was Sarah who had rekindled the spirit of success in the family. It was Sarah who had fought tenaciously for what she wanted. She had earned the right to live at the Dower House with the same motivating force that created the Fetherston family fortune, preserving it for herself and her daughter.

Yes, I deserve to live here, she thought, gazing around her new kitchen, at the yards of pine. She glanced at her watch.

'Oops!'

She opened the Aga door, pushed in a cake, sprinted to the copper tray, tearing off her apron as she ran and grabbed her keys. I've earned our new life, and I'm loving it!

Mary shot off up the stairs as if catapulted from a sling, not stopping at the half landing, instead accelerating up towards her bedroom. The navy-blue school cardigan was swinging from where it was tied round her waist by the sleeves.

'Mind you don't trip, little one,' called out Sarah from below.

'I've so much to do before dance class. I must practice for the auditions for "*As you like it*," yelled down Mary, charging up the steps.

'I can drop you instead of you cycling. Save time.'

Mary leaned over the banister, grinning down at her mother from the first floor. 'Thanks, but I should be fine, I'll just have to pedal a bit faster!'

Sarah headed for her new kitchen. By six o'clock, she had iced a Victoria sponge cake and the last chocolate cake was in the oven. An egg-shaped timer – dark red with white spots – sat beside the kettle, ticking down the minutes until the cake was ready. Supper was also made and in the warming oven. Freddy was later than usual for a Tuesday; she wasn't worried, sometimes he lost track of time. His supper would keep if needed; it wouldn't be the first time she and Mary ate alone, Freddy turning up when Mary was licking her way through a bowl of ice cream.

She dialed his mobile. It went straight to voicemail. Was he still working? Had he forgotten to switch it on? Or maybe he was in a rural reception blackspot? Mary wasn't back either, but Sarah didn't expect her for another ten minutes. Mary had left in a whirl of excitement, her dance costume straggling from the little backpack slung over one shoulder.

'Helmet, Mary,' she'd chastised her child, pushing the dangling dance clothes back into the bag.

'Got it,' she said, raising her left hand and waving the helmet. 'Don't fuss, Mummy!' she moaned, leaning over to wipe a finger round the mixing bowl. 'Yummy, chocolate, is there going to be one for us too, there's not much left of the one in the larder?' she asked, dashing back out, leaving the green baize door swinging behind her.

Sarah tried Freddy again. No answer. She tossed the phone onto the copper tray, pausing to stare for a moment at the invitation and started laying the table. The doorbell rang, sending a ripple of pleasure through her. Now she was the one who passed down the corridor – it was *her* octagonal hallway she crossed before opening the glazed doors onto the short inner hallway and sliding back the lock, to answer her imposing front door.

She popped the ticking timer into her apron pocket, feeling it trembling against her body, wondering who she would be admitting. She wasn't expecting anyone, but she had fast learned that owning the Dower House brought responsibilities and plenty of visitors. She embraced her new position as the respected lady of the big house. The villagers expected support for local causes, and she gave it willingly: both her time and, where necessary, money. People regularly dropped by, hoping to be invited into the house for a cup of tea as they tapped her for a raffle prize or thrust a crumpled sponsorship form into her hands, a shy youngster shuffling by their side. She always asked callers inside, enjoying their gawping at the sheer size and opulence of her home.

Her first visitor had been one of the church wardens, dropping by to welcome the new family to the community. 'Just wanted to leave one of our information leaflets, let you know about upcoming events, prayer meetings, Bible classes, and of course when the church services are!'

'Thank you, how thoughtful. I'm Sarah Fetherston, do come in for a cup of tea if you've time,' said Sarah, inviting the lady to introduce herself.

The visitor accepted, wiping her feet zealously on the doormat and tiptoed into the hallway.

'Oh gosh, thank you ever so, I'm Susan Johnston, I've never actually been invited into the big house before!'

Susan was 'astonished' and 'amazed' and 'astounded' every step of the way to the morning room. It took fifteen minutes to cross the octagonal staircase hall! For over an hour Sarah poured tea and fielded Susan's stream of questions while the visitor wandering round the morning room pointing at each vase and every picture. This woman had never stepped beyond the velvet rope before; fifteen years ago, neither had Sarah.

'Are all these things really yours? I don't mean yours personally; I mean do all these beautiful objects belong to your family?'

'Yes. They do now.'

'Wow, aren't you lucky. Mind, I think I might be a bit nervous of the dusting!'

Sarah held up the teapot. 'You get used to it. More tea?'

'Oh, ta very much,' said Susan passing over her cup. 'You inherited, didn't you, I mean the house, you inherited the house?'

Sarah handed back the full cup. 'Yes. It used to belong to my mother-in-law.'

'That's one of life's most precious gifts, isn't it, family. You can have all the money in the world but there's no point without your family. Children?'

'One daughter, Mary, named after her grandmother.'

'Awww, that's lovely, that is. Did she leave you all the furniture too?'

Sarah stood up, shaking the empty teapot then staring at the carriage clock on the mantlepiece. 'Heavens, is that the time!'

Susan took her cue and Sarah was able to close the front door on the guest, vowing to learn how to curtail future house tours without being rude.

Each time Sarah answered the front door, she felt the corners of her mouth twitch recalling that first visitor. Who would it be tonight? Sarah closed the door to the octagonal hallway, humming to herself as she slid back the bolt and opened the front door.

There were no villagers outside, just Mike, and he was covered in blood.

Chapter Twenty-One

Mike was bent over, his hands on his knees, panting heavily, exhaling little white puffs of warm air. Sarah rushed outside.

'Mike!'

He lifted his head, squinted up at her. There was a large gash above his left eye and a stream of scarlet was running over his face and trickling down his neck into his jumper. There were splatters of blood on the flagstones.

'Sarah,' he panted. 'Thank God you're home, help me, please.'

She stepped closer. 'Whatever's happened?! Come in, I'll call an ambulance.'

He swiped at the cut with his sleeve, pushing blood up into his hair, then propping himself up on one of the pilasters, made a stop sign with his other hand.

'No, don't call anyone. There's been an accident.' He paused, breathing heavily to catch his breath then puffed out, 'Freddy?'

Freddy! Her heart pounded; she felt her throat tighten. Freddy, that was why she couldn't reach him, why he hadn't answered her calls.

'No! Where? Is he all right?' she cried, her hands flying involuntarily to cover her mouth.

Mike shook his head, and then wheezing as he did so, stood upright, leaning his weight against the plaster column, still panting.

'It's not Freddy.' He caught his breath then explained, 'Wanted to check he wasn't home.' He took in a deep breath then continued, 'Please just come. I don't know what to do.'

'Come where? Where are we going?'

She was talking to his back – Mike was shuffle-jogging off. She followed, leaving the front door open. In the dusk, Sarah couldn't see where she was going, she could just about make out Mike lumbering down the path towards the Walled Garden. She heard a loud clapping noise and jumped, but it was just the beating wings of a pigeon disturbed from its roosting spot in the trees. She shuddered and picked up her pace, trying to keep up but treading carefully on the unlit path. Her teeth started to chatter, and she wrapped her arms around her chest. It was still winter, and she was wearing a thin blouse and skirt with just an apron as a jacket: she wasn't well dressed for this adventure. At least she was wearing pumps.

A light was shining in the distance, casting a creamy white triangle into the darkness. It was coming from the potting sheds, the middle one – the door was open. She saw Mike come to a stop in the doorway, waiting for her. Crossing the back drive, she glanced down the lane, and saw a car driving past, its headlights illuminating a gap where her gate should have been – the gate was propped wide open. Why?

'Mike, what is going on? Where's the accident and why is the back gate open?'

'Over here,' he called softly.

The back gate! She looked at her watch and yelped as if she'd been scorched. 'Mike, quick, Mary's on her way home from dance class, and if she sees that gate open, she might use it.'

Nick! His words, that night he'd broken into the Long House. *Sort your priorities out, Sarah.* Was leaving the gate open carelessness on Mike's part, or deliberate on Nick's? Was Nick out here somewhere in the pitch dark? And what were either of them doing here at this time of night - it was hardly school hours! She was already running, stumbling in the dark as she struggled over branches littering the back drive. One of her shoes came loose and she fumbled in the dark, hopping on one leg trying to shove the shoe back on. She could hear Mike crunching his way down the track behind her, and then she heard a thud and Mike cursed. She didn't stop.

The road in front of her became a carpet of light. She moaned then sprinted towards the gate. Sarah saw the bonnet of a car hurtle round the corner and she froze, and then screamed. She started to run again, crying out, 'NO! Mary, NO,' just as the timer sounded from her apron pocket.

Freddy came to a stop by Sarah's car. He pulled a notebook out of the glovebox and sat for a few minutes jotting. What had fuelled the royalists' unwavering loyalty to the Crown during the five years of "interregnum" despite the strength of support for the Republic? Would his students be tempted to draw parallels with Churchill's "We shall never surrender" speech in 1940? He believed it was closer to the sixteenth century Catholics risking lives and fortunes to practice their religion, resisting Henry the XVIII and the horror of converting to the Anglican faith. Still pondering the analogy, he locked the car.

Why is the front door open?

Closing it behind him, Freddy called out, 'Hi girls, I'm home. Someone's been naughty and left the front door open.'

He pushed at the green baize door; the lights were all on, but the kitchen was empty.

'Sarah, Mary! I'm home!'

He gazed around the silent kitchen. His eyes fell on a pile of cutlery dumped in the middle of the kitchen table. He finished laying the table and fetched himself a glass of wine. No one joined him. Freddy paced the house but there was no sign of Sarah or Mary. He dialed Sarah's mobile; it rang and rang then he heard her message system. He kept calling, only stopping when he checked the kitchen again and heard the phone ringing. The sound was coming from the copper tray. Why would she leave the house without her phone? Where are they?

Freddy sniffed.

Phew, what's burning?

His phone rang.

'Sarah?'

'Freddy, it's Penelope. I can't reach Sarah.'

'Neither can I. No idea where either she or Mary are.'

He heard Penelope inhale.

'Well, that's the thing. Mary was here, she was with Angus, but they've disappeared.'

'Disappeared, as in *missing*?'

Penelope was not her usual calm self. Freddy started to breathe a little faster.

'Her bicycle is still here, but I went to take them something to eat over an hour ago and couldn't find them. I've searched the whole house, and the outbuildings. It's dark and I'm getting worried.'

'Blimey. Does Sarah know? Is she out searching for them?'

'I can't reach her. She's not answering her phone.'

His hand reached down to scratch the side of his trousers.

'What does William think? Have you telephoned the police?'

'No. I wanted Sarah to know first. William's rushing back from a committee meeting.'

'Ask William to call me when he gets back. I must find Sarah.'

She couldn't have gone far without her phone. Maybe she forgot to collect the eggs; she's been so tied up with that blasted charity dog show. Why didn't she find someone else to run the wretched event when she knew we were moving house? Or tell blasted Sandra to do some of the heavy lifting. He pocketed her phone, set his own on torch and ran outside cursing "Mrs. Delegator". Sarah's attention was deflected, she was allowing Mary too much freedom and that lackadaisical approach had come home to roost. Where could the youngsters have gone? Penelope was too upset to press for more details, he would ask William – although he was only just sixteen could Angus drive? And were any of the estate vehicles missing?

Freddy started his search in the old stables, yelling out for Sarah and shining the phone into each cubicle in turn. Not there. He was jogging past the back drive, towards the potting sheds, still calling out her name, following the bobbing path of light from his phone when he heard her answering call.

'Freddy!'

'Sarah!' He swung the torch about, finding her feet, then travelling up past a chocolate-smeared apron to her face, which was pale. Maybe she already knew.

'You haven't seen Mary, have you?' he asked.

'She'll be on her way back from dance class. The back gate was open, I just closed it.'

He shook his head. 'She didn't go to dance class, she went to meet Angus at Langton, and Penelope can't find either of them.'

Sarah gasped, 'She went to see Angus? I didn't realise Mary even knew Angus was home schooling this week after a tummy bug. Is Penny sure?'

'Yes. She said her bicycle is there, they were rehearsing a play.'

'They must be there somewhere!'

His phone vibrated in his hand. *William!* 'Found them?'

'No, but I haven't conducted a thorough search. I don't want to offend the ladies, but I think it's best if we leave them to man our respective forts, just in case either of the rascals comes home, while you and I search.'

'I'm on my way.'

He handed Sarah her phone.

'I'm coming too,' she protested.

'No. One of us needs to be here in case she comes home,' he ordered, sprinting back towards the house.

Sarah followed, picking her way back down the path by the light of her own phone torch. She heard footsteps behind her and turned round. Her eyes were drawn to the gash on Mike's forehead. She blew out a long slow breath, she'd forgotten about Mike and his problem.

'You should get a doctor to look at that. You might need stiches.'

He dabbed at the cut with his fingers, 'It'll keep. I've padlocked the back gate. It's all safe; she'll have to go round to the front. Can we go back to the shed now?'

'Bit of a drama of my own now,' she said.

'Please.'

She had her phone. If Penelope had news, she would call, as Freddy would if he came across Mary cycling home; she should at least find out what had happened to Mike.

'Five minutes,' she said.

He scarpered off to the open potting shed. She caught up with him, standing in the doorway with his arms wrapped around his ribcage, shaking. Sarah peered inside: it was chaos! Somehow the shelving unit had come loose from the wall and fallen onto the floor, throwing bags of cannabis randomly across the room. It looked like the aftermath of a pillow fight, but with bags of brown leaves and buds replacing feathers; a large pile was trapped beneath the heavy metal shelves and Mike was staring as if hypnotised by those bags.

Sarah gazed at the bags of drugs, then up at Mike, then back down at the brown jumper she had mistaken for bags of cannabis. Her eyes travelled up the jumper towards the head of the wearer. It was a man, but the heavy shelving unit concealed most of his face.

Why does my potting shed resemble a scene from an Agatha Christie movie?

'Mike?'

She heard him clearing his throat.

'It's Nick.'

For the second time that evening, her hand shot up to her face, covering her mouth.

'He looks badly injured.' she mumbled through her fingers.

Mike swallowed.

'He's dead.'

Her hand dropped to her chin, and she turned towards Mike, her eyes wide and questioning.

'Dead?! Mike, he *can't be*, it's just a shelf unit. He must be unconscious. We need to call an ambulance.'

'No use,' he sobbed. 'His head hit the concrete. It was the most terrible cracking sound. I'll never forget it.'

'Are you sure he's not just unconscious?' she suggested.

Mike closed his eyes, shook his head, then spoke calmly.

'There's no pulse. I did check.'

'Wow.'

Mike was gushing, telling her it was an accident. Sarah tried to concentrate, but her mind was starting to wander – where is Mary, has she had an accident, is she lying injured somewhere? She should get back to the house just in case Mary showed up. But Mike was telling her Nick was dead! She detested the man, but he didn't deserve to die, he could only have been in his forties.

'I had me suspicions,' Mike was saying. 'Thought he was cheating, has been for months. He was being paid and he wasn't passing on the money. I followed him here and we had a fight. He hit me with a trowel.'

Mike was fingering the gash on his head, grimacing with pain, and then he pulled his bloodied hand away, wiping it on his trouser leg. Sarah may have loathed Nick, but they couldn't leave him lying here in the cold in a pool of blood. There was a wife – Sarah had helped Nick choose her last anniversary gift – Mrs. Henderson was probably expecting Nick home for supper.

'I pulled the shelves over. Thought it would give me a head start. He's much younger and fitter. It hit him on the head, and he fell over, and then this awful cracking noise.'

She took deep breaths, trying to calm her heart. It was throbbing so hard she was sure Mike could hear it.

He turned to face her. 'What are we going to do?'

'Mike. Did you just say what are *we* going to do?'

William met Freddy outside the front door, and from the look on the Colonel's face, there was no point asking if the youngsters had turned up. Telling himself she was a sensible girl, and wouldn't have gone far, promising not to punish her and that he'd just get her safely home where they could talk it all through in the morning, Freddy listened to William's plan of action, grateful that at least Mary had chosen the son of an ex-army officer to go missing with. Spotting the pink bicycle leaning against the paneled wall of the entrance hall Freddy felt a lump in his throat. For a few moments, he let his hand rest on the seat Mary had so recently occupied. *Where was she?*

They started with the house.

Penelope reported she'd last seen the pair in the library, rehearsing for *"As you like it",* Angus reading the part of Orlando to Mary's Rosalind. The room was warm, the fire was still glowing. William switched on the lights, illuminating two copies of Shakespeare's play lying face down on the floor in front of the fender.

'Nearly out, and the logs are seasoned oak. No one's fed that fire for a good two hours. Come on, basement first, then we'll work our way up to the attics.'

An hour later, with no sign the pair had been anywhere other than the library, Freddy was finding it difficult to fight off a mounting sense of panic. Sarah was pestering him for information every twenty minutes, and Penelope was following the men round like a faithful Labrador, offering cups of tea or slices of toast. She suggested a glass of wine, and William snapped.

'Pen, Freddy's not here on a social call! His daughter has gone missing on *our* estate, with *our* son. And given that he's three years older, I suspect this was his idea. When we've found them, you can fetch us all a brandy. Until then we need sober heads.'

Freddy asked, 'How old is this house?'

The owners of Langton were eyeing each other, William's lips pursed; did they think he'd forgotten why he was here, allowed his thoughts to slip back a few centuries when something so serious was at stake? Is that the way our friends see me? Is that the way my family see me? Was that part of the reason Sarah wanted to be here because she doesn't trust me to focus on anything that's not rooted in the seventeenth century?

Penelope fiddled with her Alice band, and then answered, 'Parts of the house date back to the doomsday.'

'Did your family ever break with Rome? Is there a priest hole?'

'Of course!' shouted Penelope, doing a U-turn and dashing off like a terrier who's spotted a squirrel.

The men followed, and the party thundered up the back staircase as noisily as a troop of roundheads sniffing out a hidden cavalier, William bellowing to his son to shout if he could hear them. Freddy was thinking the youngsters could be trapped inside the hiding place, the silly clots. Sometimes these hidey-holes can only be opened by a contraption hidden on the outside. Despite no answering call, Penelope prised up a floorboard and depressed a lever. A panel sprung out of the wall, and the threesome crowded together, peering into the dark.

Sarah took another look at Nick. His right hand was out-slung, loose around a trowel that lay nearby. She took a step closer and then stopped. Should she touch the body to check for a pulse?

'You promise me you have checked he's dead?' she whispered.

She heard Mike exhaling slowly. 'He's dead, all right.'

What should she do? She must get this right, think about Nick, his family and herself, not just consider what Mike wanted. Should she call the police, stick to her line about storing gardening kit, turn Mike in and hope he didn't shop her? Until tonight Sarah had believed she was finally free, reasoning that, even if the police noticed Mike or Nick using the back drive, even if they suspected they were growing or storing drugs at the Dower House, got a search warrant – she could deny knowledge of everything. Freddy would back her up; if she stuck to the story she had allowed Mike to keep some gardening tools in one of the sheds for a few months, that she was horrified to discover what was really in there. Without Mike's help no one could ever trace the money he had paid her, and he had no reason to help the cops. Provided she copied Freddy's reaction in the headmistress's office – she was confident she had shaken off her past. But now there was a body surrounded by drugs – would she ever be free?

Sarah closed her eyes; she didn't want to see Nick's body. 'I can't think about this now, Mike. Mary's missing.'

'Oh, luv, I am that sorry. The lanes round here can be confusing, maybe she's taken a different route home and got herself lost?'

She didn't want to discuss her problems with Mike. Sarah screwed up her eyes, choking back tears, but she heard it in her voice as she said, 'I must get back in case she comes home. Can you call Nick's wife?' she hesitated, 'And the police,' she closed her eyes, 'or do you want me to make that call, it is my potting shed?'

'Leave it to me, I can sort this.' He patted her arm. 'I was just in shock. Panicked. I'll pull m'self together luv.'

Sarah dialed Freddy as she walked back to the house; Mary hadn't been found.

'Not yet,' Freddy said.

Clinging to that last word, Sarah let herself into the morning room, switching on all the lights, then opening the curtains and dragging one of the chintz armchairs over to a window. She sat staring at the cedar tree, willing Mary's pink bicycle to free wheel to a stop next to her car and trying to conjure up innocent explanations for where Mary could be. It was difficult not to dwell on the fact that Mary was with Angus, and Angus was linked to Nick. Even though Nick couldn't be involved, surrounding him was a network of the sort of men Mary should never come across, and one of them might have something to do with her disappearance. Sarah may have enabled Angus to escape his press gang, but they would know where the teenager lived, and Sarah couldn't rule out one of them having an old score to settle.

Sarah let her eyes roam around the beautiful room, up at the intricate cornicing: acanthus leaves their tips curled over; across at the marble fireplace with the oval painting by Angelica Kuaffman in the middle of the apron; down at the polished oak floorboards. She would trade it all in a heartbeat for her child. Please let Mary be unharmed. Sarah reasoned with herself that the youngsters might have been collected by one of Angus's older friends who could drive, or possibly called a taxi to take them to someone else's house. Except Angus would have told his mother where they were going if they had voluntarily left Langton.

Sarah couldn't think of a single innocent reason why Mary was missing.

The youngsters were not in the priest hole. Together the men searched the outbuildings. No trace of either of the children. It was now four hours since Penelope last saw the pair and to Freddy, it seemed as though William was beginning to panic. They stopped for coffee and a cheese sandwich in William's study. Freddy drank the coffee but looking at the food and thinking of Mary, he couldn't muster the appetite to swallow a bite.

'I think it's time we called in the experts,' said the colonel, putting down his own half-eaten sandwich. 'I'm running out of ideas.' He picked up his coffee cup. William opened his mouth, as if to speak, and then shut it again. He was regarding Freddy over the rim of the mug, a strained expression on his face. He sucked his breath in and said, 'I was hoping to avoid this, but I think it's time I told you. A few months back, Angus got himself into a bit of bother.'

Freddy swallowed.

'We think he may have got himself mixed up with some druggies. He was smoking dope, and I do wonder if they were using him to peddle the stuff.'

'Angus, peddling drugs?'

William pushed his sandwich away. 'We can't be sure, but it's only fair you know, and I intend to mention this possible angle to the police. They need to know everything we know.'

'Are you suggesting drug dealers may be involved in their disappearance? That they may have been taken against their will!'

William put down his mug. 'I don't want to alarm you.' He cocked his head, looking straight at Freddy. 'But yes, that's possible.'

Freddy gaped at the other man. 'She's only thirteen!'

'I'm truly sorry.'

Sarah's phone rang. She jumped, fumbling to answer.

'Yes!' she cried.

'It's me again, sorry to disturb you so late.'

Sarah recognised the voice, and it was not one of the two she wanted to hear. 'Sandra,' she said.

'I've just put the phone down to Daisy Thomas. She's got a horrid sore throat and Dereck's not well, taken to his bed.'

Another two helpers off sick. Sarah tried to inject a note of sympathy into her response, but she was struggling. Mr. and Mrs. Thomas were ill, not dead, and neither was missing.

'Do you think Freddy would volunteer to help?'

Sarah made a strangled snorting noise and replied tersely, 'No.'

She needed to get rid of Sandra; her phone must be kept free in case Mary called or someone, anyone, with news of where Mary was. But Sandra wanted to discuss possible replacements for the Thomas's: did Sarah think Penelope's husband would step in? Talk of William sent Sarah's mind into a frenzy of worry, what if Freddy was this minute trying to get through to her?

Who cares about the bloody dog show, Mary's been missing for four hours, and a man is lying dead in one of my potting sheds!

'What about Rachel's partner?'

Sensing that the chairlady might have a list of possibilities and a large glass of wine, and was viewing the call as a quasi "girly chat", Sarah yapped back,

'Sandra, now is not a good time. Why don't you call Rachel and ask her? I must go but I'll see you in the morning.'

As soon as the line was free, she called Freddy, and nearly cried when she heard his voice trying to sound calm and confident.

'Nothing yet, darling, but we're still on it. Don't fret too much!'

That was easy for him to say, because he didn't know what she did, and Sarah was reluctantly accepting that Mary's disappearance might have something to do with drugs. Thinking of drugs momentarily diverted her to Nick's body – surely the police had been and removed it by now. Mike must have directed them to the back drive. Why hadn't they been over to interview her and why hadn't Mike called? She answered her own questions – Mike would have told the police the owner of the shed was aware of the accident but hadn't seen anything and was currently fretting about a missing child, and for all his faults Mike wouldn't call and clog up her line like Sandra had.

What would the police do about the drugs?

It was not a problem for tonight.

Sarah picked up the phone to call Freddy and then put it down again. What if one of Nick's goons did have a score to settle with Angus, and decided to extract revenge tonight entangling Mary in the process? It would be Sarah's fault. If something had happened to Mary, she would never forgive herself, and how could she ever explain to Freddy that she was responsible for putting their daughter in harm's way?

At Langton, Freddy was still digesting the revelation Mary's boyfriend might be ensnared in a drug ring. Penelope's head appeared round the side of the door. Freddy's eyes flicked to his uneaten sandwich; would it offend her?

'Is Molly in here with you, boys?'

'No dogs in here. Has she gone missing too?'

'She wasn't with the others when I went to put them out for a last pee.'

William stood up, shouting at his wife, and dashing out, 'Got 'em! Pen, you get a map for Freddy, while I get the Landy. Meet you both out the front.'

Penelope was rummaging in a drawer. She tossed a map at Freddy and sprinted out. He followed her down the paneled corridor. He could hear the Land Rover idling outside, and turning into the entrance hall, saw fumes spewing out of the ancient exhaust pipe. William was standing to attention with his phone in his hand.

'Map!' he bellowed. 'I reckon they're in New Wood.'

Freddy felt the map snatched from his hand like a badly trained dog, seizing a treat. William threw it onto the hall table, and bent over, stabbing at it, alternating glances at his phone then the map. 'Come on, Freddy!' he hollered, sprinting out to the Land Rover.

Freddy was still belting himself in, but William tore off with the engine revving, the tyres scrunching, and pieces of gravel spraying in multiple directions. Freddy was jostling forwards and backwards, from side to side as he stabbed around in the dark, trying to do up his seat belt. The belt clicked into place, and he asked, 'New Wood?'

'Planted in 1815, to commemorate the battle of Waterloo. Quickest route is across the park, so hold tight!'

Freddy grabbed the dashboard as the car bucked its way over the uneven landscape, the headlights alternating between illuminating the dark sky and the majestic ancient trees, their leafless branches waiting for their spring cloak to unfold. A hare shot across their path, and the engine started to struggle as they climbed a steep bank. Freddy asked why they were headed for New Wood.

'They've taken Molly, she's Angus's favourite. And she's a mischievous little monster. She thinks "come" is an optional command. Her collar's fitted with a tracking device that links to my phone. Why they've gone to the wood in the first place, let alone not come home, I've no idea.'

'It's the play.'

'Eh?'

'*As You Like It* – it's set in a wood.'

Freddy heard barking, then the lights picked out a black and white dog bounding towards them, its ears flapping up and down like wings. William slowed the car, opened his door and the animal jumped then settled herself on his lap.

'Where are they, old girl?'

'There!' shouted Freddy, catching sight of Mary sitting in a heap on the grass.

Chapter Twenty-Two

'The entry price does include tea and cakes, sir,' explained Sarah through the open car window. She tried to smile, hoping it didn't look more like she was sneering at the unattractive man with his long jowly face and bushy overgrown eyebrows. His jowls twitched. 'Hmmm, I thought at a charity dog show, we just paid for the events we entered dogs into, and bought a few pints. Didn't realise you intended to fleece the humans too.'

Sarah's hands tightened around the wad of tickets; wouldn't she just love to plant her fist smack in the middle of those jowls? She shouldn't be here; she wouldn't be here if she hadn't been running the event. Not after the combined dramas of last night. Did the police just collect Nick's body and tape off the shed? Were the drugs still on the floor? Who had told Nick's wife, was that Mike or did he leave it to the police? Imagine answering the door to a policeman knowing from the expression on their face you are about to be told something devastating. Feeling a wave of sympathy for the woman, Sarah tried to muster some for the man in front of her. She scanned his car; there wasn't even a dog. Old flappy jowls intended to tip up for a few cheap pints and a chat with his equally tight-fisted chums and chalk it up as "doing his bit for charity".

She counted out four tickets in exchange for the driver's proffered notes.

'Where do we park?' he asked, wrinkling his face so that his eyebrows met in the middle, one long hedge.

Sarah pointed to a sign, in clear view of the entrance gate: 'PARKING' was stenciled in big red letters across the white background. The man huffed, put the car into gear, the window closed, and he pulled away.

'Thank you very much,' she muttered, then turned to deal with the next visitor.

'Sarah! Up here, Sarah!'

She spun round. Fifty yards away, Sandra was standing on a grassy bank just above the spur to the parking field, her stout legs in thick brown woollen stockings sticking out from beneath her beige calf-length skirt like the ends of two telegraph poles. Her heaving bosom was squashed behind a tight pink apron that hung down to her knees, contrasting with the last eight inches of skirt and bearing the rather questionable motto 'Domestic Goddess'. Sandra's face was flushed purple with the exertion of transporting her bulk halfway down the steep bank; did the chair lady intend to complete the descent?

Sarah mouthed 'Won't be a moment' at the driver in front of her, and then jogged up the hill towards the pink apron.

'Jolly popular day,' she said when she'd reached Sandra. 'How's it all going up at the tent? Is everyone following their lists?'

'Yes yes, that's all very well, but why can't you hurry them along a bit, girl? Do get a shuffle on and get them all *in,* so we can start!'

Sandra waved her arms about as if directing the traffic at the front gate, indicating what was required of her subordinate. Sarah snorted – so, it was her fault the snaking line of impatient patrons was progressing at a trickle; nothing to do with the fact that the agreed plan – Sarah's plan – to avoid congestion was to have three volunteers on entry duty and a fourth at the spur to deal with those prickly customers who managed to miss the prominent directional signs to the parking area. Sarah hadn't even been on the original list for the gate. At least she'd volunteered! Arriving earlier that morning Sarah had discovered that overnight, all four gate sentries and the two marshals who should have been directing traffic in the parking field were felled by the flu bug. The other ladies – looking at the drizzle and darting knowing glances at each other as they unloaded their cars, muttering about this being frightfully inconvenient but frankly people who didn't get the flu jab were downright irresponsible – hid behind their boxes of baking and marched off in the direction of the tea tent.

'I'll see what I can do – maybe if someone could be persuaded to join me?' she suggested. Why was she here at all after last night's twin ordeals?

'Yes well, all right, but we are jolly busy too.' There was a loud tut then Sandra murmured, 'If you can't manage, I suppose I will have to see if I can spare someone.'

Sarah watched Sandra head back, leaning forward as she dragged her weight up the hill. She gave her head a quick shake. She still felt groggy from that sleeping tablet Freddy had insisted she took – washed down by a mug of hot chocolate – when at two in the morning the couple finally finished discussing what to do about Mary, deciding to gate her for two weeks.

Last night, sitting hunched over staring out of the morning room window, images of the hideous men Nick always mixed with flickering in her mind, she'd leapt out of the chair when her phone rang for the second time. It was Freddy!

Her fingers were trembling and slithered off the buttons, but on the third attempt she answered.

'Freddy!'

'Got 'em.'

She cried out, 'Oh Freddy, thank God! Can I speak to her, is she all right? What happened, where did you find them?'

For the briefest moment she promised herself she'd call Sandra back to apologise for snapping, but then she heard her child's voice on the line and couldn't think of anything else but Mary. Mary was sheepish, explaining that the pair had only meant to reconnoiter the wood as a possible setting to stage the play, fortunately deciding to take Molly with them. Angus got his foot caught in an animal hole and twisted his ankle, and in the dark, struggling to support Angus's weight, Mary had slipped on a downhill stretch of the path – a slippery carpet of wet oak leaves – and collided with a fallen tree, spraining a wrist, twisting her own ankle, and they discovered after a trip to the emergency department and an X-ray, cracking a rib. This last injury had offered Mary multiple opportunities to display her amateur dramatic skills. Back at the Dower House, Mary oozed "wounded heroine" as her father – carrying her as carefully as a tray of champagne flutes – took her up the staircase to her bedroom amid several moans of 'Mind my cracked rib', and 'Careful, ouch, not my rib'.

Last night, praying for news of Mary, expecting the police to ring her front doorbell at any moment and tell her there'd been a tragic accident in her potting shed, Sarah's attention had been laser-focused on Mary. In the morning as she helped a hopping Mary into the shower, her thoughts kept drifting onto Nick and his family. How was Nick's wife? Did her potting shed now have police tape across the door- she must go and check. Sarah passed Mary a towel, wrapped the child back into a dressing gown, and held out her arm.

'Come on let's get you dressed and off to school. Quickly now, your father's dropping you and picking you up and you don't want to make him late.'

Mary grabbed her mother's arm and shuffled down the corridor. Sarah picked up the pace, 'Ooch, not so fast, mind my rib, Mum!'

Sarah gritted her teeth.

In Mary's bedroom, Sarah dressed the lower half of her child while Mary managed her top half. Freddy's head appeared round the door, 'All set?'

'Nearly, can you take over? I just want to check on the chickens.'

She shot out, ran down the stairs. Her hand was on the back door when she heard the green baize door swinging behind her. Sarah turned round. Freddy was standing catching his breath.

'Darling, thank goodness I caught you. Where's her rucksack?'

Sarah huffed, 'Well, where did she put it?'

'She can't remember, can you come and help look?' He was shooting her one of his engaging smiles, 'Please, we need to be off.'

'Oooh, really, can't you two find it without me? I need to get cracking too. I've the cakes to load, and I must get to the dog show on time, we're short of helpers.'

Sarah stomped out of the kitchen and back up the stairs. Ten minutes later, the missing rucksack was located tucked under Mary's bed. Sarah dragged it out and passed it to Freddy. 'If you step on it, she won't be late. But I will be.'

Freddy was smiling at her, he tossed Sarah her car keys, 'I've put the Tupperware boxes on your back seat, off you go. I'll lock up; Mary's got a decent excuse to be late.'

She leapt in her car and shot off round the cedar tree. Driving to the dog show, she called Mike, but he didn't answer. She left a message saying she would be out for the day, and could he please let her know what had happened and did she need to do anything?

It was two hours since she'd left that message and Sarah still hadn't spoken to Mike. Just as Mary had discovered last night when she and Angus trekked to the highest point on the estate searching for a signal to call for help, today Sarah didn't have a signal on hers. Maybe Mike stayed the night with Nick's wife, so she had someone there if she wanted anything; his phone could have run out of battery.

A car honked. Sarah clambered back down the bank, treading carefully to avoid slithering on the greasy slope as Mary had done so damagingly last night. Balancing herself when she reached the road, then biting back her rage – there was a hand being held down on that horn – Sarah made her way towards the noise; they really were an odious bunch today. Or was it just today? She waved a hand in apology at the man who was now leaning out of his car window shouting at her.

'Oi, come on! I don't mind doing my bit for charity, but must we be kept here like sheep lined up to be dipped?'

He sounded just like Harry.

'Sorry, sir, just coming. We're a bit short-staffed today.'

'Well, that's your problem! Let's keep it that way, eh!'

She looked at "Harry's" face, imagining how pleasurable it would be to stuff her ticket book into the gaping mouth, to shut the whining voice up, and then she tore out the tickets.

'Right, now where do I park?'

As the taillights of "Harry's clone" disappeared she turned to the next car.

'It's not very efficient today, is it? Are you new?' moaned the lady driver, leaning an elbow on the open window and resting her chin in a cupped hand. She had thinning grey hair, cut in a fringe, and a small, pinched face. Sarah looked blankly at the woman on whose thin face she had mentally pasted the cold unwelcoming Amy's.

'Well, answer me dear.' She spoke slowly and loudly, 'Are you new?'

Sarah gawped at the driver as she rattled on.

'Is that why we're all being kept waiting, sitting like peasants, when we are all wanting to do our bit for charity!' demanded the pinched face.

Sarah remained silent.

The woman huffed and turned her head, announced to her carload, 'A bit more courtesy and respect wouldn't go amiss. We're all here doing our bit for charity, and not a word of thanks for our generosity. I shall have to have a word with Sandra about this.' She turned her attention back to the window, addressing Sarah. 'That's your chairlady, I know her from the bridge club. Mark my words, Sandra will hear all about this fiasco! Now, where do you want me to park?'

Sarah pointed to the parking sign and then slowly exhaled. She wanted to take off her apron and wrap it round the neck of the next person who forgot to say 'please'. She'd had enough of today and it had only just gone eleven o'clock, she should have left them all to it and gone and seen Nick's wife. Except how would Sarah explain to the widow how she'd met her husband?

'Coo-ee, the cavalry's arrived,' shouted a female voice.

Sarah looked round. Two ladies whom she'd last seen hiding behind their Tupperware boxes were striding towards her. She raised an arm and waved.

'Sandra says you're to go on up to the ring and start selling tickets for the dog show,' explained one of the ladies, eyeing up the long line of cars snaking down the drive. Good, thought Sarah, maybe she'd get a signal up there!

'No prizes for guessing who's going to be in charge of the megaphone, announcing each class!' added the second.

'Right, I'll be off then, head up to my new station,' mumbled Sarah, unstrapping the money belt from around her waist and handing over the unsold tickets and purse full of change. 'They're not a very endearing lot today. Hope you've both brought your sense of humour with you.'

Should she just go home? If this hadn't been her event, she would have. She was a little uncomfortable about having left Mike with the mess on his own, but it was his mess, and her cover story was much more credible if the police "informed her" of the shocking contents of her potting shed. She set off up the hill, to where the guests were assembled in a field, mostly congregated close to the hog roast and the beer tent. If only she could reach Mike and check what was going on at her house. She held her phone up high and peered at it – nothing. Could she borrow a phone off someone on a different network? Sarah searched the crowd for a friendly face; they were dressed in identikit shapeless padded or waxed jackets, wellington boots and waterproof hats, regardless of their sex. Most had canine entry tickets at the end of brightly coloured slip leads, and there wasn't much variety displayed there either. She didn't know anyone well enough to borrow a phone.

Despite the slightly gloomy weather and the time, the men held plastic cups, slopping lager onto the grass, and the women were mostly drinking Pimm's, their glasses crammed with slices of orange and sprigs of mint. The charges strained at leashes, occasionally tugging their handlers along a random pace or two, keen to persuade their owners to stop dawdling and investigate the multiple tempting aromas of roasting meat, spilt beer, and other dogs.

Sarah spotted Rachel weaving her way through the crowd, charming people into buying raffle tickets. Rachel will lend me her phone.

Sandra's irritating voice boomed out, each syllable enunciated precisely,

'All entries for the best Labrador to the ring now, please. Calling all entries for the Labrador class.'

'This will be a big class!' chortled Rachel, stopping at Sarah's side.

'Have you got a signal? I must make a call and I can't get one.'

Rachel pulled her phone out and clucked an apology, 'Neither have I.'

Together the friends watched couples untangle their dogs then drift over to the far end of the field where a section was fenced off with rope, still carrying cups of Pimm's or beer. The judge marshalled everyone into a line, then, one by one, the entries were invited to entertain the spectators, trotting round in front of the judge. Most exhibitors handed their drink to a friendly competitor before setting off; some balanced a cup on the grass; a few of the men jogged round, juggling a drink in one hand as their dog trotted obediently by their side, beer slopping on their coat.

'Not exactly Crufts, is it?' smirked Rachel, folding the spent part of raffle tickets and letting them fall into a bucket by her feet.

'They're doing a roaring trade in the beer tent, though. How are you getting on?'

'When the beer tent thrives, so do I!'

The crowd clapped. The handlers ducked under the rope and the Labradors led their owners back towards the beer tent. Rachel set off in pursuit, her wispy grey hair dancing in the wind, her quarry now marked out by the winning rosettes pinned to their chests.

Sarah removed the crumpled program from her pocket. She should be doing more to sell tickets, but today she had so many problems of her own, why was she trying to solve other people's? Mary would be off dance classes for a few weeks while her rib healed, but there would be no lasting damage, unlike the casualty of last night's other accident.

'All golden retrievers to the ring, please. That is, all goldies to the show ring now, please.'

Listening to the affected voice of her chairlady, Sarah threw the events program on the ground. She couldn't stomach that woman. Why had she structured her life so she spent all her time surrounded by people like Sandra?

Later, driving home, Sarah's foot kept straying across to the accelerator. Why was there still no message from Mike? Worse, there were no missed calls from his number, no texts, and no WhatsApp messages. He hadn't even tried to return her call. She slowed down and tapped her fingers lightly on the steering wheel, as her car was forced to chug along at a sedate twenty miles per hour behind a tractor. Why was Mike ignoring her? What if despite his offer, he'd changed his mind, didn't do anything last night and Nick's body was still lying in the potting shed, while his widow fretted? Sarah cocked her head, straining to glimpse round the tractor. Judging it too risky, she sat back, and groaned.

Spotting an opportunity, she pulled out past the green beast and accelerated away, turning, and screeching in through her front gate. Freddy was already home, his car parked under the cedar tree. Turning off the engine she paused with her hands on the car door. Was there enough time to run to the potting shed? The front door opened.

'Darling, good day, how much did you raise? What's for supper? We're both starving; I've fed the chicks for you!'

She tutted – she had to make supper from scratch; there was nothing she could defrost. Damn Mike. She kissed Freddy, left him in the octagonal hallway and walked alone to the kitchen. Her eyes fell on the post, heaped up on the table next to Freddy's coat and briefcase. She put the kettle on and slit open their first quarter's electricity bill.

'Heavens, they must have made a mistake here,' she exclaimed, carrying the bill over towards the singing kettle. 'It can't possibly be £3,000 for just a few months!' She poured water over the teabag and left it to stew, returning to the post and selecting another at random. It was a quotation, not an invoice. The contractor estimated that to repair the six-foot piece of guttering detached during a recent storm would necessitate the hire of a cherry picker. Whatever that machine was, it explained why cherries were so expensive: the hire was estimated at £450 before VAT. For a few hours! The replacement gutter itself was budgeted at £75, and the contractor proposed to charge a modest £150 for his time, but that was still a combined total of close to a grand to replace a six-foot piece of pipe.

The green baize door swung open, and Mary limped in, leaning against her father.

'Hello little one, how are you?' asked Sarah.

Mary sighed, drawing out the action, 'My rib's sore, Mummy. Is there any chocolate cake left from last weekend?'

'Do you think that might help the pain little one?' Sarah waved the estimate at Freddy. 'Bills, just lots of bills!'

'T'was ever thus, darling. These old houses are all the same, pits to throw your money into.'

He helped a hopping Mary towards her mother.

'It's so much more expensive than the Long House,' exclaimed Sarah.

'There's a good reason why they are called money-guzzling old stacks, darling.'

She threw the letter at the table and reached out a hand to help Mary into a chair, pulling out a second and propping the injured ankle onto the seat.

'I think there might be a small slice of cake left in the larder, let me go and check.' Glancing over her shoulder at a smiling Freddy, she asked, 'Could you manage a piece if there's enough?'

Out of sight, Sarah stretched her hands over her head, yawning. She bent over to cut the remaining wedge of cake in two, blinking back tears. I have built my own monster, she thought, and like Dr Frankenstein I must find a way to deal with it. I have arrived at my destination: here we are, living in this amazing house, but Freddy would rather still be in his study at the Long House. He'd shown zero interest in the At Home.

She'd tried to discuss the invite list, but he pulled a face, saying, 'It's your party, darling. Have who you want.'

'It's not *my* party, it's *our* party, our celebration for moving to the Dower House.'

'No, it's definitely your celebration for moving here, not ours,' he said, handing back her guest list.

She chewed her lip and asked, 'Don't you feel a thrill at being back in a proper house?'

'I get a thrill out of your happiness, not out of your pride in living in this house.'

She would have to organise the party herself – when she had the energy. These charity events were so draining. Today's had been unrewarding: leaving her feeling flat, almost used, spat out like a discarded toy. She had fought so hard to move her family to this gorgeous house, to create the right setting, to demonstrate her social value. Freddy and Mary weren't impressed with her efforts, and she wasn't sure she cared if the Harry clones were, anymore.

Freddy studied Sarah. She was standing at the sink draining vegetables, steam drifting up from the sieve and fogging up the window as she jiggled the water free. Even from behind there was something odd about Sarah; her shoulders were sagging, her neck slumped, and she was standing lopsided, as if one side was propping up the other. He'd suggested sending out for pizza, but she insisted she was fine and wanted to cook, claimed it would relax her. He wasn't sure she was telling the truth.

Tonight, there was no sign of Sarah's usual calm order. She was plodding through tasks she normally tore through, starting one chore, then abandoning it and dipping into another. The dishwasher was half unloaded, the door down, the drawer pulled out; the countertop was a mess: small islands of pastry lay abandoned, forming an archipelago amongst a dusty sea of flour; the vegetable peelings lay heaped on a chopping board waiting to be divided between the tastiest scraps for the chickens and the debris for the compost bin.

He got up and went to the dishwasher. The house move had taken its toll on her, and he was to blame. He'd been no help. He'd allowed her to organise every detail, barricading himself in his study, just docking in the kitchen for his meals. He shouldn't have been so cruel; she'd hankered after a manor house ever since he'd first taken her to Ashe Hall. He'd created that desire, and then allowed it to fester into a quasi-need. He shouldn't have punished her when she finally had the means to achieve that dream, just because he disapproved of the deal with Mike. Sarah negotiated with Mike; neither he nor Harry had challenged their adversary. And she was right: his brother had never taken to her – neither Harry nor Amy ever welcomed her in the way they did him – had he been unreasonable suggesting they divide the proceeds of her efforts equally with his brother?

Freddy pulled out the cutlery basket, unsure of what to do with the contents in the comparatively new kitchen.

'Come on, Mary,' he said. 'You can at least direct traffic from the sick bay. Where do these go?'

Mary pointed to the pine dresser. 'Second drawer along,' she said.

Her face fell back towards the screen. He picked up a group of forks, allowing them to free-fall into the drawer, making a crashing noise. He heard a yelp and turned around; over by the sink, Sarah's face had drained of colour.

'Ohh, sorry, that noise startled me.'

Sarah was fishing around, picking potatoes out of the sink, and dropping them into a colander; the heat was rising off the potatoes, and he crossed to the sink, putting his hand over hers. He smiled an apology.

'Sorry about the noise, darling. Let me get those for you or use tongs. They're hot.'

He ran his eyes over a haggard-looking Sarah. Her face was white, her eyes dull. The cutlery hadn't made that much noise! It wasn't just moving house that was bothering Sarah, combined with the stress of Mary disappearing last night. You are overworked, he thought, you are letting people push you around, shouldering other people's responsibilities. He should have insisted, after just a few hours' sleep, she'd called and cancelled this morning, but when he suggested it, Sarah told him it was irresponsible with so many volunteers off sick with flu, saying she felt so lucky Mary hadn't been seriously injured she wanted to help others less fortunate. Looking at his gaunt wife, Freddy thought the chairperson was irresponsible; if they were that short-staffed, they should have postponed.

Should he call Penelope? Or maybe William was a better foil – ask him to speak to Penelope and get her to stand up for Sarah at these wretched committee meetings if she wouldn't do it herself, stop these blasted 'delegators' from driving Sarah to a nervous breakdown. Maybe Freddy should take her away for the weekend, or on a proper holiday. When had they last taken a family holiday?

He hung up the final mug, then spotting Mary with the fingers of her uninjured hand pressing lightly against her phone balanced in the bandage-clad one, said, 'Away now, Mary, please.'

She wrinkled her nose at him. 'Can I just finish sending this? I can't write as fast with my left hand.'

'Phone away *now,* please, your mother's about to serve.'

'Don't show your age, Dad, we hardly ever use the phone function,' she boasted, slipping the device into her pocket.

'Your loss,' he said, sitting down and shaking out his napkin. 'Your generation may be less familiar with this custom, but we are now going to enjoy the ancient pastime of conversation.'

He sniffed as Sarah doled out slices of homemade chicken pie. The savoury perfume was mixed with the unpleasant tang lingering from yesterday evening's burned chocolate cake. To be accurate, it was this morning's blackened mess that Freddy had dragged, still smoldering, from the Aga at two a.m. With a pan of milk warming on the Aga to make hot chocolate for him and Sarah, Freddy stood over the bin, scraping out the cake, examined the tin, and then threw that in too.

Sarah sat down opposite him, picked up her cutlery, and sat there, her fork hovering over her food like a fly selecting a landing zone.

'Tuck in, darling,' he coaxed. 'Smells delicious, don't you think so, Mary?'

'Sorry it's a bit rushed tonight, we were short of helpers, and after a late night I'm just a bit shattered. How did you manage at school today?' Sarah asked Mary. 'Are you OK with the pie? Or do you want me to cut it up for you, so it's easier with one hand?'

'Miss Jones, the hockey coach, is livid with me, we've such an important match against St Pips coming up. She says I really should have been more careful,' said Mary with a note of triumph, stabbing at a potato with her left hand.

'She's quite right there,' said Freddy, pushing his peas into the pie. He put his fork down and looked at Sarah. 'I may be a bit late to this party, but darling, what were you doing on the back drive without a coat last night?'

'I was closing the gate.'

'Why? It's kept locked shut, who opened it, and why?'

Sarah froze, staring at him with her mouth open, and then she let her gaze fall to her plate.

'Not me,' confirmed Mary. 'It wasn't open when I cycled past it to see Angus.'

'So who did open it?' Freddy pressed. 'Sarah,' he nudged.

She was looking at him vacantly, as if staring at a blank television screen. He wouldn't push; she really was on the edge. She knew the dangers, so she couldn't have done it, but why would a stranger open their back gate? Had someone done it by mistake? But how could they without a key?

'Who won best in show?'

He saw Sarah lift a forkful of pie, then lower it. Why wasn't she eating anything? He asked about the dog show again.

'Sorry?'

'I was just asking who won Best in Breed?'

'Should have been Sandra, our ghastly chairwoman,' she quipped tartly.

Mary chortled, stabbing another potato. Freddy grinned; this was more like Sarah.

'That was naughty of me. It's been a long day.'

'Darling, if you feel that way, why not resign? Let them find someone else to push around.'

'I can't,' she said, staring at her plate.

'You can,' he said firmly.

He insisted on clearing up, shooing Mary and Sarah into the morning room. He lit the fire and fussed around them both, propping Mary's bandaged ankle on a little footstool, plumping up a cushion behind Sarah's back.

'I'm not going in tomorrow,' he announced, 'I'm taking the day off. You can have a lie in while I take Mary to school,' he continued, dancing around the room switching on lights. 'Talk to your mother, make her happy,' commanded Freddy as he drew the curtains on his girls. 'I'll be back with hot chocolate.'

Standing clutching the door, he asked if Sarah would prefer a glass of wine.

'No thanks. Hot chocolate would be heaven.'

'Coming up,' he said closing the door behind him.

The fire spat and crackled as the wood caught; Sarah half listened to Mary explaining the plot of '*As you Like it*' gazing into the flames – seeing the logs blacken and grey ash start to form along the glowing edges. Was there anyone at the dog show she liked? Just Penelope and Rachel and she liked them for who they were not what they were, or what they represented. It wasn't just the committee members; she didn't rate the visitors either. Maybe Freddy was right, and she shouldn't devote her time to all these charities. What had that clone of Harry's shouted at her today?

Her days were dominated by the unpaid, unappreciated demands of other people. When and why did she allow herself to become subsumed by other people's aspirations? She had done what so many other mothers had, she gave up her independence to care for her baby, and when that role became less demanding, freeing up her days, she allowed other causes, less worthy of her time, to fill the void.

When the family retired to bed, Freddy suggested a second sleeping tablet. Sarah refused, settling down beside him: the hot chocolate would work its magic. It did: not on her, but on Freddy, who was soon snuffling contentedly, little puffs blowing warmly into her back as she lay on her side, willing herself to sleep. She pulled back the duvet, slithered out and groped around in the dark for slippers. She slowly pulled the bedroom door closed, gazing at her husband.

Freddy didn't move.

The moonlight shone through the glazed cupola, bathing the staircase with dim but sufficient light to illuminate her descent as she crept down, clutching the banister for support, and then groped her way down the corridor to the green baize door. She switched on the overhead lights and the kitchen came to life. Freddy had left it spotless. Dear Freddy. She didn't want to put him and Mary through the humiliation of her downfall if she was caught. Unlike his brother, Freddy would never treat anyone with the arrogant rudeness she'd endured at today's dog show. Was that why he immersed himself in the seventeenth century, to escape people like that? He must find it strange his wife courts them.

Sarah made herself a mug of chamomile tea. She was beginning to think Nick's body was still in her shed and Nick's wife was still unaware of her husband's death. If Mike had told the police, they would have been to the Dower House by now. She took her tea through to the morning room, where the fire still glowed, and fished out a few small pieces of wood from the log basket, rebuilt the fire and sat on the fender with her mug, staring in, as the glow became a solitary flame then, gradually, more flickers licked up around the logs, recreating a warming blaze. She shouldn't be fashioning her life around Harry lookalikes.

She drank the tea and then returned to the kitchen for a refill, collecting instead her laptop and a cup of coffee. She flipped open the screen, registering that it was two in the morning – a second night of sleep deprivation. Her fingers fluttered above the keyboard like a pianist waiting for a sheet of music to be turned, as she spun different phrases round her mind, dismissing them all, and then tapping in:

'Receiving money from a crime'.

Chapter Twenty-Three

Sarah stretched out her arm; tepid water splashed onto her palm. She swung the dial to the left and then stepped underneath, turning her face up to the icy cascade, screwing up her face and wincing as the cold swept down her face, through her hair and over her back. She counted the seconds aloud until she reached twenty then jumped backwards out of reach. Shivering, she reached for her towel, shaking droplets of water onto the bathroom floor from her soaking wet hair. Wrapping the towel round her head in a turban, she pulled on her thick winter dressing gown and padded back into the bedroom to drink the cup of tea Freddy had left earlier, pointing to the mug, and saying, 'Drink. Doctors' orders, you are shattered!'

'I didn't sleep well.'

His head had poked round the bathroom door; he was staring at her intently. *She must look dreadful!* Then she heard the hum of the shower and his voice floated out, 'Have you slept at all? Stop worrying, things will be fine, the rib will heal. Drink the tea, then go back to sleep, I'm on the school run.'

She'd listened to him showering, then he'd dressed, dropped a soft kiss on her head and left.

Sarah tightened her belt, picked up the mug, cradling its warmth in her hands as she sauntered over to the bedroom window. Below her, Mary was leaning on her father, folding herself into the passenger seat of his car. The crutches were stowed on the back seat, then Freddy climbed into the driver's side, the brake lights came on, and the car with its precious cargo disappeared down the front drive. Sarah reached into her dressing gown pocket for her phone and dialled Mike's number. He had a right to know, but no more than that. Mike wasn't going to direct her life anymore; she was. Mrs. Henderson must be put out of her misery.

Staring into the flames at two in the morning, it had occurred to

Sarah that Mike may be deliberately avoiding her calls. The accident was in Sarah's potting shed, there was nothing to link Mike to it unless she compromised her own freedom. Maybe when her crooked business partner turned up on her doorstep covered in blood, he hadn't really been asking for help at all, just alerting her to the mess before abandoning her to sort the problem of Nick and the drugs.

Now, listening to his phone ring, she asked herself if Mike could be that cruel. She reached his voicemail greeting but didn't leave a message. She scrambled into comfortable clothes, a pair of thick tights, old baggy trousers, a gardening shirt then a sweatshirt she kept for grubby jobs, decorated with splodges of paint. She was like a walking "artist's palette" with different colours splattered across her torso.

She had visited Tiddleworth farm only once before, to deliver the picture of Lady Mary a few days after the house exchange and it was still in the satnav memory. Once she agreed to Freddy's suggestion of gifting Harry £100,000, securing Harry's agreement to alter the terms of the Will had been straightforward. That day she'd helped Mike hang the family portrait, prominently in the cosy farmhouse sitting room, the gilded frame rather grand over the simple brick mantel of the room's fireplace.

'She is a spectacularly beautiful picture,' exclaimed Sarah, standing back to check Lady Mary wasn't lopsided, then tugging the bottom left-hand corner a fraction downwards. 'You appreciate her more when she's not lost amongst all the other family portraits, don't you?'

'I always appreciated her,' said Mike, running a finger over the edge of the frame. 'And she was always Mary's favourite.'

'That's probably why she left it to her granddaughter. But Mary isn't exactly into paintings yet!'

For a few moments they stood side by side admiring the eighteenth-century beauty.

'Did Freddy and Harry come to blows over them pictures?' Mike asked.

'It got a bit prickly, but they sorted things out. I think both are quite happy with who they've got on their walls.'

'And which is your favourite? Did you get who you wanted?'

'Uncle Tom. Did we ever tell you about Mary's fixation with her brother? She kept calling him Thomas, towards the end when the disease had really taken hold?'

'Did she?' He gasped. Mike's mouth had fallen open, and Sarah sensed a guilty rush of shame. He didn't like discussing Mary's demise; like her, he wanted to recall the good parts of Mary's life, not the worst.

'Yes, it surprised us too. We never did get to the bottom of why.'

'Can't help you there, luv. Her mind was a mystery by then.'

'I became rather fond of Uncle Tom, as a consequence. And I don't think those two dead brothers should be separated, so we've got both.'

Sarah yawned as she followed the Satnav's directions, crawling down the single-track lanes, nervous a local car would be unphased by the narrow road and might hurtle round each corner; with five hours sleep in the last forty-eight she didn't trust her reaction times. Fifteen-minutes later she drew up to a wooden five-bar gate. It was closed. She tooted the horn and sat staring through the bars.

The red-bricked farmhouse was to the right-hand side, set back twenty feet from the road. There was no smoke coming from any of the chimneys. Directly in front of her was a strip of tarmac, sloping downwards which hadn't been there last time. It led to the polytunnels, located sufficiently distant to obscure their view from the roadside, but Sarah had seen them from the kitchen when she dropped off Lady Mary. Behind the farmhouse was a fenced-off field laid out in a series of large rectangular beds. There was green fuzz to several of the closet rectangles; Mike had been hard at work.

She gave another blast, but the car horn was no more successful in summoning Mike than the phone had been. Leaving the engine running, Sarah hopped out, undid the latch, and swung open the gate, kicking a boulder over to wedge it back against the fence. She ran back to the car, sniffing at a smoky smell: someone was having a bonfire.

She wasn't expecting Mike to be inside but tried the farmhouse first. Dwarf daffodils stood behind the wilting snowdrops which grew beside the neat weed-free footpath to the front door. Had Mike already copied the succession of seasonal bulbs that lined the entrance to the

Dower House? The telltale dark green leaves of bluebells poised to release their flowers answered her question.

She rang the bell. There was no reply, so she skirted round the side and rapped on the back door. From the doorstep she could see down the track to a small metal barn, and beyond that sat the two black polytunnels, their doors firmly shut. She gave a last hopeful look at the door, then jumped off the step and set off down the track, calling out, 'Mike, where are you, Mike? It's Sarah.'

Close to the polytunnels, she saw the remains of a bonfire, a scorched black circle by the side of the track, a pile of grey ash forming a six-inch mound. She sniffed, dipped her shoe carefully into the pyre, and then leant over pushing a finger experimentally into the powdery residue. There was no heat, just the whiff of smoke. Sweet smoke, what was that strange smell?

She reached the polytunnels, recalling the first time she'd walked into one nearly two years ago: if only she had never gone inside, just stayed in the Walled Garden until Mike came out. Sarah unhooked the first door and peered in, expecting to be hit by a blast of heat and to see Mike bent over his precious hoard or harvesting buds from the taller more mature specimens, maybe adjusting the feed tubes, or altering the overhead lamps to shine directly above the plants.

It was cold, there was no Mike, and there weren't any plants either, simply rows of empty metal trays where the plants should be. The overhanging lamps were turned off, and the feeding tubes dangled in mid-air, like forlorn party streamers the morning after an event. It was like looking at a stage set, full of props, waiting for the actors to join, for the performance to commence. The second polytunnel was the same.

'Mike!' Sarah hollered, jogging back up the track. 'Mike, where are you? What the devil is going on?'

She turned towards the fields; there was no sign of life apart from the cackling sound of crows roosting in a nearby beech tree. Sarah reached the farmhouse, and circled it, searching for a way in, peering under flowerpots for a key. She checked under the front doormat then beneath the black metal boot scraper, then picked her way across the front lawn and peeked in through a crack in the curtains into the sitting room. There was no one inside. There were no lights left on, no discarded mugs or plates. Sarah looked again, something was missing; she sat down on the front doorstep and laughed, wheezing as a cathartic process worked through her body.

The picture of Lady Mary no longer hung above the fireplace.

She had driven round to tell Mike she was going to call the police, not wanting to bounce him into her decision. Mike had been less considerate. It was no accident he hadn't replied to any of her messages, nor answered the phone. He had packed up his favourite things and destroyed the evidence of his own illegalities by burning all the cannabis plants, no doubt fuelling the bonfire with bags of dry harvested leaves; that was what the sweet smell was. The local wildlife must be stoned with the amount of cannabis drifting about. Selfishly he had protected only himself, dealt with only those difficulties he was compelled to, ruthlessly leaving Nick's wife speculating about her husband's fate and Sarah to deal with the body and the remains of the little enterprise.

Standing, unlocking the front door, she heard her phone bleep – had she misjudged Mike? But it was a text from Freddy. Mary was safely at school; he was calling in for coffee with William and he would be home in an hour.

Her eyes were assaulted by the bank of pine units in the kitchen; she had yet to settle in this space. Although substantially larger, it lacked the welcoming atmosphere of her Long House kitchen. It was also colder, and being north- facing, even a little darker. She tossed her car keys onto the copper tray and dragged herself yawning over to the fridge; the only thing to pass her lips since her shower was the early morning cup of tea Freddy had brought her.

She made herself two slices of toast, spread butter, dolloped on a spoonful of honey, and added a carafe of coffee to the tray, then left the cold kitchen for the morning room. She took alternating bites of toast and gulps of coffee as she re-laid the fire for the second time that morning, then wiped her butter-stained fingers on her trousers, leaving a smeary streak of grease to match the paint-spattered top. She poured another mug of coffee, sat down, and dialed.

The phone was picked up immediately.

'It's Sarah Fetherston. I don't know if you remember me, but you recently helped me—'

Lesley Bridge's voice interrupted her.

'Of course, I remember you, how are you, a tad more relaxed now that your ordeal is over?'

'If only.'

'Sarah?'

Sarah squeezed her eyes shut, breathed deeply, but she started to cry, gulping down the phone. She hiccupped to a stop.

'Sarah, whatever is the matter? You know whatever you say is covered by client confidentiality.'

'Where do I start?' She doubted Lesley had expected repeat business from her. Sarah took another swig of coffee. 'Mike appeared at my doorstep covered in blood, then he took me to one of my potting sheds and there was a man, except it wasn't a man, just a body.'

'A body?' There was a pause then Lesley's voice rose, 'You can't be sure this person is dead. You need to dial 999 and get an ambulance and the police.'

Sarah closed her eyes, visualizing Nick's lifeless form stretched across the floor of her shed. 'There's no need for an ambulance.'

'If you say so, but you still need to call the police. They'll want to know what happened. Where is this Mike and who is he? Do you know who the victim is?'

This was where Sarah should explain her business relationship with Mike and the victim. She tried to speak clearly, but she could hear her words were slightly garbled as she trotted out the tale.

'Mike was married to my mother-in-law. There was a fight; the other man, was much younger and fitter, and hit him with a trowel. Then there was a struggle. Mike told me he pulled over a wall unit, which hit the other man and he fell and cracked his head on the concrete floor. I think he's telling the truth; the victim had a trowel near his hand.'

'Sarah, have you been drinking?'

Sarah squeezed her eyes shut tight. Where has my energy gone?

'Sarah, you must call the police immediately and cooperate. There's clear evidence of self defence. Your father-in-law is not going to be in trouble, provided he cooperates. He's perfectly entitled to use reasonable force to escape what he judged was a life-threatening situation. Call 999 now.'

That all sounded very reassuring, but it left Sarah with two big problems. Mike wasn't there to reiterate her story, and she hadn't yet told Lesley about the drugs surrounding the body.

'Sarah, are you still there?'

'Yes. I'm not so bothered about what happens to Mike, he's not here anyway. It's the victim's family I care about.'

'Where has he gone? He needs to give a statement to the police.'

'I've absolutely no idea. He's not at his house and he's not answering his phone.'

Sarah heard her lawyer clearing her throat.

'Right. Let's take a step back here. Just when was it Mike rang your doorbell covered in blood?'

'Tuesday night,' Sarah said, reaching into the log basket and tossing more wood on the fire.

'The fight was *thirty-six hours ago?*'

'Yes.' Thirty-six hours during which I have hardly snatched a wink of sleep.

'What's happened to the body?'

'I don't know. I guess it's still out in the potting shed.'

A silence followed; the fire spat out an ember, Sarah got up and stamped on it.

Eventually Lesley said, 'It's not a criminal offence to fail to report a crime, but you do have a moral obligation to do so, and you must think about the victim's family.'

'I've hardly stopped thinking about his family!'

'I urge you to contact the police and cooperate with their investigation. Would you like me to come over, and be with you when they get there?'

Sarah got up off the fender, being so close to the fire was making her uncomfortably hot.

'You haven't been back to the potting shed since Tuesday night?'

Sarah shook her head, then mumbled into the phone, 'No I haven't.'

'To your knowledge, has anyone else been back to that shed since Mike showed you the body?'

Sarah pinched her nose, closed her eyes, and shook her head, but she couldn't clear her fuzziness. 'No, nobody's been to the shed. I'm sorry, I haven't had much sleep for a couple of nights, I'm not thinking straight. My daughter had an accident, and I didn't get to sleep until three on Tuesday and last night I gave up trying to sleep at three, so I'm running on empty.'

'I understand. Good. No, that's not good that you haven't slept. But good you didn't go back to the body. I don't want you to go back to the shed at all. It's a crime scene and mustn't be disturbed. Now call the police. Are you sure you wouldn't feel better if I was there when they arrive?'

Why couldn't she tell her lawyer the full story? Unless she came clean, she couldn't ask Lesley to be with her. She rubbed a hand over her face and pinched her eyes, then said in a quiet voice, 'No. I'll be fine. My husband's home soon, he'll be here when the police arrive, but thanks anyway.'

'If you're sure, but you only have to ask, and I will drive over. I've no court appearances scheduled today, so I can be with you within the hour.'

'That's kind,' said Sarah.

'If for whatever reason the police caution you, call me immediately and don't say anything until I get there.'

She thanked her lawyer and poured the last of the coffee – a short trickle that formed a pathetic inch-high puddle – into her mug. She needed more caffeine than that to get though the morning. Placing the spark guard in front of the fire, she went in search of one of the energy drinks Mary drank. Had the conversation with Lesley been helpful? What had she learned? Mike wouldn't be arrested for murder, but as she had no idea where he was, and about the same level of sympathy for him, she didn't care. It was Nick's wife she cared about.

In the kitchen Sarah stole one of her Mary's fizzy drinks. There was a chance Mike had done what he'd promised and for some unknown reason, contacted the police and they simply hadn't got around to speaking to her yet. She had to check. If the shed was taped off, she wouldn't have to touch anything; if it wasn't she'd only be touching the doorknob, maybe the light switch, and she could have handled both of those on Tuesday, anyway. She pulled the ring on her drink and took a long swig, feeling the ice-cold drink fizz in the back of her throat, then shook her fuddled head and hurtled out the back door, carrying the can closely for support.

A few paces from the potting shed, Sarah stopped in her tracks. There was no hazard tape on the door. She tapped the can against her hip. *Dead bodies can't harm you.* She was frozen, unable to take another step. She stood, shaking, staring at the shed door, clutching the can of fizzy drink, as if stuck in quicksand, unable to move forwards or retreat.

Freddy pulled up next to Sarah's car. Good, she was still at home. She'd been goggle-eyed with lack of sleep this morning, why did she allow everyone to push her around? Maybe it was Sarah who should be gated, not Mary – that had been William's advice: 'Confine her to barracks. Let her spend time in that walled garden, there's nothing that relaxes Pen more than spending time in the greenhouse, sowing seeds and dreaming of the summer harvest.'

'She takes on too much. Why won't she stand up to this Sandra woman?'

'Ahhh, Mrs Delegator. Let me have a word with Pen. She doesn't take any nonsense from the old crow. Pen's very fond of Sarah, we both are.'

Freddy let himself inside, and went in search of Sarah, thinking it was becoming a bit of a habit. When she wasn't in the bedroom or the kitchen, he went straight outside again. He soon saw her, standing near the potting sheds with her back to him; she wasn't moving. He called out, 'Darling there you are.'

She turned round to face him, and Freddy suppressed a gasp. What on earth was she wearing? Where had those tattered trousers come from and were those smears of grease down the front? He'd never seen that sweatshirt; it looked like it had been used by a five-year-old for a painting exercise. A few steps closer, he noticed Sarah's eyes had a vacant but pleading look that reminded him of his mother in her later years. Her face was white – why was it always white these days – with dark bruised circles under the eyes; and she was carrying a can of fizzy drink. She never drank soda. This was seriously odd.

'Darling! What on earth's wrong?'

He must get her back inside, into bed, and telephone the doctor.

Why was she just standing here in the middle of the garden, as if waiting for a bus?

'Oh Freddy, there's been a disaster.'

'Yes, I know, it's all been a bit of a shock, but Mary will be just fine. The doctors wouldn't have advised us to send her back to school unless they were confident of the speed of recovery. She's hamming it up at school, enjoying the limelight, but that's only to be expected, given her love of acting. There's absolutely nothing for you to concern yourself with at all.'

He reached out his arms, folding her into an embrace, hugging her close. She was icy cold!

'What are you doing outside anyway, and again without a coat?'

'I must tell you what's happened. I need to tell you, please.'

She was wrestling to get free, but he held firm.

'There, there, everything will be just fine, I promise.'

He took hold of the fizzy drink she was clutching, prising her hands away then emptying the contents onto the path and crushing the can in his hand, pushing the flattened tin into his jacket pocket.

'Please, Freddy,' she whispered into his shirt front.

He took her by the hand, stroking it as he led her down the path, past the back drive, towards the house. It was like taking a reluctant puppy on its first walk: each step forwards accompanied by a little tug on his hand, jerking him backwards, as she tried to pull him in the opposite direction.

'Freddy, please, we need to stay out here. I must show you something.'

He put his arm around her waist, propelling her forwards. 'Now let's get you into the warmth. Why were you outside without a coat?' he asked, opening the back door, and posting Sarah inside. 'I think you should head upstairs for a rest. Can I warm up some milk for you, darling, to make you sleepy?'

He blinked back the tears, watching her climb the stairs in front of him slowly, methodically, as if each step was an enormous effort. This wasn't Sarah, this was a shell of the woman he married; how could he help her if she wouldn't tell him what the problem is?

Chapter Twenty-Four

Freddy unfolded the letter, looked at the coat of arms, reread the contents for the fourth time, then refolded and returned the sheet to the envelope, pushing the flap back down and running his fingers over the seal, as if pressing the problem away. He must reply, just not right now. He sat silently, staring over the familiar expanse of his desk and out through the window at a scene he was still unaccustomed to. Over the top of the cedar tree was a view of the pale-brown and green expanse of winter-scorched lawn, and beyond that the herbaceous border just emerging out of its winter slumber: the early tulips just taking over sentry duty from the daffodils.

Something was seriously amiss with Sarah; this bizarre behaviour couldn't just stem from lack of sleep. Or could it? Was he being overdramatic? Should he call the doctor? Getting her into bed had been a real struggle like trying to convince a kitten it was time to stop playing: first resisting being put in its basket, then, suddenly, feeling it go limp. For a few minutes he'd sat stroking her arm, checking she was asleep, and then he tucked the limb back under the duvet, and tiptoed out of the room. He would wake her at lunchtime, check if she was any better. If she wasn't, he would call the doctor. Sleep might be the tonic she needed.

Freddy wanted to have a proper discussion with Sarah. His family needed him more than he had realised. Mary should never have gone to see Angus without seeking permission from either him or Sarah. But how could she have asked her father; even when Freddy was at home, he was holed up in his study living in the past. Their daughter needed both parents involved in her upbringing, he must stop being so selfish, start spending a little more time with his family and live in the twenty-first century. He could provide a decent income for his ladies without allowing his passion to be all consuming. But his ties with the past didn't explain Sarah's peculiar behaviour. Would it help to get Sarah away from Devon? Was Devon the lurking problem behind this mystery? He tapped the envelope against the desk.

Behind him, Sarah stood in the doorway, staring at Freddy's back. His hands were clasped behind his neck, propping his head upright. Freddy's new study was a beautiful room. Through an arched window, framed either side by inset niches, the desk had a glorious view of the garden; the walls were lined floor-to-ceiling with carved bookshelves. Freddy had already made himself comfortable, spilling his papers across the floorspace, but he looked incongruous in this Regency setting. After twenty years of sitting in the dark, low ceilings of the Long House, this light-filled room appeared wrong. She watched as Freddy opened the long middle drawer of his partners' desk, pushed an envelope in, and then shut the drawer. Did he find it easier to write in this room with the natural light, or did the juxtaposition of the architecture with his chosen period affect his concentration, like asking a Jane Austen heroine to perform in a Victorian dress?

'Hi,' she said, clearing her throat to attract his attention.

He turned round.

'Darling,' he said, in a warning voice, '*you* are supposed to be asleep. I only left you a few minutes ago.'

Sleep. She did try, she longed to sleep, but that wasn't possible, not with pictures of Nick's wife appearing each time she closed her eyes. Sarah imagined an anguished lady repeatedly dialing Nick's mobile – as Sarah would have done – peering out of a window every few minutes, praying for her husband's return.

'I know,' she said. 'But that's not going to happen while my veins are pumping more caffeine than blood. We need to talk.'

'Yes, I have something I'd like to discuss too,' he said. 'Sit down.' He suggested, indicating one of a pair of green library chairs opposite his desk, miraculously free from paperwork.

He pulled open the desk drawer, fished out the envelope she'd noticed him put inside a few moments earlier.

'The thing is—'

She cut him off. She didn't want to hear about an invite to another guest lecture, no matter how prestigious the university.

'Don't, Freddy, not now. Whatever you want to talk about can't be as important as what I have to say.'

'OK. You go first,' he invited.

She sat down, took a deep breath, and told him what had happened on Tuesday evening: from Mike's arrival dripping with blood, to her discovery of the open back gate, then being shown the dead body. She told him how she had spent yesterday trying and failing to reach Mike, and she finished with her trip to Tiddleworth Farm and her discovery that Mike had fled, taking his most precious possessions with him. She confessed she had not spoken to the police but intended to. He didn't interrupt, letting the story unfold like lava seeping down the mountainside: more and more danger as the volume gathered and the intensity mounted.

She sputtered to a halt.

'Is that it?' he asked.

She was sitting slumped in the chair, her arms hanging limply off the armrests they had been gripping at the start of the story. She huffed, lifted her eyes towards him. 'Isn't that enough?'

He stood up, walked round his desk, and removed the stack of papers from the chair next to hers.

'Let's go through this one slowly. What was Mike doing here on Tuesday evening?'

Like a driver avoiding patches of black ice, Sarah had skirted round the drugs and dodged mentioning the victim's name. Neither Freddy nor her lawyer had the full picture. How to answer Freddy's question.

'I'm not precisely sure,' Sarah stammered.

She was silent for a few moments – staring out of the window as if she was hypnotised.

'Remember I did say he could keep one or two bits and pieces in the potting sheds until he got himself straight at Tiddleworth.'

'Right, so he was round here collecting some gardening equipment, was he? Why? What could have been so urgent, what did he need for his garden when it was already dark?'

She bit her lip, feeling pinpricks of tears, then spread out her hands and shrugged. 'I don't know, I didn't ask,' she murmured.

'And who was this mystery man? The man Mike had a fight with and ended up killing? Was he a fellow gardener? Did they have a disagreement about a plant exchange?'

She took in the gentle sarcasm, then looked into his eyes and saw his disbelief. He was treating her as if he was the parent and she the child fabricating a story to try and dodge blame for starting the fisticuffs with her friends.

'I don't know.'

'And Mike has . . .' He paused and didn't contradict her, finishing his sentence by suggesting the missing Mike had gone away.

'Yes, Mike has scarpered. Leaving me to sort this mess out on my own, the little rat.'

Freddy was standing. She tried to smile.

'I'll just go and have a squint in this shed of yours,' he said. 'You stay here.'

She stood up too, put out a restraining arm. 'You can't, Lesley was adamant. It's a crime scene and it's not to be disturbed!'

'Lesley?'

'My lawyer.'

'I thought Percy was our lawyer.'

Sarah shook her head. 'Percy isn't the right man for this, not his bag. Lesley is the partner who deals with criminal law,' she explained.

His mouth fell open. 'When did you acquire the services of a *criminal* lawyer?' he asked, sitting back down.

Should she tell him about her previous brush with the law? She could skip the part about eating the spiked brownie . . .

He was looking at her again, and there was concern in those hazel eyes. 'Are you sure Mike hasn't reported this already?'

'Can't have, else we'd have had the boys in blue round here.'

'Well, darling, if you recall, we were both out most of yesterday, weren't we? They could have come then.'

'Don't be silly. The police wouldn't just come to our home, clear away a dead body and not want to question the owners of the property about it, would they?'

His idea was silly, but probably the whole story sounded silly to him.

'You are telling me the truth, Sarah, aren't you? I don't want us to be done for wasting police time. You didn't just have a nightmare, sparked by the shock of Mary's accident? Whatever this Lesley lady advised, are you sure it wouldn't be better just to check the potting shed before you dial 999?'

'Chance would be a fine thing. I've hardly slept – no time for a nightmare! And no, I don't want to see that body again. That's why I was out by the potting shed. I thought I should go back there, but I couldn't bring myself to do it.'

'Do you want me to call the police?' he offered.

Dear Freddy, she could tell he didn't believe anything she'd said, but he was still prepared to make the call.

'No, it's my drama, I will call. I'd rather do it alone.'

She stooped over and kissed him, her lips lingering on his for a fraction, as if recharging her batteries off his. She stroked the side of his face, then left. If she didn't make that call now, her nerves might get the better of her.

Freddy watched Sarah pacing around the cedar tree. She had her phone with her, clamped to the side of those grubby trousers. Should he pop out and check the potting shed? It didn't matter if Sarah had spoken to this Lesley lawyer or not; everyone knew not to tamper with a crime scene. Except he wouldn't be tampering with a crime scene if there wasn't a body. Where had she dreamt up this ridiculous notion – there wasn't a dead man in their potting sheds! If he needed any further proof that Sarah had changed her mind about reporting the crime, she was now just trudging round the cedar tree as if in a trance.

He sprinted down the stairs and out the back door. If he was wrong, he wouldn't touch anything. If he stuck to the path, just looked in through the window, he wasn't tampering with evidence. He slowed down as he passed the back drive. Of course, if it was true, this could explain why the back drive had been open on Tuesday evening – either Mike or the mysterious dead man could have come in that way – but why had they been at the Dower House and how had they opened a locked gate? Freddy walked the final few steps slowly, examining the path before he took each step, just in case there was something peculiar, something he shouldn't disturb. He hadn't asked Sarah which shed the mysterious body was in. He might have to check all three.

The potting sheds were built against the Walled Garden, with its south-facing wall doubling as their back. He reached the first and stopped. They weren't large buildings: only ten foot high at the back, sloping downwards so the front was a few feet lower, and six foot in depth, each one maybe twelve feet wide. The windows were tiny, no more than two feet square, and set to one side of each of the three green doors. He peered into the darkness of the first window. It was grimy; the bottom six inches entirely obscured by a dense matt of cobwebs stretching back over the width of the windowsill, as if someone had left a folded cloth there. He couldn't see a thing. He moved along to the next shed, where he had the same challenge. The last was a bit cleaner: he could see a brick perched on the inside windowsill, but nothing beyond that; he couldn't see into the shed itself because he was staring from the light into the dark. If he wanted to discover what lay inside, he would have to open the door and probably switch on the light, and he couldn't do that, not when there was the faintest chance he could be contaminating a crime scene. He took a final look at the sheds and returned to his study.

Alerted by the wail of the siren, Freddy glanced up to see a police car shoot round the corner and pull up by the cedar tree. He ran back down the stairs and out the open front door. Had Sarah forgotten how to close it? He couldn't leave this to Sarah, not when she was so fragile. He stood with his back to the door catching his breath, his arm around Sarah, as a policeman walked towards them, switching on his body camera.

Freddy extended his hand.

'Good morning officer, my name is Freddy Fetherston, this is my wife Sarah, who called in the incident.'

'Yes, thank you, Mr. Fetherston, I'm sergeant Grindley,' he said, shaking Freddy's hand but then addressing Sarah, speaking to her as if they knew each other. Maybe they had met at one of her charity events.

'Please take me to this shed, Mrs. Fetherston. I have an ambulance on the way.'

A second police car rounded the corner, drawing to a swift stop beside the first. Oh dear, why two of them? We are diverting the police from their proper duties. The sergeant talked over his shoulder at his colleague who slammed his car door shut and trotted over to join the gathering, straightening his jacket, and pulling out a notebook as he ran.

'I told you,' Sarah said. 'Tragically, the victim is already dead.'

'I think we will be the judge of whether the victim needs assistance, madam,' said the first officer. 'You've no medical training.'

Freddy held Sarah round the waist and pulled her close. He should have suggested she showered and changed. What must they both be thinking? All this bizarre talk of bodies from a woman with tousled hair and rumpled, stained clothes. But the police were used to seeing people at their worst, maybe they ignored your appearance, thankful to find someone with clothes on at all – they must respond to some domestic incidents to find people stark naked.

'The man is dead,' Sarah said, 'I don't need medical training to know that. Anyway, he's been there nearly two days, so it's a bit late for a doctor.'

'Why didn't you call us as soon as you discovered him?' asked Grindley firmly.

Freddy squeezed Sarah's arm.

'Hold on, officer,' he said. 'There's no need for that accusatory tone of voice. We're trying to do the right thing here. My wife has had a bit of an ordeal these last few days. She wasn't the one to discover this body, and I think she naturally assumed the person who alerted her to its presence reported its existence to you. On the same evening our daughter had an accident, and since then she has understandably been preoccupied with our daughter's welfare. It's only since no one has shown up to investigate, and she can't get hold of the person who told her about the body, that she's called the incident in herself.'

'Right sir, I understand. Now let's go and have a gander, shall we?' suggested Grindley.

They walked towards the Walled Garden, Freddy holding Sarah's hand, encouraging her to lean on him. She was still freezing cold. He stopped and took off his jumper, putting it over her sweatshirt with the same care he used with Mary when she was too young to be able to dress herself: pulling each of Sarah's arms up, threading them in turn into the sleeves and tugging the jersey back down.

Freddy took Sarah's hand again, squeezing it. 'Come on, darling, chin up, eh! The police will sort this out for us.'

The group passed the back drive and reached the end of the path; the row of potting sheds lined up in front of them like a train carriage. Sarah leaned into the comforting warmth of Freddy. What would he say when he saw all those bags of drugs? She should have told him the whole story, she'd missed the best opportunity to confess, beg his forgiveness. If Freddy and Mary forgave her, she didn't care what anyone else thought of her. She swallowed realising that no one was going to believe she hadn't seen those drugs on Tuesday night, or that she didn't know what they were. There was only one explanation for her omitting that part of the story, and she just didn't have the strength to deny it anymore. Poor Freddy, he was going to witness her being handcuffed and driven off in a police car.

Both policemen were staring at her, she felt Freddy pat her arm. 'Which one, darling?'

She blew out a short breath and whispered, 'Middle.'

Sarah held Freddy's hand tightly. The policemen took the last few paces alone and stopped outside in front of the middle green door. Grindley pulled on a pair of thin plastic gloves, flexing his fingers to ease them into place, and then he passed a pair to his colleague, and turned the handle.

'The light switch is inside on the left-hand side,' she said, closing her eyes as the door swung open on the chaos.

She opened them to see the sergeant's arm moving up and down as he groped around the wall, to locate the light switch. The overhead strip lights flickered, illuminating the room briefly in a few short flashes, before settling and flooding the small room with bright light. The policemen were blocking the doorway. Beside her Freddy's neck was stretched upwards, enabling him to peer over the heads of the officers. Being shorter, Sarah couldn't see into the shed, but through the gaps of the men in front of her, it looked like there was more in the shed than she remembered. Out of the corner of her eye she caught Freddy gazing down at her, a concerned expression on his face. She took a step closer, and Grindley's voice boomed out from inside the shed.

'Mrs. Fetherston, please could you step in here for a moment?'

She inched forward slowly. Freddy was standing behind her now, his arms resting on her shoulders. She felt him stroke them gently as she stepped into the doorway.

The room was crammed full, but not chaotically. Against the back wall was a series of large black plastic buckets, each filled with green metal hooped plant supports, organised in ascending order of height. In front of these containers was a short, fat body dressed in bright clothing. She was sure Nick was taller than that, and he'd not been wearing buttercup yellow! She took a tiny step forward. It wasn't a body; it was four blue and yellow bags of compost piled one of top of each other. She ran her eyes over the rest of the room – where was Nick's body? By the side wall were green and black plant pots, stacked inside each other in precarious three-foot-high towers. There were assorted lengths of bamboo canes, a small rotovator and a jerrycan of fuel. There was no body. There was no *space* for a body – there was hardly room for the two officers to stand in there, let alone one of them to lie down, unless they curled up in a foetal position on top of the bags of compost.

There was no body, there were no drugs, and there was no blood on the floor. There was no evidence of anything remotely sinister. She wheeled round towards Freddy, who was staring at her with a puzzled expression, then turned back to the policemen, opening, then closing her eyes, as if blinking in slow motion.

'Where precisely was this body?' asked Sergeant Grindley.

'I, I, well . . .'

'Madam, are you sure it was the middle shed? It must have been quite a shock seeing a body; it's easy to forget points of detail when you're in shock,' suggested the younger officer. 'Was it one of the other potting sheds? Or – you've got quite a bit of ground here, Madam – maybe it was in one of the other outbuildings?'

There was a long silence.

Had she made a mistake? Was the young policeman right, had the drama unfolded in one of the adjoining sheds? She stepped further into the room, forcing the officers to shuffle up: the younger against the bags of compost, the senior moving into the corner of the room beside one of the stacks of plant pots. No, there'd been no mistake; they were in the correct shed. Between the two policeman she could see one of the holes in the back wall where the screws fixing the heavy shelf unit had been wrenched free of their home, a jagged black gap in the red brick. She dropped her gaze to the floor; why was it newly swept? And those bags of compost, had they been strategically positioned to cover up where she recalled Nick's head lying in a pool of blood? If she nudged that blue plastic bag to one side, would it reveal a dark stain?

Was this why Mike had ignored all her attempts to reach him? He must have been thrilled when he received her message apologising for being out all day at the dog show. He was busier than her on Wednesday. What has Mike done with Nick's body and why didn't he tell her what he was doing?

Sarah raised her head. Three sets of eyes were trained on her, like a pack of terriers waiting for a rat to move before they pounced. She sniffed, what was that? Couldn't the men smell what she could? She inhaled again, short sniffs so she didn't, attract anyone's attention. Someone had been spraying room freshener – there was a faint whiff of pine where she should be smelling dope.

She ran her eyes across the three men. Freddy had his head cocked to one side. Dear Freddy, he wanted her to explain what's happened to the body. The younger officer was putting his notebook away; she didn't blame him, he must be thinking he's been called on a wild goose chase by a weird middle-aged woman with not enough drama in her life. Sergeant Grindley was stroking his chin, squashed into the damp corner of the shed.

'Right, let's all get outside, it's a bit crowded in here,' suggested the sergeant, pushing past. 'Now then, Mrs Fetherston, on Tuesday night, did you recognise the victim?'

Trooping back outside, Freddy heard Sarah stuttering a response. 'I don't. I mean to say, I can't, I . . . I . . .' then she tailed off in a slur of gibberish, he turned round, and she sagged into his arms. He tried to catch the senior officer's eye, as he held Sarah up under the armpits. Was she about to faint?

'Now, darling,' he said, 'why don't I get you back to the house? I think the policemen can probably finish off by themselves, can't you officers? I think we can trust them to shut the door on all this precious gardening equipment.'

He grasped her shoulders with both hands and steered her away from the shed, tossing a look back at the police, mouthing, 'Back soon, sorry,' then adding, 'Have a good poke round, take your time, we've nothing to hide.'

He took Sarah in through the back door, ushering her through the kitchen; it was like trying to shoo a child through a toyshop.

'Freddy, I'm so sorry, all this mess. I must clear up.'

'Not now.'

'And what about lunch, what do you want for lunch?'

He took both her hands and locked his eyes onto hers, like connecting two magnets. 'Upstairs, sleep!'

In the bedroom, he sat her in a chair in a corner and darted around the unmade bed, straightening the sheet, and shaking out the duvet, dashing from one side to the other like a collie dog shepherding the cover into position. Then he dug out a pair of silk pyjamas, carrying them over to Sarah. She sat slumped, sagging like an overflowing bag of laundry.

'Right, darling, it's time for a nap.'

He knelt on the floor unlacing her shoes.

'I love you,' she said.

'I know, darling.'

He felt her hands in his hair, her fingers running through his curls. He stood up, tugged off her trousers; she pulled off her own sweatshirt passing it to him, and he tossed it onto the heap of clothes on the floor.

'In you pop, warm and cosy,' he said, handing her a pair of bed socks.

'I'm not a child, Freddy.'

He put his hands on his hips. 'You are not well.' He poured a glass of water from the bedside carafe and handed it to her. 'Drink,' he commanded, 'I'll be right back.'

He returned from the bathroom with a small white tablet and sat down on the edge of the bed. 'You must sleep,' he said softly. 'I will deal with the police. You and I can talk about all this when you've had a proper rest. We'll sort it all out together, whatever the problem is. When I said for better for worse, I meant those words.'

He waited for her to put down the glass of water, then handed her the sleeping pill. She took it from him, holding it between finger and thumb, then peeked up at him as if seeking permission to take it.

He held out the glass of water. 'Down the hatch, please, darling!'

Freddy circled the bedroom, closing the wooden shutters then pulling the curtains tightly across them, plunging the room into darkness. Leaving the pile of discarded clothing in a heap on the floor, he stumbled towards the door, blew a kiss across the room, and left.

It was all imaginary; Sarah was having a nervous breakdown.

Walking back down the path he saw the two officers, by the potting sheds; one was talking into his radio, the other was laughing. What a fiasco! He slowed down, giving them time to finish talking to each other. Freddy had his hands stuffed into his pockets, but removed one, and riffled his hair.

'Officers, I can't apologise enough. My wife has been under an enormous amount of stress. There isn't a *body* here, is there?'

'No sir, there doesn't appear to be any evidence of any crime anywhere on your property. We have made a thorough examination of the grounds, as you suggested.'

'I'm sorry for wasting your time.'

The officers exchanged a glance. 'Does your wife have any problems with her mental health, Sir?' asked the Sergeant, politely.

Freddy's brow was furrowed.

'No. She is normally a very competent, well-organised person.'

'What sort of stress has your wife been under, Sir? Is it just your daughter's accident? Or is there something else troubling her?'

'These are all good questions I have been asking myself, and I will ask her in due course.'

'Do you think she feels guilty about the trial?'

'*Trial?* What trial?'

He saw the officers exchange a glance. The senior officer muttered that he must have made a mistake, thinking he'd recognised Mrs Fetherston from a driving incident he'd overseen.

Was that what this was all about, had Sarah been involved in some sort of accident, and it had gone to court, and she'd not told him, but why not? Why wouldn't she have told him if she was in trouble?

'I'm sorry for wasting your time,' Freddy said again.

'These things happen, Sir,' said the Sergeant.

Freddy walked the officers back to their cars and apologised again. He stood in the entrance porch watching the cars disappear down the drive, then turned and opened the front door, scuffing with the toe of his shoe at a spattering of dark brown stains on the flagstone that he didn't recall noticing before.

Chapter Twenty-Five

Sarah floated to the cusp of being awake, and then allowed herself to be tugged back down – like a parachutist, gently hauling the silk folds of his chute to the ground – into the welcoming cocoon of deep sleep. She shifted her head on the pillow, gave a little snuffle, and slept on.

She was dreaming of a camping holiday with her parents. The family was in Devon. They had eaten breakfast: bacon rolls dripping with butter, the crispy bacon fried by her father on the little camp stove with its pale blue canister of gas. Her parents were either side of her, each holding one of her hands, walking her towards the beach. Her mother was wearing her nurse's uniform: a dark blue dress and white belt with its shiny metal buckle; her father was dressed in jockey silks: a bright-yellow top and purple shorts, and a jaunty cap in the same clashing colours. The beach was getting closer; they were walking past sand dunes with long fronds of dark green marram grass bent back in the onshore wind. She could smell the tangy scent of the sea, feel the cooling breeze, and hear the cries of the seagulls swooping over the incoming waves searching for mackerel caught in the shallow waters. Then the birds saw the family and swerved, gathered, and flew straight at them. Her father dropped her hand – he was running towards the protection of a sand dune. She tried to follow, but her mother was tugging at her hand, trying to drag her in the opposite direction. She was being torn in two; she could feel the muscles in her arm ripping. Sarah's feet were stuck. She lost grip of her mother's hand and watched as the blue uniform ran off. She looked down at her feet, but she couldn't see them; she was sinking into the sand. With tremendous effort she pulled one leg up above the sand, shaking it clear amid a haze of crystals; but with a jolt her body slid back down, and she felt the prickly heavy sand around her knees. The gulls formed into a V-shape and flew directly at her: a slice of bright white, the hooked beak of the closest bird aimed directly at her. She covered her face with her arms and screamed out to her parents for help.

Sarah woke up thrashing her arms free of the constricting duvet. Her heart was pounding, her chest heaving with the effort of sucking in deep breaths. She could still see those birds' dark-red beaks. She threw off the bedclothes and sat bolt upright, her hands behind her, supporting her body. She closed her eyes, waggled her head, and reached over for her glass, quaffing down the slightly warm water. Would she ever get a proper night's sleep again?

There was a note written on the back of a used envelope, propped up against the carafe.

Morning, darling. All under control, sleep tight. Come find me when you're awake.

And it was signed simply 'Freddy', with a little heart and a single 'X'.

She swallowed and lay back down. Then she sat up again, reaching for her phone. It wasn't where she usually put it: on her bedside table, behind the pile of books, where it would force her to sit up in the mornings rather than hit the snooze button. What was the time? How long had she been asleep? She levered herself up and headed for the bathroom, then tripped over a pile of clothes and fell onto the end of the bed.

The door opened a crack, the side of Freddy's face appeared, and then the door was pushed fully open. He spoke softly, 'Awake or still drifting?'

'Awake.'

His eyes smiled at her.

'Tea?' he offered.

She ran her tongue around the inside of her mouth. It was dry despite the water.

'Please. What time is it?' she asked, yawning.

'Just gone eleven.'

'Gosh, how long have I been asleep for?'

'Since midday yesterday. You must be hungry, toast? I could manage tea and toast in bed?'

'OK, why not.'

'You run yourself a bath, room service may be a while,' he explained, retreating behind the door, and shutting it.

Downstairs, Freddy walked into the unfamiliar kitchen. He put the kettle on, found the bread and slotted four slices into the toaster. *Tray, where does she keep the trays?* He dashed out to the dining room and the silver cupboard, found his mother's silver teapot and matching milk jug, buffed them up with his sleeve and jogged back. The toast was standing proud, it looked a little blonde, so he popped it back down, spotting the trays stacked neatly on top of the microwave.

What's missing? Toast rack!

He searched in every cupboard in the kitchen, and then ran back to the dining room. Kneeling in front of the silver cupboard, he picked up a toast rack with hooped dividers, put it on the carpet and reached for another more elaborate one with crossed golf sticks to separate the toast slices. He weighed up the two alternatives for several minutes and chose the hooped rack – it was larger with eight sections, and he was a bit nibble-ish himself.

He smelt the burnt toast before he saw it. Why was there always something burning in this kitchen! It was that burnt cake when he'd first noticed Sarah behaving oddly – she never burned food at the Long House. No, it wasn't that night. She may have been distraught with Mary missing, but any mother would be, she was probably distracted and forgot about the cake, and she'd been rushed but quite calm when she left for the charity dog show in the morning. Was it when she returned that evening when the frazzled look appeared?

He dropped a spoon onto the tray, debating adding a platter of fruit – he wanted sugar in her – and turned to hunt through the fridge. He found an apple and a satsuma, deciding it was the evening of the dog show things became peculiar. Had something happened there? Had someone said or done something to upset her? Should he ask Penelope? Just where had this ridiculous story about a body come from?

He examined the breakfast tray. Tutting, he crossed to the fridge, mumbling, 'Butter and marmalade,' and shuffled round the contents, searching for preserves. Yesterday he'd telephoned Mike to ask if he could cast any light on Sarah's delusions, but annoyingly the man had yet to return his call. Maybe it was best if they severed connections with Mike. They had nothing in common with him, not since Freddy's mother died.

Standing with a second plate, and a knife in his hands gazing at his mother's silverware, Freddy was lost in thought. Ma loved living at the Dower House and Mike waited on her hand and foot, but that was no reason to keep in touch with him. He would leave Mike a message and ask him to come and collect the last of his gardening equipment. There was to be nothing to remind Sarah about the embarrassing incident with the police.

Carrying a serrated knife, Freddy went out into the garden, and cut off a daffodil – shaking the flower free of the dew still clinging to the stem and petals – and carried it back inside. He added folded linen napkins to the tray, placing them neatly on the side plates, and laid the flower gently on top of one.

What's still missing?

'Ah, toast!'

Upstairs, Sarah ran a bath. She squeezed bubble bath into the tumbling water and watched the pressure create a thick foam of cloudy bubbles. With just a few inches of water, but a decent head of froth, she climbed into the tub and lay still as the water level crept up, covering her body with its warmth, but she could not relax. What has Mike done, why did he move Nick's body, where is it and has Mrs Henderson been told? After just a minute in the water she stood up, dusting off the bubbles from her body, and reached for a towel.

The bedroom door opened; a tray appeared which Freddy lowered with a majestic flourish onto the duvet. He perched on the bottom corner of the bed; Sarah sat diagonally opposite, propped against her pillows, wrapped in a fluffy bath towel and the couple had a serious conversation over the breakfast tray.

Sarah let Freddy start; she felt groggy – the lingering effects of the sleeping tablet? She chose a piece of toast and spread butter then marmalade and took a large bite.

He shot her a smile, but Sarah's eyes were drawn to his hand massaging his trouser leg. Freddy's eyes tracked hers, downwards to his hand. The massaging stopped. Freddy fiddled with his hair, ran his hands over his face, and shut his eyes.

'Thanks for the toast,' she said.

He straightened his back.

'I have made a doctor's appointment. It's next week. I'd like to come with you so we can discuss this together, as a couple.'

'Whatever have you done that for?' she asked, pouring strong tea into a cup.

'Darling, what happened yesterday, you don't need to talk about it now, but we do need to take care of whatever has caused this little wobble.'

She shot him a look then switched her gaze to her plate and finished her slice of toast.

He stumbled on.

'No, this is wrong. We should talk about it now, there's no stigma to mental health anymore, it happens all the time, you've just been under a lot of pressure and then Mary disappearing, well it was just your tipping point.'

She buttered a second slice of cold toast; she wasn't interested in discussing her mental health. 'And just what would you have done if there had been a body in that potting shed yesterday?' she asked.

He tutted. 'There wasn't. But it doesn't matter, what we need to accept is that you *thought* there was, and I believe you genuinely did think there was a body and I applaud you for calling the police.'

'But, if there *had* been – and say I didn't have an explanation for why it was there – what would you have done then?' she probed, biting into her slightly soggy toast.

'I don't think this is helping you, darling. All I want to say is that I am here for you. I am not the best house husband, and if it all gets a bit topsy-turvy, we can hire a professional housekeeper for a bit, but I will try my best while you recover your equilibrium. And when you have, well I'd like to spend a bit more time with you and Mary.'

Sarah listened to Freddy tiptoe round his chosen topic. It was like one of those phone-in competitions on the radio, where the contestant isn't allowed to use certain specified words and is then thrown questions that cry out for those banned words as answers. Freddy's forbidden words were "nervous breakdown", and he was doing very well, but what Freddy wanted to discuss was entirely different from

Sarah.

'OK, so theoretically, if the police had turned up and arrested me because I had no explanation for why the body was there, what would you have done then?'

The bed creaked. Freddy stood up, picked up the tray and moved it the floor, then sat down beside her.

'I'm not sure why you are so fixated with this body in the potting shed lark, but let me repeat what I said yesterday. You are my wife. I married you because I love you. I still love you. Whatever happens to you happens for a reason, and I will stand by you, for better for worse, for richer for poorer, in sickness and in health.'

Sitting in the back of a taxi two days later, Freddy was trying to decide what it was about the message from his brother that irritated him the most. Was it Harry's indifference to parting with something he'd so recently claimed to cherish, or the obvious failure to consider the impact his change of heart might have on his sibling?

"Just thought I'd let you know . . ."

Freddy played the voicemail twice to check he hadn't misunderstood, but no, there it was, in a dull monotone, as if reporting the weather forecast, Harry's message revealing that in a little under twenty-four hours the portrait of Great Aunt Sybil would be sold by a reputable auction house as lot 505.

In London.

Freddy called the auctioneers and tried to arrange a telephone bid, answering a stream of questions.

'Which lot, sir?'

'505, please.'

There was a pause in the flurry of questions about his personal details.

'Aahh, you've made a mistake with the lot number, sir; you mean lot 504 don't you sir?'

'No, I think I mean lot 505. It should be a picture of a young lady with a small dog in her lap.'

Wretched Harry, he can't even be trusted to get the lot numbers right, thought Freddy, I should have checked the online catalogue.

'Ah, yes, lot 505. Yes, that is a picture of a young dark-haired lady wearing spectacles, and she has got a dog in her lap. It's listed as a portrait of Sybil Fetherston.'

'That's the one!'

'Sorry, sir,' came a firm voice from London, 'but we can't accept a telephone bid for that lot. We're all booked up with the previous lot; no one would have time to get hold of you before the bidding started.'

Then there had been a helpful suggestion of either leaving a commission bid or attending in person. Which was why Freddy was in a taxi, having been forced to cancel yet another day of tutorials and catch the early morning train to London. He wouldn't let Great Aunt Sybil down, risk her ending up hanging on a stranger's wall.

Waiting for his bidding paddle, Freddy watched a gaggle of excited people gather by the entrance doors to the auction room. The top half of each door was glazed, and through the crowd he had a clear view into a large room where row after row of people were staring at a man standing at the rostrum, with a focus Freddy wished his students would evidence in some of his lectures. By the doors, the audience swelled. There was an air of festivity as if the group was counting down the hours to the start of a bank holiday weekend. They were talking and laughing; Freddy kept hearing them ask each other – *'What do you think she'll go for?'*

He reached the doors. A lady wearing a black suit with a name tag identifying her as Bella shoved them open, announcing in a cheerful voice, 'Right, in we go, change of auctioneer, we're getting close!'

The crowd shuffled in, fanning out across the back of the room. Freddy swept his eyes around, but there were no empty seats, so he stood next to Bella and toyed with his bidding paddle. Everywhere was a rumble of chatter. No one got up to leave. There was a loud scratching sound, followed by a high-pitched electronic whine, and a little cough. 'With you shortly, ladies and gentlemen,' promised a voice.

At the rostrum, the new auctioneer fiddled with papers.

'Are you bidding for her, Sir?' asked Bella.

Freddy looked down his nose in reply. *'Her?'*

'Yes, lot 504. Only I'm against you if you are, I'll be taking one of the phone bids.' She pointed to a man who had squashed in beside Freddy, forcing him and Bella to shuffle sideways so that now

Freddy was standing behind a tall man restricting his view to the back of the man's navy-blue blazer. 'Richard here was involved in the cataloguing,' said Bella, as proudly as if she'd been introducing the artist.

'I even took the call from the seller,' boasted Richard.

'No, I'm here for lot 505,' replied Freddy. *What was all the fuss about?*

Richard rattled on, crowing about the phone call from the mysterious owner, and how he'd helped with the thorough and detailed research into ownership and provenance before the auction house accepted Lot 504. *'Property of a Gentleman'* was apparently how the seller specified the picture should be described in the catalogue. Freddy feigned interest, wondering why everyone was blithering on about lot 504.

'The owner wants to sell so he can retire and live a life of luxury in the sun,' Richard said.

'Who can blame him?' asked Bella.

Hemmed in between Bella and her friend Richard, and behind the tall man, Freddy couldn't really see the auctioneer, but heard him clearly as he restarted the auction.

'Right, ladies and gentlemen, we recommence at lot 490. A pretty portrait isn't she, there's been some interest in this lot, and I have to start the bidding at three thousand pounds. Three thousand, three anywhere?'

For the next few minutes Freddy listened to the auctioneer coax people, stroking egos, dragging the tension out and the prices up. At lot 495, Bella excused herself, walking down the aisle. Softly he said, 'good luck,' and shuffled over to take her place, giving him a decent view of the auctioneer and the left-hand side of the room, towards a bank of ten people. Bella was in the middle. All ten were standing, phones glued to their ears, with their eyes trained on the auctioneer – like trigger-happy athletes at the start of a race waiting for the gun to sound.

'Now we come to lot 504,' announced the auctioneer.

There was a low growl of noise, like a distant sound of thunder. The audience shifted in their seats, whispered to each other, and fanned themselves with their paddles. Freddy felt a jolt of excitement shoot through the room like a scramble of shoppers bursting through the doors at the start of a Black Friday sale.

'There has been considerable interest in this lot, which is a portrait . . .'

'Here we go . . .' muttered Richard, cutting across the auctioneer.

The room fell silent.

The bidding opened at a staggering two million pounds, and then raced ahead by another million. The auctioneer swept the room from his vantage point on the rostrum: his eyes circling cautiously, like an eagle seeking out hidden prey. A catalogue was raised by the tall man in front of Freddy.

'Three million, three.'

Freddy saw Bella raise her arm; she was waving at the auctioneer.

'Three million, five,' she called out.

The auctioneer dropped his eyes to his desk, scanning something hidden from view.

'Three million, seven,' he replied, slowly.

The bidding whizzed up past four million, with bids coming from the phones, the man in the blue blazer, and someone hidden from Freddy's view on the right-hand side of the room.

'She's going to bust the guide price. Not surprised, what a prize!' exclaimed Richard.

Freddy had no idea what the tussle was over, but he felt the adrenalin coursing through him. The tall man standing in front of him – blocking Freddy's view of the prize – faltered at four and half million.

'One more, Sir?' encouraged the auctioneer.

The tall man shifted his stance.

Freddy stroked his trouser leg, willing the man upwards, but the tall man shook his head.

Four and a half million pounds!

Freddy was spellbound listening to the right-hand side of the room battling against the phone bidder, clawing their way up another five hundred thousand pounds.

'On the telephone at five million pounds. Do I hear five million one? ' wheedled the auctioneer.

All heads on the left-hand side of the room were aimed rightwards, as if waiting for a return shot at a tennis match, but the opponent couldn't quite reach the ball.

'Going once at five million pounds,' announced the auctioneer slowly, staring at the underbidder hidden from Freddy's view. 'Going twice . . . going for the last time . . . at five million pounds . . . to the telephone bid . . . fair warning.'

Smack down came the gavel.

'Five million quid. What must it be like to know you were worth that amount of money?' asked Richard.

Freddy didn't reply, didn't care, he was readying himself for his own lot and inched forwards, his hands slightly damp around the bidding paddle hoping there wasn't quite so much interest in Great Aunt Sybil.

Freddy was gazing around the entrance foyer for information on where to collect Great Aunt Sybil. He spotted Bella, still buzzing from the auction, who offered to show him where to pay.

'I had a good horse, a serious collector,' she explained, leading the way down a set of stairs, to a short queue in front of a kiosk. 'Thought I was going to lose out to the man in the navy-blue blazer and then there was that lady bidder who came in towards the end and just wouldn't drop out!'

'Why did the picture sell for so much?' Freddy asked, shuffling closer to the kiosk.

'Impeccable provenance – been in the same family since she was painted.'

'Is that so very unusual? My brother and I own all our family portraits.' And they still did today, no thanks to Harry. Freddy was going to have a firm word with his brother about the other pictures; if Harry was intending to drip-feed them onto the market to supplement his income, they needed to come to an arrangement. Freddy didn't want a repeat of today's little excursion to rescue other relatives.

Bella stood aside to let a customer pass. 'It is unusual for a portrait by Gainsborough!' she said.

Freddy was at the front of the queue and passed his paddle through the window.

'Ah yes, well no, we don't have any of those!'

Chapter Twenty-Six

Sarah telephoned, texted, sent WhatsApp messages, but Mike didn't answer. She gave up; Henderson was a common name, and she had no idea where the woman lived, and even if she did find her, what could she do? The woman wouldn't appreciate being told her husband was dead, especially with no explanation of where his body was. Consoling herself that Nick's wife was probably aware of her husband's nefarious sideline and the potential dangers it exposed him to – recalling Nick's jest that his wife would end up identifying his remains on a trolley – Sarah reverted to her old routines, the weight of her former double life lifted.

She was tidying the morning room, rearranging the cushions, bouncing them off her legs to puff more air into the sunken feathers, when the landline rang.

'The Dower House, Sarah Fetherston speaking,' she said in a cheerful voice.

'Mrs. Fetherston, my name is Benjamin Trencher. I'm doing a little research into the recent sale by your family of an interesting portrait, and I wonder if I may ask you a few questions.'

'Ahh, Benjamin, you have the wrong branch of the family. It's probably my brother-in-law in Suffolk you're trying to reach,' she explained. What has Harry sold now? Why can't he offer the family pictures to his brother before sending them to auction?

'No, it's the Devonian branch. The man who sold the picture definitely lives in Devon. Don't shop my source, but my girlfriend Bella works at the auction house.'

'But we haven't sold any pictures.'

She heard the caller clucking his teeth then he asked, 'Are there any other branches of the Fetherston family in Devon? I'm after the branch related to Lady Mary Fetherston. I want to find out what it's like to live with a Thomas Gainsborough, to know it's been in your family since it was painted, and then decide to sell.'

'A Gainsborough,' she spluttered.

'Yes, Lady Mary, painted by Thomas Gainsborough.'

Sarah gasped and sank down onto the sofa. Thomas! It was not Uncle Tom her mother-in-law had been desperate to talk to them about, but Thomas Gainsborough! Sarah stared out of the morning room window at the cedar tree, recalling the first time Mary tried to talk to her about Thomas. It was just after her mother-in-law hosted the antiques art expert for the weekend. What had that man said to Mike? *"Take great care of her for me!"* and Sarah had assumed the man meant Mary. He hadn't; he'd been referring to the Gainsborough. The man probably spotted the portrait, admired it, and revealed the artist to his surprised hosts. Mary hadn't left her money equally. Her mother-in-law tried repeatedly to warn the family who had painted Lady Mary, but despite her efforts, she was defeated by that cruel disease.

When Benjamin told Sarah what the portrait had sold for, she dropped the phone.

A tall man wearing a collar and tie pushed open the door and walked towards where Sarah was chewing her lip, sitting on her hands to prevent her adding her nails to the menu.

Lesley stood up, saying in a low voice to Sarah. 'I know him.'

'Ms. Bridges, I understand your client would like to report her involvement in a crime.'

'Yes, this is my client, Sarah Fetherston,' said Lesley, placing a hand on Sarah's shoulder. 'She would like to confess to the crime of money laundering.'

Sarah rose slowly, keeping her head bowed as if dipping her head in respect. Lesley had warned her, but seconds later Detective Constable Thompson arrested her, right there, in the station foyer. A chill shot down her spine; this moment would return to trouble her for decades. For the third time in her life she was cautioned, then DC Thompson took her by the arm and led her back out of the entrance door and over to a tall metal fence. Lesley followed.

The officer used a security fob to open a gate, stood back to allow the women through, then entered, pulling the gate shut behind him. It closed with a decisive click; to Sarah, it sounded both loud and life-altering. She was taken through another door and told to sit on a short varnished wooden bench. The detective didn't linger, using his security fob for a second time and exiting the other side of the room. Sarah sat down and folded her hands in her lap, squeezing in her arms to create more space for her lawyer to sit next to her – the room was the size of a broom cupboard.

Lesley held up a warning hand, pointing towards the ceiling.

'You're on camera. There are also voice recorders, so if you want to say anything important, wait until we can be private.'

Sarah stared at Lesley; this was her world, she was completely at ease, seemed as familiar with the geography as Sarah was with the layout of Mary's school. What must she be thinking of the mess Sarah had made of her life? Does she ever wonder why her clients end up here, or is it like being a doctor in an accident and emergency department where you just do your best for a patient but never allow their world to collide with yours, for their problems to become yours?

She heard a rustle of keys; it was almost like being in the county jail of a Wild West movie, with a Sheriff and a bunch of cell door keys hanging from his belt. There was the sound of muffled voices, then the door opened, and DC Thompson allowed them out of the tiny room into a space that was brightly lit, silent and modern. A reception kiosk stood in front of her, and Sarah walked towards it as if her feet were shackled together at the ankles.

Her handbag was taken off her; Lesley reached out to claim it, and then stood to one side. Sarah was led the final few steps to the cubicle. It was curved with no sharp edges. A poster hung on one side of the kiosk, explaining her rights and her language options. Sarah stood still responding to the questions and her details were tapped into the computer. She could have been at a reception desk in a cheap airport hotel spelling out her name and address.

Sarah said goodbye to Lesley – who promised to stay – and was led away down a wide corridor. It was remarkably like the entrance to a hospital ward, except instead of *'Florence Ward'*, or an equally innocuous name, Sarah spotted the words *'Detention Cells'* picked out in black letters. After her photo and fingerprints were taken electronically, she was walked to the end cell. It was larger than she expected, ultra-modern and spotlessly clean – she couldn't dispel the ridiculous thought she might be asked to leave a review of the cleaning standards like for an Airbnb rental.

The door shut behind her and she was on her own.

There was a bench bed, eight inches off the linoleum floor with a loose bright blue mattress reminding Sarah of an exercise mat from the gym. There was also a much smaller thicker mat, was it intended as a pillow? Would she be there long enough to find out? There was nothing else in the cell except for a push button loo and sink, and the omnipresent cameras on the ceiling prevented her from using either of those.

Strangely, initially, she felt at peace; there was an inevitability to sitting waiting for the interview. She was part of a process and there were no more decisions to make. Sarah was offered all three, but with the cameras in mind – declined anything to eat or drink, nor did she want anything to read. There was plenty to occupy her mind, sitting silently reflecting on why she was there, and the consequences of her decision to confess. She angled the "pillow" against the wall and sat back against it with her feet sticking out over the side of the bed. They hadn't taken her shoes off her, so she kicked them off, and sat staring at her stockinged feet, thinking of Mary still at school, and of Freddy. She imagined him taking a tutorial, enthusing about the zeal of the royalists striving to restore England to a familiar way of life, risking their lives and family wealth to rid themselves of the horror of Oliver Cromwell – would Freddy understand Sarah's motive to hide her one-night stand as he did the Royalist's? How had she allowed herself to be manipulated, for an ancient mistake to land her in a police cell?

Could she expect Freddy to stand by her when he learned the real reason he was collecting Mary from school? How would she explain this to Mary? She screwed up her face, shuddering as she recalled lecturing Mary about the perils of drugs – Mary hadn't questioned her mother's moral authority then, how could she expect Mary to take advice from her now? After the Caroline WhatsApp incident, Freddy returned from introducing Mary to his mature student – the former heroin addict – with a contrite Mary, who hugged her mother and said, 'Sorry, Mum.' Maybe Sarah should have gone with Mary and shown herself the misery drugs inflict and given herself the courage to confess before Nick was killed.

The minutes ticked by and the connected implications of being a convicted criminal kept floating uninvited into her thoughts. It was like discovering a tendril of bindweed in one of her raised beds, recognizing the threat and pulling it out, then digging down deeper and deeper, pulling out the network of white roots, each trowel full of earth revealing yet another nasty threatening strand. The tears fell. She wiped them away with her sleeves. She had no right to feel sorry for herself.

An hour later, the cell door opened. She pushed herself forward off the bed and bent over to replace her shoes. Sarah was escorted by DC Thompson along the silent deserted corridor and outside, down metal steps surrounded by high security fencing with cameras at the corners angling towards her and the officer. Turning into the corridor of interview suites she shuddered at the sense of familiarity sweeping over her. A door was opened. She looked round the compact, windowless room, and then she saw– like a warm welcoming fire on a cold winter's evening – Lesley standing in a corner.

The starkness of the room wasn't a shock, it was the same one she'd previously been interviewed in, but today the central heating was on, and the room was hot and airless; she picked at her blouse, at the patches which had stuck to her arms. She glanced down at the wrinkled sleeves that had earlier soaked up her tears and scoffed at herself for worrying about her appearance – it hardly mattered now! DC Thompson indicated the wooden bench, and Sarah sat down, pulling herself upright. The officer grabbed hold of one of the two heavy wooden chairs opposite the bench and dragged it into the corner for her lawyer.

There was the same state-of-the-art black recording machine, squatting on the side table, poised to change her life.

Earlier, her lawyer had warned her about what to expect. Lesley sat listening without interrupting to Sarah spilling out her sorry story – *all of it* this time. Sarah ended by telling Lesley about discovering Nick's body was gone, and then dropped her eyes, staring at her lap as if in apology.

Lesley stood up and walked towards the telephone. 'Technically, your first crime – taking the money – is an offence under section 328 of the Proceeds of Crime Act,' she stated, as unemotionally as if she had been reciting a shopping list.

'What will happen? I mean, once I've told all this to the police –
what happens after that? Do they keep me at the station?'

Lesley picked up the phone receiver. 'Before we do anything, I
want you to understand the implications of confessing and establish
precisely what you want to confess to. Don't feel obliged to confess
to anything, or everything. You were coerced into taking the money
and later into making deliveries.' Lesley spoke into the phone, 'yes,
and biscuits too, please. Thank you.'

After hanging up she walked back to the table. 'They probably
won't detain you; you're not much of a flight risk. It's Mike they'll
want, he's committed a much more serious offence; he was the one
conducting the underlying criminal activity. He was growing and
supplying a prohibited substance and receiving money from those
crimes. And then there's the question of what happened to Nick and
what Mike's done to destroy the evidence. Where is Nick's body?
Any ideas?'

Sarah shook her head. Mike wouldn't have taken the body to
Tiddleworth, incriminating himself; apart from the farm, her guess
was as good as anyone else's.

'I'm not sure his wife knows she's a widow!'

Lesley pulled a face. 'In my experience criminal's wives are
much cannier than their husbands give them credit for. Bet she knew
exactly what Nick was up to and has worked out for herself he's not
coming home.'

'I concealed his body.'

Lesley shrugged.

'Did you? Personally, I don't think you should concern yourself
about that one. It's hardly in the public interest to prosecute you when
you did your best. Technically you did report the body. It's not up to
you to insist you are right if the investigating team don't believe you
and choose not to look more closely for evidence.'

'Will I go to jail?'

Sarah tried to research this question on the internet herself but
found the reports confusing and decided it was better not to speculate.
Lesley was better than Google. The room fell silent; the lawyer
stroked her chin and Sarah fiddled with her hair, winding strands

round her fingers, and then tucking it behind her ears.

Lesley inhaled; Sarah leaned a little closer.

'Certainly not for the death of Nick. I don't think you'll be charged with anything there. If you confess to the other offences . . .' she paused, tapping her pen on her legal pad while Sarah listened to the wall clock ticking away the seconds. It was only her lawyer's opinion, but to Sarah it felt like waiting for the foreman of a jury to speak, '. . . my hunch is not.'

'Phew!'

'There are mitigating circumstances, you didn't do this out of greed. My belief is because you are providing the evidence that will convict Mike – but incriminating yourself in the process – you will get off with a suspended sentence, a lot of community service hours and maybe a fine. You've only committed a minor motoring offence in the past; you're of "previously good character", as we term it.'

There was a knock at the door. A metal trolley was wheeled in, the teacups clattering against each other as they bounced their way towards the ladies.

'Just here on the table would be marvelous, thank you,' directed the lawyer.

Sarah watched a man offload a teapot, a plate of biscuits wrapped in cling film, cups, and saucers, and then the trolley – which had a slightly squeaking wheel that the shaking crockery had masked – was steered away.

'It's none of my business, of course, but why do you want to confess to your involvement in these crimes?' enquired the lawyer, taking off the lid of the teapot and poking the contents with a spoon.

'I want my life back.'

The lid was replaced; Lesley steepled her hands and was gazing at Sarah across her fingertips.

'Mrs. Fetherston, the last thing this confession is going to do is give you your life back. Life for you, as you know it, will be irreversibly changed. You will have a criminal record, and don't expect your friends and acquaintances not to judge you for what you've done. Even family may treat you differently.'

Sarah looked sideways, out of the window, down at the Exeter traffic: ordinary people going about their daily lives; how many were hiding guilty secrets? She should have told Freddy once she'd forgiven herself for her infidelity, she should never have let that lie fester at the heart of her marriage. The truth would have hurt Freddy, damaged their marriage, but it would have been a dent compared to the blow she would be forced to land now. She watched Lesley unwrap the biscuits, balling up the cling film and throwing it at the bin.

'I don't mean I want the life I've lived for the last fifteen years back. I mean I want my real life back.'

Stirring milk into her tea, Lesley suggested Sarah sleep on their discussion, advising her to talk things over with her husband.

'I know why you are saying that, but, no, I have made my decision: no more lies. Would you be able to come with me now to the station?'

The lawyer asked repeatedly if Sarah was sure. Sarah wasn't just sure, she was determined. Which was why, just two hours later, Sarah was watching as DC Thompson loosened his tie with a finger, pulling the knot down a fraction, then reached out and turned on the recorder.

Sarah prepared herself for the onslaught of questions. Lesley had advised her to keep it factual and simple, not to be afraid to ask for a private moment with her lawyer if she was unsure how to reply and under no circumstances to answer, "no comment". Apparently, it was the worst reply she could give; she might just as well say "yes". An innocent person would simply say no, a guilty one would either deny it – if they were a hardened criminal that didn't mind lying – or as she mistakenly had in her first time in the interview suite, say "no comment". The police could spot the difference between an ordinary housewife and a hardened criminal.

'Mrs. Fetherston, do you want to tell me what's been going on?'

The recording machine was flashing and making a dull whirring noise; Sarah's voice drowned the sound out. She started in the Walled Garden, saying she wished she'd reported Mike two years ago.

'Mike?' enquired DC Thompson.

'It's not Mike, his real name is Darren Smith, and his address is Tiddleworth Farm,' she answered crisply.

That had been the crucial mistake: not following her instinct to shop the horrid man; she'd allowed him to manoeuvre her into a position where instead of him, it was her that was trapped. She couldn't do anything to him without punishing herself too. She explained that at the start she'd convinced herself Mike wasn't really a bad man and that he was a victim too, being forced into his crimes by Nick.

'Nick?' prompted the officer.

'Nick Henderson,' Sarah replied. 'Mike and Nick were in the business together: growing, storing, selling-on the cannabis.'

'When and where were they growing and storing these drugs?'

'I don't know when it started, but I discovered it in June nearly two years ago. Everything was happening at the Dower House, where Mike – sorry, where Darren – lived. The cannabis plants were being grown in two huge polytunnels in the Walled Garden, and once it was picked it was stored in the potting sheds.'

'What specifically was stored in those potting sheds? What part of the plant was it?'

'It was the flower buds, and separately the leaves.'

'You saw this yourself?'

'Yes, on more than one occasion.'

She'd seen it and chose to say nothing. The truth about Mike was obvious once the Will fraud was exposed, cheating Freddy out of his inheritance; Mike was never a victim. Yet despite the evidence of his calculated meanness, she was duped again, deftly deflected by Mike's acceptance of the idea of gifting them the house. She'd failed to question why. When he had the upper hand, when the fraud had worked, and neither Harry nor Freddy was going to challenge him, why was Mike prepared simply to hand over the Dower House when she asked him to? Nothing had altered her position: regardless of the threats she made, she still couldn't expose his crimes without exposing herself too. She'd never asked why he would donate the proceeds of the fraud to her family. She'd convinced herself he was telling the truth, that he just wanted to punish Harry. As if!

Sarah looked at the flashing lights – she was still being recorded. Was DC Thompson wondering what drove her into the arms of the criminal world? Why someone so obviously well-to-do was tempted to risk their ordered life by dealing with a pair of crooks?

'When was the most recent occasion you saw the buds and or the cannabis leaves being stored in the potting sheds of the Dower House?'

When Mike killed Nick! That probably was an accident, but what did Mike do with Nick's body, and why did he move it? It takes a cruel, calculating mind to deprive a family of a body. Everyone has their limit, and for Sarah it had been that phone call from the journalist. She was so blindly focused on the prize of the house, she'd accepted he just wanted the picture of Lady Mary as a keepsake. That crook had stolen a million pounds from the family, and then swindled young Mary out of an additional five million. And unlike the sons, with no inheritance tax to pay – by varying the Will, the portrait had been left to him by his wife!

Sarah looked up at DC Thompson, chewing her lip.

'Three nights ago. That's when I last saw drugs in the potting shed.'

The officer sucked in his breath, making a hissing noise. He exhaled, puckering his lips, and leaned towards her. 'Mrs. Fetherston, you have given your own address as the Dower House. You told me your family moved there in December. Are you saying this operation persisted under your ownership of the property?'

'Not the growing, that part was moved to Tiddleworth Farm.'

'But the cannabis was being stored at your property with your consent?'

'Yes,' she mumbled.

'Clearly, please, for the record.'

She cleared her throat then said crisply. 'Yes, the cannabis was being stored with my consent on my property.'

'Mrs. Fetherston, is your husband aware of what is going on in your potting sheds?'

Sarah started to laugh.

'Lord no, Freddy has no idea what's been going on these last few years. I told him I'd allowed Mike to store a few gardening bits and bobs in one of the potting sheds for a few months.'

DC Thompson called for a break when Sarah mentioned discovering Nick's body.

Once they were left on their own, Sarah asked Lesley what would happen next. Did the police have enough to catch Mike? Lesley assured her the police would track down Mike and arrest him. Sarah wasn't so sure. How would they find him if he wasn't at Tiddleworth? With the combined proceeds from the drugs and the sale of the portrait, he probably wasn't even in the country. Was she sacrificing herself in vain? Were they going to catch the real villain?

Chapter Twenty-Seven

Sarah stopped outside the hotel and peered in through the window; she was early, but that didn't mean she was first. The glass was bleary, obscuring her view across the room towards the bar. She cupped a hand over her eyes, focusing her vision as she scanned from left and right. There were no single women inside. She walked the last few steps to the entrance door, propped open with a door jamb, and into the hotel lobby. There were two attendants wearing dove-grey jackets behind the reception desk: talking loudly into their telephones as if justifying how busy they were, explaining why they couldn't attend to the man standing in front of them with his arms crossed and a scowl on his face. Sarah walked past them all, ignoring the background noise, as she pushed open the door to the bar.

The bar wasn't busy. There was an elderly couple at a table in the centre of the room, wearing fawn-coloured raincoats. A white tea service was spread across the table, the remains of a cream tea: plates with blobs of jam and butter, a ramekin dish of clotted cream and a single forlorn-looking scone waiting for its fate to be decided. A man sat in a corner reading a newspaper folded over and held with just one hand, enabling the fingers of his other to dip like a pecking bird's beak into a porcelain bowl on the table in front of him, regularly transferring snacks to his mouth, hidden behind the paper. A pint glass kept the bowl company: a creamy froth still forming the top half-inch of beer.

Sarah didn't know any of these people, it was only her second time here, but she hadn't known anywhere else to suggest meeting. Apart from those two glasses of white wine with Percy nearly a year ago, she hadn't been anywhere in Exeter on a truly social basis for over fifteen years. She'd spent hours in the city at committee meetings, and far too many days and evenings there at charity events as part of the unpaid helping team, but neither activity gave her an insight into the development of Exeter's hospitality sector since she'd worked there for a salary and knew every pub, bar, and restaurant, all the interesting places to enjoy a glass of wine with a friend.

Sarah no longer sat on charity committees. Nor was she invited to any of their events. Apart from Penelope, all those ladies had shunned her once they discovered what she'd done, once she was a convicted criminal. Sarah took control over that portion of her life; severing the connection was her decision, not theirs. She emailed out her resignation letters and derived a weird sense of pleasure from hitting the 'delete' button without opening any response, depriving her former "friends" of their spiteful comments. Sarah was prepared to pay – and had paid – her dues to society for her misdemeanours but would not tolerate being judged by *Society*.

Telling Penelope wasn't as traumatic as Sarah had expected. Her friend's widened eyes and repeated interjections of *"how could he do that to you"*, were as comforting as a large glass of wine at the end of a hard day. Sarah told her friend about Angus confirming Penelope's suspicion her son was being used to ferry drugs. Sarah explained how she had stepped in to protect the child; her friend threw her arms around her, holding her tightly and breathing into her hair. 'How can I ever repay you for what you've done? Thank you, you are a true friend.'

Sarah accepted the six-month sentence – suspended for two years – and willingly undertook her hours of community service work; the owner of the fish and chip shop where she'd scrubbed away the graffiti politely thanked her and the two other offenders, even bringing them lunch halfway through each day. He hadn't judged any of them or asked why they were there, merely been grateful for their help.

Mike hadn't got off so lightly. He'd bolted, set up his new life in Portugal, but not being a professional criminal, he failed to be diligent enough with his planning. Tiddleworth was searched but it was empty. He'd arranged for his possessions to be collected, boxed up and stored by a specialist firm from Bristol, but the CID painstakingly contacted every storage facility in the southwest, uncovered his hiding place, and put a tracker device inside one of the boxes. A month later, a Portuguese van collected his furniture from a depot in Lisbon, where the Bristol firm was told to deliver to and drove it down to Mike in his smart new villa in the Algarve. The truck was escorted by the Portuguese police, accompanied by a plainclothes CID detective inspector who served him with his arrest warrant.

Mike was serving a ten-year jail term. Ironically, if he hadn't removed Nick's body, and with it the evidence that Mike had acted in self-defence, the sentence could have been considerably shorter. They found Nick's body; Mike told them where he hid it in a disused quarry. It was covered in Mike's DNA, and the jury didn't believe his story about a fight with the younger, fitter victim whom he claimed attacked him. Sarah didn't lie at Mike's trial, but she didn't help him either.

Sarah chose the same table in the window that she had sat at with Percy. She picked up the drink's menu in its shiny plastic wallet, running an eye down the wines offered by the glass. She heard sounds from the reception lobby, saw the door open fully, and stood, pushing away her chair with the backs of her legs.

'You haven't changed much!' she said. 'You can never tell from social media. No one updates their photos, do they?'

The other lady tossed her coat and bag on the table.

'I've put on a few pounds since I had the kids. Can't find the time or the energy to shake the last few off.'

'What'll you have? Are you going back to the office? Would you prefer tea, or do you have time for a glass of wine?'

'What a good idea. Afternoon tea is a vastly overrated drink.'

'White?' suggested Sarah, standing up and reaching for her purse.

'As always,' said Kate, her old flat mate.

'Muscadet?'

'Whatever!'

Sarah walked to the bar, trying to recall the last time she had stood at a bar ordering a drink, let alone buying one for a friend too. She returned, as Percy had, with two small glasses of wine, and several porcelain dishes.

'Sod the extra few pounds, tuck into these,' she said offloading her bounty and handed her friend a glass. 'How's the world of estate agency?'

'I've had a pig of a day. Had to call one of my elderly clients to tell them the buyer is ready to exchange but has decided to have a late nibble at the price. No explanation or excuse offered, just take it, or leave it. My poor client didn't really understand, thought everything was agreed and the legals were just a formality. I had to advise them to accept the reduced price – what's the alternative? You're back to the start and re-marketing and that nasty cash buyer knew that too.' Kate lifted her glass towards her friend. 'Cheers.' She took a swig, then asked, 'Go on, satisfy my curiosity – how much did you make?'

Sarah gulped down her own mouthful of wine. 'I didn't make anything. I gave it all away to charity.'

'I'm still curious. How much?'

Sarah gave a quick tut. 'I didn't tot it up, maybe a hundred grand.'

'Really? I made twice that flipping a London pad!'

'That's your specialist area though, Kate.'

Her friend laughed. 'Well, let's find you a new one! Don't want you sticking with drugs!'

Should she ask Kate to sell the Dower House, Sarah wondered. She was keen to sell. She wanted to join Freddy and Mary in the small flat in London the family was renting as a stopgap. They wanted Mary to start at her new school at the beginning of the academic year, not halfway through the autumn term, and anyway it wasn't practical for Freddy to commute to his new professorship. They would find a house to buy as a family – choose together, enjoy the search. They didn't know what they were looking for, only that it wasn't going to be Georgian.

She'd made her full confession to Freddy in his study – sobbing and shaking and begging his forgiveness. He held her close, murmuring into her hair, 'Hush, hush, for better for worse darling.'

Then he sat her down and removed an envelope from his desk drawer and revealed the offer of a professorship at the prestigious London School of Economics. Mike had been wrong about Freddy. He'd stood by her, forgiven her for what she'd done, and they were going to start a new life together hundreds of miles away.

'To old times,' said Kate, taking a small sip.

'To old times,' Sarah chimed, raising her glass in a toast.

Acknowledgements

Firstly, a heartfelt thankyou to my editor Susannah for her insight, guidance, and boundless reserves of enthusiasm. I do have so much fun working with you. I owe a big debt of gratitude to Lee for explaining the investigative process after a fatal road traffic accident, and to Kiara for sharing her knowledge of police interview procedures and giving me a guided tour of the Barnstaple police station.

Thank you to James, Joe, Chris and Stefan for all their work to bring this book to fruition.

I am deeply indebted to my early readers for debating plot lines and encouraging me to press on – KT, Davo, Jane, Fiona, and Lucy.

Thank you to Veronica Henry for her kind supportive words; to Niamh Mulvey and Richard Arcus who helped me turn a story into a novel; Jessica Brody for the inspirational advice in her book; and to Ivan Mulcahy of MMB Creative for his invaluable early advice and introductions.

Lastly to my husband Martin, without whose support and unwavering belief, none of this would have happened, and to my little pack of dogs for enduring being parted from compelling scents to enable your mistress to write.

A Thank you from DCR Bond,

So, to all the readers who have picked up (or downloaded) my book, despaired at Sarah's lack of judgement, smiled at Freddy's ineptness and perhaps sent up a small cheer as horrid Harry met his comeuppance, a huge thank you.

I promise to keep weaving tales that will make you smile, think and surprise you with an unexpected twist. I sincerely hope you'll continue to read, enjoy, and support my writing.

In a world cluttered with so many distractions and obligations it is humbling to me that you've taken the time to immerse yourself in my novel. I hope it provided you with a much-needed escape from reality, even if only for a little while. We all face challenges in our lives but it's comforting to know we aren't the only ones battling along. If Sarah can overcome her obstacles so can we and I trust her journey reminded you of the power of love and forgiveness.

Several readers have asked what inspired me to write this book. Was it personal experience? Well, full disclosure, I do have a (modest) Polytunnel, in which I spend much of my free time, but my most exotic produce to date is heritage tomatoes!

I felt compelled to write the plot line about Mary's Will from a personal family Will drama. Please be careful if like Sarah you too have a relative afflicted with dementia!

I want to ask you a very big favour. Please can you visit my website www.dcrbond.com and sign up for my newsletter. Please do share your thoughts with me – leave me a review, it's wonderful to receive personal feedback. In return I would like to share with you a few free short stories, snippets of forthcoming books, and let you know about events I am attending in your neighbourhood. There are also some suggestions for questions you might want to pose if you are reading this book as part of a book club.

Lastly, I would like to thank you for all the reviews and messages you've sent my way. Your words of encouragement and support mean so much. Its gratifying to know that my book has touched you in even a small way and that you had as much fun reading it as I did creating it.

DCR Bond